MW01138089

The Star Hunters:
Light
Runner

K. N. Salustro

DEDICATION

For Ben, who
somehow managed to
survive me writing this one.

For Mom, Dad, and Jacki, who
were there at the start. There
would be no books
without you.

And while
it may seem selfish,
this one is also for me.
Sometimes, we need
to remember

what we're capable of.

CONTENTS

CHAPTER 1: PULSE

Lissa sat in the control room of the silver, blue and black ship, listening to the rhythmic hum of the systems as the ship bled stars and planets across its trail. It was a solid, comforting sound, steady as the beating of a strong heart. It helped keep her own heartrate in check.

As she studied the coordinates she had wrestled out of the communication logs lifted from the Seventh Sun ship on Sciyat, her thumb traced back and forth across the collar around her throat. Her nail scraped and bumped over the seven white stars.

Seven stars. Seven leaders for the Seventh Sun.

Subtlety was not a defining characteristic of the Neo-Andromedan organization, but when it came to hiding their leaders, they tended to employ more tact.

Particularly when it came to *this* leader.

Lissa knew she'd found at least one of them. But rather than giving her a sense of purpose, the discovery had tightened nerves until they were brittle with dread.

It's probably not Rosonno.

She told herself this as though the idea of postponing her next meeting with him could give her any comfort. He still haunted her nightmares, and sometimes, she had the feeling he would stay with her long after he was dead.

If he didn't kill her first.

Or send her back into an Awakening machine.

Welcome to the fight for me, Little Light.

Lissa closed her eyes against the voices in her ears. She pulled her hand away from the collar around her throat, took a slow, steady breath, and refocused on the sounds of the ship.

She was safe for now. She had to remember that.

She opened her eyes again when she heard Lance approaching the control room. She always picked him out by his footsteps, which were nowhere near as quiet as he thought they were. They were especially loud and erratic this time, and Lance kept muttering something under his breath that sounded like curses. Lissa swiveled in her seat, half-expecting to see Lance limping and rushing to tell her that someone had managed to sabotage the ship's defenses and get inside. It took her a moment to register what was actually happening, and a moment longer to release her hold on her energy pulse pistol and relax again.

Lance stumbled toward the control room, holding two trays of food above his head as he dodged around Blade and Orion. The arkins had their eyes locked on the trays, and their muzzles kept straining upwards whenever Lance tried to rebalance himself. Orion got his head between Lance and the doorframe, and one of the trays almost tipped into Blade's waiting mouth. The black arkin's teeth snapped closed on air as Lance jerked his arm back. That made him pause and look back and forth between the two arkins.

"I think I liked it better when you two were trying to maul each other," he said.

Orion gave a frustrated grunt as Lance pushed past him, then settled for lying down and blocking the only way out of the control room. Blade stood guard behind him.

Lance offered Lissa one of the trays. Slices of dark meat and something charred and green sat precariously on the surface, and Lissa had the feeling that Lance had lost some of this meal to the arkins on his way back from the galley.

He had insisted on purchasing enough fresh meat for all of them, arkins included, the last time they had put into port. The Star Federation had accustomed him to decent, fresh food once in a while, although without a galley cook, neither he nor Lissa had known what to do with the meat. Lissa was conditioned to cheaper, preserved meals that were high in nutrients, low in flavor, and easy to find almost anywhere that sold basic supplies. Looking at the unseasoned, slightly burnt meat Lance had finally produced, she was not sure that the result was worth the price.

"I haven't figured out how to cook yet," Lance admitted, taking a bite from his own tray and grimacing. "But it still beats space food."

Lissa sniffed experimentally at the burnt food. In spite of her doubts, her mouth began to water. Then her stomach flipped and Lissa lowered the tray to her lap.

Lance caught the movement. His laughter faded as he took the seat next to her and studied her expression. "What did you find?"

Lissa reached for the datapad that held the translated communication logs and the coordinates she had lifted. "You're not going to like this," she warned Lance.

And he didn't.

He spent so long studying the coordinates and checking them against one of the ship's starmaps that Orion crept into the room and stole a bite off of Lance's tray. Lissa finally gave into hunger as well, and found that Lance was right; a burnt meal of fresh food was lightyears beyond the preserved meals.

Lissa chewed slowly, allowing Lance to take his time. His unfamiliarity with the written Neo-Andromedan language blocked him from verifying her translations of the communication logs, but the coordinates were more straightforward. There were no errors for him to find, but for that brief moment, Lissa allowed herself to hope that he would. She knew what they needed to do, but if there was one hunt she wanted to turn away from, this was it.

The target's coordinates were in an uncharted area, a piece of the galaxy too riddled with neutron stars, black holes, and other hazards for anyone to safely travel. Even renegades avoided unmapped territories unless near-certain death was a preferable alternative to capital punishment at the hands of the Star Federation. Lissa had checked and rechecked her translations and the coordinates until her eyes ached, but everything pointed to the uncharted sector.

And Lissa knew that only a Seventh Sun leader could be there.

She could not refuse this hunt.

Surprisingly, Lance did not question the coordinates. "Is this right?" He asked, pointing to one of the translated communications instead.

Lissa saw the name *Sciyat* near his finger. She nodded. "Whoever this is, they helped coordinate the attack on Sciyat."

Lance took another bite of food, too distracted to comment on the taste this time. "I suppose," he finally said, "an uncharted sector is the best place to hide your leader."

Lissa stopped her hand from straying back up to the collar. "One of them, at least."

He saw the gesture. His green eyes flicked over her tense posture. "Do you know who we're going after?" There was a layer of caution to his tone that snagged Lissa's attention, but she didn't know quite what to make of it.

She let it go and shook her head. "I only knew some of the Sun's leaders by reputation before Aven and I left, and that was a long time ago. If they're all still in power, I can't see any of them ordering strikes from a place like that."

Especially not Rosonno, she thought, remembering the dark night on Yuna when he had stood over her in the desert and promised to Awaken her.

Lissa shivered against the memory.

Lance was focused on a starmap and missed her distress this time. Relieved, Lissa gave herself a moment to take in the hard lines of his lean face and the determined set of his jaw. He'd let his hair grow a bit longer than the Star Federation's regulated length, and there was a gentle wave forming in the blond-brown locks. He did not take his attention away from the starmap when Orion's muzzle edged towards his tray again, but he placed his hand on the arkin's head and gave Orion a gentle but firm nudge away. The gray arkin snorted, and his yellow eyes narrowed against the black slash of fur across his face.

It's safe here, Lissa reminded herself, glancing over at Blade.

The black arkin had settled across the doorway, lying as stretched out as she could manage in the little space that remained in the control room. One wing was tucked neatly along her back, but the other rested awkwardly against her side, reminding Lissa that the Seventh Sun could and would always find her, and they could hurt her as easily as the ones she cared about.

Lissa looked back at Lance and Orion and wondered when exactly that had extended beyond Blade and Aven.

We're safe for now, she told herself.

But that was a dangerous, complacent thought. Aven was only safe because he was dead. And Lissa was taking Blade, Lance, and Orion to an uncharted territory to hunt a Seventh Sun leader.

Lance interrupted her thoughts before they could turn darker. "How long has this leader been at this location?"

Lissa took the datapad back and scanned through the transmissions she had marked. "I don't know," she admitted, "but I found one that dated back almost a full sidereal year. Same transmission signature, and I pulled the same coordinates from it. So at least that long."

Lance nodded. "That's a good sign." At Lissa's skeptical look, he continued. "They're comfortable where they are. And they know that they're protected by the location alone." Lance sat back and considered her. "It would be as dangerous for them to try to leave as it would be for us to go into that system. Whether or not they know we're on their trail, I'm betting they're not going to move for a while."

Lissa frowned. "That's not how people generally act when they're being hunted."

Lance started to say something, changed his mind, and said, "I only mean that if they've run, they're already gone, and it's not worth going in there trying to find them."

"And if they haven't?"

"Then they figure they're safer there than anywhere else in the galaxy, and they won't move until something forces them out. Something like us. If we somehow manage to get into the system and we're not completely prepared, we could lose the target. Maybe permanently."

He made a good argument, but Lissa sensed that there was something more than hunter's logic behind it. "You want to keep on track for Phan," she murmured.

Lance nodded, then quickly added, "Only because I think Dr. Chhaya could help with..." He gestured to the collar. "If there's any sign of the Star Federation, we leave."

Lissa saw the sense of the suggestion, but she balked at the idea. She had not been able to pull another target from the data, and as dangerous as this one was, she did not like the idea of letting it go.

But we're not letting it go. Just... putting it on hold.

Her hunter's instinct screamed at her to resist that temptation and throw the starship into the unmapped sector. Her caution and fear told her that would be a terrible, deadly mistake.

And if they stayed on track for Phan, that could give her more time to find another target in the communication logs. Maybe one that lived on a planet that was easier to reach.

"All right," Lissa finally agreed, "we'll go back to Phan."

She did not need to say anything about the risk of running into the Star Federation. Once, she would have been certain that Lance was trying to lead her into a trap and reinstate himself within the military's ranks. Now, they both would find themselves staring down the barrels of enerpulse rifles as Star

Federation soldiers tried to shoot them down. She knew that Lance understood that.

He nodded in response, not hiding his relief as well as he could have. Then he took another bite of meat, wrinkled his nose, and muttered, "It's worse than space food when it's cold."

He tossed the last of his meat to Orion, who snapped it out of the air and swallowed it whole. Blade groaned her disapproval and looked at Lance as though he had betrayed her to a mortal enemy. Her gaze softened as he approached her with the empty trays. She accepted his peace offering and curled her paws around the trays as she began to lick them clean. Lance gave her an affectionate pat on the shoulder, then almost fell into her when Orion headbutted him in the back. Lance retaliated by twisting around and grabbing the gray arkin around the neck. Blade groaned and flattened her ears when Orion pushed Lance into her side, and then all three of them were wrestling on the control room floor.

Lissa was surprised to find herself smiling as she watched them. It felt wrong, but she let herself enjoy the security of the moment.

She knew it could not and would not last.

CHAPTER 2: LIGHT

Rosonno had been right. The purge *was* good for the Seventh Sun.

Barely hours after the Star Federation had formally declared the genocide, Neo-Andromedans were already reaching out to known agents, a great many of them begging the Seventh Sun to relocate them and their families back to the original stronghold out beyond the Andromedan Reach, as far away from the Star Federation's grasp as they could imagine. Most of those requests were denied, of course. The Seventh Sun had spent the last few years moving the Neo-Andromedan population off of that dying base and spreading them in secret throughout the galaxy. But there were the few odd requests that came in from very promising individuals. People with valuable skill sets that were sorely needed. Those people were moved beyond the Reach. First Lit Zeran would find use for them.

The rest of the applications were filtered through Sekorvo's network, and the more interesting ones were passed on to Rosonno.

As the days slipped by, his database saw close to a five percent increase. A considerable number when he thought about all the Neo-Andromedans that he hoarded information on, regardless of whether they were alive or not. As a rule, he never deleted anything. The behaviors of the dead helped him recognize patterns and flows in the living. And with the main bulk of his starship's computer customized to his needs and demands for information, he had generations' worth of data at his fingertips.

Usually, that made him feel powerful.

He only needed to call up an individual's file to see the scope of their full life. From there, he could see how they would act and react in any situation.

Almost any.

Alone in his private quarters, Rosonno stared down at Lissa's file without seeing it. He'd been rereading her information quite a lot these days, but no matter what, he could not find the break in the pattern that had turned her into the merciless hunter that was coming after him.

There was a beauty to it, he had to admit. A terrifying but iridescent cut that made him uncertain about her. No matter which way he looked at Lissa, he could not puzzle out what she would do next.

She was unpredictable.

And for that, she had to be destroyed.

Unfortunately, that had proven to be a very difficult achievement. Even with Syreth's handling team set on her trail, Lissa was eluding the Seventh Sun with alarming grace. Syreth's team had finally managed to identify her ship's signature, but that had taken them several long, sidereal days to accomplish, and twice they went after the wrong starship before untangling Lissa's signature from the others. They were following her now, but they were so far behind that Rosonno doubted they would catch up before she had done more damage.

Rosonno was far from ready to admit defeat, but he knew that Lissa was out of his reach for now.

With a heavy sigh, Rosonno pushed the datapad with Lissa's file up to the top corner of his desk. The datapad lived there permanently now, and would remain there until he had total confirmation of Lissa's death.

He would not make that mistake twice.

Rosonno sat back in his seat, stretching. His shoulders creaked and popped with the motion, and he winced at the sharp mix of pain and pleasure. The feeling reminded him to focus on what he could control while he waited for Lissa's downfall.

Even if Lissa was hunting him and the other leaders, it would take time before she found anyone. Plenty of time. Until then, the Seventh Sun had work to do, and their first major strike was rapidly approaching.

Arrevessa had been very closed off about the details, keeping the final coordination of the strike between herself and Tyrath now that her secondary strategist Ereko was gone. Rosonno's thumb brushed against the single red star on his collar as he thought about the dead First Lit, but a bubble of excitement formed in his chest.

He may have been excluded from the planning of the attack, but he would get to see the strike himself. All of the First Lit would.

Such a special occasion had merited a selection of agents to broadcast the strike to the First Lit straight from the battlefield. Precautions had been taken to ensure that no one would ever be able to trace the First Lits' locations should the worst happen, but Rosonno doubted that would truly be a risk. His own broadcasters were excellent field agents, all highly skilled in combat and more than ready for the attack. Rosonno silently ran through their names in his head as his thumb traced the remaining white stars on his collar.

There were three agents that he was particularly looking forward to watching: Yvenna, Auroso, and Kidra.

All three agents were in peak physical condition, and were fiercely loyal to the Seventh Sun. They lived and breathed for the future of Neo-Andromedans.

They would give him a show of Star Federation blood.

All he had to do was wait for it.

CHAPTER 3: FADE

Jason stood on a private starship port overlooking Yuna's solitary oasis, which had long since lost the last traces of its toxic water. He imagined that, once, this private port had been the envy of the owner's neighbors, stretching out over the oasis and suspending the ship over the life source of the planet. There were a few other private ports poking out over the empty space that water had once filled, but all Jason could see when he glanced left or right were silent buildings standing guard around the dead oasis. The city was completely abandoned now. Even the animals had disappeared, leaving only empty nests behind. Jason knew there was no one left to save, but he was reluctant to leave the burning, barren world.

Orders had already come through from his commanding officer, and how Jason loathed them. Fleet Commander Keraun was all too eager to see purge efforts pushed to their limits, and the Hyrunian had ordered Jason to Firoden, a nearby world in the Andromeda Reach. Though small, Firoden had once been a rich and prosperous planet famous for its mineral and textile exports. At the onset of the Andromeda War, the wealthy had fled from Firoden and other worlds within the Reach, taking their businesses and their bank accounts with them. Many planets, Firoden included, had not recovered. It was now a hostile haven for roving renegades. Much like Yuna had been.

Where Keraun's intel on Firoden had come from was a mystery to Jason, but the Hyrunian fleet commander was convinced that there was a healthy pocket of Neo-Andromedans on Firoden. With the purge on, it was the responsibility of Keraun's officers to root them out, but the Hyrunian had saved this particular mission for Jason. He had not forgotten the modifications Jason had made to the Ametrian memorial speech.

Jason doubted that there were any Neo-Andromedans on Firoden, much less a solid population of them. Keraun was keeping Jason away from the bulk of purge activity, and while that suited him just fine, Jason knew that it was not done out of respect or sympathy. Keraun was up to something, and Jason was willing to bet that a dishonorable discharge would be the least of his problems if the Hyrunian had his way.

This strike on Firoden reeked of failure. If Jason was not very careful, he could damage the Star Federation's reputation along with his own. Firoden was dominated by humans, and Jason had a strong premonition that they would not submit to Star Federation authority even with their lives on the line, purge or no purge.

He silently cursed the Hyrunian for sending him to that planet.

Stalling for as long as he could, Jason stared out over the dead oasis. Heat shimmered through the air, warping the far shoreline into oblivion and hiding the rest of the abandoned city behind a mirage. He kept coming back to this place, kept standing over the oasis long after it had dwindled into nothing, wondering what else he could possibly do to push the Star Federation and himself down the right course. His soldiers still respected him, even if some of them resented his more sympathetic views toward Neo-Andromedans, views that surprised even himself. They had only fully come to light when he'd been forced to give that sham of a memorial speech. The words he had been instructed to say were nothing more than thinly veiled propaganda in favor of the purge and going to war against Neo-Andromedans.

His small rebellion against the speech had not won him any allies, but for now, he was all right with that. It was one thing to hold on to before he went to Firoden.

Jason's personal communicator came to life, shattering the scorching silence of the dead world. "Final sweep of the city is complete, Captain Stone. We wait for your orders."

He couldn't stay any longer. "Double check the roll call and make certain all crew are accounted for. Then ready the ship for departure. I'm on my way back."

After one final look at the dry pit of sand that once was the lifeblood of an entire planet, Jason turned and began the trek back through the empty city to the ground port. Sandstone buildings loomed overhead, throwing dark shadows into the streets. Grit scraped against Jason's goggles as the hot wind pulled at the robes and headscarf that protected him against the worst of the glaring sun.

People lived here, he thought as he wound his way around small dunes scattered throughout the city. Now that there was no one to maintain the generators powering the forcefield that kept the sand at bay, the dunes had built up with eerie swiftness, warping Jason's sense of direction and threatening to trap him within the spiraling maze of the city.

He could not imagine life in this place.

And yet it had been here, until the Star Federation had failed to protect it from the Seventh Sun.

Jason picked his way through the empty city, feeling the evidence of that failure press through the silence.

When he finally reached the ground port, he saw that the ship was already alive with power. Even with the hard glint of the sun on the hull, Jason could see light spilling out from the open airlock. Heat blazed out from the engines, shimmering against the desert and the yellow sky.

The starship was a mid-sized cruiser, usually too large for a ground port this size, but with all the other ships gone, it had been able to land without trouble. It was a bulkier craft than what the Star Federation usually provided to its officers, but the evacuation efforts had demanded the extra room. A small fleet of these ships had gone to Yuna, and all but this one had left with refugees filling the livable spaces.

Jason and his soldiers had searched all over the city, but if there was anyone left, they did not want to be found.

That left Jason free to set a course directly for Firoden. He'd kept as many of his trusted junior officers with him as he could, but Lieutenant Reed—one of Keraun's personal favorites—had been directly assigned to the Firoden mission. Lieutenant Reed was a scarred, hostile man who took too much pleasure in the dangerous side of the Star Federation's work, and Jason had come to know him well as a persistent pain. The evacuation efforts had left Reed bored, and he'd made minimal contributions to getting as many civilians as possible off of Yuna.

Reed had also been present when Keraun had murdered Aven, an unarmed Neo-Andromedan sick to near death with the Banthan virus.

Jason pushed that memory to the back of his mind. It wasn't good focusing on it. Not now. He had phantom Neo-Andromedans to hunt down, and actively fueling his desire to punch Reed in the face would only distract him and make him sloppy. He could not afford that on Firoden.

As Jason drew closer to the ship, he picked out the figure of a waving soldier inside the airlock, gesturing for him to hurry. His communicator came to life again, crackling with static disruption.

The soldier informed him that a sandstorm was moving in.

Jason quickened his pace, noticing that the wind had picked up. The loose end of his scarf cracked and whipped behind him, and sand was rolling across his feet. He made it to the ship with time to spare, though a large, dark smudge was visible on the horizon as he climbed into the airlock.

"All crew accounted for," the soldier told Jason as she shut the airlock behind him. "A direct course for Firoden has been set, and we are ready to depart."

Jason moved into the interior of the ship, unwrapping the headscarf and peeling the goggles off. Sand crumbled to the ground around him. "Signal the bridge to take us starward."

The soldier obeyed, but she stopped him before he set off for his personal quarters. "A message came in for you from Sciyat." She held out a small datapad.

More sand cascaded off of Jason's robes as he turned to regard the datapad with trepidation. Erica was on Sciyat, he knew, and he was not eager to receive a message from another fleet commander. But when he took the datapad and glanced at the screen, he saw that the message had been marked as personal correspondence. He made to thank the soldier, but stopped when he saw the look on her face.

Her eyes were fixed almost hungrily on the datapad, and though she held herself at attention out of respect for his higher rank, there was a resigned slope to her shoulders and her breathing hitched slightly.

"You have family on Sciyat?" Jason kept his voice gentle, though he already knew the answer to the question.

The soldier raised her dark, upturned eyes to his and nodded. She was human, and looked to be in her late twenties, with black hair drawn back into a tight, regulation bun. Her skin was pale ochre with cooler undertones picked up by her gray uniform.

"Have you heard from them?"

She swallowed hard. "No, sir."

The datapad suddenly felt heavier in his hand. He shifted it behind his back. "What is your name?"

"Diana Wu, sir." She drew herself up to her full height. "Ensign."

Jason nodded. A shudder ran through the ship, and there was the slightest shift in Jason's balance, signaling that the starship had lifted off the ground and angled skyward.

"I can't promise anything," Jason told her, "but I will try to find out what happened to them."

Hope sparked in her eyes, but it flickered away immediately. "I am not the only person with family on Sciyat," she said evenly, but there was sadness in the words.

Jason nodded, understanding. He had tried to get word from Sciyat regarding any of his subordinates, but information was reaching them at a steady trickle at best. He felt a heavy feeling wash over him as the ship's artificial gravity system came online, but it faded as the ship broke free of Yuna's pull.

"I greatly appreciate your offer, Captain," Wu quickly said before he could speak again. "But it would not be right."

By which she meant, it would not be fair.

Jason considered Ensign Wu for a moment, but dismissed her without offering again. As he watched her walk away, his conscience twisted painfully. But he knew that she was right, and beyond what he was already doing, he did not have much else to offer. The best he could do was to keep trying for all of his subordinates.

Whether or not it proved to be enough.

Back in his private quarters, Jason pulled off the loose Yuni robes, took a quick shower, and changed into a fresh uniform. Plainer cut than his dress uniform, the clothes were designed for easy wear, thermal comfort, and performance efficiency. All of the soldiers wore them when out in the field, though modifications to the structure of the uniforms were needed for many of the non-human species that made up the Star Federation. But every uniform was the same signature gray of the military, and all sported the insignia blazed on the front, which was placed over the heart on human uniforms. Jason pulled on the top half of his uniform and ran his thumb over the golden wings circled by a ring. Two bars floated beneath the insignia, signifying his rank as a captain, as did the two bands on the shoulders of his uniform.

Stand and Protect, he reminded himself.

His eyes fell on the datapad resting on his cot. It took him a moment to make his arm cooperate, but he reached for the datapad and brought up the personal correspondence message. He already knew that his sister Ranae and her family were safe. His rank as captain had afforded him the privilege of a special inquiry, though once it had been confirmed that his family was all right, that advantage had been squeezed off. But learning from a clinical report from a soldier on Sciyat that Ranae, his brother-in-law Tomás, and his niece and nephew were safe was a very different experience from reading a direct message written by his sister. Some pieces had been redacted, giving the message a jarring flow, but enough was left to ease a part of Jason's heart that he had not known was ratcheted tight.

Ranae's censored message was soothingly calm, updating Jason on Tomás's status. He had been injured by stray enerpulse fire at the onset of the attack on Sciyat, but it was not a severe wound and he had already been discharged from the hospital. The family had been temporarily relocated off-planet for their own safety, but while they had been given clearance to return home, they had elected to charter passage to Earth instead.

The planet's name had been cut out of the message, but the family's intention was to visit Tomás's mother and stay with her until some of the chaos had died down. Carmen Ramirez was Earthborn, and Jason knew that Earth was where she would spend the rest of her days. The woman hated the idea of space travel, and Jason had the feeling that part of her resentment of Ranae stemmed from her and Tomás setting up their architecture firm on Sciyat rather than Earth. After his last conversation with Ranae, he was surprised that she was willingly visiting her mother-in-law, but as he read on, he understood.

It seemed that Mamá Ramirez wanted to make amends. The attack on Sciyat had reminded her of just how easy it would be to lose her son and his family—all of his family—and she felt that she was at least partially responsible for driving Ranae and Tomás away.

I didn't think she had it in her, Ranae had written, *but she actually used the words "I'm sorry." Even Tomás said he doesn't remember ever hearing her say that, but fear does strange things to people. Usually, it brings out the worst in them, but sometimes, you end up seeing the best.*

Jason didn't fully agree with that idea, but he was glad to know that Tomás's mother would at least make an effort to accept Ranae as she never had before. It was far less than his sister deserved, but it was a start.

Jason read Ranae's message through twice more, then hashed out a quick response. He kept his words as neutral as he could, knowing that his reply would be scrutinized for any scrap of information that could compromise the Star Federation, his captain's rank be damned. The censors might scrub a few words here and there, but he was confident that the bulk of the message would get back to Ranae. Eventually.

As he sent the message off, the communication terminal in his quarters came to life, and a soldier informed him that they were on track to reach Firoden after a few days of travel. The teams chosen to lead the search for the Neo-Andromedans were waiting for him to coordinate their plan of attack.

Jason struggled to keep his voice neutral when he said, "I'll be there shortly."

Not for the first time, he found himself missing Major Miyasato. She was a junior officer and they kept a respectable distance, but she'd proven trustworthy, and under different circumstances, Jason liked to think that they would have been friends. He could have used her candid ear now, but she'd gone on one of the refugee transport ships. Her medical expertise had been needed, and while she and several other officers would be rendezvousing with Jason now that the evacuation of Yuna was fully complete, it would be some time before he could confide in her again.

He was certain that Miyasato shared his gradually evolving views on Neo-Andromedans. Once, he had considered

Nandros a deadly scourge to the galaxy, and might not have been so against the idea of a purge. Now, he knew that the war the Star Federation waged was not as black and white as Keraun, Erica, and the other Star Federation leaders believed.

As he made his way to the deck where the leaders of the ground teams waited for him, Jason tried to remember what, exactly, he was fighting for. He thought of Ranae and her family, but he could not protect them by killing innocent people. That much he was certain of.

CHAPTER 4: HEARTBEATS

Sciyat's sky burned blue and clear. There were no clouds, just the yellow-green silhouette of the lunar world's parent planet hanging almost directly overhead. Starships and shuttles carrying returning evacuees streaked across the sky, cutting glittering crisscrosses against the blue. Erica watched one of the shuttles swing around and slip towards the surface, bringing the next wave of Sciyatis home.

The Nandro attack had shaken Sciyat to its very core and left grief and paranoia thick on the surface of the lunar world. The Star Federation was there to keep order and protect the civilians, but Erica knew that the presence of her soldiers was fueling the anxiety.

It wasn't the curfew or the patrols that was aggravating the Sciyati population. This went farther than interruptions in the civilians' lives. Erica could feel the heavy glances that followed her gray uniform and settled for long, uncomfortable moments on the rank bands on her sleeves and the fleet commander insignia pinned over her heart. Sciyat was deep within Star Federation territory, and a solid chunk of the population was comprised of veterans and military families. The population was familiar with the Star Federation insignia blazing across visiting starship hulls.

What they weren't used to was the Star Federation not being able to protect them.

And that, Erica had to admit, was something the military had failed to do in a truly spectacular fashion.

We should have seen this coming, Erica thought as she watched the shuttle touch down in a designated landing zone. *We should have done better.*

Soldiers moved into position and stood at the ready as the shuttle's airlock cracked open and a weary crowd filed out. All returning evacuees, young and old alike, were shepherded towards the soldiers that stood waiting with the hologram disrupters and identity scanners. In the scramble to get as many civilians to safety as possible, checking for hidden Nandros had not been a priority. Now that the crowds were returning to Sciyat, no precautions were spared. Every returning evacuee underwent the test, even the non-humanoid ones, much to their irritation.

But doing better started here, with these tests.

Reports from the battles had indicated that while particularly vicious Nandros had attacked the population, they had not come to this planet unassisted. Sleeper agents from the Seventh Sun had sabotaged Sciyat's Monitor systems and allowed the drop ships into the atmosphere. Those agents had been on Sciyat for an unknown length of time prior to the attack. Years, maybe even decades, but without more information—or *any* information—the Star Federation could not know for certain.

Erica felt the Seventh Sun's hidden presence woven over Sciyat, like one of the spider webs she had stumbled into as a young child living on Earth, long before she had ever considered joining the Star Federation. The webs hung between trees and fence posts, invisible from almost every angle, and Erica had sprinted through a web more than once, the sticky threads clinging to her skin and hair long after she thought she had brushed the final one away. Those strands tickled her mercilessly until blind luck allowed her to swipe the last one clear; she could never find them otherwise. Eventually,

Erica had stopped running and started looking hard for the webs. When the light hit them just right, she could see the gleaming, intricate patterns suspended in the air. She'd gotten quite good at detecting spider webs, but standing now on Sciyat, watching her soldiers pat down civilians and perform quick but uncomfortable DNA tests, she felt the clinging threads and knew that the Star Federation had run straight into the web.

They weren't caught, not yet, but Erica couldn't help but wonder how many other webs the Seventh Sun had spun throughout the galaxy.

She was so engrossed in the thought that she almost did not notice the steady tone in her ear, informing her of an incoming transmission. Sciyat had been nothing short of chaotic ever since she had killed the last Nandro, and she'd traded her standard communicator for one of the specialized ones that clung to her ear and always kept her ready for incoming news. It was an annoying thing that managed to not fit her ear quite right, but it was necessary for now.

Erica murmured a word to accept the transmission.

"We found something, Commander," an eager voice told her.

It took Erica a moment to connect the voice with a name. When she did, her spine went ramrod straight. "I'm on my way."

She cut the transmission and turned on her heel, moving towards the sleek, narrow, hovering land cruiser that had been provided to her by the Sciyati police force. Cooperation from local law enforcement had been seamless. Top-of-the-line land and sky cruisers had been turned over for Star Federation use with little to no resistance, along with any other resources Erica and her officers had asked for. The rehabilitation was running smoothly, save for the Star Federation's failure to find any Nandro agents.

All they had were the corpses of the berserk Nandros that had been loosed on Sciyat during the initial attack. Something was different about them, had made them deadlier than

Nandros already were. Erica hoped the autopsies would shed some light on the matter.

That transmission promised as much.

Erica signaled to her three escorts as she closed the remaining distance to her land cruiser. They were two Star Federation soldiers and one Sciyati officer, the latter of which had been chosen to help Erica navigate the city streets and provide information when needed. The Sciyati officer was a firm, stocky man, obviously shaken by the Nandro attack but mentally and emotionally resilient. He had rebounded strong and proven eager to help, and always with a level head. Erica liked him. She wished more people were like him, although a particular two came to mind.

As Erica and her escorts mounted their individual cruisers and steered their way towards the city, Erica's mind slipped towards Jason Stone and Lance Ashburn.

She hadn't thought about Jason much these past few days, but she had not shaken the feeling that Jason knew something about Nandros that no one else did. The last time she had seen him, he'd been on the verge of telling her something, then swallowed the words on some misguided morality. If he had withheld something that could have saved Sciyat...

She did not believe that, not even now. Jason would not have risked the population of an entire world for a secret. He was not that kind of man. Whatever it was that he had not told her, it was about Nandros and related to the Seventh Sun, but it wouldn't have changed Sciyat's fate.

That blame rested with someone else.

Wind pulled at Erica's uniform as her land cruiser bolted through the city, the drone of her escorts' cruisers cutting through the whistling stream of the wind. Clear paths were marked for cruiser transportation, but with the Star Federation in control and the attack still fresh in everyone's minds, civilian activity was reduced to a minimum and the streets were empty. Erica could have ridden along the pedestrian paths without trouble, but more out of habit than precaution, she remained in the cruiser path. She knew the route back to the Star

Federation camp by now, and as she took the corners without pause, she silently cursed Ashburn.

She'd lost count of how many times she'd damned his name as she followed his trail across the galaxy. After he had deserted the Star Federation and allied himself with the Shadow, Erica had chased him across star systems, losing soldiers along the way and deepening the rift between herself and Jason. She did not regret it, and instead let it drive her on.

Ashburn was a traitor, and he had let Sciyat be attacked.

He may have even facilitated the strike. Who better to help the Seventh Sun navigate the security of a Star Federation world than a former fleet commander?

But then, who better to bring the traitor and the Seventh Sun down than the Star Federation's newest fleet commander? She'd doubted herself before, thinking that her promotion had been purely superficial, but even if that were true, she had a sworn duty to the galaxy, and she would see it through no matter what.

Erica's grip tightened on the land cruiser's controls, and the machine raced on. Buildings whipped past, silent and empty, though the speed did not hide the holes left by pulse cannon fire during the Seventh Sun's initial attack. They cut black, angry lines across the peripherals of her vision. And sometimes, there was a pile of rubble where a building or two had collapsed from the damage, too distinct for her to ignore.

Stand and Protect, Erica reminded herself.

The land cruisers slowed from a hearty drone to a soft thrum as they came into the Star Federation camp. Set up around a four-block radius surrounding the worst of the Nandro attack, the soldiers had been granted access to some of the least damaged buildings as a means of shelter, though many had pitched tents in the streets. Most of those tents were filled with soldiers trying to reunite families that had been separated in the attack, relocate those who had lost homes when their buildings had been hit, and provide medical aid to those who needed it. The severest injuries had already been taken care of, either treated by Star Federation medics or airlifted to secure hospitals, but minor, non-lethal wounds were still being patched up and monitored for signs of infection. But there was one medical tent, larger and sturdier than the rest, that had been set up away from the others. This one was kept under heavy security day and night.

Erica parked her land cruiser near the large tent and swung off the vehicle. She pulled her helmet off and brushed sweat and her short, blonde hair off of her forehead. The two soldiers from her escort dismounted, but the Sciyati police officer's head swiveled towards the tent, and he remained on his cruiser. He knew he was not allowed inside.

"If you're hungry," Erica said to him, "you can grab a bite to eat in camp. We'll contact you when we're finished here."

The officer nodded and steered his cruiser away.

Turning back to the tent, Erica led the two soldiers to the security checkpoint at the entrance. This had been implemented on her own orders, as had the strict instruction that even she must undergo the identity scan before entering, no matter how impatient she may seem at any given moment. She did not want anyone sneaking in here and seeing what she had a small team working on, Sciyati civilians or otherwise. Today, she resented her own caution while the soldiers checked her, and then the two soldiers accompanying her. They were granted access, and ducked inside.

The air inside was still and hot, but cleansers had pulled the smell of decay out of the tent. Lights hung overhead, bright and harsh, and additional lights were angled over tables from every direction. Soldiers in scrubs were bent over their work, pausing barely long enough to glance up and salute Erica as she stepped towards the middle of the tent.

A small room walled entirely with unbreakable glass stood in the center, accessible only by a single decontamination checkpoint. Inside the glass chamber were five human medics. Three were bent over the still form spread across the lone table. The other two, both majors, stood a couple of steps back, talking with each other.

Erica knocked hard on the glass.

The majors turned at the sound, then one moved towards the decontamination checkpoint. The other stepped back into the group and accepted an instrument handed to her by another medic.

Erica moved to meet the emerging soldier. He removed his gloves and facemask before stepping out of the chamber, and gave Erica a crisp salute.

"As we said, Commander," the major began, "we finally found something for you." He peered over her shoulder at Lieutenants Kim and Mohanty. "Current party has your full clearance?"

Erica nodded.

The major motioned them to a data station set up at the far side of the tent. He accessed the terminal, quipped brightly, "Brace yourselves," and brought up an image from an autopsy of a Nandro.

One of the lieutenants made a displeased noise, but Erica did not flinch. She had seen enough carnage to be unfazed by an open chest cavity, even if it did look startlingly human.

"Isn't that a perfect picture?" the medic purred. "Gives us exactly what we need." He narrowed the focus to a spot near the exposed heart. "Like this little guy."

"What is that?" Mohanty asked, her voice low. "Some sort of gland?"

"Exactly." The medic enlarged the image to show the small, pale organ. It was shaped like a bean, connected to the heart by a very narrow vein, and made remarkable only by its confirmed existence. "This," the medic said, looking at the gland with cautious admiration, "just might be the key to the whole Nandro puzzle."

Erica frowned. "You mean this is what makes them so dangerous?"

"Yes and no. In this state, that little gland is not doing anything. The only reason a Nandro might have any sort of advantage over one of us humans is for the basic biology reasons." The medic pulled back on the image to show the full chest cavity again. "Slightly stronger bones, slightly stronger heart, a bunch of slightly little things that will add up, but you know, if you shoot a Nandro, you're going to get the same result as when you shoot a human." The medic dipped back into the database. "But when that little guy up next to the heart gets excited, that's when we get this."

Another image came up, and this time, Erica drew in a sharp breath alongside her lieutenants.

The second image showed another open chest cavity, but the gland that had been unremarkable and almost overlooked in the first image was nearly twice its size in this one. The vein connecting it to the heart was engorged and angry purple in color, and the arteries branching out from the heart looked swollen and overburdened.

"The first image was one of those calm Nandros that the soldiers brought in early," the medic told Erica, crossing his thick arms over his chest. "Said something about finding the Nandro just sitting in the middle of the street looking dazed before they shot him dead."

Erica nodded, remembering the reports. "And the second?"

"That was one of the ones you brought down, Commander. One of the wild ones that was almost untouchable."

She almost shivered at the memory of the Nandro dodging energy pulse fire, drawing closer to her and her soldiers, eyes blazing with bloodlust before a shot finally connected and brought it down.

"We're pretty certain that the extra gland is responsible for the Nandros' berserker mode," the major said. "Or that it plays a key part if it's not directly responsible. But seeing as this was the only wild Nandro who came in without a damaged chest, we've had to make some educated guesses." He deactivated the terminal and the grisly images disappeared. "We could confirm if you managed to bring in another undamaged one brought down while it was going crazy, but no offense, Commander, I'm not betting on that one."

Erica agreed.

The major paused delicately before saying, "Best thing you could do for us would be to bring in a live one."

Erica met his gaze, but did not bother dignifying the request with a response. Everyone in the tent knew that, even with a purge going on, there were some acts that were unforgiveable. Maybe not within the Star Federation, but if Erica wanted to maintain her ability to travel freely through the independent territories that were not under Star Federation control, she could not flirt with those kinds of war crimes. The Star Federation would certainly forgive her, but protests and resistance from independent territories was something they could not afford.

Her jaw tightened as her thoughts turned briefly back to Mezora and how those so-called law enforcers had blocked her from Ashburn's trail. Because of them and their fondness for spiting the Star Federation, she had lost Ashburn.

Her anger must have shown on her face as the major cleared his throat and moved back towards the glass chamber in the middle of the tent. "For now," he said, "we've taken it upon ourselves to try the next best thing. We're seeing what it takes to stimulate that gland."

"Any luck so far?" Erica asked, coming up beside the major.

"None, but we are working with an alien corpse. There's a hard limit to what we can understand. I've got my hopes up for electrical stimuli, but for now, best I can promise is we'll keep at it for as long as we can."

Erica nodded. This finding did not change much. Thanks to the brutality of the first purge and the new development of the berserk Nandros, this was the first time an autopsy had been performed on a Neo-Andromedan. There was still much to learn, but until there was something solid to report, Erica thought it best to keep this project within the small circle that was aware of it. That included the admiralty board. They wanted to know exactly what the galaxy was up against almost as badly as Erica did.

But after seeing those images, Erica had the feeling she'd be of more use elsewhere. She'd done what she could for Sciyat, and she would leave the lunar world in capable hands. But there were Nandros prowling among the stars, and she could not let them hurt anyone else. It was time for her to move on.

CHAPTER 5: NANDRO

Putting into port on Phan was easy. The Star Federation had lifted the bulk of its surveillance, and beyond the usual routine check-in from Phan's Monitor team, the silver-and-blue starship breached the Phanite sky with no trouble. Lance knew all the right lies to tell, and they coasted past security with nothing more than a firm warning to get their ship named and registered as soon as possible. They docked at the public port, choosing to hide in the open with proper security clearance, and Lance and Lissa donned hologram disguises to mask their identities before setting out. Blade and Orion whined when told to stay onboard the ship, and the black arkin loosed a snarl as the airlock hissed shut behind Lance and Lissa.

"I'm sure they'll be fine," Lance said as they moved away from the ship.

"If they break anything, they're sleeping in the airlock," Lissa returned.

They focused on weaving through the thick crowd of the ground port. Gray clouds tangled with weak sunlight and light breezes as Lance followed in Lissa's wake through the press of bodies. He took the opportunity to take in the feel of life on Phan.

He immediately felt the shift from his previous visits. The last few times he'd been on Phan, tension had rippled through the crowds whenever a Star Federation insignia appeared, but life had ground on, unremarkable but secure.

Now, the drone of the crowd was muted. Crews from different ships kept among their own mates, shooting wary glances over their shoulders or avoiding eye contact all together. Gazes lingered on humanoid forms, and more than once, Lance saw grips tighten on weapons that, in the not so distant past, had been carefully concealed instead of placed on hostile display.

There were some who acted with deliberate nonchalance, but they were a bit too openly dismissive of the attitudes around them to fully mask their own unease, and they worked the hardest to avoid meeting a stranger's eye.

And then there was the female Vareesi who stalked up to Lance, refused to let him pass, and forced him into trouble. "You got funny-looking eyes," the Vareesi proclaimed loudly, and activity around them came to a standstill.

Lance shook his head. The projected build of his hologram disguise was the same as his natural frame. His pale olive skin was the same, his facial structure was similar save for the more pinched nose, and he'd even given himself an unshaven jaw to match his own scratchy stubble. But he'd given himself brown hair and mud-brown eyes. There was nothing remarkable about them.

He moved to step around the Vareesi, but she would not let him go so easily. Built like a centaur from the myths of old Earth but with limbs segmented like an insect's, she lashed across his path, blocking him with the length of her body. Her four legs were wiry but hard with muscle, and her spine curved before him at his eye level, turning the length of her body into a living wall. A nubby tail flicked with angry anticipation, and her torso was ratcheted straight upwards over her front legs. She had drawn herself up to her full height to tower over Lance, and her yellow eyes glared down at him.

Bewildered but recognizing the danger, Lance dared not break eye contact with the Vareesi. In his peripherals, he saw the crowd press in around him, hungry for confrontation. He did not know where Lissa was. She had been a few steps ahead when the Vareesi had cut across his path.

"I said," the Vareesi hissed again, voice deep and heavy, "you got weird eyes."

Lance held her stare and said, "You got weird everything."

A snicker ran through the crowd. Good. He needed them on his side. If the Vareesi hit him, she hit him, but if the crowd liked him, they might hold back from rushing him. They wouldn't help, but they wouldn't jump at the chance to kill him, either.

The Vareesi stamped her back leg. Muscles rippled under her purple hide, and the white, symmetrical markings on her head and neck looked like an armored mask of bones. Her long snout curled into a snarl, and Lance couldn't help noticing that the thick horn at the tip of her nose and the ones on her head were chipped and cracked with heavy use.

Lance regretted speaking.

But as the Vareesi opened her mouth, a snarl half-formed in her throat, the barrel of an enerpulse pistol knocked against her jaw and came to rest against the soft patch of velvety skin at the base of her exposed throat. The Vareesi's yellow eyes were wild with surprise and pain as they swiveled around to settle on Lissa, who stood almost leaning against the Vareesi's hard, flat chest, one arm fully extended to hold her enerpulse pistol in place.

Lance remembered that he had advised Lissa to craft a better disguise. All she had changed was the color of her eyes, opting for a brown so dark they were almost black. Lance had not thought that would be enough, but the Vareesi had proven him wrong. Lissa's disguised eyes were a sharp change from her natural silver, but at that moment, they were not so different from her Neo-Andromedan eyes; they glittered with the promise of death.

"Move away," she murmured to the Vareesi.

After a tense moment, the Vareesi took a hesitant step back, then another, then wheeled away. She rammed her way through the press of bodies, and Lance watched her horned head bob and weave over the top of the crowd.

He turned back to find Lissa staring at him, along with the crowd that had gathered around the excitement.

"You've got shit-brown eyes," Lissa loudly informed him with a smirk, "but that's better than shitty Nandro eyes."

The crowd laughed and Lissa bared her teeth with them, but Lance heard the catch in her voice when she used the slur, and her darkened eyes looked dead behind the smile.

As the crowd dispersed, Lance and Lissa set off again for the main city and the hospital where Dr. Chhaya worked. They ran into no more trouble, but Lissa's walk was tense and alert, and her silence was grim.

Lance tried to think of something, anything to say to her, but he wasn't certain the right words even existed.

CHAPTER 6: COLLARED

Ever since the day Lissa had stumbled into this particular Phanite hospital, half-dragging and half-carrying a wheezing, nearly unconscious Aven over the threshold, very careful arrangements had been made for Lissa's visits. A select portion of the staff knew that she was Neo-Andromedan, and there was always someone ready to help her and alert Dr. Chhaya to her arrival.

She expected a different reaction to her arrival today. When Lance had given her Aven's broken navigation sphere after the events on Sciyat, she'd had a premonition that her brother was dead, and knew the staff would look at her with sad, sympathetic eyes. She was ready to deal with that.

She was not ready for the looks of fear that she got instead.

"Dr. Chhaya is with a patient," a receptionist informed her in a hurried, quiet tone, avoiding her gaze. "You'll need to wait for him."

Lissa stood at the desk for a moment, remembering the warm smile the receptionist had given her the last time she had been here. How helpful the others who knew that she and Aven were Neo-Andromedan were. The feeling of security that had enveloped the hospital, promising safety from the Seventh

Sun, from the Star Federation, from civilians with Anti leanings. Looking around now, Lissa only saw heads turn quickly away and spines tense with fear.

"It's going to be a while," she informed Lance as she sat down next to him in the old but clean waiting area.

He had not said a word since the incident with the Vareesi, and he only gave her another lost, pained look.

She turned her head away. She wasn't sure how many more looks like that she could take, and she could not explain to him what it was like living a life made up of moments like that. The Vareesi had given him a taste, but if he wanted to understand more, it was up to him, not her.

Minutes ticked into an hour, and Lissa's disappointment shifted towards anger. She maintained her composure, but as she watched others come and go around her, she felt her temper turn brittle. Lance said nothing, only waited with her, occasionally sneaking a sidelong look at her. The receptionist and other staff members made a point of not looking at them. The staff edged around them, reluctant to move within five steps of them, hurrying past when necessity demanded it. They kept that up for the better part of the hour that Lissa was forced to wait, until a human nurse with cream-colored skin and auburn hair emerged from the restricted areas of the hospital and paused at the front desk. Round in face and figure, she smiled with easy warmth as she said something to the receptionist. She was handed a datapad in response. As the nurse turned to walk back through the decontamination checkpoint, her gaze caught on Lissa, and her eyes widened in recognition. The nurse changed direction mid-stride, and walked directly towards Lissa and Lance.

Lissa shot to her feet. "Keera," she breathed, relief washing over her.

She was—had been—one of Aven's main nurses, trusted with the full secret of his identity. Warm and protective, Lissa had always liked her, and true to her nature, Keera cast a searching glance over Lance as he got to his feet. She looked back at Lissa questioningly, but relaxed when Lissa gave her an encouraging nod. "Does Dr. Chhaya know you're here?" Keera asked softly.

Lissa glanced at the receptionist, who pointedly looked away. "No."

Keera followed her gaze and chewed her bottom lip as she took in the cold, distant attitudes of the other staff members. "He just finished with a patient and is waiting for this." She brandished the datapad in her hand. "I'll take you to him."

With Keera leading them, they moved quickly through the hospital, though there was a delay when Lissa ran her enerpulse pistol past security. What was once a routine check-in for Lissa's previously approved alias stretched for a suspiciously long time, long enough for Keera to duck into the clerk's office and try to find out what the problem was. Several minutes later, she came back shaking her head, but with clearance for Lissa to carry her weapon beyond the initial checkpoint.

Lissa did not ask about the delay; she already knew the reason why.

What she didn't understand was the hospital staff's reluctance to let her see Dr. Chhaya. As they rounded a final corner and saw the doctor at the far end of the hall, she asked Keera why the barriers had been thrown up.

"Honestly, I think they were trying to protect him," Keera answered.

Lissa stiffened. "From what?"

Keera winced and said nothing, but as they drew closer to the doctor, Lissa understood.

Kyle Chhaya was an older man, with healthy brown skin lined with wrinkles and a head crowned with wiry gray hair. He had a solid build softened by age, and kind brown eyes matched by a demeanor that Lissa had always liked. What he did not have was any sort of rusty injury or bad muscles, and yet there was a distinct limp to his walk as he moved towards them, and one of his arms was in a sling. Worst of all, there was a dark, swollen bruise under his left eye.

Lissa looked at all of these badges of pain, and murder pounded through her heart. If she ever learned who'd done this to Dr. Chhaya, she'd kill them with her teeth.

The doctor read her rage. "I'm all right, Lissa," he assured her, keeping his voice mellow, but the edges were ragged with exhaustion.

"What happened?" she demanded.

Chhaya sighed, eyeing Lance's hologram disguise. "Mr. Ashburn, I presume?"

Keera tensed. "Ashburn… of the Star Federation?"

Everyone nodded, and Lissa added tersely, "He's with me."

"It's a long story," Lance said to Keera.

The nurse looked at Lance for a moment, then understanding bloomed in her eyes. "Oh, you're the one who talked to Aven before…"

"Before whatever killed him, killed him," Lissa put in. At Chhaya's and Keera's stares, she said, "I know he's dead. I'm accepting it. But what happened to *you*, Dr. Chhaya?"

The doctor stood in silence for a moment, but Lissa pressed him again, and he finally told her that ever since the official initiation of the Star Federation's purge, Phan had become a lot less safe for people like him.

"People like you?" Lance murmured.

"Neo-Andromedan sympathizers," Chhaya said.

"Someone on your staff leaked that?" Lissa demanded, remembering the cold treatment earlier.

Chhaya quickly shook his head. "They've all been keeping their heads down ever since…"

Lissa waited, but the doctor seemed reluctant to go on.

"It seemed like we were all right at first," Keera supplied, "even though some threats were coming to the hospital. We thought it was a lot of hot air but we stepped up security to be safe, and everything was fine until Dr. Chhaya showed up late one day, looking like…" She glanced at the doctor uneasily.

"I looked like someone beat the hell out of me," he finished, and then added, "Which they did."

Lissa must have looked ready to commit a crime, for the doctor rushed to assure her that even though they had surprised him, his attackers made a point of leaving him alive, and he was able to make it to the hospital. "Someone finally stopped to help me when they saw me bleeding and hobbling down the street, and my staff took care of me here. I'm okay, really."

"Groups of us have been walking together since then," Keera added. "We watch out for each other."

"How long until that's not enough?" Lissa asked quietly. She felt Lance shift uneasily next to her, but kept her gaze locked on the doctor and the nurse. Her voice was hot with anger. "This is a hospital, a sanctioned service center. You should be under protection from the Star Feds." She had intended to say more, but the look that passed between Chhaya and Keera stopped her. Cold clarity settled over Lissa, and the way the staff had treated her came into sharp relief. "It was the Star Feds that did this," she said, "wasn't it?"

Chhaya's silence and Keera's nervous shifting of her weight were answer enough.

That was why Lissa was suddenly a threat to Dr. Chhaya. If the Seventh Sun had attacked, maybe the hospital would be crawling with Star Federation soldiers, maybe it wouldn't be, but Lissa's status would have been unchanged. The Seventh Sun had always been a threat, and Dr. Chhaya and his trusted staff members had always known that. But if the Star Federation had invaded, had marked Chhaya as a potential threat, then any associations with Lissa would brand him a human traitor, a Neo-Andromedan sympathizer, a purge target.

And yet, the hospital was painfully empty of gray uniforms and winged insignias. Which meant they knew that the Neo-Andromedan connection here had already been severed.

"Who was it?" Lissa asked, her voice jagged. "Who killed Aven?"

Keera looked at her so sadly that Lissa's skin started to burn under that well-meaning, pitying stare.

Chhaya hesitated, but after sizing up Lissa's distress, decided to give her the truth. "Fleet Commander Keraun."

Lance stiffened, and Lissa's eyes finally darted to him. "Keraun is the Hyrunian fleet commander," Lance told her. "The only Hyrunian officer in the Star Federation. He's ruthless."

"He's the one who initiated the purge," Lissa said, remembering the newscast they'd heard after the events on Sciyat. Her anger drained to numbness.

Lance gave a single, solemn nod.

Lissa lapsed into silence and slipped out of focus. She was dimly aware of Lance asking Dr. Chhaya and Keera questions, but her mind kept wrapping around her inability to keep Aven safe.

All those years spent running and hiding from the Seventh Sun interrupted only by the brief happiness with the Fangs on Terra Six, all that time and money pushed into fighting off the Banthan virus, all those bounties, all those nights spent chasing targets and running from phantoms, looking over her shoulder, waiting for Rosonno's agents to catch up. The day Rosonno finally did catch up, beginning with the betrayal of the renegade captain and his crew—*His name was Montag*—and the ambush at Ametria when the Seventh Sun took the opportunity to slaughter a squadron of soldiers under the command of a golden fleet commander—*When I met Ashburn*—to the follow-up surprise attack on Yuna where Rosonno had confronted her in person—*In PERSON*—all the way to her capture on Phan and Awakening on Daanhymn—*Fight for me, Little Light*—to Mezora, to Jetune, to Sciyat, all the enerpulse shots that dotted a path between those worlds, racing for a way to bring down the Seventh Sun before they caught up again, only for Aven to fall to soldiers screaming *Stand and Protect!* instead of agents whispering—

"Lissa?"

Welcome to the Light.

Dr. Chhaya's hand was gentle on her shoulder, grounding her in the hospital again. Lance and Keera were watching her closely. "Are you okay?"

"Fine," she managed to scrape out.

She shifted, and Chhaya immediately withdrew his hand. He did not look like he believed her, but he did not press her. His voice was frustratingly gentle when he said, "Mr. Ashburn said you came here because you needed something removed?"

Lissa tugged down the high collar of her shirt and lifted her chin, revealing the ring of black that choked her neck. Keera and Chhaya both pulled in a sharp breath, leaning in for a closer look at the Seventh Sun's collar.

"It's been hitting her with sedatives whenever someone activates it," Lance said. "Neither of us knows what would happen if we tried to take it off, but it seemed dangerous to try."

"I guarantee it is," Chhaya muttered, stepping closer. "May I?" he asked Lissa. She nodded and gathered her hair in her fist, pulling it clear of the back of the collar. Chhaya brushed the fingers of his uninjured hand against the black surface. "Total seal, no seams anywhere," he murmured as he studied the collar. After a thorough inspection, he stepped back. "Do you remember feeling any particular spot where the collar injected you?"

Lissa scratched at the left side of her neck, where her skin was most raw. That was where the pain had come from on Sciyat. She remembered that much.

"This is beyond me," Chhaya told her. "I can't take it off, but we have a specialist who can. She doesn't have Anti leanings as far as we know, but keep your head down, just in case." He paused delicately. "What's left in Aven's treatment account should cover all costs of the procedure."

Lissa nodded, not trusting herself to speak.

"It won't take long," Chhaya assured her. At her continued silence, he promised to wait with her. Keera made to give him the datapad, but Chhaya shook his head. "Leave it outside the room, I'll get it on my way in."

Keera nodded and wished Lissa well before turning to leave. She smiled an uncertain goodbye to Lance, and went on her way.

Time blurred for Lissa. She didn't know how long it was before she was meeting another human doctor who poked and prodded at the collar around her throat, wondering aloud why it was there to begin with, but she didn't seem terribly interested in the answer.

"You're not our first renegade," she told Lissa dismissively, then led her to a menacing chair with an uncomfortable number of saws and laser cutters near it. She pushed Lissa into the seat and strapped her wrists down without missing a beat. More restraints closed around her shoulders and forehead, locking her head and neck in place.

Lissa had to bite back a scream at being restrained again. Her heart thudded wildly in her chest, threatening to pulverize her ribcage. Her breath became hard in her lungs, and heat rose under her skin, flushing the natural golden brown hue towards mahogany. Then Lance's hand closed over hers and Lissa froze, surprised. After a moment, she laced her fingers around his. The nails of her other hand dug into her palm.

The collar is coming off, she told herself.

But the memory of a Seventh Sun agent slipping it around her neck haunted the moment, and Lissa focused hard on Dr. Chhaya standing before her, absorbing the details of his white doctor's coat as he relayed the facts of the collar to the specialist.

"This is going to have to come off in two parts," she told Lissa, "but I need to make three cuts. Two around the injectors to isolate them, and the last one to cut you free. It's very important that you hold still for all three."

Lissa did not remember responding, but the next few minutes were filled with tests on the collar and concentrated frowns as the specialist determined where to make the cuts. Then there were light whirring sounds as the lasers dove in once, twice, three times, and a searing pinch at the left side of Lissa's neck followed by the pressure of a gauze pad against the wound. The restraints were lifted, and Lance released her hand.

The specialist dropped the two halves of the collar into Lissa's lap. "There you go," she said, pleased with her triumph over the alien technology. "The design isn't as clever as it pretends to be, but this piece was tricky." She held up the small section that contained the injectors, and Lissa saw light glint off of tiny silver probes sticking out of the collar. "Put up a bit of a fight coming out of you." The specialist eyed the piece thoughtfully. "I'd like to keep this," she said. "We could get some good use out of reverse engineering it."

Lissa turned the pieces of the broken collar in her hands, feeling cold and nauseous. She traced the line of white stars, and then her hand wandered up to her neck. Her bare skin felt almost foreign to her, soft and vulnerable without the hard collar there. She lowered her hand and found Lance and Chhaya both staring at her. It took her a moment to realize the specialist had offered to dispose of the collar for her, and she had tightened her grip on the broken pieces in response. Quickly, Lissa surrendered the smooth, unadorned back half of the collar, but she hesitated over the other bit. She flipped it over, stared hard at the seven white stars, and slowly closed her fingers around it.

"Keep your piece," Lissa said colorlessly, "and I'll keep mine."

Lance and Chhaya both shifted uneasily.

Sometime later, Lissa stood before Dr. Chhaya in the hallway, the broken collar secured in a pouch on her belt. It didn't quite fit and the outline was visible against the flexible fabric. Lissa could feel the stars on the surface whenever she pressed her fingers against the narrow bulge.

Chhaya pretended not to notice the new habit, though his pointed effort to look anywhere but at that particular place was far too obvious to Lissa.

Lance only watched her face. Lissa did her best to ignore him.

"—may feel a little groggy," Chhaya was telling her, "since the collar didn't come off as cleanly as it could have, but she did very well and you'll recover fully once the last of the tranquilizer leaves your system. Be on the watch for symptoms of withdrawal." He directed that statement more to Lance than to Lissa. "It's unlikely that it's addictive, but since you won't stay overnight for observations, you need to keep an eye out."

A small silence played out.

"We should be going," Lance murmured. He looked between her and the doctor. "I'll let you say goodbye."

Chhaya nodded his thanks as Lance stepped away, though the ex-Star Fed did not stray too far. He waited for Lissa twenty paces away.

She turned her head from him, but was all too aware of his attention on her.

"I suppose this is our last goodbye," Chhaya said after a moment. His brown eyes searched her face, looking for something, anything.

There was only numbness.

Disappointment slipped into Chhaya's expression, but his voice remained gentle. Deep and gentle and comforting, as it always had been. "I know you have been through a lot, and you still have a long way to go." He made as if to touch the fingers that traced the broken collar in its pouch, but clenched his hand and let it drop again. "I want you to know that I admire your strength."

The statement jolted her, and she focused sharply on Chhaya now, taking in the tired droop of his shoulders counterbalanced by the high thrust of his chin as he met her gaze, trying to make something of their final goodbye.

He smiled sadly at her. "I remember your face the day you learned that the only way we could treat your brother was if you could cover the expenses. You hesitated, wrestled with doubt, but when you made your decision, you accepted it fully and never looked back." He took a deep breath. "I don't agree with what you decided to do to meet the price of Aven's treatment, but I have always admired your fighting spirit, and your refusal to give up. I know Aven was… reluctant to accept your help, but he…" Chhaya wiped his uninjured hand over his brow. "Something was broken between you two, but he did love you, Lissa. You were all he had for a very long time, and even though he made it seem like he resented you for keeping him alive, I think he just wanted you to be free. He…"

"He didn't like being a tether," Lissa finished.

Chhaya nodded. "He wasn't a good person, in the end. I don't know what he was like before the Banthan virus ripped through him, but I know what loss is like, and I am truly sorry for yours."

Lissa ran her thumb over the pouch on her belt and counted seven bumps under her finger. "I can't tell you that you'll be safe now," she told him. "You're marked as a sympathizer, and people won't be kind to you."

Chhaya shrugged. "I like to think that you and I have something in common when it comes to conviction. I don't pretend to have your strength, but I will never turn away a Neo-Andromedan."

"Thank you," Lissa said, voice dry in her throat. She wanted to say more, but Chhaya's admiration had thrust into her gut like a knife, twisting sharp and painful. Seven stars burned under her fingertips. She had to drop her eyes from Chhaya's open, earnest gaze.

"What will you do now?" the doctor asked after a long moment. "Where will you go?"

Lissa took a deep, steadying breath. She raised her eyes again, and her gaze fell past Chhaya, snagging on Lance as he waited. He met her stare patiently.

"Forward," Lissa told Chhaya. "Whatever that means."

CHAPTER 7: SUBMISSION

Vinterra spent most of her days on Daraax Beta creating a stabilization serum from the stores of pollen samples from Daanhymn. First Lit Tyrath was hungry for results, but without a steady source from Daanhymn, Vinterra's progress crawled at a grinding pace. The pollen from Daraax Beta had lost its vibrancy over its journey across the light-years, fading from brilliant blue to dull gray. The samples that had completely lost their color were useless, Vinterra soon learned, and she focused on the fresher samples, rationing where she could. Until the Star Federation cleared out of the Paradise Void, Daanhymn was inaccessible, and there was no way to safely bring more pollen samples to Daraax Beta.

Sometimes, Vinterra found herself slipping out of her work, thinking about the vivid sunsets and glowing, swirling blue pollen from the night-blooming flowers that now felt more like dreams than memories. Real or imagined, they offered her no comfort.

She did not know how long she had been on Daraax Beta. On this world, it was easy for the days to blend together. Venturing outside of the base was dangerous, and Vinterra found adjusting to mornings without sunrises difficult.

Even if Vinterra could have gone outside without wasting resources and the time of an entire escort team, and least of all risking exposure to dangerous radiation from the Daraaxi sun, there wasn't anything on this cold, dead planet that could bring Vinterra any sense of peace.

She buried herself in her work, making no friends among her colleagues but no enemies, either. The other Seventh Sun agents assigned to Daraax Beta were coming to know her by reputation as the scientist who had discovered the stabilizing effect the Daanhymn pollen had on the in-stasis Awakened, and they regarded her with unspoken awe.

In another life, Vinterra might have enjoyed that kind of quiet respect, but now, after everything that had happened between her and Haelin, it made her skin itch.

Luckily, aside from the lingering glances and occasional approach for invitations to meals and recreational activities— not all of which she could refuse, if she wanted to stay in the good graces of the base, and so suffered through—the other scientists left her alone for the most part. This was, she suspected, more out of the sheer amount of work to be done than respect for her wish to be alone. Currently, there was no real data on how the pollen affected active Awakened, but First Lit Tyrath had expressed high hopes for moving towards field tests very soon, and she was pushing the science teams firmly in that direction.

That alarmed Vinterra.

If the Seventh Sun wanted to turn the serum on active Awakened, then the in-stasis Awakened would not maintain that status for long.

And there was the very real chance that Haelin would be lost.

Vinterra thought about this often. She tried to keep herself calm, but her heart raged.

After learning of Haelin's self-sacrifice so Vinterra could live, Vinterra had spent several long, sleepless nights trying to find a way to recover her partner. Haelin had survived the Awakening process long enough to go into stasis, and through a seemingly casual request painstakingly worded and timed, Vinterra had managed to secure Haelin's transport to Daraax Beta. She was lucky that First Lit Tyrath was far too busy with her own work to review the request, but even with that good fortune, Vinterra knew that the Seventh Sun was moving towards an open strike against the Star Federation.

Her suspicions were confirmed as her pool of test candidates began to shrink.

Vinterra's team adjusted to the changes, though she was the one who struggled the most. There were a few murmurs of disappointment from her colleagues over some of their favorite candidates being pulled from the list, but beyond that, no one voiced any resistance. Vinterra suspected that her team was more excited by the prospect of shifting focus to active Awakened than they were disappointed by losing a few test subjects, but for her part, she only felt anxiety.

She knew that she could not keep constant watch over the transportation of Haelin's group of in-stasis Awakened without drawing attention, but when the test pool began to shrink, Vinterra's resolve crumpled. She began to check on Haelin's progress every day, but as her ship drew closer, Vinterra's dread only grew.

It finally burst when Haelin's transport ship changed course, and her group of Awakened were marked for fieldwork.

This time, Vinterra did not even try to keep the anger inside. This time, she sought out a target for her rage.

The moment she saw that Haelin's ship had turned, Vinterra stalked out of her laboratory, not bothering to come up with an excuse for leaving her team. She passed the other labs, the kitchens, and two common areas before she came to the massive, central room that made up the bulk of the base. She was dimly aware that the packs of agents in the hallways were stepping out of her way as she passed. She knew her expression must have been murderous, but her anger kept her feet moving. It took her past the gaping maw in the middle of the room without the familiar, paralyzing fear. Vinterra held on to the anger.

Looking around, she saw people everywhere, talking in pairs or groups or walking solo as they went through the motions of their days. Their predominantly dark clothing stood out in sharp contrast against the pale walls and floors, and Vinterra flicked her gaze over everyone, waiting for her attention to snag on the sparks of color she knew she would find.

She tipped her head upwards as she moved around the pit that held the stasis chambers, making sure she kept a wide enough berth around the edge. Logically, she knew there was a ramp in place that would stop her from falling to her death if she wandered over the edge. Emotionally, she could not bring herself to trust it. But she made herself ignore the drop and pay attention to the balconies that ran around the second and third levels of the base. People stood at the railings, talking with each other and sometimes gazing down into the darkness at the center of the room.

And there, on the top floor, dressed in vibrant purple slashed with white, and leaning carelessly against the railing, was First Lit Tyrath.

Vinterra almost ran up the ramp that joined the first two floors. She hurried past the group and private living spaces of the second story, making her way up to the final level. The third floor of the base was dedicated to storage space for the most part, but a little more than a quarter of the entire level was sectioned off for First Lit Tyrath.

The First Lit lived alone, but her quarters were open to the rest of the base with only three walls sectioning off the space. If she wanted privacy, she simply retreated to the back of the three-walled room and stayed out of sight. That was rare, however. Tyrath immersed herself in the daily routines of the base, and made sure to check in with every team as often as she could. That, of course, made it difficult for Vinterra to hide her attempts to track Haelin, but she had to grudgingly acknowledge that Tyrath did care about her subordinates. She took requests for unusual supplies very seriously, including tools, food, and even games. As long as the work was done, Tyrath let the agents do as they wished in their free time.

If the work wasn't done, Tyrath crafted tailored punishments, and rained them down with crushing force.

Vinterra paused just before she reached the top level. She'd done her work, but she'd also snuck around and tried to bring Haelin back. If Tyrath knew...

Her anger faded into fear, then snapped back.

If Tyrath knew, then she was the one responsible for ripping Haelin away.

Vinterra took a deep breath and stepped on to the third level.

The First Lit stood at the railing in front of her living space, speaking to two agents as she gazed down at the rest of the base.

As she approached, Vinterra stole a glance over the railing and felt her stomach drop as she gazed into the depths of the pit that held the Awakened.

The holding chamber was brightly lit near the top, filled with in-stasis Awakened resting in suspension pods illuminated with a sterile blue glow; a mark of Vinterra's work with the pollen samples. The color was nothing like Vinterra's memory of the flowers on Daanhymn. It scraped against her brain and sent a shiver of wrongness up her spine. The most chilling aspect of the chamber, however, was the fact that it was a mark of failed ambition.

The pit had been dug to hold far more Awakened than the Daraax Beta base had ever seen. Lift systems ran all the way to the bottom, and the pods that spiraled down were fully functional, but after the halfway point, they remained dark and empty. Cold lights that were the wrong shade of blue clustered near the top of the holding chamber, and blackness ruled the bottom.

Vinterra had made a point of never venturing farther down than the third-to-last row of Awakened, but even that close proximity to the unyielding darkness made her uneasy. As she looked into the holding chamber, she felt an unsettling pull towards the edge, but she forced herself to tear her eyes away and focus on the First Lit.

Vinterra kept a firm grip on the railing as she approached Tyrath, and the knuckles on Vinterra's hand were clearly visible beneath her dark brown skin. Even with the vertigo from peering over the railing, Vinterra felt heat flushing her face, and try as she might, she could not calm herself.

The First Lit did not notice her approach, and that only fueled Vinterra's anger.

Tyrath stood with her arms resting lightly on the railing before her, leaning over to stare into the depths of the stasis chamber. Her long, straight hair fell in a dark cascade down her back, a few glossy locks swinging forward over her shoulders. They stood out in stark contrast against her fair skin.

Vinterra saw the First Lit's mouth moving as she spoke to the agents standing beside her, both men entering frantic notes on datapads as she calmly rattled off orders. Vinterra was less than three steps away by the time she picked up on any of Tyrath's words, but the First Lit abruptly cut off and jerked her head around to stare at Vinterra. Her upturned, red-and-gold eyes drilled into Vinterra's, anger sparking behind them before a cool, pleasant smile replaced the hostility.

"We'll finish this later," Tyrath informed the other agents as she straightened and turned away from them. They looked ready to protest, but a single glance from the First Lit was enough to send them into a quick retreat.

As Tyrath turned back to Vinterra, she saw that the First Lit knew everything. Vinterra pulled her anger above her fear, drawing herself up to her full height as she forced herself to meet the First Lit's gaze and deliver a quick but respectful greeting. Tyrath's mouth twitched into an amused smile. She crossed her arms, her hands disappearing into the folds of her long sleeves, and waited.

Not for the first time, the First Lit's sharp, strong jaw reminded Vinterra of something predatory. Not quite like the Awakened, she had decided a while ago, but something a step *above* that level. Somehow, even after watching an Awakened escape and massacre the Daanhymn team, the First Lit's expression was more threatening.

Vinterra felt another flash of terror, but lifted her chin and kept her voice calm when she said, "My team has noticed that you have pulled some of our most promising test subjects out of the pool."

Tyrath cocked an eyebrow. "Your team?"

"Yes."

There was a long pause as the First Lit's eyes swept over Vinterra. She could not help but feel a pang of regret for not cleaning herself up before seeking out Tyrath. Her clothes were disheveled after another night in the lab without sleep, exhaustion pulled at the skin beneath her eyes, and her grip on the railing betrayed her unsteadiness. Vinterra forced herself to release the bar and stand straighter, but the First Lit's eyes had already turned away again.

"They were perfect candidates," Vinterra pressed on, not certain why she kept up the lie. "All recently Awakened and entered into stasis. None of them were—"

"When I told you to ask for anything you needed," Tyrath cut in, "I meant it. Granted, I expected you to restrict yourself to tools and colleagues to help you with your projects." The First Lit turned away from the railing, and seemed to float across the distance separating them.

Vinterra took an involuntary step back.

"I did not expect," Tyrath said, still smiling but with hard, cold eyes, "you to go behind my back and try to spirit your traitorous lover to Daraax Beta."

Vinterra opened her mouth, but her voice had hidden itself somewhere deep in her gut. She closed her lips again without a word.

"You must know that I want you to succeed here," The First Lit said as she halted less than a step away. She held Vinterra's eyes for a long moment, letting the hostility fall away. Vinterra was more than a little surprised by the genuine warmth in Tyrath's gaze. "Your work is very important to me,

51

Vinterra. I know that you're brilliant, and you could help the Seventh Sun do great things." The sharp smile returned. "As long as you stay focused on your work."

Tyrath turned away, and Vinterra closed her eyes and let out a long breath.

The First Lit returned to her place at the railing, resuming her vigil of the darkness far below them. "I'm willing to overlook this… *misstep*, provided you return to your work in earnest." She fixed Vinterra with another cold stare. "You had better start now."

Vinterra felt a reply rise to her lips, but this time, she willingly bit back the words. She dropped her head in what she hoped was a sufficiently submissive gesture, then turned to leave. Clearly, she would need to find another way to ensure Haelin's safety, if not reunite with her.

"And Vinterra?"

She froze, then slowly turned back to the First Lit.

Tyrath was not smiling now. "Try to remember what Haelin's selfishness cost us. Cost *you*." She cocked her head, considering Vinterra. "You were happy on Daanhymn, weren't you? I'd like you to be happy here. You can't do that if you keep fooling yourself into thinking that Haelin cared about anyone but herself."

"You're wrong," Vinterra whispered before she could stop herself.

Tyrath's eyes narrowed. "You know I'm not. If I was, would you be here right now?"

Vinterra's vision blurred, and she had to trust her feet to bring her back to her private quarters. When the door was closed behind her, she cried, remembering the note Haelin had left her that proved the First Lit wrong. And she remembered all the other things Haelin had done that proved Tyrath right.

Vinterra had never been as brave as Haelin. She'd never been as strong or as cunning. She'd botched her attempt to bring Haelin back, and now, as far as Vinterra could tell, Haelin was being sent into the field to fight.

Vinterra collapsed on her bed, tears rolling down to stain her pillow. If their positions were reversed, Haelin would have figured out something to do by now. She worked best through instinct and improvisation, and would have known what to do by now. Some smaller, subtler way to change the fate of her Awakened partner.

Vinterra tried, but she could not think of another way. Her mind had always focused first and foremost on her projects, and those required a very different kind of thinking. Hypotheses formed on existing data. Variables controlled to bring new findings into light. Small-scale tests in case something went wrong.

Vinterra was not Haelin. She could not approach this the way Haelin would. She had to figure it out on her own, and in her own way, before it was too late.

After allowing herself another minute of frustrated crying, Vinterra forced herself to get up, strip off her soiled clothes, wash herself, dress in fresh clothing, and find something to eat. She still felt exhausted, but being clean and fed helped clear her mind.

She still did not have a plan, but she had a theory about how she could see Haelin again.

All she had to do was risk the wrath of the entire Daraax Beta base along with her life, but as far as she was concerned, she wasn't really living, anyway.

CHAPTER 8: DISTANCE

Lance had hoped that Dr. Chhaya would be able to help Lissa. And he had, physically. But after Lissa had learned who had killed Aven, she slipped into silence. After they left Phan, she spent the next full day locked behind the door to her private quarters. Lance understood her pain, and let her be at first. Then he found Blade shut out of Lissa's room, lying against the closed door and whining softly. Lance tried to draw Lissa back out, but she was curt with him, saying that she was working on the communication logs and did not want to be bothered. She kept herself isolated for days. He did not know if she slept or ate, and she refused all offers of food.

When she finally emerged from her room and stalked into the control room, the look on her face was enough to set Lance on edge. It was the same guarded, mistrustful stare she'd given him when they'd first met, but this time, it was strained with the memory of Ametria and the pain of Jetune. Lance fought the urge to reach for an enerpulse pistol as Lissa sat down next to him at the controls. He noticed that she was not carrying the datapad with the communication logs, and her hands shot towards the navigation controls.

"Did you find another lead?" he asked, struggling to keep his voice as neutral as possible.

"No." She finished entering a set of coordinates, overrode the warning block the ship put up, then rose from her seat and turned to leave the room.

Lance did not need to look at the starmap to know where they were heading. He shot out of the control room after Lissa and stopped her with a hand on her arm. She pulled out of his grasp, but he shouldered into her path. "We can't go there, Lissa. It's suicide."

She turned away, but with Lance blocking the hall and the arkins watching from the control room, there was nowhere for her to go. "I can't do nothing," she said quietly.

"I understand, but stop long enough to think about what you're doing. This isn't like you. You don't rush into things."

"I don't hesitate when I get the chance to shoot, either." Her hair was tied back from her face, high on her head, and Lance found himself looking at the exposed golden brown skin at the base of her neck. He kept expecting to see a line of black where the collar used to be. "You're taking that from me," she said, low and hard.

Lance was too stunned to say anything for a moment, but he found his voice quickly enough. "*I'm* taking that from you?"

She rounded on him, and her smile was more like a snarl. "You keep stalling but you should be happy, Ashburn. We're doing what the Star Federation wants and going after a Seventh Sun leader." She took a step towards him, and Lance had to force himself not to recoil. A brightness was creeping into her eyes, and he thought of her on Daanhymn, when she had been out of control and starved for blood. "You should be thrilled," she growled.

Lance pushed away the memory of Lissa Awakened and focused on her now. The brightness had stalled. She wasn't at the point of losing control. Not yet.

"This isn't about the Star Federation," he said. "This is about you and your people, and your future."

"What future?" she snapped. "We have no future. We spend our terror-filled lives running from place to place, until something catches up with us and kills us." The brightness ebbed away, leaving her eyes cold and steady. "For Aven, that was you."

Lance's eyes narrowed. "I don't remember ever pointing an enerpulse pistol at him."

"You chased me from Ametria to Phan. You showed the Star Federation where to look. You led them right to him."

"By that logic, *you* led the Star Federation to your brother." The words cut, Lance saw, deeper than he had intended, but he made no attempt to soften the blow.

Lissa's voice was quiet when she said, "Yes, I led you, and I led the Seventh Sun. But the Sun didn't kill him."

"I know that," Lance said. "But you *cannot* blame me for what Keraun did."

Lissa's face twisted as she moved to step past him.

Lance caught her by the shoulders, moving back into her line of sight. "Listen to me. If I had thought for even one second that Keraun would go after Aven, I would have left you alone, even after what happened on Ametria. No one deserves to be helpless before Keraun. No one. And I'm sorry that's what happened to Aven. I truly am."

Lissa's eyes were hooded when she finally looked at him again.

Lance took a firmer grip on her and pressed on. "But I have no control over what the Star Federation does. You cannot hold me responsible for Aven's death. I am willing to be your ally in this, but not if you won't trust me."

She was still for a long, silent moment. Then she reached up, touched her fingers lightly against the skin of his wrists, and shoved his hands off her shoulders. "The next time we put into port," she said, "maybe you should go."

He stared at her, stunned, but as the words sank in, he shook his head. "You don't get to throw off responsibility for ripping my life apart. You don't get to dump me when I become inconvenient for you. You pulled me into this, but you don't get to say when I get out. This isn't just your fight anymore, and you need to think about what will happen after we go into this system, after we—"

"There are *no afters*," she snarled. "Why don't you understand that? There is nothing *after* we do anything. There is only this moment, the one we live in, and the chance that we live or die. If we live, then we think about what to do next, but never after. There's no end, there's no after. There's nothing but what we do now, and I can't do nothing!"

"You can try to find someone else to hunt. It doesn't have to be this person."

Lissa shook her head. "No. No more waiting. No more stalling. We go to the uncharted system, and I do what I need to."

"And then?"

"Then you can leave." She pushed past him and flung over her shoulder, "If you're still alive."

CHAPTER 9: TRIGGER

Firoden was a beautiful planet. Deep blue oceans spanned most of the surface, surrounding a massive, lush, green continent that stretched from the northern polar cap all the way to the southern one. Islands pockmarked the other side of the planet, visible through an atmosphere so clean and pure it looked like it did not exist. Severe storms were rare on Firoden thanks to the planet's slow rotation, and a single Firodeni day lasted nearly five sidereal days. All good supporting elements for a high-production society.

As Jason read through the Star Federation database entry detailing the history of the planet, he found it hard to believe that this idyllic world was home to some of the most dangerous renegades in the galaxy, but Jason suspected that territory wars would destroy the small paradise within the next few sidereal years. Intelligence gathered on the planet suggested that four major families ran the world, but allegiances were breaking and forming between them and other satellite renegades with increasing frequency. Paradise was destabilizing, and Firoden was on the cusp of its own war.

Against that, Jason had brought one mid-sized transport cruiser with reinforcements stationed lightyears away.

Yes, this should go wonderfully, he thought wryly. But between the demands of the evacuation efforts and his mistrust of the soldiers that had come from Keraun's ranks, this was all he was comfortable bringing in.

Luckily, Jason had stealth on his side. The Star Federation always equipped its soldiers with top-of-the-line technology, and while the black markets may boast a more advanced piece here and there, Star Federation tech swept the competition aside across the board. His cruiser came armed with pulse cannons, a good set of thrusters, plenty of room in the hanger for fighters and a few dropships, and a cloaking system that would have made most bounty hunters seethe with jealousy. Jason utilized this last system as the cruiser breached the sky and landed on the coast of a mountainous island. There were no safe touchdown points anywhere else on the island. Multi-passenger land cruisers would take him and his soldiers to the strike point.

Keraun's orders had required Jason and his soldiers to move in for a precision strike. Otherwise, Jason would have been sitting in the captain's chair, watching as his soldiers turned pulse cannons on the settlement Keraun had targeted for purge efforts. He was not sure which he would have preferred, but the thought of any purge activity left a sour twist in his stomach.

At least this way, there was a chance they would not find any Neo-Andromedans.

When the ship touched down, Jason and his soldiers were already in the land cruisers. Three of the large, open-sided vessels shot out of the ship, tearing down the shoreline. The day was warm, and Jason felt sweat forming on his brow and back. He wore the lighter, more flexible battle armor that had gaps in the plating around his joints, but it blocked nearly all of the wind from the cruiser's speed and left him at the mercy of Firoden's blue-white sun. Jason stood holding one of the overhead supports, watching sunlight wink off the ocean as the cruiser sped down the beach. In the distance, a hazy island rose out of the sea. Then the cruiser banked and took them away from the beach, over foothills covered in a carpet of thick, green plants disrupted only by the strikingly vibrant skins and feathers of the local fauna.

The beauty of Firoden made Jason uneasy long before they reached the strike point, but when they arrived, he could not help but wonder if there had been some mistake.

The ground cruisers slowed to let Jason and the other soldiers jump out and quickly form up. They started off at a brisk jog through the plant growth, but Jason held up a hand and called his units to a halt when he saw the small cluster of residential buildings and the clear-cut paths that led to them.

Private homes. Every single one of them.

None of them were taller than a second story, but they sprawled over the land, twisting into unexpected shapes to avoid presenting a window to their neighbor. They were built predominantly of wood, painted brightly in all different colors but with the same pale trims. Dark, flat roofs soaked up the sunlight and sent solar energy pulsing gently into the homes. Once, this had been a picturesque retreat for a powerful family. When Jason looked closer, he saw that the paint was old and chipped, and almost all of the houses had makeshift additions that did not match their original designs. Most of these were the second stories.

Jason stared at the houses, trying to make sense of things. Keraun had ordered him there on purge efforts, and demanded a precision strike due to the presence of humans in the area. Jason knew that the caution was more out of a desire to appease the human officers in the Star Federation than out of any level of concern for the residents of Firoden. Given the planet's current state, a remote strike would have made more sense, and most likely been forgivable.

Why, then, had Keraun ordered him to search and purge such a small residential area?

Jason could not even see a retail outlet of any sort, just the houses, all equipped with a small hanger. A few hangers stood with their doors open, boasting at least three flashy sky cruisers each.

There was not a soul to be seen.

There is something very, very wrong with this mission, Jason thought as he moved forward once again.

Bringing his hand up to activate the communicator in his helmet, Jason opened a transmission line back to the lead land cruiser. "Have you scanned this area?"

A soldier answered immediately. "We have, Captain."

"And?"

"Threat level minimal. We picked up energy signatures of pulse weapons inside the houses, but nothing above the level of a rapid-fire rifle."

That was enough to damage light Star Federation armor, but only if the soldier wearing it stood perfectly still and let an assailant shoot them a few times at pointblank range.

"Are there people inside the homes?" Jason asked.

"Yes, sir."

"How many?"

"Twenty-seven in total. All humanoid."

Less than half the number of soldiers that flanked Jason. If the Star Federation had reason to open fire today, this would be a slaughter.

His mind tripped, falling back to the memory of the ambush at Ametria. Far fewer Seventh Sun agents had overpowered over one hundred soldiers then. It was a mistake to think that numbers would protect Jason and his soldiers now.

But the "slaughter" part still applies, he thought grimly.

Jason covered the rest of the distance to the homes at a deliberate walk, watching for any sign of movement. He gave a sharp signal, and his soldiers fell into formation behind him, spreading out to cover more ground and open their sightlines. They maintained total silence, but Jason could sense their confusion. There was a halting rhythm to their gaits that mirrored Jason's reluctance. But they were all under orders from a fleet commander, and they moved forward to carry them out.

Jason's armor weighed heavy on his shoulders.

K. N. SALUSTRO

When they were less than thirty paces from the door of the first house, Jason stopped again. He gave another signal, and his soldiers took up firing positions. Glancing left and right, Jason saw how out-of-place the armored soldiers were, all hard gray figures glinting under a brilliant sky, clutching enerpulse weapons, and crushing the thick green plants underfoot.

Jason's communicator gave a soft tone as a requested transmission from the ground cruiser pilots came in. He accepted it, turning his gaze back to the houses.

"We're tracking movement inside the structures," one of the pilots told him. "People moving to windows with enerpulse weapons. They're keeping a close watch on you."

Jason saw the flutter of motion in one of the second-story windows of the house closest to him.

"What else do you see?" Jason asked.

"There's a few people keeping close together in your nearest building. Talking, we think. Wait, one of them is moving towards you."

The door to the home in question slipped open with casual ease, and a barefooted man wearing a sleeveless shirt over colorful shorts leaned out. He held a violet-colored drink in his hand, and sipped it thoughtfully as he leaned against the frame and looked around. His skin was equal parts bronzed and burnt red by the sun, flaking at the worst parts. Black hair was combed back and held in place by a set of dark glasses pushed up on his forehead. He regarded the soldiers with a slow glance and an easy smile on his pinched, narrow face, but Jason saw the calculations running behind his murky blue eyes.

Jason adjusted his grip on his enerpulse pistol, bringing the weapon into a more direct line with the man, although he kept the barrel pointed toward the ground.

"I gotta tell ya," the man called as he moved out of the doorway to the edge of the porch, leaning casually on the painted railing as if he were talking to a neighbor, "this is a hell of a greeting." His eyes fell on the red-and-gold insignia blazed on the chest of Jason's armor, narrowing slightly as he added, "Officer."

Before Jason could speak, another few doors banged open in quick succession, and three men and two women strolled out of the houses further down the line. They advanced abreast toward the soldiers. They ranged in height and skin tones, but they all sported tan lines and sunburns along with an enerpulse rifle each.

"Drop your weapons!" Jason shouted. The helmet distorted his voice a little, but he knew the order would carry.

Around him, soldiers turned their own weapons on the advancing group. The men and women did not slow, only curled their lips in disgust as they stared the soldiers down. They kept their rifles slung across their shoulders, barrels to the sky and hands away from the triggers, but there was a hard set to their postures and their steps were certain.

"It's their property," the man on the porch called. "They can carry eight rifles each if they want." He took a slow, noisy sip from his sweating glass. "'Specially when a bunch of armored Star Feds show up on their front lawns and look ready to turn the neighborhood into a shooting range."

"They have permits for all those rifles?" Jason snapped back.

The man studied him for a moment, then shrugged. "Maybe." He pushed off the railing and moved down the steps, approaching Jason directly. He never once looked at the pistol Jason now had trained on his chest, but he stopped a comfortable, calculated distance away that was meant to show that he was not a threat to Jason. Or at least not an immediate one. "But somethin' tells me you're not here for illegal firearms—" his eyes flickered to Jason's insignia and narrowed again, "—Captain."

Jason risked letting his attention wander, taking in the advancing group and the silent homes beyond them. He saw shadowy faces in the open upper story windows, betrayed by the slant of the white-blue sunlight as they tried to stay hidden. The men and women with the rifles moved to flank the sun-stained man in front of Jason, forming up next to him like guards around a leader.

No, Jason thought, *that's* exactly *what they are.*

The renegade leader smiled easily at Jason. "Suppose we could get back to enjoying our day, Captain?" The smile hardened. "Unless you want to tell me why you walked on to my vacation property in battle armor and turned a pistol on my family."

Jason eyed the snipers in the houses again. The day could either end shamefully, or bloody.

He decided to try for the former.

Lowering his pistol and giving a quick signal, Jason heard the clacks of armor against rifles as his soldiers followed his orders and shifted out of attack stances. None of them holstered their firearms, but Jason could sense the hard stares that focused on him as he lifted the visor on his helmet, offering the renegade leader a view of his face, and a skilled sniper a target.

"Sorry for disrupting your vacation," Jason said, keeping his tone and posture easy. "Seems we were given some faulty information."

"I got eyes. That much I can see."

Jason gave a warm, apologetic smile that was lightyears away from sincerity, but he had plenty of practice at that kind of smile. "To be on the safe side, we'll take a quick look around, and then we'll be on our way."

The leader let his eyes drift skyward, as though he was seriously considering the idea. "Maybe if you told us what the hell you're lookin' for, we could tell you all the places you're not gonna find it." He jerked his head at the row of homes behind him. "Like my family's vacation homes."

"I'm afraid that's classified," Jason told him, still smiling. Inwardly, he wondered what was taking the ground cruiser crews so long to give him an accurate read on the situation. He had not closed his communication line with the pilots, and he could hear them murmuring as they continued scanning the houses and tracking movement inside.

The renegade leader rocked back on his heels, turning his head to address the men and women behind him. "'Classified' like private, like our homes are supposed to be."

One of the men gave an amused sniff.

The leader turned back to Jason. "If you don't tell me what you're lookin' for, I'm not letting you anywhere near my house."

Definitely hiding something, Jason thought, *but maybe not Neo-Andromedans.*

He studied the leader, taking in the patchwork sunstains across his exposed skin and the hard, defiant set of his jaw. He was someone who had come up against authority before, and sneered at it until it fell silent before him.

Jason let his fake smile fall.

"It wasn't a request," Jason told the leader. He reached up and lowered his visor again before signaling his soldiers. They clapped their weapons back into firing positions and waited for his next signal.

The renegades did not flinch.

"We were told that something we're looking for is on your property. We can't leave until we've conducted a satisfactory search, and that's all you need to know." Jason shifted his stance, bringing himself up to his full height and facing the leader squarely. "You can either stand aside and let us look, or watch from the ground with your hands cuffed." Jason tilted his helmet as though he was looking towards the upper windows of the houses, trusting the mirrored visor to shield his face. He never took his eyes off the renegade leader. "And we'll take your snipers down before you can say, 'Fuck you.'"

The leader stared at him for a long moment. Then his lips cracked into a genuine smile. "Damn shame I like you, Cappy." He hooked the thumb of his free hand into the waistband of his shorts. "Makes this next bit so unpleasant."

A warning from the ground cruiser pilot informed Jason that some of the snipers in the houses were being joined by gunmen with heavier artillery. The kind that the Star Federation had tried and failed to wipe from the black markets after discovering that the solid ammunition had the capacity to pierce field armor at a much higher rate than enerpulse fire.

This complicates things, Jason thought.

"I'll tell you what," the leader said, taking another slurp of his lavender drink as he stepped forward. He gestured with the glass at the soldiers behind Jason. "You take your friends here, you leave, maybe you send me a little something to make up for the trouble, I forget any of this happened." He closed his hand on Jason's shoulder, as though the armor was not there and he was talking to an old friend.

Marking me, Jason thought. *First target.*

"What do you think, Cappy?" The leader's smile was all teeth and no warmth. "Take your toy soldiers, go back to where you all belong, and keep gettin' yourself some pretty gold bars to spiff up this armor of yours, huh?" He slapped the insignia burned into to the chest plate of Jason's armor.

"We still need to look," Jason told him flatly.

The leader laughed with exasperation, rolling his head and arms dramatically. "What the fuck are you lookin' for, Star Fed?"

One of the men behind the leader suddenly stepped forward. When Jason's attention snapped to him, he slowed and made a show of raising one of his hands and dropping the barrel of his rifle to the ground, but he kept moving all the same. He reached out and grabbed the leader's shoulder, coming up close to murmur in his ear.

The language was a Firodeni dialect, but Jason's helmet caught the words and translated for him.

"The Star Feds are purging," the man told the leader. "They're here for Neo-Andromedans."

And with that, the leader blanched under his suntan, open horror invading his expression before he smoothly locked down his emotions and gave Jason another easy smile. But there was real fear in his eyes now.

"Ah, maybe we should just let you look around," the leader said to Jason in the Galactic Unified Voice, his tone steady and congenial, "and maybe we could show you a little better hospitality. Get you a drink." He raised the glass of purple liquid in salute. "Maybe some sugarleaf?"

Jason had no idea what was in the glass, but he knew it was not the sweet, green drink enjoyed throughout the Andromeda Reach that was commonly known as sugarleaf. It had to be a codeword, and Jason glanced up at the windows just in time to see the snipers heft up one of the armor-piercing weapons and swing the barrel towards him.

His helmet toned again, and the ground cruiser pilots informed him that there was a lot of activity inside the houses now. It looked as though people were grabbing supplies and moving underground, either to bunkers or to escape, but they were taking weapons, too. The snipers were all taking aim at the soldiers.

So much for no bloodshed.

Jason lunged forward and grabbed the leader's arm, spinning him around. He pulled the leader close, turning him into a shield between himself and the snipers. He brought his pistol up and fired a shot before the leader's guards had time to swing their rifles around. His shot took one down, and his soldiers polished off the others.

A sniper shot clipped the hip of the man Jason held, and the armor-piercing round ripped through flesh and bone and sent a spray of blood across the ground. The shot missed Jason's leg by a hair's breadth. The renegade leader screamed in pain, crumpling in Jason's grip. Jason let him fall. He jumped away and ran out of the direct line of fire, curving towards the side of the house. He signaled for the soldiers near him to do the same, then tapped his helmet to switch frequencies.

"Search the houses!" Jason barked, and his helmet transmitted the order across the unit. "They're hiding Nandros inside. Watch for snipers, they're armed with heavy ammo."

The soldiers burst into motion, some charging toward the houses while others traded volleys with the snipers. Jason saw two soldiers take direct hits to the chest, their armor tearing like tissue paper under the armor-piercing rounds, but this time, the Star Federation did have the advantage through sheer force of numbers. Their shots burned the windows, leaving dark, smoking patches where they'd hit the siding. Moans of pain came from the upper floors of the houses where the snipers had gone down.

Jason led a small group of soldiers along the side of the house, circling back around to the front now that the remaining snipers had no clear shot. He ducked under the lower windows, then launched himself over the railing and on to the porch. His soldiers formed up around the door, and as Jason reached for the controls, he saw that the rest of his unit had already infiltrated the other homes.

The door slipped open without any resistance, and Jason charged inside, sweeping the barrel of his pistol across the room. A man and a woman were waiting for him, both armed, and they opened fire the moment he stepped over the threshold. Their shots slammed into his chest, but other than cushioned impacts and a few scorch marks, the enerpulse shots left no damage. Jason returned fire, and the two went down.

Jason's soldiers found the escape door almost immediately. It had been left open in haste, and the ground cruiser pilots informed him that the route led to an enclosed space, not an exit.

Rather than charging down and facing more enemy fire, Jason gave the order to smoke the fugitives out.

The smoke grenade thudded its way down the stairs, and then there was a hiss as it released the thick gas. Dark smoke wafted up and curled out of the bunker door, and Jason had his units stand back as unsteady footsteps pounded up the stairs.

The first to emerge was a woman, coughing hoarsely. She fell to her knees as she came through the smoke. Tears ran down her face as a soldier stepped forward and secured her hands behind her back with a set of laser cuffs. She was lifted roughly to her feet and pushed towards the front door, but she began to fight the moment she found her footing again. Jason saw the flash of her eyes—bright, burnished bronze seething with hatred and defiance—then she was gone and the rest of the group was stumbling out of the smoke.

Some had brought weapons with them, but between their ragged breathing and streaming eyes, none were able to fire. They were disarmed, cuffed, and taken away.

Silence fell after the last coughing prisoner was led away. Jason and the remaining soldiers waited with their weapons trained on the smoky doorway, but there was no movement or sound beyond Jason's own breath in his ears. He reached up and tapped his helmet again, asking the ground cruiser pilots for a scan of anyone remaining in the bunker.

"We're showing two or three people still down there," came the response.

"Two *or* three?"

"They're sitting close together, maybe even on top of each other. We can't get a clear read."

Jason spared a moment for a silent curse. "Are they conscious?"

"Seems that way," one of the pilots said. "We suspect they had a few gas masks down there, but not enough for the full crowd, or maybe they were the only ones who were able to grab them before the smoke became too much."

"What's the situation outside?"

"Under control," another pilot answered. "We're circling around to begin extraction of the surviving prisoners."

Jason signaled to the soldiers with him, then led the cautious descent into the smoke-filled bunker. His armor's respirator filtered out the gas, and infrared scanners in his helmet activated as the light closed off. Bright patches of yellow and orange appeared, marking the enemy's positions.

There were three, he realized. Two in the corner, huddled in a defensive position, and one out in the open, standing ready to fire. The rifle was a dull red against the brilliant yellow infrared imaging of the person who held it, but Jason recognized the length and general form as an enerpulse weapon. His armor would hold up against that.

With a final signal to his team, Jason charged down the last few stairs, opening fire as he came around the corner. He clipped the aggressor in the middle of the room, and enerpulse shots from his soldiers streaked white-hot across his vision. Jason swung his attention around to the two in the corner, squeezing the trigger of his pistol as he brought the weapon around.

It only occurred to him after he had fired that one of the figures in the corner was far too small to be an adult. And then the screaming came, high-pitched and panicked, and Jason knew he would carry that sound with him for the rest of his life as the small body collapsed, writhing in agony.

Jason's shot had not been clean, and it took a few minutes for the child to die.

The screams faded to whimpers, and then into silence as the life drained from the room.

Jason stood frozen as his soldiers inched forward, pressing toward the three bodies.

A soldier breathed a curse as he bent down to check the small form for vitals, then gave a negative signal.

All three holdouts were confirmed dead.

Jason could not tear his gaze away from the child.

After what felt like an eon but was only a moment, one of the soldiers roused Jason with a tentative, "Captain?"

They were waiting for his orders.

Jason knew that during a purge, it was protocol to take every target into Star Federation custody, no matter if they were alive or deceased. He was not supposed to leave them, but moving this child felt unforgiveable. As though he had not already crossed that threshold. But he could not bring himself to give the order.

Then one of the soldiers moved toward the child's body, reaching for it.

"No," Jason snapped, and the soldier looked at him. "I'll take it," he said quietly. "Help move the others."

The soldier obeyed, and Jason stepped to the small form. He could not tell the gender through the infrared scan, but the body was light in his arms. Jason could almost pretend the child was sleeping, if he denied that the last few minutes had happened, that he had pulled the trigger.

The thought made him sick.

He carried the body up the stairs, taking the rear this time. As he emerged into the light, the infrared scan switched off, and Jason fought a wave of dizziness as his brain tried to rectify the sudden change in his vision.

Everything felt slow and muted as Jason followed his soldiers out of the house. They carried the adult bodies between them, struggling only a little under the weight of the dead. They moved down the porch, across the lawn, and placed the two adult bodies at the end of the line of casualties pulled from the other houses.

A very small group of surviving prisoners sat huddled and cuffed a short distance away, staring silently at the line of bodies.

Almost silently.

The leader was sprawled on the grass, moaning in pain, maybe not all of it physical as he stared at the dead arranged before him. He was bleeding heavily from the nose, Jason saw, not just his hip. One of the soldiers must have hit him at some point. Jason made a mental note to find out who that was, and see them disciplined.

Then the leader's eyes fell on Jason. The man saw what he carried, and his moans changed to shrieks.

Jason tried not to look at the black, ragged wound his enerpulse shot had left in the small torso as he slowly carried the child to the end of the line. As gently as he could, Jason laid the child down, but with that task complete, he had to face what he'd done.

It was a boy, Jason saw now, dressed in blue shorts and the remains of a white, short-sleeved shirt. Above the scorched pit of the enerpulse shot, Jason saw vibrant yellow swirls, the top part of some graphic design. The child's bare arms were brown and smooth, and the over-sized gas mask covering his face lent a chilling, inhuman sense of finality to it all.

71

Jason felt his stomach churn as he stood above the small body, but he forced himself to look. He burned the image into his mind, and swore that he would never do something like this again.

Somewhere in the middle of his silent oath, he became aware of what the renegade leader was screaming.

"My son! That's my son!"

Jason turned around, and saw a soldier half-heartedly restraining the renegade leader as he tried to drag himself across the grass. Someone had placed a rudimentary bandage around his injured hip, but it was coming loose as he struggled against the soldier.

"Let him go," Jason said, crossing to the leader. The soldier backed away at his approach, and Jason tried to pull the renegade to his feet.

The man screamed and swatted at Jason, his gaze pure venom as he stared into Jason's mirrored visor.

Jason stumbled away, and the renegade fell back to the ground. Groaning, he resumed pulling himself across the grass, and did not stop until he had reached the child's body. Crying openly in front of the soldiers that watched his every move, the renegade leader pushed himself to an awkward kneel, his injured hip rotated oddly and leaving his leg splayed uselessly. Fresh blood stained his bandage as he tried to tug the gas mask from his son's head. When it was off, he pulled his son's lifeless body to his chest. He threw his cuffed arms over the child's head, getting as close as he could to a hug around the boy's shoulders as he buried his face in his son's thick, black hair.

A minute crawled past as the soldiers watched the renegade mourn.

Then the ground cruisers returned, and it was time to move the surviving prisoners, and destroy the bodies of the dead Neo-Andromedans.

Purge protocol was exacting.

It took two soldiers to drag the renegade leader away from his son. He howled as they took him away, growing paler as the exertion on his injury took its toll. By the time they'd taken him to the ground cruiser, he was unconscious.

But Jason's attention was locked on the boy again. He and his soldiers stood around the child, looking down at the young face.

The boy's eyes were open and staring, already clouding over, but that did not hide the colors of his eyes. One was dull blue, an exact copy of his father's eye color. The other was bright, burnished bronze.

Jason and his soldiers all regarded the child in silence. They all knew what they were looking at. They all knew that purge protocol dictated that they leave this particular corpse intact, and bring it back to the ship for further study. And they all knew that, given the chance to grow up, this child would have become as dangerous as at least one of his parents. Quite likely both, given his father's nature.

But the fact that the child was a human-Neo-Andromedan hybrid justified nothing in Jason's mind, and he reached down to do the only thing he could think of in that moment: he gently brushed the boy's eyes closed.

It was a useless gesture, he knew, and one that was selfish, meant more for himself than anyone else. Jason felt a little part of his humanity die that day.

This was what the Star Federation demanded of him during a purge. And as a soldier, he had to obey.

CHAPTER 10: TORN

Lissa barely slept as the ship stalked closer to the uncharted system. Every time she closed her eyes, she kept seeing Aven and Rosonno. In the dream, she was running towards them, but time was sticky and she could not move fast enough. They ignored her, and Lissa tried to shout to them but her voice was small and weak in her own ears. So she ran. As the ground ebbed away under her feet, she saw that Rosonno and Aven were speaking, but the words would not carry to her. Tension and uneasy familiarity rippled and shimmered between them like heat through the air as they stepped toward each other. Aven raised his pistol, and Lissa screamed a warning, but it was too late. Rosonno had already shot him. But when he turned to Lissa and trained his weapon on her, it was not Rosonno who stood there laughing, but Fleet Commander Ashburn. The Star Federation insignia was blazed over his heart, and his green eyes smoldered with hatred as he stared down the barrel at her.

She always woke the moment he pulled the trigger and filled her vision with white.

She knew that Lance had not killed Aven, but every time she looked at him, all she could see was the memory of the nightmare, and the less sleep she got, the more the line blurred between her dreams and reality.

Welcome to the fight for me, Little Light, voices whispered in her ear.

Groaning, Lissa rose from the cot in her room. She stretched as she rose, feeling her muscles creak in protest. Her stomach growled faintly, but the thought of food made her nauseous, and she substituted a meal for a splash of cold water across her face. Then she hurried to the control room.

It was time for them to enter the uncharted system.

Even if she'd slept a full sidereal day, navigating unmapped territories would have been difficult at best. The ship's autopilot could not carry them through, and Lissa switched to manual piloting as they entered the dark system. Lance was beside her in the control room, keeping one eye on readings from the ship's scanners and the other on her.

She avoided his gaze at all cost, not trusting herself to keep the nightmare version of Lance separate from the real one. If she looked at him, she knew she would make a mistake. She focused on piloting the ship and tried to mentally prepare for the upcoming hunt.

Reluctance pulled at her. She knew indecision would kill her, but two facts kept drumming through her head.

One, the Star Federation had killed Aven.

Two, the Seventh Sun had not.

She tried to convince herself that the Star Federation had simply found him first, that the Seventh Sun would have ended his life if they had been the ones to reach him. She knew that was not true. The Seventh Sun had been on Phan alongside the Star Federation. They had known where he was. They must have found him. They must have.

And then they had walked away.

Welcome to the fight for me, Little Light.

Lissa did not know who she was hunting now. She did not know their role within the Seventh Sun, did not know if they dealt with Awakenings, did not know if they had been involved in the decision to hunt down Lissa and Aven after they had fled the organization all those years ago. She tried to remind herself that, no matter who this target was, they had played some part in everything that had brought her to this moment.

She tried, but she kept seeing the Star Federation insignia burning over Aven's body.

Blade and Orion both sensed Lissa's tension. The arkins kept close to her, but not close enough for her to reach out and touch them. They were wary of her, maybe even afraid, and their eyes were wide and alert as they watched her.

Lissa tried to ignore them, too.

She ran on pure adrenaline as the ship tore through the uncharted sector. Lance urged her to a slower speed, but she only shook her head, her grip tight on the controls as he fed her information from the scanners on the locations and severity of obstacles. The ship responded beautifully to Lissa's touch, but under her straining nerves, she could not appreciate it. She was only aware of the pull on the ship from unseen traps.

It was a long, tense ride through the system, ending with a neutron star almost claiming the ship. The gravity warp came on so fast that there was no time to arc around the collapsed star, and the ship rattled and screamed as Lissa fought to bring them out of the dead star's grasp. She pushed the thrusters up to top speed, angled the ship, and dove further in to the neutron star's gravity field. She used their momentum to skim around the edge of their ship's safe zone within the field.

Lance gripped the edge of his seat as the ship shuddered violently, and the arkins howled as alarms shrieked. Lissa grit her teeth and pushed the ship forward. It rocketed past the neutron star, curved with the gravitational field, and soared free, straight into a slender fringe arm of a nebula. The dust cloud confused the sensors, and something hit hard against the ship's shields, but then they were through and coasting to their destination. The target coordinates had led them to a quiet little star with one lonely planet in its orbit, blue and tranquil and totally oblivious to the dangerous chaos that existed beyond this little pocket of the universe on the edge of a nebula.

Lissa slowly released the controls, her fingers stiff and sore. Her hands were shaking and exhaustion pulled at her eyes. She reached for the navigation system, more than ready to surrender the ship back to autopilot, but Lance's hand was already there. It took her a moment to realize that he was speaking, but he paused and waited for her to look at him.

She finally did, not sure if the sternness in his eyes was from concern or anger. She did not know which to expect anymore.

"You need to sleep," he said. "And eat."

Lissa shook her head, turning away. "We can't waste time."

"We won't," Lance said. "I'll take us in to land, but I need to go over the hull before we try. That trick you just pulled could have damaged something, and breaching the sky could cripple the ship." He studied her for a long moment. "It was good flying, Lissa, but we need to make sure we can leave that planet before we land on it. I won't let this become another Ametria for us."

Lissa frowned at the name of the red planet. She wanted to point out that when they had gone to Ametria, Lance had gone against her warning and alerted the Seventh Sun to their presence, and then hackers had grounded their ship on the surface. Then Lance had blown up their base with the pulse cannons from a crashed Star Federation ship.

Now they were here, drifting towards the atmosphere of an unnamed planet in an unnamed ship, a bounty hunter and a Star Fed getting ready to kill more Neo-Andromedans.

Not so different as he pretended.

Welcome to the fight for me, Little Light.

Lissa shook her head violently to chase away the voices, but they lingered, and so did the memories.

She needed to act, before they overwhelmed her.

She made to rise, ready to fight Lance for the controls if she had to, but she swayed dangerously on her feet, and her knees buckled. Lance was there immediately, steadying her and leading her away from her seat, towards the control room door.

In that moment, she realized that, more than anything, she was afraid to shut her eyes, was afraid of what her nightmares would show her.

"I can't sleep," she whispered. "I can't."

Lance paused, and she felt his eyes on her face, searching. "Okay," he finally said. "No sleep, but rest. Try to relax. I'll take care of the ship, and I'll get us on the ground." He sank down with Lissa to the floor, encouraging her to lean against the wall near the door. "Just rest. Please."

She met his gaze then. His eyes were anxious and concerned, but soft. Not hard and scoffing like in the dreams. She nodded, and he stood up.

Blade shoved into the space the moment he was gone, lying down and pressing her side against Lissa's. Relieved that the arkin was not shying away from her and grateful for the soft warmth, Lissa let herself slide down against Blade. The arkin's breathing steadied her, and in spite of everything, Lissa's eyes slipped closed.

She jerked awake when she felt a hand on her shoulder.

Lance kneeled in front of her, a ration of food in his hand. "Here," he said, offering her the package. "We'll breach the sky in a few minutes."

Lissa took the ration and sat up to find Orion curled up against her legs. The gray arkin flicked an ear in annoyance as she pushed to her feet.

Her head swam as she stood. As it cleared, the dizziness was replaced by a gnawing emptiness in her stomach. She bit into the food ration eagerly. "How long was I asleep?"

"A little over four hours," Lance said, leading the way back to the seats at the control panel.

Lissa nearly tripped in surprise, and her sore back flared in confirmation. She winced and stretched as she chewed the thick space food. "How's the ship?"

"Sturdier than I thought," Lance said. "There was a minor breach in the outer hull from when that neutron star almost ripped us apart." He paused. "I took a spacewalk and fixed it."

Lissa froze, only halfway into her seat. "You spacewalked while I was *asleep*?"

He shrugged, watching her sidelong.

"Why would you risk stranding yourself in space? What is *wrong* with you?"

"The hull needed to be fixed, and you needed to sleep." He turned away. "These things needed to happen in that moment. And you're the one who said we needed to exist only in the present." His hand brushed the controls and the ship's navigation system brought up a display of the peaceful planet they were about to raid. "So that's what I did." He faced her again in challenge.

Doubt started nibbling on her mind. Lissa slowly sank into her seat, watching him closely. "You didn't spacewalk."

"No, the hull was fine."

She frowned. "Then why...?"

Lance rested his elbows on his knees, leaning towards her. His eyes managed to be both fierce and gentle at once. "You risked stranding us in an uncharted system. I needed to know if that's because it's *your* life you don't care about, or everyone else's."

Lissa said nothing.

After a long moment, Lance sat back in his seat and gestured towards the display. The light of the star cast a warm yellow glow on the surrounding nebula, throwing light and shadow around the contours of the dust clouds and turning the area into an eerily beautiful spacescape. The oblivious little planet spun on.

"Are you sure you want to do this?" he asked.

"I can't do nothing," Lissa whispered.

"I know, but are you sure you want to do *this*?" He looked at her, but she would not meet his eye. "We can still walk away. It's not too late."

Lissa took a shallow breath, her attention locked on the display from the navigation system. Somewhere on that lonely little planet, one member of the Seventh Sun played with the lives of Neo-Andromedans across the galaxy. Not Rosonno, but someone.

Welcome to the Light, a voice snarled in her ear.

Lissa flinched out of her seat, breath caught in her chest. Lance made to rise, but she shook her head, trying to hide her sudden fear. She'd heard Rosonno's voice in her ear that time.

Rosonno.

"Too late was back on Ametria," Lissa told Lance, "when we blew up that base. Too late was on Yuna, when I was ambushed. Too late was when the Seventh Sun tried to have me hand-delivered to them by Montag's crew." She gripped the back of her seat, feeling the padded material give way under her fingers. "Too late was when Aven ran to Banth because he had nowhere else to go. Too late was when we ran away from the Fangs. Too late was when we escaped from the Seventh Sun the very first time." She finally looked at Lance, and heat flared through her heart. "Too late was when we were born."

Lance said nothing. And the longer the silence stretched between them, the more doubt started to worm its way through her gut. The Seventh Sun had pulled them into this life, but they had not killed Aven.

Don't think, she told herself. *Act before the chance is gone. Be unpredictable.*

"Put us on the ground," she told Lance. "I'll go in by myself if I have to, but I'm doing this. It's all I can do."

She left the control room then, heading for her private quarters to change and ready herself for the hunt. Blade followed her at a cautious distance. As she listened to the soft sounds of the arkin's slow and reluctant footsteps, Lissa knew that she had failed whatever test Lance had given her. If they survived the nameless planet in the uncharted system, she doubted he would remain with her the next time they put into port.

Regret chased her, but as long as she kept moving forward, it would not catch up.

CHAPTER 11: RUMORS

Moving the hybrid child's body out of the Firodeni system was a heavy task. Taking a dead child away from his grieving father, off of his home planet, and finally to a Star Federation analysis table reeked of disrespect and desecration, but Jason forced himself to bear the weight of it.

He had been the commanding officer on the field. And he had been the one who shot the child.

He still heard the boy's screams.

Jason personally oversaw the treatment and preservation of the body, ensuring that it was handled gently and disturbed as rarely as possible. Once the corpse was onboard the cruiser and frozen in a transport container in the securest part of the cargo hold, there was no need to tamper with the body further, but Jason still found himself watching over the boy protectively, checking the ship's logs for every movement in and out of the cargo hold.

He knew that the soldiers were too well-trained to disturb the body, even the ones from Keraun's units who were borderline disrespectful to Jason, but he still felt a small prick of panic every time he found that someone had entered the cargo hold. No one did anything to the child's body, and for the two-day journey from Firoden to the rendezvous point with the main ship, the boy rested peacefully.

In between his obsessive monitoring and trying to clear his head of the child's screams, Jason filled his time with plans for further purge activity. He gathered his junior officers and began to allocate resources to the ones who were willing to go back into the Reach and chase down the few other leads Keraun had supplied them with. Most of those leads were shaky at best, and Jason made a point of giving them to the more levelheaded officers. The last thing he wanted were his trigger-happy subordinates looking for Neo-Andromedans where there were none. Those soldiers he assigned to the more promising leads, the ones that did not demand observation, objective judgement, and potential infiltration.

Lieutenant Reed was assigned to one of the brute-force missions, and to Jason's surprise, he accepted the orders with only a flicker of subdued hostility. It seemed even Reed had his limits.

Jason hoped against hope that none of them, including Reed, would come back with more dead children.

What seemed like an eternity passed for Jason as the cruiser carried him through space, and then time caught up with itself when they rendezvoused with the *Argonaught IX*. Resources and soldiers were transferred in a blur of activity from one craft to another, and Jason swore he had not blinked before he was suddenly standing in the control room of the dreadnought. Reed and his assigned unit took the cruiser back into the reach. A few smaller crafts were released from the docking bay and shot off to their destinations. And Jason stood with his breath tight in his throat, watching the soldiers enter the *Argonaught IX*'s next destination.

When they were finished, Jason delivered the dead hybrid child to Major Malia Miyasato in the medical unit.

Miyasato gave an audible sigh when she saw the young boy's face, but she had seen too many fatal enerpulse injuries to be disturbed by his death. "It could have been worse," she murmured as her team readied the equipment that would rob the hybrid child of his final dignity.

Jason's eyes lingered on the gleaming dissection tools before fixing on Miyasato again.

She only shrugged. "If you'd captured him alive," she said softly, "my job would still be the same."

Jason's stomach turned at the thought, but he was far from comforted. He knew Miyasato had not meant it as a form of forgiveness, nor did he want to take it as such. They both knew that it was the lesser of two evils.

Before he left the medical bay, Miyasato drew him out of the room. She found a corner of the medical bay that was away from the rest of the activity and dropped her voice low. "I overheard something when we were transferring the Yuni refugees. It's more rumor than anything else at this point, but it's something you should know, Captain."

"Go on," Jason said, wary but also grateful for the news. Out in the Reach, it was hard to keep a finger on the pulse of the Star Federation. His main source of information came from other officer's reports, and his rare but terse orders from Keraun.

Miyasato glanced at a medic as he walked past, but his attention was fully absorbed in his datapad and he barely registered the edge of the doorway as he bumped his way through to the next room. Miyasato waited for him to disappear before she continued. "There's talk that the Yukarians have agreed to develop special defensive technology for Star Federation ships, and that they're basing it off of the recovered data from the *Argonaught IV*."

The implications sent Jason's mind racing. "If the Yukarians are developing special tech to counteract Seventh Sun hacking," he said, shaping his thoughts aloud, "then they're either giving the Star Federation exclusive tech, or first access to it."

Miyasato nodded.

Jason fell silent again, reflecting on the possibility of the Yukarians breaking the technology trade lockdown and giving the Star Federation an edge. It was possible that the hyper-intelligent race was recycling tech that they'd already had for years, decades even, but developing it specifically to block the Seventh Sun? That demanded new twists, developments, and improvisation to meet the requirements, leading to what was, essentially, brand new technology, even if it was based on something old.

The Yukarians openly feared Star Federation dominance over the galaxy, and they held a stable but complicated peace with both the human-dominated military and the Hyrunians. Jason knew that they would never give that kind of technology to the Star Federation freely. It had the dangerous potential of giving the military an edge over both the Yukarians and the Hyrunians. If the rumors were true, that tech would come at a high price.

Jason could not even guess at what that might be.

The more troubling aspect of the rumor was the basis on the crashed *Argonaught IV*. As that ship had been brought down by the Seventh Sun, it was the perfect starting point, but it fell firmly under Keraun's authority. If the Yukarians were using that starship, that could only mean that Keraun was brokering the agreement between the Star Federation and the Yukarians.

He asked Miyasato if she'd heard anything about Keraun specifically, but she shook her head. "There wasn't much to the rumor," she told him, "which is why I think it might be true. But nothing about Keraun, even though he has to be the one leading the collaboration."

"It would explain his recent silence," Jason reflected. He looked over his shoulder at the doorway that led back into the room where the hybrid boy would be torn apart and studied. "I expected *some*thing in response to my last purge report. There's been nothing."

Miyasato shifted uncomfortably, but she was nodding in agreement again. "As a fleet commander, it does make sense that he can speak directly with the Yukarians."

"Sure, but since when is he on such good terms with the Yukarians that he can get them to offer up custom tech to the Star Federation, and within a few months of recovering a crashed starship?" Jason frowned. "Keraun isn't just a Star Federation officer. He's also a *shekdan*. Working with him would risk angering the Hyrunians, and the Yukarians have always put that alliance first. Why would they work with him?"

Miyasato had no answers for his questions, but she did agree with him. "There's something happening with Keraun at the center," she said, mirroring Jason's hard frown. "The admirals have to know, don't they? Maybe even the other fleet commanders?"

"Maybe," Jason had to say, because he had no other explanation.

But neither he nor Major Miyasato were convinced by the argument, and as Jason left her to focus on her grizzly task with the hybrid child, he felt that there was something out-of-focus in front of him, something that he could not even begin to hope to describe.

All he knew was that it did not sit right with him.

CHAPTER 12: UNNAMED

Lance wanted to help Lissa. He truly did, but he had seen this before: trauma consuming someone until there was nothing left but a husk; a numb, lifeless body that could only act in desperation. They became reckless, welcoming death, often charging headlong to meet it. The Star Federation had not cared for some of its soldiers as well as it could have, and this emotional decay was all too familiar to Lance.

There was some hope for Lissa. She had been upset when she had thought that he'd risked his life on a spacewalk without anyone to monitor him, and he'd seen the way Blade's presence had comforted her and allowed her to sleep. Lance knew that Lissa was plagued by nightmares, but after Phan, she'd stopped talking about them. She had stopped talking about everything when she'd learned how Aven had died.

Lance had known that hunting the Seventh Sun would be particularly dangerous for her. He'd known it ever since Jetune, when he'd seen her kill Neo-Andromedans and scream for an Awakening to be shut down.

He should have known it since Daanhymn, when the Seventh Sun had successfully Awakened her, but he had been too eager to fuel her desire for vengeance to see anything else.

Now, Lissa was right: it was too late.

He could help her stay alive on this unnamed planet, maybe even get her out of the uncharted system again, but he did not know if he should expect her to resemble her former self anymore. His mind slipped back to when he had first met her. The Seventh Sun had ambushed his dreadnought after manipulating a small renegade crew under the command of a man named Montag. Lissa had been reserved and cautious back then, thinking over everything carefully. She had considered situations from every angle, waited for her opening, then took it when she knew she could succeed. She had escaped from the Star Federation and the Seventh Sun, and even though they had both caught up with her again, she had maintained control, and slipped beyond their grasp.

Lance wondered if she remembered what she had been like back then. Silent, restrained, and dangerous, but in total control. He worried that part of her was lost forever, drowned in light.

She'd told him, once, that Awakenings did that to Neo-Andromedans. Drowned them in light. He did not fully understand what that meant, but more than anything, he wanted to help her back into the safety of the dark.

He doubted this raid on an unnamed world with the intent to kill an unknown target was the way to do that.

But here they were, and if they did not do something, Lissa would shatter. All Lance could do was direct the ship towards the lonely planet and hope this did not push her over the edge.

The past had taught him a hard lesson about the Seventh Sun's hacking abilities, and Lance avoided initiating a scan of the planet. Instead, he waited for the ship to pick up on any sort of energy signature radiating out from the world. He'd seen very few Seventh Sun structures, but they had all been built in impossible locations and been impressive in their own ways. And they needed a lot of power to run.

Sure enough, the ship caught a source within the northern hemisphere, right in the heart of the planet's autumn. Red and brown was splashed across the green land, and Lance couldn't help but think that this world was not so different from the

Terra colonies or even Earth. Humans would have liked to live here, if they dared make the journey to the planet and survived the trip, as the Seventh Sun had dared and done.

Lance felt a grim respect for the Neo-Andromedan organization as he set the ship on a new trajectory. They had risen from of a ruined race and were carving out their existence wherever the rest of the galaxy could not hope to touch them. They were surviving, they were enduring.

They were also killing people, he reminded himself.

He paused then, remembering Jetune, and Ametria, and his career in the Star Federation.

It was so easy to blur the lines.

He knew this raid would not set things right, but if he did not let Lissa off the ship, he feared what she would do next. So, with a heavy, reluctant heart, Lance pushed the ship into the planet's atmosphere, and felt the jolt as they breached the sky.

Lissa stepped into the control room a few moments later. She had found new thermal wear to replace the outfit that had been taken from her on Daanhymn, and she had changed from her loose traveler's clothes to her hunting garb. The fabric was tight, but so black that it absorbed all shadow and light, making it difficult to pick out her form, even as she stood next to his shoulder.

"How long?" she asked.

One gloved hand rested on the enerpulse pistol holstered at her hip. Her hair was drawn back severely from her face into a tight bun at the base of her skull, slicked into place with gel. Her attention was fixed on the navigation system's display.

"Minutes," Lance told her. "There's a clearing not far from the base. It'll be a half-hour's walk at most from there."

Lissa's eyes narrowed. "They'll see us coming."

"Probably," Lance agreed, too drained to worry about her dissatisfaction. It was the best he could do, and she would have to take it if she didn't want a five-hour walk instead.

"Drop me from the airlock," she said, turning to go. "I'll take Orion."

"You will not," Lance told her, twisting around to meet her stare.

Tension stretched between them, and Lance heard one of the arkins sigh.

"Risk yourself all you want," he said, "but you will not pull me and Orion down with you."

Lissa said nothing, but light flickered behind her eyes. For a moment, Lance thought—and almost hoped—that she would fight him, physically or verbally. They could break the tension, maybe get some closure out of this. Lissa needed a release, something other than hunting and killing her own people, no matter what they had done.

She did not take the chance.

Instead, the light went out of her eyes, leaving them cold and distant. She left the control room without another word.

Lance breathed out, hard, and almost overshot their landing zone.

No attacks from the Seventh Sun came as the ship lowered to the thick grass, but they must have detected the starship landing so close to their base. Even in this remote area, they had to be on constant alert. It would be stupid not to be.

A soft beep from the ship told Lance that Lissa had the airlock open before the starship had fully touched down. He quickly finished the landing procedure, set the ship's security and alarms, ran for the enerpulse rifle he had cached in one of the lockers just outside the control room, and chased Lissa out of the ship. The arkins were already outside, Orion reveling in the sunset and stretching his wings against the burning sky. Blade was calmer, warier. She stared hard at Lissa, who hesitated at the edge of the clearing, just before the dark tree line.

Hope flared as Lance jogged to Lissa's side, but he quickly realized that there were no second thoughts. She was only waiting for her navigation sphere to point her in the right direction. The black sphere hovered over her palm, taking longer than it usually did to project a display.

Lance had seen Aven's navigation sphere trace the signature of Lissa's navisphere all the way from Phan to the Paradise Void, nearly to the planet Daanhymn, but this unnamed world in the uncharted sector was confusing the device.

Evening had enveloped the clearing by the time the navisphere beeped and displayed the exact location of their target's coordinates, tracing out a path for Lissa to follow. The sky was red with the last traces of the dying sunset as Lissa stepped into the forest.

Fallen leaves crunched under Lance's feet as he followed her.

"You don't have to come," Lissa said quietly. She glanced over her shoulder at him, and at the two arkins stalking close behind. "None of you do."

"No," he agreed, "but I want to make sure you don't get yourself killed."

She did not respond.

As Lissa led them through the dark forest, Lance strained his eyes to keep her in sight. It was almost impossible with her black hunter's clothing, and he finally had to send Orion ahead to keep track of her. With their keener eyesight, the arkins could pick her out from the trees, and Orion's coat was just light enough for Lance to follow. He shifted the rifle slung over his shoulder as he followed in Orion's wake, checking behind them every so often for unwanted followers.

The ground sloped up under their feet as they neared the Seventh Sun's base, cresting in a small hill that overlooked the clearing where the Neo-Andromedans had chosen to build. Lance and Lissa dropped to the ground and crawled to the top, rustling as quietly as they could through the leaves and keeping their heads low as they took in the sight below.

The base was almost disappointing compared to the others Lance had seen. It pushed towards large but not impressively so, and was built with sloping roofs to keep rain and snow from pooling in the winter. Light burned through the sparse windows, and floodlights illuminated the ground around the building, catching on the tall, yellow-green sea of rippling grass.

It almost looked like a residential structure, Lance thought, one with an elevated, private starship hanger connected to the side. It was something Lance would expect to see on human-populated planets throughout the galaxy.

But this planet had no humans, only the Seventh Sun's agents. And as Lance looked, he saw them patrolling just beyond the reach of the floodlights, weapons glinting with their movements. The grass had been allowed to grow wild, and it filled the clearing right up to the walls of the building, standing thick and tall, reaching past the waists of most of the Seventh Sun agents. They prowled slowly through the grass, watching the trees. A few stood with rifles trained, tense and waiting, and when Lance looked harder, he saw two snipers positioned on the roof. They were forced to lay on their sides as the slope of the roof was too steep for stable footing. Prime targets for a counter sniper, but deadly for anyone trying to break through the line of prowling agents on the ground.

Lance studied the positions of the agents, then frowned. There were far fewer here than he had expected. He supposed that the others could be inside the building, but if he had been a leader of a criminal organization and knew that people were coming to kill him, he would have placed more than nine agents on patrol.

Lance heard Lissa shift next to him, and her hand came forward, enerpulse pistol in her grip. He put his hand over hers before she could take aim. He felt her tense, but she did not pull away. He slowly leaned in close until his lips were almost touching her ear. He kept his eyes trained on the Seventh Sun agents as he whispered a plan to her, and after a long pause, she gave the smallest nod before creeping back down the hill. He heard her murmur an instruction to Blade, and then there were soft footfalls as Lissa moved north and the arkin turned south. Orion followed Blade after a quick signal from Lance.

When the others had safely moved away, Lance dipped below the crest of the hill and readied his rifle. He'd practiced with the weapon several times after purchasing it, and it was a familiar, solid weight in his hands now. He glanced left and right, seeking a better position, and found a thick patch of grass a short crawl away. Sheltering in the overgrown shoots, Lance nosed the barrel of the rifle forward, parting the grass as slowly as he could. He caught a glimpse of the prowling Seventh Sun agents just in time to see one pause, head turned to where Lance lay.

Lance froze, but the Seventh Sun agent turned fully towards him, rifle swiveling towards his hiding place. Lance knew he had been seen, but he held his ground. Sweat broke out on his forehead despite the cool air as he saw the Seventh Sun agent shift into a firing stance. An insect chirped somewhere near Lance's ear as the rifle trained on his patch of tall grass. Lance held his breath.

An arkin's roar tore the night apart.

The Seventh Sun agents all whipped towards the sound, weapons training on the far tree line in desperate confusion. One of them shouted and pointed to the sky, and Lance glimpsed Orion silhouetted against the yellow nebula and the emerging stars. He was high, too high for anyone to get an accurate shot at him, but Lance's heart was in his throat as rifles pointed up and began to trace Orion's flight path.

Lance went for the snipers first. He missed his first shot, but it landed close to the agent, startling them and sending them slipping down the roof, rifle falling uselessly away to the ground far below. His second shot hit the other sniper, and the third took out the first sniper as the agent dashed over the roof, making a wild grab for their fallen companion's weapon.

With the snipers down, Lance retreated from his compromised hiding place. He darted through the trees, squeezing off shots at the agents on the ground. From his vantage point on the hill, he saw agents from the far side of the building running towards the commotion. He also saw the ripple through the grass, shooting towards an agent standing several paces away from the others. With most eyes trained on Orion and the rest searching for Lance, no one noticed Blade until she leapt from the grass, tackled the lone agent, and went for the kill with an angry snarl.

A scream was cut short, and then agents were stumbling away, weapons sweeping the grass as they looked for Blade. Light breezes treacherously played with the tall grass, and Blade flickered away.

Orion roared again and banked towards the tree line, ready to touch down and join Blade as she stalked through the grass and picked off loners. Lance fired into the tight group of agents that was forming, hitting one and scattering the rest.

He ducked behind a tree and scanned the grass again, this time looking away from the knot of agents. He saw another rippling line, but this one moved straight to the building. He had just enough time to see Lissa burst from the grass and charge for a door before an enerpulse shot landed in the tree next to his head, sending pieces of scorched bark flying and momentarily blinding him.

Lance dropped to the ground and felt his way down the hill, letting his eyesight recover before running to a new position and harrying the Seventh Sun agents again. One by one, he picked them off with Blade and Orion. He did not see if Lissa had made it inside the building, but he had to trust her to finish what she'd started.

He focused on his own task, and fired another shot.

CHAPTER 13: STILLNESS

There had been no security features on the door. There had been no one guarding the entrance. There had only been the agents outside, and Lance and the arkins distracting them.

Lights were on throughout the building, washing over everything and rendering Lissa's hunting clothes useless. There were no shadows to hide in here. After a steady look around the room, she began to cautiously move forward.

The characteristic austerity of the Seventh Sun had carried even to this untouchable planet. The room was far more open than Lissa had seen in other structures, with dark wood floors and woven rugs, but although everything was clean, it was all worn and would clearly be used until it fell apart. The few pieces of furniture were small and scattered, though a small cluster around a low, bare table suggested an eating space. As Lissa moved slowly through the room, listening intently, her eyes wandered past storage lockers, a cooking space, and an open door leading into some sort of gathering room. There was a communication terminal in that room, but it was silent and dark. Nothing moved inside the base.

A shout from outside made her whip around, pistol drawn, and a face flashed past the window. Instinct kicked in and Lissa scanned the room again for a nonexistent hiding place, but then she heard the muffled growl of an arkin and saw another face flash past, too intent on escape to look through the window.

It wouldn't be long before one of the agents tried to barricade themselves inside the building and sealed Lissa in with them.

Moving faster now, Lissa stalked through the base. Her mind kept slipping back to Jetune. That base had seemed empty, too, but every last Seventh Sun agent had been inside the Awakening room, trying to push a boy into the Light. Lissa snuck a glance up at the lights in this base. They were bright and burning with power. No Awakenings were happening here.

The voices were still on the edge of her mind. *Welcome to the fight for me, Little Light.*

Lissa shook her head violently, trying to scatter the whispers, but she kept hearing them, and now something else was creeping in. A low-pitched, haunting sound. It sounded like—

Music?

Lissa stepped forward, her footsteps silent on the woven rugs, and heard the slow melody drifting down from an upper level. She moved towards the back of the building and found a narrow staircase leading up. It was darker at the top, though not quite entrenched in shadow.

The music drifted down to her from the dark space. She could hear higher notes now, slicing through the lower melody.

It all felt so wrong.

Another shout from outside followed by rapid enerpulse fire reminded her that she needed to move.

Pushing aside the feeling of dread, Lissa forced her feet up the stairs. There were soft creaks as she went, and the sound scratched out no matter how she shifted her weight or how lightly she stepped. She could only hope the music would drown the noise out.

The next level of the based was much more closed off, consisting of a long hallway with several rooms on both sides.

The ceiling was lower than Lissa had expected. She could have reached her hand up and brushed her palm against it as she walked, but she kept her attention on each room she passed. She saw neatly made beds in most, four to each room. Far more beds than there had been agents outside.

Lissa hesitated, turning the discovery over in her mind, but she moved on without exploring further. If there were more agents in the base, she would find them soon enough.

She passed more bunks than she cared to count, but the two rooms at the far end of the hall were different.

One of those rooms stood wide open. Empty racks that had once held enerpulse pistols and rifles stood in the middle of the small room. From the structures of the shelves along the walls, Lissa guessed that there had been a few other items in there as well. She did not have time to hope that Lance and the arkins were holding their own against agents armed with a full arsenal.

Then she paused again.

That was too many weapons for the agents outside. There had to be an ambush waiting for her somewhere.

Lissa turned to the other door across the narrow hall. It slid open at her touch, and the music spilled out to envelop her. It rooted her in place.

She remembered the silence of Daanhymn, after she'd killed all the agents while she'd been Awake. She remembered the hum of the Awakening machine on Jetune. There had been life on both of those worlds, but it had been dedicated, driven, unable to indulge in simple pleasures.

Or maybe that was just what Lissa had thought. All she'd known were the agents trying to Awaken her. It was too easy to lock them into those roles and refuse to let them be anything else.

The music was making that impossible this time.

It made her stop and wonder who was up there.

Lissa shook herself free. Step by cautious step, she moved up the smaller staircase. As her head came level with the floor, she peered around and found herself in another open room with a higher ceiling than the hallway below. It followed the slant of the roof of the building, coming to a point overhead. A large sheet of glass offering a view of the dark sky made up the entire far wall, and the lights were dimmed to almost nothing to let the natural radiance of the night take over. The nebula that surrounded this world's tiny pocket of tranquility turned the sky into patches of ethereal yellow light and shadow, sparsely dotted with newborn stars.

Tearing her eyes from the large window, Lissa saw another communication terminal set into the wall at the lower end of the sloped ceiling, dark and void of power. A few tables were scattered throughout the room, some displaying hologram projections of starmaps, others covered in datapads and printouts of information in the Neo-Andromedan language.

Lissa stepped off the stairs, into the maze of tables. In the center of the room, she saw a large, half-circle desk. A simple lamp offering soft light illuminated the surface of the desk and picked out the form of a woman seated there, bent over her work. There was no one else in the room.

Beyond any doubt, Lissa knew that this was who she was looking for.

Moving quickly now, creaks and footfalls obscured by the instrumental music, Lissa searched for a better vantage point. The starmaps were disrupting her view, and it was hard to tell if they were purely holographic displays, or if they were projected through thin sheets of glass. Lissa did not want to risk the second scenario, and she moved around the tables until she found a clear line of shot.

As Lissa stepped into position, pistol raised, the Seventh Sun agent suddenly sat back in her seat. She pushed her dark, tightly curling hair out of her eyes, fingers coming to rest at her temple, just obscuring Lissa's shot. Lissa moved to adjust her vantage point, but the agent's other hand waved dismissively, and the music cut off.

Lissa froze, halfway through a step. Her weight distribution was all wrong for the shot, but she needed to take it before the chance slipped away. She sighted as best she could along the barrel, knowing she'd need two shots for this kill, but before she could squeeze the trigger, the agent spoke, her voice soft but clear and intense.

"I'm so sorry, Lissa."

The agent dropped her hand, and her eyes swiveled to Lissa, pinning her in place. They were clear silver, bright against her tawny skin, somehow more metallic than Lissa's own burnished eyes. Her cloud of dark hair pulled them into an even stronger contrast, and their severity matched her straight, unforgiving posture as she rose to her feet and turned to face Lissa fully. "We should have left you and Aven alone."

Lissa's gaze traced over the woman's clothing, searching for the telltale bunch and snag of a concealed weapon. When she saw that the agent was unarmed, Lissa allowed herself to breathe again. She shifted into a better shooting position and kept her pistol trained on the agent, but she did not fire. The agent's words were thundering in her skull.

I'm so sorry.

In the space of her hesitation, the Seventh Sun agent pressed her advantage. "I know that anything I say to you now will never undo the damage the Seventh Sun has done to you and your brother. If you shoot me, I won't pretend that I don't understand why. But I am truly, truly sorry.

"It's easy to look back and see what we have done wrong, and what we should have done to ensure the best outcome for everyone, regardless of their status as Neo-Andromedans. But more than anything, I should have seen how obsession was clouding our objective. Namely, the obsession of one of our First Lit." She tilted her head slightly, never breaking eye contact with Lissa. "You know whom I speak of."

Lissa's grip tightened on the pistol. She said nothing but still did not fire. She heard weak shouts from outside. With the music gone, she found herself focusing on the voices. She forced herself to wrench her attention back to the agent before her.

The agent took Lissa's silence as confirmation and continued on. "It was Rosonno's obsession with you and Aven that led him to spend years and countless resources to tracking you both down." The woman allowed a mournful shadow to pass over her bright eyes. "I should have recognized that, and stopped him. We should have left you two alone, and let you live your lives as you saw fit."

"Do you think we would have ended up any other way if you had?" The words were out before Lissa could stop them, but she managed to keep her voice quiet and smooth. "Our lives were shaped by fear. We didn't need Rosonno in our shadows to become what we did."

To her surprise, the agent looked thoughtful at this, as though actually considering the idea. "I suppose that is true," she said after a long moment, nodding in solemn agreement. "We made a mistake with you."

Lissa's mouth twisted into a snarl, but the agent continued before she could respond.

"We should never have inducted Rosonno as a First Lit. He is too easily wounded by failure, and too arrogant to admit mistakes. His obsession cost us dearly."

Lissa's attention hitched on the agent's quickness to place the blame on Rosonno's shoulders. She'd admitted to the Seventh Sun making a mistake, but put Rosonno at the heart of that deadly error. No willingness to assume responsibility of her own.

Lissa allowed her gaze to flicker around the room and take in the various starmaps and the private communication terminal. She couldn't help but wonder what it was that this agent did. The agent struck her as a person with ultimate authority, unafraid to face her opponents but far too calculating to do it unarmed.

Which she was.

Only physically, Lissa realized. *Mentally...*

The mental match had begun when this agent had sent all of her guards outside, and let Lissa into the building to find her way upstairs unchallenged. Lissa had come prepared to hunt and kill, not stroll in without firing a shot to find music and a conversation.

This agent was unpredictable.

She has to be a leader, Lissa thought. *A First Lit. She's too dangerous to be anything else.*

"Perhaps if we had let you completely escape us," the First Lit said with a thoughtful sigh, "you might not have come to resent us as you have."

Shifting her stance a little, Lissa bit down on the question of whether or not the Seventh Sun agent had forgotten that, even without Rosonno, her and Aven's lives had been damaged beyond repair.

But the First Lit plowed on. "Perhaps, if you'd truly believed you had escaped, you might have come to understand what it is we are trying to do. Maybe you would have even made your way back to us someday."

Lissa did not try to stop the words this time. "We never would have believed we had escaped."

The First Lit shook her head. "We could have shown you, somehow. Perhaps made an example of the man who had so desperately pursued you." She tilted her head, studying Lissa closely. "Maybe let the Star Federation have him. Word of that retribution would have reached your ears, I'm sure. The whole galaxy would have known of it."

"You'd betray one of your own so easily?"

"If they were as much of a threat to our future as Rosonno is, yes."

Lissa swallowed. "Then where's his retribution now?"

The agent smiled a little sadly. "You most likely won't see it, but it will come."

Tension shot through Lissa's arm. "Most likely?"

The First Lit dipped her head almost submissively. "It won't be as public as throwing him over to the Star Federation. He is too entrenched in the Seventh Sun to be an example now. It will need to be... quieter. So, yes, you most likely won't know of it." She raised her head again. "I imagine that will be somewhat disappointing."

Lissa allowed herself to relax enough to stop her arm from shaking. She loosened her vice grip on the pistol. She understood what the First Lit was doing now.

The agent was trying to appeal to Lissa's nature as a selfish hunter, trying to stir her thirst for blood and send her tearing after Rosonno. But the First Lit had made another misstep. Lissa's hunts had always been for someone else, up until this moment. She wasn't the hunter that this agent needed her to be.

Maybe that's why I haven't pulled the trigger yet, Lissa thought.

It was what she wanted to believe.

"What's disappointing," Lissa said, as much to herself as the First Lit, "is that you seem to honestly believe you'll make me see the Sun as anything but a nightmare. You destroyed my life, and you took my brother from me." *Mostly. That was mostly you.* "You won't drown me in your Light."

The First Lit quirked a sad smile. "We're not as evil as you believe. We've tried to do good by our own people." She slowly gestured with one brown hand at the starmaps around the room, but Lissa kept her gaze riveted on the agent. "Even after the Star Federation's attempts to destroy us, Neo-Andromedans have spread in secret across the galaxy. Our numbers have grown. Our population is not large enough to be healthy, but we have made progress. What's more, we have made room for our own culture once again."

Lissa almost snorted.

"It's true," the First Lit said with urgent sincerity. "We built this entire facility from the ground up with the resources this planet had to offer. Powered by solar energy, built from wood from the forest and materials from the ground. Self-sustaining, self-powered, and now that we can survive, we're learning how to live again.

"We finally allowed ourselves time for creative pursuits. We wove the rugs you saw downstairs, we built the furniture you walked past, we even composed the music you heard." She smiled with a fondness that rang false. "That all came from us. We're learning creativity, and this is something that has been denied to us by a history that demanded we put survival before all else. It's time for us to have a secure future, and room for more than just surviving."

"Pretty things will not undo all the horrible things you've done," Lissa snarled. She advanced toward the First Lit, and took satisfaction in seeing the agent recoil. Hunter instincts reminded Lissa to keep a clear shot, and she took three quick steps to the right to keep a starmap out of her line of fire. "You've killed countless Neo-Andromedans, and that's just the ones you *didn't* feed into the Awakening machines. The things you've done to your own people, and you dare say you're fighting for their future?"

Lissa's feet carried her forward, bringing her within striking distance of the First Lit. To her credit, the agent did not budge, but real fear crept into her eyes this time.

"The Seventh Sun hunted my brother and me across the galaxy," Lissa said. "The Seventh Sun drove him to Banth and then threw *me* into an Awakening machine. And you, you're one of their leaders, and you let them do that, and then you *dare* tell me you're sorry?" Lissa did not know when she had dropped the barrel of her pistol, but for the first time in her waking memory, she did not want this target's death. She wanted her pain.

Lissa forced herself to a halt. This was where mistakes were made. She allowed herself a deep breath, and her fist unclenched at her side.

The First Lit still had fear in her bright eyes, but they had become cold and clinical once again. "Revenge is such a beautiful motive," she said quietly, "but it is also cloudy." She straightened with slow caution, raising her hand a little toward Lissa in what was meant to be a soothing gesture, but it lacked any real empathy. "It's the most powerful force in the universe, but it drives us to terrible judgments. For my part, I regret everything I've done to hurt our people. I thought they were necessary sacrifices—no, evils. I am not too small to see my own faults.

"I convinced myself they were necessary evils, Lissa. I convinced myself that this was the only way for us to survive, but living beyond survival is so much harder when you can look back and see how quickly revenge led you down the wrong path. How it made you trust the wrong people, and lose the ones who were good."

There was a pause, punctured only by Lissa's heavy breathing.

"I can't help but wonder," the First Lit murmured, "how you came to trust a Star Fed, especially one like Ashburn."

"I don't trust him," Lissa spat, only realizing the truth behind the words as she said them. "I never trusted him," she finished softly.

The First Lit gave an encouraging nod. "There are so few people left who you *can* trust, Lissa. And the Star Federation took one of them from you, didn't they? They killed him while he was lying in a hospital bed, weak, unarmed, and helpless."

"And he was there because the Seventh Sun chased him there."

The First Lit cocked her head. "Did we?"

Lissa wanted to say yes, but her memory snagged on Aven's arrogance, his enjoyment of the hunting game and his willingness to seek dangerous thrills towards the end of his time as the Shadow. He'd gotten himself into trouble on his final hunt, and he'd taken himself to Banth. The only people who had been chasing him were the ones he'd tried and failed to kill. Not the Seventh Sun.

But we followed that life because the Seventh Sun put us on the path.

Aven had taken up bounty hunting to keep himself and Lissa on the move. It wasn't safe for them anywhere, between Anti-Neo-Andromedans and the haunting promise of the Seventh Sun finding them again. Hunting had made their lives focused but unpredictable. It had kept them one step ahead of the Seventh Sun.

One step ahead of them.

One step ahead of their—

Mind games.

Lissa pulled herself out of the trance the First Lit had lured her into and finally recognized the emotional trap. She refocused her attention, trying to see what she'd been forced to miss. She had just enough time to register the silence outside to realize that the battle was over, and then there were footsteps in the hallways below. They hit the stairs and bounded up, heavy and creaking and fast. Too fast.

Lissa surged away from the First Lit and raised her pistol again. She brought the barrel up to follow the dark silhouette of the man who came surging up the stairs and turned into the room, and when he registered her weapon trained on him, he moved to dodge out of the way. His hip clipped the edge of a table and he went down hard, the rifle in his hands skittering away over the floor. Lissa rushed forward and cleared her shot line, but before she could focus her aim, two animal bodies jumped into view, coming to rest protectively over the man. They were arkins.

Orion stood with his head bent low, lip curled into a snarl. Blade stood tense and whining, amber eyes focused on Lissa's face. Looking past them, Lissa picked out the shape of the man on the floor, but she knew it was Ashburn even before he twisted to face her. Her breath stopped when she saw the fear in him.

Shame flickered through Lissa's heart before rage took over, and she turned to face the First Lit again. The agent stood with her hands clasped behind her back, watching Lissa closely.

"You have more control than I thought," the First Lit said, "but those attachments will only drag you down." She tilted her head towards Ashburn and the arkins. "Cut yourself free, and come back to us, Lissa." She smiled, cold and cruel. "We'll welcome you back to the—"

"NO!" Lissa screamed, and threw the barrel of the pistol up. She took the shot too early, and it sailed below the First Lit's torso, heading for her legs.

The agent made no move to dodge as the shot passed clean through her and struck the edge of the desk.

The agent flickered and distorted for a bewildering moment, but Lissa's brain registered the disrupted hologram projection long before she was ready to accept the realization. Then she finally saw the small communication device sitting on the floor against the side of the desk, projecting a perfect holographic representation of the First Lit.

"—ve that out of your system now?" the agent said as the hologram reformed and the distortion cleared.

"You were never here," Lissa said weakly. She felt as though her own legs had been shot, and she had to brace against one of the tables to stop herself from falling.

The agent quirked an expression that was more disgust than amusement. "Did you really think you could ambush me? I am Arrevessa, leader of the Seventh Sun, and I will never fall to someone like you."

Lissa's mind did not want to cooperate any more than her legs. "Were you *ever* here?" she heard herself ask. She wondered why the answer mattered.

Arrevessa closed her eyes and shook her head, as though dealing with a particularly stupid child. "I left days ago, and can promise you that you'll find nothing at that base. No logs to trace, no data to steal, nothing." She opened her eyes and gave Lissa another wicked smile. "Except the gift I left for you: the signature of a starship. You know whose it is. Do with it as you will, Lissa, but stay out of my way."

Arrevessa's intense glare pinned Lissa in place, even as the hologram faded into nothing. Lissa found herself staring at the place where the First Lit had been—had not been—and trying to make sense of everything she had done to bring herself to this moment. Silence roared in her ears, until the whispers wormed their way back in.

Welcome to the fight for me, Little—

"Lissa?"

She turned to see Lance standing next to one of the tables, holding a datapad. Both arkins stood between him and Lissa, backs to Lance as they watched her closely. Their eyes gleamed yellow and amber in the darkness.

They were protecting him.

From her.

Lance said her name again, and Lissa forced herself to focus. He turned the datapad's display toward her, showing her a few sets of coordinates listed below the wavering starship signature Arrevessa had promised. "All of the datapads have the same information," he said, gesturing to the small batch on the rest of the table. "They've been wiped clean of everything else." He extended the datapad he held to her.

Lissa said nothing, and made no move to accept the thin machine.

After a moment, Lance slipped the datapad into his waistband and muttered, "We should go." He retrieved his rifle without looking at Lissa again, and led Orion back downstairs.

Blade gave a soft whine, and then followed Lance and Orion.

Left alone in the room with nothing but the whispers in her ears and the sound of her own breathing, Lissa sauntered to the window that made up the far wall. She stared up at the nebula and the bright bursts of its infant stars. She wondered how much further she could push herself before she broke everything and everyone around her, leaving her alone with herself.

CHAPTER 14: VENOM

Rosonno was hunched over his desk in his private quarters with his attention buried in Awakening candidate files when the transmission came in. It took a few minutes for the blinking light on his private communication terminal to register at the edge of his mind, and even then, he assumed that Tyrath could wait a few moments longer. That the delay would almost certainly irritate her was a happy coincidence for him. He took his time straightening the files on his desk and stretching before strolling to the terminal.

He smiled as the hologram projection came up, ready for Tyrath to launch into another complaint about what she felt was a shortage of Awakened—the Seventh Sun had more than enough for what was to come, Rosonno knew—but when the face in the projection came into focus, Rosonno's heart stuttered and the breath he sucked in was sharp and painful.

Arrevessa looked back at him over the connection. Her usual unbreakable calm was in place, mirror smooth over her features, but her silver eyes blazed. Even through the hologram projection, her gaze burned into Rosonno, and it was all he could do to keep himself from throwing up an arm in defense.

"You said you knew how to kill her," Arrevessa said in place of the customary greeting. Her voice was serene, but to

Rosonno, there was a distinct note of menace undercutting her every word, though, and move.

Rosonno swallowed his surprise and trepidation. "I'm afraid I don't know what you're talking about."

"Lissa," Arrevessa said. "You said you would eliminate her before she did any further damage."

Rosonno went cold. Arrevessa herself had extracted that promise from him in front of the other First Lit after the Sciyat strike, after First Lit Ereko had died by Lissa's hand. Rosonno did not know what Lissa had done since then, but he was certain that he would fulfill his promise to see her dead, no matter what.

He took a moment to gather himself, thinking hard on how to best phrase his next words. Arrevessa was, after all, the Seventh Sun's primary master strategist. Their *only* master strategist, now that Ereko was gone. Until that role was filled again, Rosonno knew that he needed to keep himself in Arrevessa's good graces. If she wanted him gone, she need only hint at her desire for his elimination to the other First Lit. He would be quietly removed within three sidereal days at most.

"Lissa is elusive and unpredictable," he said, "but I have a special team tracking her down."

Arrevessa's lips tightened, and she slowly shook her head.

"Syreth's handlers can find anyone," Rosonno pressed on, "and with their record, he'll finally have his chance to——"

With a disgusted groan, Arrevessa sat back and gave a cutting signal to someone out of the communication terminal's range.

Rosonno fell silent.

"We are out of time," the leader of the First Lit said. Her voice took on a disinterested, dismissive quality. "Because of your failure, you have cost us far more than Ereko's life."

In spite of his fear of Arrevessa's authority and what she could do to him, Rosonno's anger began to seethe to the surface. "I have *not* failed. I know exactly how to handle her."

Arrevessa's eyebrow quirked. "You really believe that, don't you?"

"I'm doing what I said I would!"

"Then why did Lissa and that ex-Star Fed Ashburn arrive on my planet, kill my agents, and chase me out of my home?"

She found Arrevessa's outpost? And made it there alive?

Rosonno found that he had temporarily lost the ability to speak.

Arrevessa's tilted her head and studied Rosonno. Her eyes were bright against her tawny-brown skin, and his skin crawled under the intensity of her gaze. "You do know," she finally said, "that you have jeopardized everything we have worked for?"

Rosonno frowned. He failed to see how this was purely his fault, but something told him that resisting the accusation would only land him in deeper trouble. He held up his hands in mock surrender. "I admit, it was bad luck that Lissa was able to pull data from Ereko's ship. That must be how she found you." He lowered his hands and squared his shoulders. "But I do know her, and I *know* she cannot have much left to go on. Sooner or later, she'll run out of leads to chase."

"I agree," Arrevessa said. "That's why I gave her the signature of your starship."

"You…" Rosonno actually felt his heart stop, then beat fast and painful in his chest to make up for the lost time. "You WHAT?"

"I gave her something to chase." Arrevessa considered his stunned expression for a moment. "I did give you a fighting chance. She'll need to trace the signature from old coordinates and track your ship for a while before she can close in on you. If you move quickly, you may be able to find yourself a new ship before she finds you."

Rosonno sputtered for a moment before the words exploded out of him. "All of my work is housed on this ship! I deal with far too much data to transfer it anywhere else." The very thought of losing his ship, his haven, sent Rosonno's mind into a panicked spiral. "I would lose too much time finding a replacement ship. I could lose part or even *all* of my work, I would have to halt the Seventh Sun's candidate recruitment, I would—"

"Yes, yes. You, you, *you*. Always you, Rosonno." She drew herself up to her full height, but true to her nature, she kept her anger under control, allowing only a small sliver of it to color her voice with harshness. "You have always put yourself before the Seventh Sun. I thought that, given the right opportunity, you could break yourself free of that selfishness, but clearly I was wrong."

Rosonno's voice fled from him, and he stood there gaping at Arrevessa.

She gave him a bitter smile. "You have a choice to make now, Rosonno. Either you continue to believe that you should come before the Seventh Sun, that you can somehow operate as you do and live free of the consequences, and that you are not a poison that will rot us from the inside, all because you could not give yourself over to a selfless fate."

Her words were calm and steady, but Rosonno felt as though she had screamed at him. He felt very, very small before her fury.

After a moment, Arrevessa settled back again, and regarded him with the cool, calculating expression that she normally wore. "Or," she said, softly again, "you abandon your ship. You leave your work, and you step down from your position as First Lit. You are free to hide yourself from Lissa, or at least try to. You will spend your life running, always wondering when she will catch up. But you will know that the Seventh Sun will not pursue you, nor will we do anything to expose you to Lissa, because you removed yourself from your position to do us harm."

Arrevessa looked off again at someone Rosonno could not see, and nodded. "The choice is yours, Rosonno. And your choice will either let the Seventh Sun succeed, or destroy it."

She cut the transmission and blinked out of his life.

Rosonno sank to his knees in front of the communication terminal, sheltering his head under the edge as though it could shield him from the fallout that was only beginning.

Arrevessa had condemned him, that much was clear, but she had not ordered him removed.

Or had she?

No, she'd given him a choice.

She wanted him to remove *himself*.

Because of Lissa?

Of course it ties back to Lissa, Rosonno thought, working his way through the doubts. *It's because of her that we lost Ereko. She must have scared Arrevessa when they met.*

That easily could have sent the older First Lit into a panic. Arrevessa was a brilliant strategist, but Rosonno had never known her to be anywhere near the battles she planned. She was always safe and secure in her uncharted sector of the galaxy. Rosonno could only imagine how she had reacted when she'd learned that Lissa, a notorious bounty hunter, had touched down on her isolated little planet.

Fear. That's all this was. Irrational fear.

And she had tried to instill it in him with that bluff about his starship signature. It had to be a bluff. Arrevessa must know that she could not simply throw him away if she wanted the Seventh Sun to succeed. He was too important.

But Arrevessa was afraid, and she had decided to turn Rosonno into her scapegoat.

Rosonno could not combat that directly, but once Syreth's team took out Lissa and Ashburn, he knew it would sooth Arrevessa, and this whole exchange would be forgotten. It had to be. They had to move forward.

And Rosonno had work to do.

Returning to his desk, he sank his attention back into the files on strong Awakening candidates. He intended to use them to restore the ranks of the Awakened after the Seventh Sun's next victory, for they were certain to suffer at least a few losses. This next strike was a bold move, one that required the full care and attention of all of the First Lit. He could not let Arrevessa's tantrum distract him now.

But there was a small part of Rosonno's mind that kept wandering back to his conversation with Arrevessa, and how she had communicated with someone he could not see. It bothered him that he did not know what that meant.

He decided that, after Lissa was dead and he had the chance to speak with Arrevessa again, he would ask her about it.

CHAPTER 15: CONFESSIONS

Leaving the uncharted system was easier than going in, although Lance kept the ship well below Lissa's suicidal pace on the return trip. It took them longer to trace their way back to navigated space at the slower speed, but the starship performed beautifully and carried them to safety with little more than a shudder near the neutron star that Lissa had used to slingshot them into the nebula.

Lissa chose to spend the journey in her private quarters, and Lance let her be. He did not know what to say, and he was too tired of being pushed away to try again. And he was a little afraid.

It would be all too easy to say the wrong thing, he knew, and he was straining himself to exhaustion wondering and worrying over whether or not she might try to kill him now. He knew she hated the Seventh Sun, but he'd found her talking with that agent, and he'd heard the order to cut all attachments and return to the organization. Lissa had refused, but she would not tell him anything else about her exchange with the agent. All Lance knew was that the interaction had left Lissa deeply disturbed.

She had been on the verge of a breaking point before. Now, she was hardly eating, and sleeping even less. Shut inside her room, she struggled through nightmares that Lance heard from his own quarters, and they were growing worse from the sound of them. Not even Blade could give Lissa comfort anymore, and Lance sometimes found the arkin outside of Lissa's quarters, lying pressed against the locked door and whining softly.

The signature and coordinates from the base on the unnamed world rested within the datapad Lance had taken. Lissa had put the datapad inside a storage locker just outside the control room, and it had not been moved since then. Lance did not bring it up.

He could sense that Lissa was on the verge of abandoning the hunt for the Seventh Sun leaders, but he had not wanted her to do it like this. Not while she was broken.

He did not know how to help her.

Lance did the only things he could: he made sure Blade stayed fed and exercised; he set the ship on a course for a peaceful, neutral system where they could safely put into port; and he gave Lissa time and space.

Lance doubted any of that would help.

Finally, as they approached the planet he had chosen as their next destination, Lance accepted that there was nothing more that he could do. He was alone, having left the arkins to spar and play and nap in the more open space of the main storage hold. Lance stood between the two seats of the control room, lost in idle thought as he stared without fully seeing the displayed starmap from the navigation system. He tried to figure out where they—or he—could go next, but his mind came up blank and his thoughts slipped into silence.

That was when he became aware of Lissa behind him. She'd come up on completely silent feet, but he could feel her watching him. She still managed to startle him when he turned to face her.

There were dark circles under her eyes. Her black hair hung wild around her face, and she wore loose, oversized clothing that was disheveled. She leaned heavily against the doorframe, as though afraid that she would fall without its

LIGHT RUNNER

support. Her eyes burned into his with surprising intensity
through her exhaustion.

"We need to land," she breathed. "I don't care where."

Lance looked at her for a long, silent moment. "I already
found a port. We'll be on the ground within an hour."

Lissa's gaze softened fractionally. She nodded, turned, and
slipped away. Lance did not follow. He spent the time running
through lists of their supplies, checking what could be traded
and what needed to be restocked. The hour passed and they
did not see each other again.

The ground port was built in a field a short distance from a
large town with a thriving but quiet population. Night had
fallen on this side of the planet, cold and clear with a thick
dusting of stars across the sky. Tall grass waved in a soft breeze
all around the port, with open landing spaces picked out in
white lights to signal the borders of the designated starship,
shuttle, and cruiser spaces. Lance steered them towards one of
the midsized starship spaces, but before the ship had fully
touched down, he heard Lissa call for Blade, and then the ship
beeped to signal that the airlock had been opened.

Lance did not rush after her. Not this time.

When the ship was down, he found Orion waiting for him
at the gaping airlock. The arkin blinked at Lance as he came
up, then turned his head back out to the dark land beyond the
illuminated port.

Lissa and Blade had disappeared.

Lance took a few minutes to gather up the items he had
marked for trade, cloaked himself in a simple hologram
disguise, and then set out for the town to see what he could
find. He let Orion loose in the field near the port, giving the
arkin the chance to stretch his wings and hunt. He trusted the
arkin to keep himself safe, but Lance hurried into town and
spent less time than usual haggling through his trades. He was
more worried about Orion dropping out of the sky and
catching unwanted attention than getting a fair deal on fresh
food. It was quiet on the streets, quiet in the stores that were
open to moonlit trading, and Lance moved quickly through it

115

all. He returned to the ship with a few less articles of clothing than he would have liked, but he'd found enough food for another decent trek between star systems.

If he went.

His footsteps slowed as he drew closer to the ship. He had not forgotten Lissa's invitation to skip out the next time they put into port. She'd asked him to leave. He was beginning to think that wasn't such a terrible idea.

He glanced up at the sky as he wandered on, the pack of supplies heavy against his shoulders. He let the weight drag his posture back a little, turning his face more fully towards the stars. There were so many places where he and Orion could slip away. So many places where Lance could lose himself.

He could think of nothing that he wanted less.

With a sigh, Lance pulled himself back to the present, and meandered through the thin crowd spread over the surface of the ground port until he reached their starship.

No, Lissa's starship, he reminded himself. It was her deal and her bounty contract that had secured the ship on Mezora. But she seemed afraid to grow too attached to it.

She had not even named it yet.

Lance paused to press his hand against the ship's hull. Lights from the ground port reflected off the surface, warping into streaks along the gray metal and the slashes of blue and black that marked the body of the ship in elegant sweeps, highlighting the predatory yet graceful angles of the craft.

It was a beautiful ship. It deserved a name.

Lance thought he'd suggest as much to Lissa before picking out a planet where she could drop off him and Orion. Somewhere a little less remote but not interesting enough to catch the interest of the Star Federation or the Seventh Sun. Somewhere he could start over. Nameless. Alone.

I'd prefer it if she just shot me, he thought with a grimace. He noticed that his dim, distorted reflection in the ship's hull looked more composed than he felt.

Pulling himself back to reality, Lance moved around the starship and found Orion waiting for him at the airlock. He wasn't alone.

Blade gave Lance a slow blink as he drew near. She did not move when he opened the airlock and slipped into the ship, but he felt her amber eyes on his back as he rounded the corner. He unpacked the new supplies, gave Orion a bit of fresh meat from the market as a treat, and decided to wait in the control room for Lissa, whenever she decided to return. He had just taken his seat when a warm puff of air hit his face, and he turned to find Blade staring at him.

The arkin held his gaze steadily, but with half-hooded eyes to show she meant no threat.

After a moment, Lance hesitantly stood up. Blade turned and moved towards the door of the control room, pausing to glance over her shoulder and make certain that he followed.

Orion waited out in the hall. He fell into step beside Lance as Blade led them to the airlock and back out into the night. Lance paused long enough to lock up the ship again, then followed Blade as she hopped off the illuminated platform of the ground port and stalked through the tall grass. Orion followed in her wake, and Lance traced the gray arkin's path, picking out his lighter fur in the starlight far better than the black arkin's.

Blade led them far enough away from the ground port that Lance could hold up his thumb and cover one of the larger docked ships. Here, the ground began to slope gently down under his feet, and Lance stopped to look at the shallow valley that Blade had led him to.

In the heart of the valley, a large white rock rose up out of the dark, rippling grass, pale enough for Lance to see it clearly. On top of the rock sat a figure in dark clothing.

Lissa.

Lance felt a nudge at his hand. He looked down to see Blade staring up at him. Her eyes were less hooded, but there was no danger in her gaze. She almost looked desperate.

With a sigh, Lance focused on Lissa down on the rock again. His eyes gradually picked out her posture: tight and huddled and closed off.

"I can't help her," Lance said, not certain if he was talking to the black arkin or himself. He forced himself to meet Blade's stare again so he'd feel a little less like he was raving into the night. "She won't let me."

Blade snorted and pressed her nose into his hand again. Orion whined.

With a short, heavy breath and no real sense of why he did it, Lance moved down the hill. The grass changed around him, becoming thicker with clinging burrs at the tips. He pushed his way through, feeling the burrs snag on his clothes. He called out softly to Lissa as he went, letting her know he was coming. Her head turned a little at the sound of his voice, but she did not look at him as he approached. She did not turn to him even when he had climbed up on to the rock and stood next to her, picking the burrs off his sleeves.

After a silent minute, Lance sank down and sat with his legs dangling over the edge of the rock. He did not bother searching for the right or wrong thing to say. He only waited for Lissa to speak.

The stars overhead had wheeled noticeably towards the dark horizon before she finally did. It was not what he expected.

"This isn't grass, you know."

A wave of frustration rolled over Lance, but he bit back the words and let her talk.

"You can see the spice branches on the tips. It's late in the season so most of them have fallen off, but if you look..."

She stirred next to him, and out of the corner of his eye, he saw her run her hand over her face. The spice burrs clung to her own clothing, but she'd made no attempts to brush them away.

"You can't do anything with unharvested spice," Lissa said, but her voice sounded less like her own, as though she was mimicking a memory of someone else. "It goes bad too fast if it's taken too late. You need to harvest at just the right time to get the most out of the crop. And you can't let it grow wild like this. Not if you want to stay on the honest side of the trade." She took a deep, shuddering breath and stared hard at the spice stalks rippling in the warm breeze. "It's funny what will remind you of days that were almost, maybe, happy."

Lance realized what she was linking this moment back to. He risked speaking. "You enjoyed living on the Fang's farm?"

"I did."

"And you had a good relationship with them before...?"

"Yes," she murmured. "Before."

Another silence slipped in between them.

"Aven—" Her voice hitched on his name. She coughed, tried again. "Aven said we'd stayed there too long. He said, when you hesitate, when you take too long, terrible things happen." She scraped her heel against the rock, sending a shower of cached pebbles to the ground. They landed without a sound, lost among the spice stalks. "I didn't want to believe him, but I learned that he was right, on my first hunt."

Lissa pulled her knees in close against her chest again, wrapping her arms around her legs. Her eyes hardened and her jaw clenched, but she continued on, and Lance heard the strain in her voice as she forced herself to speak. To open.

She told him about the contract she'd picked up on a lesser-known but powerful drug lord who'd begun to encroach on a rival's territory. The woman had taken over for her late husband, though from what Lissa could tell, she had been running the operation from the start, and she herself had killed her spouse when she no longer needed his name to hide behind. She was cold, cunning, and cruel, and had raised her son to be just like her.

"Spoiled little terror," Lissa growled, "a lot like his mother but with none of the quiet lethality she showed in business. He thought the universe belonged to him, and he'd scream and bite anyone who tried to tell him otherwise."

Lance shifted uneasily. "Were you contracted to kill the whole family?"

"No," she whispered. "Just the drug queen. I wasn't supposed to kill the prince."

Lissa continued the story quietly. Lance let her go uninterrupted, straining to hear but reluctant to break the flow.

"The queen knew how to protect herself. She rarely exposed herself as a target, and when she did, it was impossible to get anywhere near her. She had her own army. Scouts to patrol and clear areas, counter snipers to watch her wherever she went, guards to keep their bodies between her and a direct line of fire… The woman knew how to stay alive. She just had that one weak spot: that damned kid she could never say no to."

She paused again, but Lance sat patiently now. He sensed something releasing its hold on Lissa as she spoke, as though she'd never told anyone about this before. For a brief moment, Lance remembered his thoughts about leaving with Orion, but they evaporated. He knew that there would still be broken things in their lives, but Lissa had finally decided to trust him. He would not throw that away.

After Lissa had collected herself, she continued on, her voice soft but steady.

The drug queen's son had wanted a grand, extravagant party for his ninth birthday, but not with other children; with adults who would fawn over him and shower him with gifts and do everything they could to entertain him. He wanted it outdoors. His mother would deny him nothing. So the drug queen had arranged for such a party, insisting only on a brief pause to take a holographic portrait of mother and son to immortalize the day. It was the only time the guards dropped away from the queen, and allowed a clear line of fire. Lissa had stumbled upon the opportunity by chance, and only happened to be in the right place at the right time to take the shot by pure luck.

"And I hesitated. It was the first time I'd ever hunted. And I kept thinking, 'I am too calm. I should not be this calm before I kill someone.'" She pressed her forehead against her knees, then pulled her face back up to stare out at the wild spice field again. "Turns out I already knew how to compartmentalize bounty killings. I knew what I had to do, and I knew how it would help someone that I still cared about, and I knew that I was not taking away an innocent life. So I reminded myself of all of that, I aimed again, and I fired. One quick shot. But it wasn't quick enough, and that kid…"

Lance could guess how this story ended, but he waited for Lissa to release it.

"He didn't mean to, but he saved his mother's life. He just… ran in front of her." She bit her lip, hesitating. "I think he was trying to ruin the holoshot. Just being a spiteful, horrible little child. But I never really managed to compartmentalize that one. That one was a mistake. That one was beyond my control. But it shouldn't have been.

"I never took a contract that listed domestic sites as possible kill spots ever again. Didn't stop me from killing as many people as I needed to keep Aven alive. And that was worthless all on its own. I thought I was doing what I had to. Turns out, I just fell into some twisted, terrible pattern, and didn't even try to pull myself out."

Lance picked his words carefully. "We all have a twisted sense of nobility," he told her. "You hunted to protect your brother. The Star Federation initiated a purge to try to keep a war at bay. I pushed you to hunt your own people because I thought that would make everyone's lives a little safer." He shifted, and his shoulder brushed against hers. She did not pull away. "None of us are the grand protectors we thought we were."

"So what do we do, then?"

"Whatever we think is right. It's all anyone has ever done."

She shook her head. "I never thought what I was doing was right. Just that it was what I needed to do. I don't know how to do what's right."

"That's what happens when you're never really given the chance to try." He stood up, and offered her his hand. After a moment, she took it, and he pulled her to her feet. "I saw some pretty terrible things when I was an officer. I saw people drunk with power learn how to abuse it. I saw others who were so full of hate they acted on every little fear. There wasn't anything I could do about them, except try to hold on to why I was against them. But most of the time, I saw people do their worst when they felt backed into a corner." He focused hard on her silver eyes. The starlight brought out their natural color, making them glow without any of the harshness of an Awakening. They were beautiful. "I want to see who you are when you're not backed into a corner. I want to see who you are when you're free."

She shifted uncomfortably. "You may not like what you find."

"I'll take that chance."

Lissa said nothing. She turned back to stare at the waving spice stalks, and Lance made to leave, but she caught his arm. "Please stay," she whispered, so softly he thought he imagined it, but he put his arm around her shoulders, and stayed with her under the stars until the dawn came and chased them away.

CHAPTER 16: REBELLION

Vinterra did not know where the Awakened were going. She simply did not care enough to ask, but she overheard chatter about an upcoming strike against the Star Federation, and it promised to be a decisive one. Some of her coworkers were thrilled. They claimed that this would end the war and wipe out the Star Feds for good. Others were more skeptical, pointing out that one successful strike was unlikely to end the war.

It struck Vinterra that if anyone was giving the possibility of failure a thought, they were keeping quiet about it.

Vinterra listened to these conversations as she helped stabilize the designated group of in-stasis Awakened, and bring them out to the ships that had come to collect them.

It was a base-wide effort, with every able and available person contributing. The base swarmed with activity. Even First Lit Tyrath was helping with the removal and transport of the marked stasis pods, overseeing their movements and checking readouts alongside the other team leaders. The pods were brought up from the holding chamber via hover transports, moved into an airlock and passed on to a rotating escort team that took them out to the waiting starships. From there, the Awakened were brought aboard one at a time and loaded into a special holding bay.

From the moment she had seen the transport ships breach the sky and land on the Daraaxi surface, Vinterra knew that she had found the missing variable that turned her theory of escape into an actual plan.

Timing would be everything, but if she did it right, she would get at least a few hours head start on any pursuers that might come after her.

That will *come after me*, she amended.

After all, she was going to steal a ship.

Not one of the visiting transport ships, she had decided immediately. That would be too difficult and attract far too much attention. Least of all, she probably wouldn't even get off the ground before someone realized what she was up to. But there were other ships available.

They were reserved for emergency evacuations. Given the number of Awakened the base housed, not having a base-wide escape plan in place would have been an invitation for a massacre. Vinterra had been drilled on the evac routine within her first day of arriving at the base, and had been walked through all the paths she could take to the evacuation ships if any of the Awakened managed to break free from stasis and could not be contained.

Based on that tour, she had the sense that no one really expected the Awakened to get out. She was assured repeatedly that the stasis pods were completely secure, and even in the event of a power failure, they would not release the Awakened. They needed a direct override to their central system, and only the First Lit and a few very trusted team leaders knew how to carry out that procedure. It was the only secret Tyrath seemed to keep, but it was one that no one, even the most morbidly curious among the scientists, had any desire to probe.

With all that in mind, Vinterra did not feel too guilty about taking an evac ship and using the chaos brought by the Awakened transports to disguise her departure from Daraax Beta. She further rationalized her decision by reminding herself that she would not need to siphon off any supplies if she stole the evac ship; the vessel would already have more than what she would need, even if it was awful, long-term storage food and rations of water that tasted faintly like their containers.

The only problem was that Vinterra had no idea *when* she should go for the ship. Everyone was busy, but that included her. Swept up in the need to help, she knew that her absence would be noted if she did not slip away at just the right moment.

Anxiety roiled inside Vinterra as she worked alongside the other agents to get the marked Awakened out to the ships as quickly as possible. She lost count of the number of runs she made from the airlock to the stasis chamber, and even managed to forget her fear of the dark pit as she moved up and down the ramp, pushing and pulling the hovering stasis pods with her teammates. Data from the pods swirled across her awareness as she checked displays of vitals and verified that the Awakened she was moving were fit for the journey. She was so entrenched in the efforts that when her group suddenly found itself without any further tasks, her heart leapt into her throat.

"Looks like the last of them have already gone to the airlock," one of the scientists said, surveying the other teams as they relaxed and dissolved into giddy conversations. He wiped sweat off of his brow with the back of his sleeve before looking around at the rest of the group. "So, with that done... Food?"

There was an enthusiastic murmur of agreement, and the group began to file towards the mess hall.

Vinterra's feet felt rooted to the floor. She'd missed her moment. She'd allowed herself to get caught up in the work, so paranoid that someone would notice her that she never saw her chance to leave.

She felt sick to her stomach, but she forced herself to move as she followed her group. The other teams joined them, apparently all listening to their stomachs and heading for a very late lunch. Vinterra flowed into the crowd, but it was only when she had almost reached the mess hall that she realized something.

No one was talking to her. No one was looking at her. They were ebbing around her, jostling to get into the mess hall as fast as they could without breaking into a run. They were laughing and talking loudly, clearly relieved to be done with the work and looking forward to some rest before life returned to normal on Daraax Beta. The base so rarely took respites that nearly everyone was caught up in the happy atmosphere.

Vinterra let the crowd sweep her off to the side, edging her way further and further out of the press of bodies. She cast a furtive glance around before she fully exited the throng.

There was no sign of First Lit Tyrath anywhere, and no one was paying Vinterra any attention.

She turned and walked away.

Her heart hammered in her chest as she traced the route she remembered to the evacuation ships. She met no one on the way, and as she drew closer, her steps quickened with adrenaline and the sudden burst of hope.

Then she rounded the final corner, and came to a skidding halt. She spent a precious moment trying to understand what she was seeing, then scrambled back behind the wall. Her breathing was quick and shallow, and she took several gulps of air to calm herself before peering around the corner.

There were people milling around three of the eight evacuation ships. Agents, Vinterra saw, most of whom she recognized from the base, though she did not know any of them personally. She was not certain if she had never encountered the others, or if they had arrived with the transport ships. Regardless of where they had come from, all of the agents were darting around the ships, making last-minute checks, and the engines were already starting to glow with power from the energy cells. Vinterra watched them closely, but her mind was numb. Beyond a surface-level recognition of their actions, she could not make sense of what they were doing.

Vinterra had a reason to steal an evacuation ship and flee the Daraaxi system. These people could not all have that same reason. There was something else going on.

Before she could begin to puzzle it out, she realized with a rush of dizzying relief that they were not taking the ship she had marked for herself. Instead, they were filing inside three of the four midsized ships. A faraway thought drifted across her mind, informing her that taking ships that size would cut drastically into the base's evacuation resources. She felt a jolt of guilt at the thought of taking one of the smaller ships after this.

Even after everything, Vinterra was still bound by loyalty to the Seventh Sun. She had to marvel at that.

Then a hand closed on her shoulder, and Vinterra was spun around and slammed against the wall. She gasped in pain, and found herself staring up at a man she was surprised to recognize.

He was Malorro, one of Tyrath's most trusted team leaders. Vinterra had seen him plenty of times around the base, and from what she understood, he oversaw the engineers. A large, round man with thick black hair, pale skin, and small, burnished copper eyes flecked with brown, he stood out in Vinterra's memory as one of the few agents who wore his hair long. He kept it tied back in a straight, hard line against his spine. Though his face was round and softened by his weight, there was strength in his body, and Vinterra knew he kept himself fit.

She had no doubt that, if he wanted to, he could subdue or kill her with his bare hands in a matter of moments. And as she held his stare, she began to wonder if he was considering one of those two options.

"Are you answering the Final One's call?" Malorro asked, keeping his deep voice slow and deliberate.

Vinterra gaped at him.

Malorro's eyes narrowed. "That's a no, then." With one hand, he pushed Vinterra hard against the wall, and balled his other hand into a fist. He hesitated just long enough to shrug and say, "Sorry." Then he drew his arm back.

"I'm trying to leave!" Vinterra blurted out.

Malorro's arm jerked as he stayed the blow. He waited for her to continue, but did not release her.

"I'm taking one of the small evac ships," Vinterra rushed on. "I need to find Haelin."

In the silence that followed her words, Vinterra realized that it was highly unlikely that Malorro knew who Haelin was. There was no recognition in his eyes as he studied Vinterra, but finally, he nodded and relaxed his hold.

"You're probably telling the truth," he said.

Vinterra sighed with relief.

Then Malorro punched her in the stomach.

Vinterra dropped, pain constricting her chest as she coughed and gasped for air. Through that, she felt Malorro's hand pat her shoulder.

"You'll be all right," he said, "but we need the head start."

Then he walked away, and Vinterra heard someone call his name. The sounds of starships taking off roared through her ears a few moments later, and then there was silence punctured only by Vinterra's coughing.

When she finally recovered her breath, Vinterra pushed herself to her feet and stumbled around the corner again. The three starships were gone, and she had to move fast. One agent going rogue could have been overlooked for a little while. An entire pack of them stealing four evac ships on the same day was bound to catch someone's attention if it had not already.

As Vinterra pulled herself into her chosen ship, powered it up, and steered it toward the exit of the hanger, she tried to imagine what Malorro and the others were doing. He had mentioned a final one, but Vinterra had no idea what that meant.

Final what?

She doubted she would find an answer where she was heading, but she did not care. She had far more important things to worry about now.

She piloted the ship out of the hanger, let it coast over the dark ground until it was a safe distance from the base, and angled the ship toward the stars. The transport ships and stolen evac starships had already left the atmosphere, but she did not let herself hesitate, or think about anyone pursuing her.

As the ship carried her away from Daraax Beta, Vinterra brought up the navigational and tracking systems, and began to key in the latest set of coordinates she'd pulled from Haelin's dropship.

"I'll find you," Vinterra promised.

CHAPTER 17: BLINDSIDE

After leaving Sciyat, Erica had tapped a secure frequency that connected her to the admirals and the other fleet commanders, broadcasting the discovery from the Nandro autopsy. She'd been rewarded with a direct message from Admiral Lukati himself, offering modest, veiled praise for assigning the team to dissect the Nandro secret. He advised her to keep her eyes on the Star Federation's main mission, however, and informed her that the Intelligence Unit would be sending her updated information on potential Nandro threats very soon.

She held the datapad with a digital copy of that information in her hands before the admiral's message had finished playing.

The real problem with a purge, Erica quickly discovered, was that there were far too many leads to sift through. Even with the Intelligence Unit handling the brunt of the work back on the Star Federation space station, there was too much information for them to filter the credible sources from the noise. The galaxy was proving eager to assist with purge efforts, and a steady stream of information was passing from Monitor teams on the larger worlds to the Intelligence Unit. That was helping with the screening process, but far too many transmissions were leaping over the Monitors and slamming directly into the Star Federation.

The Intelligence Unit sent the most promising leads to the fleet commanders, but they were long lists. Erica and her peers were faced with the decisions of how to divide their attention and where to send their units.

Though she knew she'd done the right thing by focusing on Sciyat, Erica felt how far she had fallen behind the other fleet commanders. They had been communicating their movements to each other, and Erica had to play catch-up by cross-checking the most recent positions of their ships on a projected starmap in her private quarters. She sat cross-legged on her bed, her back against the wall as she waved her hands to toggle the hologram projector's display, using designated colors to follow the trajectories of the other fleet commanders and see where their efforts were concentrated.

Territory lines had always blurred across the fleet commanders, but now more than ever, soldiers were being sent across borders as fast as their ships could carry them, never quite changing command but leaving a confused sense of hierarchy where they went. Erica had to wonder how effective these frazzled attempts to cover as much ground as possible could be. Then again, the Nandros had already surprised them once. It would do no good to give them any chance to regroup and launch another attack.

As Erica studied the movements of the other commanders' soldiers, she found her attention wandering over the trails of Keraun's units. Although he had sent several officers out on purge efforts, resulting in varying degrees of success, he was keeping a concentration of his force in the Andromeda Reach.

Erica knew he was not purging the Reach. Very little data from that sector had come in, and the only suggestion of Nandro habitation was questionable at best. Even that had only extended to small pockets of Nandro civilians. There had been no evidence of enough Nandros to warrant purge efforts at this time. The Reach would be cleaned up once the main force of the Nandro population had been dealt with, but for now, it could be left alone.

It should be left alone.

Keraun was not leaving it alone. He was up to something else in the Andromeda Reach.

Erica studied the knot of yellow lines that signaled movements of Keraun's soldiers in the slender arm of the Milky Way that extended towards the Andromeda Galaxy. In her mind, she knew Keraun was wasting resources. In her gut, she was glad he was keeping his attention on that sector.

It was sometimes easy to forget that the Andromedans had entered the Milky Way through the Reach over a full sidereal century ago. They had come in secret, only allowing their presence to be known decades after their arrival. The extent of their settlement had been a startling, unnerving realization, but the Andromedans had promised amicable relations and made no move to sway the tide of galactic development. They were scientists, they had said, and only wished to study the various advanced races of the Milky Way.

The extent of those studies only came to light when, of all things, a small pirate fleet led in part by the intrepid Captain Gabriella Montoya stumbled upon the Andromedans' main research ship. That vessel had been kept carefully hidden throughout the Andromedans' time in the Milky Way, and upon breaking in, the pirate crews had found the experiments the Andromedans had conducted on several different species.

The races that had received the most attention from the Andromedans had been the Yukarians and Earthborn humans. Yukarian experiments had yielded awful results of short-lived beings too frail to exist outside of life-supporting fluids and thick-glassed tanks, but the natural intelligence of the species had proven too tempting to abandon.

Humans, however, had proven to be a strong template, and by the time the Andromedans' vile creations had been discovered, Neo-Andromedans had naturally bred into their next generation. They'd been unleashed on an unsuspecting sector of the galaxy, and advanced by their creators to the point of developing their own technology. The Neo-Andromedans were smart. They were powerful. They were highly adaptive. And they were all too ready to follow the instructions of their creators.

In the end, the newly formed Star Federation had not had the resources to perform a thorough enough purge. While Admiral Montoya and the other founding officers had chased the Andromedans out of the galaxy, destroyed their experiments, and found partial justice for Yukarians and humans alike, a chunk of the Nandro population had slipped through the cracks.

This time, the Star Federation would stamp them out.

Erica began the long, grueling task of assigning her subordinate officers missions based on the data from the Intelligence Unit. She'd set her own ship on a course for a lunar world close to the Terra Colonies when her private communication terminal beeped urgently. Erica pushed off her bed, smoothed a few wrinkles out of her uniform, and accepted a frantic message from another fleet commander.

"I received word from the planets Chandieranda and Araxii that Nandro forces have mobilized in major cities on both worlds," the commander's broadcast informed her and the other high officers. The slender tendrils that fringed his face and ran long over his skull quivered with distress. "I believe it's a Seventh Sun attack utilizing the specialized Nandros that have their secret gland active. I have redirected some of my units to Araxii and am moving to provide assistance to Chandieranda, but I expect this will not be an isolated incident. Be prepared for further attacks."

Not long later, reports of aggressive Nandro activity began to trickle in, and it was all too clear that the Seventh Sun was farther ahead of the Star Federation than anyone had anticipated. An order from the admirals came in, directing the fleet commanders and their subordinates to prioritize attacks over purge efforts. All but Keraun and the fleet commander rushing to Chandieranda returned a prompt acknowledgement, and the admirals themselves began to move Star Federation soldiers across the galaxy.

Erica rescinded the order to head for the Terra Colonies and had her crew slow their ship to a steady coast. They had not moved out of the heart of human-controlled territory yet, and they drifted between Sciyat and the Terra Colonies. As news of Seventh Sun movements reached her, she directed her own officers closest to the attacks. She waited for something to surface near her own location, but nothing came.

A fearful thought fired across Erica's mind. She reached out to her officers and the other fleet commanders, not certain if she should hope for confirmation or denial. The responses came slower now that their attentions were focused, but the reports were all the same.

The Seventh Sun attacks on each of the worlds consisted of only a few agents, and even fewer of the berserk Nandros. Each attack utilized two or three of the rampaging ones at most. Against civilians, they were a deadly force, but once the Star Federation arrived, they fell quickly enough.

These were strategic attacks, but not against the Star Federation.

Erica turned temporary command over to Captain Ventura and returned to her quarters. She had forgotten to shut off the galactic hologram map earlier, but was glad for the mistake. She slipped into a prowling circle around the map, updating the movements of the other fleet commanders and their units as well as her own, looking for some pattern that would signal the Seventh Sun's next move.

There was a seeming randomness to the attacks married to a precise coordination that frustrated her. They were cropping up in bursts, always spaced far enough apart to demand the attention of separate units, and the timing of each attack prevented any one unit from responding to more than one assault at a time.

"But why spread themselves so thin?" Erica wondered. She sank down on her bunk again, drawing her legs up under herself and tapping her fingers against her knees.

There was no logic to launching such small-scale assaults. The Seventh Sun had to know that the Star Federation would snuff out these kinds of attacks before they did any serious damage. The strikes had a similar feel to what had happened on Sciyat, with dropships leaving berserk Nandros in areas heavily populated with civilians, but the scale was wrong. Sciyat was a relatively small world, and had received a larger attack. These chosen planets were far more densely populated, and the Seventh Sun was only nipping at them.

If the Seventh Sun wanted to do heavy damage, as they had on Sciyat, they should have concentrated on fewer planets and brought more of their feral Nandros. But they had not. Damage to these worlds was not the goal.

"What are they doing?" Erica growled.

Berserk Nandros appearing across the galaxy, but only two or three at a time at most. Few enough that local police forces were containing and sometimes bringing them down before the Star Federation arrived. Some officers had reported finding only one of those Nandros, but once it had been killed, calming the population had proven to be the real time sink. Star Federation soldiers were spreading to meet the Seventh Sun's attacks, easily matching each new invasion, but for how long? How much longer could they play this game before the Star Federation was spread too thin?

Erica's fingers fell still, and she stared hard at the galactic map.

No new attacks near Sciyat, the Terra Colonies, Earth, or the Star Federation space station. And most of the Star Federation's soldiers were steadily moving further and further away from those locations as the attacks cropped up in new areas.

There was a sudden hole in the heart of Star Federation territory, and Erica felt her stomach turn as she recognized their vulnerability.

Erica leapt up from the bed and dashed to her private communication terminal, almost tripping as she tore across the room. She fired off a message as quickly as she could to the admirals and other fleet commanders, stressing the need for reinforcements to return to human-controlled space as soon as possible.

She ordered her own units to regroup within human territories.

Then she waited.

She spent the time back in the ship's control room, listening intently as soldiers brought her updates from across the galaxy. She had the ship's main navigation system display a galactic map in the center of the control room, and she stood with Captain Ventura as they watched the colors trail across the map. Not enough units were moving back into human territory.

Anxiety had festered in her gut by the time the distress call came. Erica shot towards the communication station, reaching it just as the soldier situated there received the message.

As the broadcast played out, a heavy silence settled over the control room, but it was far from numb. Erica sensed that she almost did not need to give the order to set the ship on course to meet the Seventh Sun's newest and grandest attack yet. The soldiers turned back to their stations immediately and the drone of activity resumed.

Erica stalked back to the galaxy map, her spine tight with anger. She read similar rage in Ventura's face, and they stood in grim silence as their ship began the sprint towards the Seventh Sun's target.

Erica chewed on her shame and regret. She should have known that the Nandros would be bold enough to attack the Star Federation space station.

And with most of the Star Federation's numbers scattered across the galaxy, that stronghold would fall if Erica could not get her soldiers there in time.

CHAPTER 18: BREAKOUT

Kidra felt the tremor through her seat as her dropship latched on to the outer wall of the space station. A soft murmur went through the room as the agents around her came alert. Their helmets obscured their faces, and the body armor thickened their movements, but Kidra could sense the surge of adrenaline coursing through them.

She did not feel the moment when the driller activated, but she knew that it wouldn't be long before the ship had cut through. A quick blast would remove the debris, a transport tunnel would thread its way through the hole, and then Kidra and the others would have a straight shot into the very heart of the Star Federation.

"Three minutes to unit launch," a voice cracked out over her helmet's intercom. "Prepare to disembark."

Almost in unison, Kidra and the other agents unbuckled their safety restraints, rose to their feet, and removed their energy pulse rifles from the holsters on the walls.

Kidra was familiar with the weapon's weight and lethality, but the anticipation of finally striking back against the Star Feds was dragging on her. She adjusted her grip on the rifle and swallowed past the sudden lump in her throat. The collar around her neck tightened as her nerves worked up, reminding her to breathe and stay calm.

She'd do no good for the Seventh Sun if she panicked before the battle had begun. And First Lit Rosonno had chosen her for a reason. She would not let him down.

The camera was built into her helmet, broadcasting her movements back to the First Lit via a secure frequency. It was linked to Kidra's heart rate. If she fell in battle, the frequency would be cut, then the camera would destroy itself.

Kidra didn't like to think of that possibility, and wearing the helmet stirred her apprehensions, but she did not dare voice her concerns. When she'd been selected as a broadcaster, she had decided to consider it an honor, and accepted the duty without hesitation.

"Two minutes to unit launch," the intercom voice barked. "All agents move to initial positions."

Rifle in hand, Kidra and the other agents moved towards the center of the room, boots sounding hard against the floor. Lines of agents formed up around her, and Kidra took her place in the ranks. She allowed herself to cast her gaze around the unit. The gesture was as much for herself as it was for First Lit Rosonno; Kidra was proud of the order and discipline of her group, and she wanted the First Lit to see her fellow agents before the battle began.

While they were not the largest attack force of the Seventh Sun, Kidra's unit made for an impressive group. The dim, blue-green light filtering into the room glinted on their dark, shining armor and on the rifles held in each agent's hands. As they were, ready for battle, it was impossible to tell one agent apart from another. In Kidra's mind, that was how it should be. They were all equal here, all prepared to give their lives in the name of the Seventh Sun.

"One minute to unit launch. All agents ready weapons."

The safeties snapped off of the rifles, and the energy capsules were locked into place. The rifles came alive with pure white light running in thin lines down the barrels, and Kidra murmured to herself, "White-hot, killing shot."

She felt a surge of embarrassment as she remembered the First Lit watching, but fought the feeling down and forced herself to focus. There wasn't much time now.

"Awakened ready. Deploying in three... two... one..."

Kidra breathed in, and began to count. At thirty, she released her breath, shifted her hold on her rifle, and squared her shoulders.

"Unit launch in ten seconds."

This was the first time Kidra's unit would fight with Awakened agents. They'd gone through the drills and learned all that they could, but Kidra still did not know what to expect. Self-aware Awakened were rare, and from what she understood, the waves sent to attack the Star Federation space station mainly consisted of feral Awakened. They were stronger and faster, but much harder to control. Kidra was not looking forward to fighting with them.

"Nine."

All Awakened were dangerous and unpredictable. The team leaders swore that precautions had gone into effect to ensure that none of the Awakened went rogue and attacked any Seventh Sun agents, but there was always room for error.

"Eight."

Kidra also did not like to think about how the Seventh Sun had managed to amass that many Awakened. As much as she wanted to believe it, she knew that not all of the Awakened had been willing volunteers.

"Seven."

Kidra had heard the stories of what happened to dissenters. It did make sense, she had decided a long time ago, to put the traitors on the front lines and let them take the brunt of the attack, and yet, the punishment seemed a little... harsh.

"Six."

After all, not every Neo-Andromedan could survive an Awakening. They all had the capacity to be Awake, but there were some who simply could not handle it. If they didn't die before reaching the Light, they tore themselves apart. Kidra may not have seen that happen firsthand, but she had been responsible for it, once. Or so she suspected.

"Five."

Not that she'd ever told anyone about that. She had, of course, given her superiors the name of the man who'd tried to persuade her to abandon the Seventh Sun's ideals, but she withheld the doubt he'd fostered in her heart.

"Four."

She never really knew what had happened to him, but she did know that he'd disappeared not long after she'd turned him in. If the Seventh Sun had simply eliminated him, they'd done it very, very quietly. But by then, she already knew that dissenters went into Awakening machines.

"Three."

Sometimes, Kidra had nightmares about his face. She dreamed that he was screaming, always screaming, and his eyes were burning molten-copper-hot in his skull, so hot they smoked and burned his skin.

"Two."

Whenever she had those dreams, she pushed them away by thinking about all the good the Seventh Sun was trying to do. All the good they'd already done. They'd saved her family from poverty and starvation after Anti-Neo-Andromedans drove them out of their home, and even healed her young nephew's near-fatal injuries. Because of the Seventh Sun, he would grow up. He would have a future. And Kidra wanted to do that for other Neo-Andromedans. That was enough for her to remind herself of what that man—that traitor—had wanted her to give up, of what she would lose if she chose to succumb to his way of thinking. All because of what had happened to a few dissenters.

"One."

The Seventh Sun was too important. Kidra would never forget that.

"Launch!"

The airlock hissed open, and Kidra stepped forward with the rest of her team.

The manufactured tunnel was dark with uneven, spongy ground, but light spilled in from the far end. Kidra focused on that as her unit broke into a steady trot, the material on the ground cushioning their footfalls.

Sounds of the battle began to filter in to Kidra's range of hearing. Enerpulse shots rang out continuously, and she could hear multilingual shouts from Star Federation soldiers intermixed with Neo-Andromedan orders and battle cries.

Her unit leader cried out in a clear, strong voice, "The Light awaits us all!"

Kidra joined in the rallying cheer that met his cry.

As they reached the end of the tunnel, the visor on Kidra's helmet adjusted automatically to preserve her vision. When her unit burst into the space station, she had a clear view as she took in the field.

Her team had been deployed into the main level of the station. Artificial gravity had enabled the Star Federation to abandon the rotating design of early space stations and build as they had seen fit. Their station was multi-storied, fashioned into a main pillar encircled by a delicate ring near the top. The ring housed civilian starship docks and other areas open to non-military personnel. Kidra's unit had bypassed that area and been sent to fight within the massive, central pillar that made up the core of the Star Federation space station.

As part of one of the later waves, Kidra had time to be distinctly unimpressed by her first look at the inside of the Star Fed's stronghold.

In front of her, there was an empty spread of space. Bodies dotted the ground, some of which were the unarmored forms of the Awakened, but the vast majority of the dead wore the deep gray uniforms of the Star Federation. These were concentrated towards the center of the station, where another core was partitioned off by a gray wall.

Kidra remembered from the designs shown in the mission briefing that the very center of the pillar housed soldiers' bunks, officers' quarters, the entire Intelligence Unit, briefing rooms, training areas, mess halls, the kitchens... All of the key elements of Star Federation life were inside the core. All Seventh Sun agents participating in the attack had been warned that the Star Feds were likely to retreat to this area and try to make a stand. One quick look and Kidra knew that that was exactly what they'd done.

The Star Feds who were still alive after the initial onslaught were shooting wildly at the approaching Seventh Sun agents. The armor held under the enerpulse fire, but Kidra realized that the Awakened were occupying most of the Star Feds' attention.

Kidra felt her heart squeeze as she watched the Awakened flicker in and out of space, sometimes moving too fast for her eyes to register. If one of them broke from the group and came for her unit...

She did not have long to linger on the thought.

Kidra's team began to fan out as they broke into a run, and she forced her mind away from the Awakened as she slipped into the ebb and flow of battle.

She fired her rifle at a clump of Star Feds that were backing away from an Awakened. She did not wait to see if she'd landed a hit, but kept sprinting forward. Her breath came in even draws, filling her hearing and muting the sound of returned enerpulse fire.

Her unit slammed into the Star Federation ranks, trading enerpulse fire and finally thrown punches as the close-quarter combat shifted the tempo of the fight.

The Star Feds had been caught off-guard, and with little time to prepare, the soldiers were in varying stages of dress. Some were armored, ranging from full combat plate to only a stiff vest. Others were in simple uniforms that offered no protection. They went down easily, and Kidra knew that she and the other agents would cut deep into the Star Federation's ranks long before reinforcements arrived.

Kidra shifted her rifle to one hand and brought her fist around to meet a charging human soldier wearing an armored vest. He wore no head protection. She knocked him back with a square punch to the nose, brought the rifle up again, and fired, hitting him in the leg. Before she could finish him, an Awakened came screaming out of nowhere, and ended his life.

Kidra drew back, mesmerized by the grizzly scene, but another agent hit her shoulder after a moment, shouting for her to focus. That pulled her back to the present.

The fight raged on, with Kidra's team doling out heavy damage and taking little in return. Their armor saved them from the worst of the Star Feds' return fire, though a few agents went down under concentrated enerpulse shots.

It was the Awakened that pushed things truly in the Seventh Sun's favor, however.

Moving like they were caught up in some violent but eerily graceful dance, the Awakened glided around the Star Feds, ending lives faster than the enerpulse fire could. Even as more and more Star Feds came from within the station, taking the place of their fallen fellows, the Awakened rose to meet them, almost insatiable in their bloodlust.

Almost.

Kidra saw more than one Awakened fall out of the Light, losing focus and becoming dazed and confused. They looked numbly at the battle they'd been drawn into, and some stared with real horror at the fresh blood on their hands. Enerpulse fire found them quickly enough, and the fractured Awakened died.

Far, far more of them remained in the Light, and they ripped into the Star Federation's ranks.

Kidra eventually found herself in front of a large bank of lifts. Star Federation soldiers were using them to join the battles, but Kidra took the first chance she saw to gun down a small, emerging group. She and four other agents ran into the empty lift, slammed a button for a lower level, and rode in silence as they were carried down.

The doors opened to spill them into one of the docking bays that housed Star Federation starships.

Kidra paused for a moment, taking in the vessels before her. They came in all shapes and sizes, but she realized that the dreadnoughts were missing.

Next level down, she remembered.

But this one would have to do.

There were more Star Feds down here, trying to win enough ground to board their ships and move the battle off the station. In space, they could engage in dogfights and remove the advantages provided by the Awakened. But there was no hope for the Star Feds. The onslaught was driving the soldiers away from the starships, and some Seventh Sun agents were planting explosives along the hulls of the ships they'd managed to claim.

Four starships were already on fire, blasted into empty shells that smoked and sparked. The burning ships threw orange light on the battles before them, silhouetting the fighting figures.

There was a beauty to it all, Kidra decided.

Then she charged in.

She did not know how long she fought, but moments of the battle were in sharp focus: taking a group of Star Feds by surprise as they tried to stop another ship from exploding; corralling an Awakened behind an undamaged ship and waiting for the perfect moment before releasing her to attack a cluster of Star Feds; landing an enerpulse shot directly on the insignia sewn into the breast of a soldier, and watching the metal scorch and burn.

It was going beautifully, all so beautifully. The First Lit would be pleased. The Seventh Sun would be victorious.

Then there was a commotion somewhere behind Kidra. She turned to see a fresh wave of Star Federation soldiers arrive, this time rising up from a lower level.

Strange, she thought. *Our agents there should have stopped them.*

Leaving confusion behind, Kidra ran forward with her fellow agents to meet the new threat. These new Star Feds all wore full gray armor, she saw, but no matter; they would fall.

And the Awakened would catch them by surprise, as they always did.

Kidra picked out a soldier to directly engage as the enemies drew closer. This one was an officer, she realized, with a blue-and-gold rank badge blazed on the breastplate of their armor and specialized symbols lining the arms.

What is that rank?

It looked familiar, but Kidra had not worried about the particulars of Star Federation hierarchy. She only knew that if this soldier fell, the enemy would fall a little further into chaos.

Shifting her rifle, Kidra slowed enough to fire off a few quick shots. Three hit the oncoming soldier, leaving scorch marks and slowing their charge, but the armor did its job and the soldier came on, focused entirely on Kidra now.

By some unspoken agreement of battle, everyone left them alone as Kidra and the soldier came together.

The soldier hit far harder than Kidra had anticipated, and the blow twisted her helmet and sent her stumbling. She righted herself quickly and blocked the next punch, but the officer had feinted and Kidra was rewarded with a solid kick to her middle.

The armor cushioned the blow, but those two hits told Kidra that she was outmatched. She would not win a trial of strength. She had to move quickly.

Faking pain, Kidra backed away unsteadily and let the soldier charge her again. When the Star Fed was close enough, Kidra dove forward, driving herself into the soldier's midsection and bringing them both down. They scrapped together before Kidra locked her arms around the soldier's neck. She started to squeeze, but when the soldier pulled free, leaving a piece of armor in Kidra's grip, she realized she'd mistimed the strike and caught only helmet.

Scrambling back to her feet, Kidra saw that it was a woman she was fighting. A woman with pale skin like her own, and short blonde hair that was damp with sweat. Brown, human eyes bore into Kidra's, and the female Star Fed held her mouth in a snarl.

The fight had brought them near one of the burning ships, and the firelight danced over the woman's face. There was nothing beautiful about that sight, Kidra decided. It was only terrible.

"Come on!" the Star Fed roared.

Kidra hesitated, then threw the helmet away and ran to meet the challenge.

Her last thought was that she should have paid more attention to what the Star Fed had done with her hands. If she had, she might have seen the sharp splinter of metal that the soldier had pulled off of the damaged hull. The splinter was the right size and length to slip into the unguarded spot at Kidra's throat, just beneath her helmet and above the line of her armor.

The collar with the seven white stars did nothing to protect her.

The metal splinter went in sharp and hot, and then there was nothing but darkness.

CHAPTER 19: HOLLOW

Erica stood in the main hanger bay, surveying the carnage. The battle had raged throughout the space station and over the course of a full sidereal day. Erica had allowed the fighting to carry her wherever she and her soldiers were most needed, even when they were on the brink of exhaustion, but now that the fight was over, she took a quiet moment to herself for reflection.

She had arrived in time to save the Star Federation from defeat at Nandro hands, but only barely. The Seventh Sun had caught the soldiers on the station off-guard, and the death toll was high. Too high.

This never should have happened, she told herself again and again.

She swung her gaze around, looking at the sprawling bodies and the smoking remains of starships. Her helmet—retrieved shortly after her one-on-one fight with an armored Nandro—offered her holographic data projections retrieved from a quick scan of the area. She'd come to look for survivors. There were none here.

Erica forced herself to take a step forward. Then another, and another, until she was weaving her way through the ruined

147

bodies and ships. She made herself look at the soldiers who had died protecting this place.

Some were in full armor like her, colored the deep signature gray of the Star Federation. Light glinted off the armor, catching on the golden insignias blazed over the hearts. Here and there, Erica saw the bands and flourishes of higher ranks; a few lieutenants, several majors, and at least two captains were down. She paused to lift the helmets off of those bodies, but she did not recognize the faces beneath. They weren't hers.

Other Star Federation soldiers had come to fight as they were. A few had managed to strap themselves into piecemeal protection. There were armored vests here and there, and a few had grabbed helmets. But many wore uniforms or fatigues.

Then there were the non-human soldiers who had fallen to save the station. Their bodies were twisted in death, forced into awkward forms that Erica knew were impossible to achieve in life. Spines bent, limbs shattered or missing, and everywhere the choking scent of death by scorching enerpulse fire.

Not even her helmet could completely filter out the smell.

"You made your stand," Erica murmured to the fallen soldiers. "You protected the galaxy. You died as you lived: true to your duty."

She came to a halt in front of a cluster of Nandro bodies.

They were easy to pick out from the Star Federation soldiers, clad in black armor instead of the signature gray. They were all humanoid, which was what angered Erica most. Here they were, masquerading as something they weren't, trying to claim a place for themselves where they had no right to be, always at the cost of human life. They didn't deserve to look like that, and those horrible metallic eyes...

Erica found herself staring into the blank gaze of one of the fallen Nandros that wore no armor. The eyes had dimmed to a deep bronze with green spots around the pupils, but Erica knew they had blazed bright and searing before the Nandro had died.

The Seventh Sun loved to send the berserk Nandros into battle first, and always without protection. They loved the death and destruction those Nandros brought, even when they went up against trained soldiers armed with enerpulse weapons. They loved broadcasting the message that no matter how hard the Star Federation fought, no matter how much they trained and honed their offensive and defensive maneuvers, they would never be a match for a Nandro in its natural state.

This never should have happened.

More Star Federation reinforcements had arrived in the wake of Erica's frantic rush back to the space station, and still more were coming to track down the retreating Nandros that had managed to escape in Seventh Sun starships. The admirals had commended her for spotting the vulnerability in the Star Federation, and anticipating the Seventh Sun's next move, but the praise was tarnished by bitter thoughts.

Was this to be the signature of her career? Arriving in time to turn the flow of battle, but always far too many steps behind the Nandros to stop the unnecessary deaths?

She couldn't bear the thought.

It was time for action. There were a few Nandro starships that the Star Federation had managed to bring down mostly intact. Their crews had either fallen in battle or taken their own lives rather than submit to questioning, but that was all right. Those ships had all come from somewhere. Stories about their origins were written in their signatures.

And Erica had faith in her soldier's abilities to draw them out.

CHAPTER 20: REPERCUSSIONS

Rosonno sat on his bunk in his private quarters onboard his starship. His personal communication terminal was active, but it only offered the dim glow of a blank projection and the low buzz of white noise. He stared at it blankly, not quite certain when he'd moved from the terminal to the bed, but he had not taken his eyes from the projection, even after the last agent broadcasting to him had fallen.

He had expected one or maybe even two of the broadcasters to die, but not all twenty of them. Some of them should have made it out alive.

But then the Star Federation reinforcements had arrived, led by the new human fleet commander. That officer was not supposed to have been so close to the space station. She and the other Star Feds out in the field should have been drawn away by the deployed Awakened. If her arrival had only been a few hours later...

Pointless speculation, Rosonno's mind snarled. *Do something about this.*

Forcing himself back to his feet, Rosonno stalked back to the terminal and closed the dead broadcast. He took a moment to smooth out his clothing and run a hand through his brown-and-gray hair before reaching out to Arrevessa.

He tried to tap her original frequency before he remembered that Lissa had chased the First Lit off her secluded planet.

Recovering from the misstep, Rosonno tried the frequency Arrevessa had last used to contact him. He brushed away the memory of her ultimatum. It was ridiculous, and it was time for her to face her own failure.

As the Seventh Sun's strategist, Arrevessa should have seen this coming. She was the one watching the Star Federation in the moments leading up to the space station strike. Even if she hadn't been able to prevent the fleet commander's arrival, she should have known how to counter it. As far as Rosonno knew, neither the field agents nor the other First Lit had heard anything from Arrevessa during the battle.

He hesitated, thinking. He realized that he himself had not heard anything from Arrevessa since she'd tried to blame him for the Seventh Sun's destruction.

As though the Seventh Sun could be destroyed.

Rosonno rested his hands on the terminal as he waited for Arrevessa to accept the transmission. One of his fingers began to tap out his growing frustration as the transmission went ignored.

Finally, he had to accept that Arrevessa would not speak to him.

This is childish, he thought as he sent a new transmission to Sekorvo.

As the eyes and ears of the Seventh Sun's inner network, First Lit Sekorvo would know where to find Arrevessa. His web of information extended across the entire organization. He always watched and listened for signs of dissent and revolt within the Seventh Sun, and Rosonno had learned early on that ignoring a warning from Sekorvo was dangerous, if not outright deadly.

After all, it was Sekorvo who had noticed that, given the right motivation and a gentle nudge, Aven and Lissa would flee the Seventh Sun, even as children.

Rosonno had worked hard to ensure that no bad blood had come between him and Sekorvo after that. He understood the value of the man and had no intentions of throwing that away.

Sekorvo accepted Rosonno's transmission almost immediately. As the hologram flickered into focus, Rosonno wasn't at all surprised to see the anger on the First Lit's face.

Sekorvo was a large man, solidly built with long, muscular limbs. He had dark bronze skin, close-cropped black hair, and copper eyes that burned almost as brightly as they eyes of the Awakened. Not for the first time, Rosonno wondered if Sekorvo had ever tried to Awaken himself; the man was hungry for it, and his admiration for the Awakened was notorious throughout the Seventh Sun.

After a quick greeting, Rosonno said, "I take it you were watching the battle?"

"Part of it," Sekorvo growled. "My attention was demanded elsewhere after my sixth broadcast agent fell."

That surprised Rosonno. "So, you don't know?"

"That the Seventh Sun lost the battle?" Disgust dripped from Sekorvo's words. "I know."

Of course he does, Rosonno thought. *He has eyes and ears everywhere. He'd know if I sneezed yesterday.* Aloud, Rosonno said, "In light of that, I'm trying to find Arrevessa."

Sekorvo snorted. "No one knows where she is."

"Don't *you* know?"

"No, and it's not a priority for me!" Sekorvo snapped. "I've been *trying* to trace the disappearances of key agents from the space station strike."

Rosonno felt a jolt of surprise. "What disappearances?"

Sekorvo's copper eyes flashed and his mouth pulled into a snarl, but his voice was more controlled now. "We thought they were casualties at first, but I noticed in the broadcasts that some of the key attack units were thinning out, and our losses were nowhere near high enough to account for the missing numbers. So, I started reviewing the retreat patterns of the surviving agents." Sekorvo bared his teeth again. "Some of them fled the battle *before* the fleet commander came."

Shock and anger settled around Rosonno's heart. "But why?"

"That's what concerns me," Sekorvo admitted after a moment. "I don't know why. These agents were fiercely loyal to the Seventh Sun. They went to battle willingly. They were ready to fight to the death, if that's what was asked of them. But then, even before the battle shifted in the Star Feds' favor, they left." He looked off, lost in thought. "I don't understand it."

Rosonno bit down a comment about Sekorvo's network fraying at the edges. Instead, he said, "Send me some of the files of those agents. I'll take a look myself and see if we've missed anything." A hopeful thought formed in his mind. "Were these untested field agents?"

Sekorvo shook his head. "All were seasoned fighters. They've been with the Seventh Sun since the early days. Not as long as the First Lit, of course, but…"

"But no one has been with the Seventh Sun longer than us," Rosonno finished grimly.

First Arrevessa, now loyal agents, Rosonno thought. *What is happening?*

But Sekorvo wasn't finished yet. "It's not just the field agents who have been going missing." His voice was edged with anger again. "I've been getting reports of deserters all over the organization. Almost all of them are long-term agents who have been nothing but loyal to the Seventh Sun."

Rosonno frowned. "When did this start?"

"About ten sidereal days ago. Obviously, there's always a delay between a desertion and the news reaching me, but some of the earliest reports came in barely hours after the agents ran."

Rosonno wracked his brain. What had happened ten days ago?

K. N. SALUSTRO

Final preparations for the space station strike had occupied everyone's time, and Rosonno could not remember any details outside of that. Except...

He went cold.

Except for Arrevessa's condemnation.

"Sekorvo," he said, his voice small, "when was the last time you heard anything from Arrevessa?"

The First Lit frowned. He stared hard at Rosonno, clearly trying to puzzle out the sudden change in the conversation.

Rosonno kept his face a blank mask. He couldn't let any of the other First Lit know about Arrevessa's condemnation. If he did, they would either try to kill him or force him to step down, all to bring her back. He knew Sekorvo in particular would favor the former method.

"One of her agents contacted me two days ago," Sekorvo finally said.

Rosonno nodded, as though an auxiliary agent meant anything to him. "And what about directly from her?"

Sekorvo shook his head. "She rarely contacts anyone directly. You know that."

"Yes, but *when?*"

Sekorvo frowned again, but he was quicker with the answer this time. "I have not heard from her since First Lit Ereko's death."

Rosonno nodded, giving in to the urge to reach up and touch the dark star on his collar. His eyes found the collar around Sekorvo's throat, and he saw that the same star—second from the left—was black. The other six stood out in stark contrast against the dead one.

"Her star still burns," Sekorvo said, misunderstanding Rosonno's distress, "so she still lives. She will contact us again soon, now that we need a new plan in the wake of this defeat."

He sounded so confident, so assured, that Rosonno almost believed him.

When their transmission ended, Rosonno stood at the terminal, staring off and thinking about Arrevessa. There was always the chance that he was wrong, but he could not shake the feeling that those disappearing agents were tied to her, and that there was a reason why she had not yet called another meeting of the First Lit. It should have followed on the heels of the battle, regardless of victory or defeat, but especially in the case of defeat.

The Seventh Sun had lost. Where was she?

He did not expect to find out.

About an hour later, as Rosonno struggled to keep his mind from wandering away from his work and back to Arrevessa, another transmission came in on his private terminal.

Rosonno pushed the file aside and nearly ran to the communication terminal. He was so ready to be wrong about Arrevessa, but a fresh wave of panic washed over him when Tyrath appeared in hologram form instead.

"What's wrong?" he blurted out before Tyrath could say a word.

She frowned at him. "How did you...? Never mind." She closed her eyes and drew in a deep breath. "I just spoke to Sekorvo about this, but I thought you should know, too. A group of agents has deserted the Daraax Beta base. They took supplies and ships."

Rosonno swallowed past the hard lump in his throat, and his collar tightened its grip. "I don't suppose these were all unexpected desertions from long-term, loyal agents?"

Tyrath looked at him quizzically, her upturned eyes narrowed. "I expected this from exactly one of them, but yes, the rest fell into that category."

Rosonno fought to keep his voice level when he asked, "Does Arrevessa know?" He dreaded Tyrath's answer, but he had to be certain.

She shook her head, frowning again. "I haven't been able to contact Arrevessa for days."

And with that, Rosonno's fears were confirmed.

Tyrath worked far closer with Arrevessa than any of the other First Lit did, excluding Ereko. But even before his death, Tyrath had been a close second. She handled the deployment of Awakened, and her work was integral to the strategists' plans. If no one else, Arrevessa should have been in contact with Tyrath up until the moments before the battle, and again the second it was all over.

Arrevessa was not in contact with anyone because she had deserted the Seventh Sun, and she was taking key agents with her. Agents who had been around for a long time, almost since the beginning of the organization. Agents, Rosonno now realized, who had probably been recruited by Arrevessa herself. She must have put the call out shortly after she'd condemned him. He did not doubt for a moment that she had set up some secret network within the Seventh Sun, hidden even from Sekorvo. Now she was tapping it, pulling back her own agents, and leaving the Seventh Sun vulnerable.

And she *had the nerve to condemn* me.

Arrevessa had told him that he would bring destruction to the Seventh Sun. As far as he could see, it was her selfish motives that would destroy them, not his. She may have even cost them the battle for the Star Federation space station.

"This is *your* fault, Vessa, not mine," he muttered.

"What?"

Rosonno jolted back to the present and saw Tyrath studying him closely.

For a moment, he considered telling Tyrath about the condemnation. Once, she might have defended him, and stood with him against the other First Lit. But not anymore.

He felt another hard lump in his throat as he remembered the fallout that had come in the wake of Lissa and Aven's disappearance from the main Seventh Sun base. Tyrath had told him then that he'd let ambition and arrogance blind him. Then she'd tried to have him removed from his position as First Lit. A single vote had saved him.

A vote from Arrevessa.

It always circles back around…

Aloud, he said to Tyrath, "It's nothing. I'm only… concerned that we haven't heard from Arrevessa yet." He hesitated. "Do we know who she last spoke to?"

Tyrath's frown deepened. She knew him well enough to know when he was keeping something from her, but she also knew better than to press the matter. "The last time I spoke directly to her was a few weeks ago. I have written correspondence from her up until about ten days ago. She wrote that she'd be busy before the strike, but everything was in order. She said not to take any silence on her part as a problem, and I haven't. But I don't know where she's been since then."

Tyrath shifted, and she folded her arms tight across her chest. Rosonno knew she was uneasy, and probably thinking about First Lit Ereko's death.

Rosonno found himself repeating what Sekorvo had said about Arrevessa's star still burning. He took no comfort in it himself, but it seemed to sooth Tyrath a little.

"I know," she said, relaxing her arms a bit. "But we're being hunted now." She gave him a pointed look. "I don't think all of us are going to survive it."

Rosonno had no response for her.

Shortly after they ended the transmission, a knock sounded on Rosonno's door. He opened it to find an agent holding a datapad.

"This information came from First Lit Sekorvo," the agent said, offering Rosonno the datapad. "He said you'd asked for it."

"Yes," Rosonno said, remembering his offer to look over the deserters' files. "Thank you."

The agent turned to go.

Rosonno called him back. "One more thing..."

The agent waited, but he began to fidget as the silence stretched.

Rosonno had to force his next words out. "Find a suitable replacement for this ship. I need a new one."

CHAPTER 21: SECRETS

"You're absolutely sure about this?"

Miyasato gave a single, solemn nod.

Jason sat back in his seat, staring down at the datapad the major had presented to him. She had requested a private meeting in one of the ship's smaller conference rooms, and the moment the door had closed, she had handed him the flat machine without a word.

Even after what Jason had seen on Firoden and carried back with him in the cargo hold, Jason was still having trouble accepting what he was reading.

He raised his eyes back to the major.

She returned his gaze, waiting with grim patience for his questions.

"Everything we know about hybrid races points to infertility after the first generation," Jason said. The words were robotic in his mouth; he was repeating basic schooling that predated his Star Federation training days.

Miyasato was ready with the counter. "Between species that share no common ancestors, absolutely. But everything we learned from the hybrid boy confirms that humans and Neo-Andromedans can produce viable offspring. Given the origins of Neo-Andromedans—"

Jason held up a hand to stop her, but he was nodding. "It makes sense," he said. "I just don't understand how no one found this before."

Miyasato grimaced. "I'm sure they did, but I'd bet my life that the people in control of the information were more interested in keeping it quiet."

"You think the Star Federation knew about this, and kept it from the rest of the galaxy?"

"I do." She hesitated, and Jason watched her weigh her trust in him against the next thing she wanted to say. "I think it even played a role in the first purge."

Jason frowned and opened his mouth, but the words died on his tongue. The idea of the Star Federation withholding this kind of discovery was not hard to accept.

If that information had been hidden for as long as Miyasato was suggesting, then it was possible that the Star Federation had successfully wiped the knowledge from existence. At least for a little while. Jason doubted that the boy from Firoden was the first child of such a union, but prejudices took a long time to die, if they ever did. Jason would not have been surprised to learn that the majority of human-Neo-Andromedan hybrids were a recent development.

Jason knew that this jeopardized the purge. The ability to procreate with another species exponentially increased the Neo-Andromedan race's odds of surviving a second purge, but more importantly, it was something that would make Neo-Andromedans more sympathetic. They could create viable offspring with human partners, and that made them far less inhuman than the galaxy had chosen to believe. With fertile offspring, an entire subspecies of humans and Neo-Andromedans could form.

And beyond Star Federation leadership, Jason suspected that he, Miyasato, and her team were the only ones who knew with total certainty that such a species was possible.

That put them in a lot of danger.

"We can't tell anyone," Jason said aloud.

Miyasato sat stunned for a moment, then leapt out of her seat in outrage.

Jason hurried on before she said something he knew she'd regret, if only because he was her superior in rank. "The second anyone finds out that your team discovered this, you all become targets."

The major stopped just short of screaming at him, but her anger was still burning strong, almost tangible in the air around her. All the same, she took a moment to consider his words.

"If the Star Federation really is containing this," he told her, "you're likely to end up dead long before you can get the information out."

He watched Miyasato run through a thousand different counter-scenarios in her head, trying to find the one that ended with them telling the galaxy what it desperately needed to know, but in the end, she slumped back into her seat, defeated.

Jason deactivated the datapad and slid it across the table. "Where is your team now?" he asked.

"I left them in the mess hall. Told them to wait for me there and keep quiet." She sighed and picked up the datapad. "About everything."

"Good." Jason tapped the table to get her full attention again. "Listen very closely, Malia."

She lifted her head with a slow blink, but she looked ready to hear him.

"First and foremost," Jason told her, "keep your team safe. Make sure they know the danger of sharing this with anyone outside of this circle. I'm sure one or two of them may not care, but if we're going to get this out there and walk away with our lives, we need to play this very carefully."

Miyasato blinked at him again. Then she eagerly leaned forward as she realized what he was saying.

"Your report needs to be inconclusive at best. Don't give anyone any reason to suspect that you and your team know otherwise. As for the actual information..." Jason hesitated, his plan still not fully formed in his own mind.

But Miyasato was far more ready for this than he had anticipated. "I have a contact," she said, "someone I trust. Getting this to him will be... difficult... but if I can do it, he'll take care of everything."

Jason nodded. "Your correspondence is going to be watched very closely from now on. Play this safe. Don't worry about perfect timing. I don't think there ever will be one."

Miyasato gave a half-shrug, but she did not openly disagree with him.

"I'm serious," he told her firmly. "Do *not* rush this. One mistake will cost you your life. Possibly the lives of your team members, too."

"What about you?" she asked.

Before Jason could respond, there was a sharp knock on the door. It opened a moment later and an agitated soldier spilled over the threshold. "Sorry for interrupting," he said, dropping a salute to both Jason and Miyasato, "but there's an urgent message for Captain Stone from the fleet commander." The soldier held out a datapad to him.

Jason's anger at the soldier for barging in without permission dissolved into a nervous pit. He stood and moved to accept the datapad, but he turned his gaze back to Miyasato. "Please file that report as soon as possible, Major. You're dismissed."

Miyasato rose on cue. She played along and gave an affirmative reply with her salute before slipping past the soldier in the doorway. She kept a firm grip on her own datapad as she went.

Before she was even halfway through the door, the other soldier was stretching his arm around her, almost desperately trying to give Jason the message. Jason accepted the datapad, told the soldier to wait, then closed the door. In the privacy of the small conference room, he activated the datapad and played the recorded message from Keraun.

The Hyrunian's green, horned head flickered into focus, the permanent glare of his yellow eyes smoldering with even more anger than usual. "It is a mystery to me, Captain,"

Keraun clicked out, "why you have chosen to turn off your communicator—" Jason's hand shot to his hip and he switched the device back on, which promptly beeped to alert him of three missed transmissions, all during his brief meeting with Miyasato. "—but regardless, all officers need to know that the Star Federation space station has been attacked by the Nandros."

Jason's mouth fell open and his heart forgot to beat. He almost missed Keraun's next words.

"Reinforcements are moving in from all nearby territories, but Fleet Commander Anderson has driven off the worst of the attack. Your units are too far away to be of any help. Recall any soldiers you may have in the field and stand by for further orders."

The message ended there.

Jason stared blankly at the space the hologram had filled a moment earlier. He felt too numb to respond, but to his surprise, his thoughts came trickling back with cold clarity. When he told the soldier waiting outside the conference room to send a transmission to all field soldiers and recall them, his voice sounded distant and detached from his own body. The soldier gave a crisp salute and ran off. Jason followed at a steadier pace, wondering why he felt so calm. Keraun had given him devastatingly few details, and Jason felt like he was moving through thick gel as he made his way to the control room. But his mind raced.

Even without the details, Jason knew what that kind of message meant; the unthinkable had happened. The Seventh Sun had penetrated the station and caused severe damage. He had been alerted after-the-fact, *after* Erica had managed to get there with reinforcements and drive off the Neo-Andromedans.

Jason knew what was coming next: a counterstrike.

Erica was too good a soldier to come away from a battle like that without any way to trace her enemy back to their nest. She would find a target for the Star Federation. It was only a matter of time.

Until then, Jason knew what he had to do.

In the control room, he broadcasted a message to all of his subordinates, telling them about the attack and the orders from Keraun to standby and wait. As he expected, the news turned their frustrations up to a boiling point, especially once the field soldiers returned. They had been in the middle of purge efforts and were returning with mixed results, but to Jason's relief, none of them had come back with any more hybrids.

In the days that followed, Jason and his more trusted officers worked to keep the soldiers busy. They were all angry over the space station attack, and Jason ordered extra training regimens to burn off their rage and extra energy. It helped, but not enough. On the second day, Jason heard someone mutter, "Nandro lover," as he passed, but when he whipped around, he only saw soldiers seated at their places in the control room, heads turned to their holographic displays and attention locked on their tasks.

He was not certain that he had not imagined the whispered insult.

Real or not, he did not let the hostility cut him. He made a point of training with the others; took his meals in the common mess hall instead of having them sent to his private quarters as high officers usually did; and even allowed holocard games during recreational hours, provided the soldiers gambled nothing beyond sweets and holovids picked up on their down time.

Throughout all of that, Jason kept an eye on Miyasato and her team. They were more subdued and kept to themselves. That made them stand out, which was exactly what Jason was hoping they would avoid. But when someone made a jab at them during mealtime, one of Miyasato's subordinates made a groaning, dramatic statement about the sheer amount of work medical reports demanded.

"I'm going to be the first recorded death by drowning in datapads and holograms," she proclaimed.

That earned her a few laughs, and bought Miyasato's team some forgiveness for their sullen mood. But after that, the medics put on a more energized charade. Jason suspected that Miyasato was responsible for the false cheer. He hoped they would not need to keep it up for much longer.

By the time the new orders came in from Keraun, all of the field soldiers had returned, and the ship was heavy with anticipation for the Star Federation's next move.

As Jason had suspected, Erica had found a target for them. She and Keraun were coordinating a massive counterstrike, one that called for speed and force instead of stealth. They wanted to seize control of a Nandro base, but they did not want to take any prisoners.

Jason relayed the orders to his soldiers, and his navigators plotted a new course.

They were heading to Daraax Beta.

CHAPTER 22: TRAILING

Tracing and tracking the signature of Haelin's dropship was easy. Far easier than Vinterra had expected. At first, she was relieved when she locked on to the signature, almost even hopeful. But without something to occupy her time, the journey between Daraax Beta and Haelin's dropship was agonizingly difficult and lonely.

Without any distractions, Vinterra obsessed over the dropship's trail. Every change in course brought on a new flare of anxiety. Vinterra told herself over and over again that it was highly unlikely that Haelin's ship would engage in a battle, but she kept imagining a Star Federation ship turning pulse cannons on the dropship, obliterating Haelin in precise blasts of white-hot energy.

That ship won't see battle, Vinterra repeated over and over to herself, as though the unspoken chant would charm Haelin's ship to finish its journey and land unharmed.

Of course, that only led Vinterra's thoughts down a path that ended with Haelin brought out of stasis and deployed on the ground. She would have to feed the gnawing hunger the Light put in her. If she did not starve, Haelin would live or die by enerpulse fire.

Surviving that trip between the stars, alone and sick with worry, nearly killed Vinterra. She barely slept, forgot to eat, and felt her exhausted body beginning to rebel against her. The only thing that saved her was the realization that she could not help Haelin if she destroyed herself.

Vinterra forced herself to bathe and eat with some regularity, though sleep kept eluding her. "I promise I'm coming," she whispered whenever she stepped away from her vigil over the dropship's trail to feed and care for herself.

When Haelin's ship finally settled on a course for Araxii, Vinterra felt her heart stop, then beat slow and hard and sharp against her ribs. Of all the planets that ship could have gone to, militant, fierce, Star Federation-controlled Araxii was one of the worst.

Vinterra checked the distance between herself and the dropship, then the maximum speed of her stolen ship. She ran the calculations in her head seven, eight, nine times, but they always came up short. She did not bother wiping away the tears that rolled down her cheeks.

She was too far away to save Haelin. The dropship would reach Araxii long before Vinterra caught up, and Haelin would meet her fate on that hostile planet's surface. Her flight from Daraax Beta had all been for nothing.

Crying and with her breath hitching in her throat, Vinterra watched on the stolen ship's tracking system as Haelin's dropship moved closer to Araxii. She could not bring herself to tear her eyes away, even though she knew she should give up.

She could take the stolen ship somewhere, maybe abandon it and find a way to evade the Seventh Sun.

More likely, she'd be caught long before that happened. She was surprised no one had tried to hail her yet, ordering her to ground the ship and surrender. Someone from the Seventh Sun had to be on her trail by now. Tyrath would have quickly noticed the absence of her and those other agents, even with the chaos of the strike against the Star Federation.

Maybe it was better to drift through space and let them catch up.

Or Vinterra could throw the ship into the Araxii surface. Escape all of those fates. Not have to live with her failure to save the one she loved.

If she made it that far.

Vinterra pressed her fingertips against her forehead, feeling her skin burning with shame and distress. She tried to remember life with Haelin on Daanhymn, but all she could think about was Haelin's unhappiness on that planet, and their last moments together.

She had *screamed* at Haelin the last time she saw her. Told her to leave. Left her unforgiven and unwanted.

"I'm so sorry, Haelin," Vinterra whispered.

Tears blurred her vision when she looked back at the trackers. She rubbed them away as she reached to switch off the system, but her hand froze when she realized what she was seeing.

Haelin's dropship had moved into an erratic pattern just outside of Araxii space. It was stalled now, as though it had forgotten where it was supposed to go. Or...

The tracker updated, showing that the dropship had reversed course and was speeding away from Araxii. There was another ship behind the dropship, pursuing it, but it peeled off before long and returned to the planet.

The dropship must have been intercepted by a hostile vessel. An Araxii police vessel or maybe even a Star Federation cruiser. Vinterra hoped against hope that it had not been the latter. That dropship needed to remain intact for as long as possible. Or at least until Vinterra could catch up.

Wiping her face, Vinterra threw herself at the controls, pushing the stolen ship after Haelin's dropship.

She might not even be on that ship anymore, a cruel voice whispered in the back of Vinterra's mind.

She shook her head. She knew the voice was right, but she had to know what had happened to Haelin. No matter what.

"I'm coming for you," Vinterra whispered again, and she kept whispering it to drown out the dark words in her head. She whispered it over and over, and the whisper grew to a desperate shout as the dropship settled on a direct course for Crythsia. Vinterra could get there. Maybe not before the dropship, but there was a strong chance she could land before it was ready to leave.

"I promise I'm coming!"

CHAPTER 23: FORWARD

Lance and Lissa sat at their seats in the control room of the blue-and-black starship, Lissa with her legs curled under her and a datapad in hand, Lance leaning towards her with his elbows on his knees. The arkins were sprawled across the floor, Orion half-in and half-out of the control room, blocking the doorway. Blade lay with her shoulder pressed up against his hip, bad wing resting on top of the gray arkin's side. Almost in unison, they gave a loud sigh of boredom.

It had taken weeks for Lissa to translate and comb through the rest of the data from the ship they had attacked on Sciyat. Lissa did not trust the signature the First Lit had given her, so she had thrown herself back into the communication logs.

There had not been much for the others to do while they'd waited for her to finish. Everyone was feeling the stress of too much time spent aboard a starship, but Lance and Lissa had both agreed that they should keep moving. They had no way of knowing if the First Lit from the uncharted sector was tracking them. There was a chance that their ship's signature was still safe, but neither of them wanted to take the risk. After they'd made amends, they had sprinted to a new part of the galaxy, and had kept the ship in constant motion since then.

K. N. SALUSTRO

The arkins needed exercise. Lance had run out of fresh food to experiment with and could only fill so many hours with strength training and light sparring, which he used to help Lissa develop and refine her hand-to-hand combat skills whenever a pounding headache drove her away from the data translations. And Lissa herself needed to breathe unrecycled air, even if it was just for a moment, before the staleness drove her into dangerous territory.

When she wasn't sleeping, training with Lance, taking her turn plotting a course for the ship, or trying to keep the arkins occupied, she was deciphering and translating as much information as she could. She had finally been rewarded with two leads, but she did not trust either of them.

The first lead was a starship signature. Lissa had found it through a series of transmissions sent in irregular patterns, and with little consistency in tone. The messages ranged from complex, incomprehensible data to rambling correspondence seething with anger and bloodlust. It had taken Lissa a long time to realize that those transmissions had all come from the same source. Once she did, Lissa had managed to tease out a signature for the ship within a few hours, but she did not like the idea of going after this lead. There was an unstable, unpredictable nature to it. If they chose it as a target, they would need to take it by surprise. Anything else would lock them in a deadly clash.

The second lead was a base of some sort, but there was no location attached to it, and try as she might, Lissa could not figure out where in the galaxy the transmissions had originated from. Her best guess was somewhere in the Andromeda Reach, but she could not lock in the location. They could not chase a target they could not find.

Lance agreed with her on both counts, once she had shown him the leads and explained her misgivings.

That left them with one final option, which they had lifted from their raid on Jetune: Daraax Beta.

Lance did not like the idea, but he spent a few quiet moments considering it.

170

A newscast frequency filled the background. Lance had gotten into the habit of keeping newscasts on as a way to track the major Star Federation and Seventh Sun movements happening across the galaxy. Lissa was often focusing too hard on the communication logs to pay much attention to the broadcast, but the droning monologues helped block out the other voices that kept nibbling at her ears.

Finally, Lance reluctantly agreed with Lissa's suggestion that they head to Daraax Beta. "The starship will take a lot longer to track down, and we're not far from the base." He frowned at her. "Although, we've known for a while that the Seventh Sun has been active in the Daraaxi system. After everything we've done, we should expect them to have much better security now."

Lissa nodded and reached for the controls to access a starmap. She brought up the binary Daraaxi star system, and the two planets that shared a central orbit. "I'm thinking we can hide around Daraax Alpha and try to scout the area for a bit," she said. "See what ships come and go, and what kind of base we'd be dealing with."

"What happens if it's too much for us?" Lance asked softly.

Lissa pressed her mouth into a grim line. "Then we get out of the system and go after the starship. It's the only other move we have."

"Well," Lance said, shifting back in his seat and turning his face to the ceiling, "we could still just slip away." He locked his hands behind his head, and Lissa found her eyes drifting to the side of his body that she knew had suffered an enerpulse wound. It had healed cleanly without any traces of residual pain, leaving him free to work the muscles back to their normal strength. After a minute, Lance focused on her again, but she had already shifted her gaze back to his face. "You said that the First Lit would pull back on you and let you go free, though I'm not sure you trust that offer."

"I don't," Lissa agreed. After that night in the spice field, she had told him everything about her encounter with the First

171

Lit in the uncharted sector, every word she could remember. "She played a lot of mind games. And even if she was sincere about leaving me alone, I don't think she could guarantee it." Her hand wandered to the broken collar that still resided in a pouch on her belt. She had redistributed some of her supplies to clear space in one of the larger pockets. The broken piece rested comfortably there now, no longer threatening to rip through the fabric. She felt the hard edges of the collar and the seven little stars that ridged one side. "I'll never really be free until the Seventh Sun is destroyed."

But even she could hear the reluctance in the words.

Lance was right; this wasn't what she wanted to do. Not anymore. But she didn't know what else to do, other than finish what she'd started.

Lance seemed to be at a loss as well. She knew that he did not want her to lose herself again and go charging blindly into danger. Neither of them knew what to expect at Daraax Beta, although they suspected it had to do with the Awakened. At the very least, this was a chance to cripple that part of the Seventh Sun's operations, and that was enough of a motive for the moment.

"We need to start somewhere," Lissa said, "even if that means sneaking into the Daraaxi system just to get a look at the base out there. We can't just coast through space, waiting for something to happen." She waited for Lance to argue, but he was staring at the communication terminal, a deep frown creasing his brow.

"I think something already did," he finally said. He adjusted the volume of the incoming newscast and let the words fill the cabin.

Lissa felt the rest of the universe fall away as she listened to the broadcast.

The Seventh Sun had attacked the Star Federation space station, only to be driven back by Fleet Commander Erica Anderson. She had arrived at a critical moment with reinforcements, and the news broadcasters held nothing back as they heaped praise on the officer for her foresight. It quickly became clear that the broadcasters had very little information about the attack, other than that it had taken place and the aggressors were Seventh Sun agents.

Lance switched off the broadcast as a fresh commentator offered a new perspective on the fleet commander's tactical brilliance in driving back the Seventh Sun. He swiveled in his seat to face her again. "Can we agree," he said, "that they probably used Awakened in that attack?"

Lissa nodded, her tongue feeling thick in her own mouth. She found that she was not surprised that the Seventh Sun had attacked the Star Federation like this, but the speed shocked her. It had not been that long since the attack on Sciyat.

"I know Anderson well," Lance said, tracing out a line of thought word by careful word. "It's a safe bet that she's captured some Seventh Sun agents, maybe even some of their ships."

Lissa hesitated, thinking, but Lance had not phrased it as a question. And Lissa had to agree that it was unlikely that the Seventh Sun had executed a flawless retreat, especially if they had not expected the fleet commander's arrival.

Lance continued. "There's now a very, *very* good chance that Anderson has something to trace back to an origin point."

"Which may be Daraax Beta," Lissa finished.

He nodded. "We can't rule out the possibility that the Star Federation knows about that base now." He hesitated, and his gaze flickered to the control room door as, with a loud groan, the arkins suddenly hauled themselves to their feet.

Orion stood in the doorway, making impatient grunting noises. Blade was just in front of him, silent but staring so hard at Lissa that there could be no mistaking their motives.

Dinner was late.

Lance waved them off, which earned him two glares, but the arkins contented themselves with settling down in the hallway and blocking any escape route out of the control room.

Turning back to Lissa, he said, "Anderson is not one to wait. If she has anything that will point her to Daraax Beta, she will take a fleet there and launch an attack." He leaned forward in his seat, his gaze intense. "Is the Star Federation a risk you're willing to take?"

Lissa spent a moment studying Blade. The arkin still held her bad wing out, even when she stood at attention. Lissa doubted that the injury would ever fully heal.

She faced Lance again. "No," she told him. "If there's *any* chance the Star Federation knows about Daraax Beta, we can't go there."

Lance's relief was almost tangible, but it was short-lived. "So what do we do now?"

Lissa sighed and brought up the starship signature from the communication logs, along with a fresh starmap. She marked the ship's most recent positions on the starmap before sinking back in her seat with an unenthusiastic wave at the locations. "We start hunting."

Lance rose to get a better look at the map. "Do you really think that signature the First Lit gave you was a trap?" he asked as he looked over her shoulder.

Lissa considered the question for a long moment. "I'd be surprised if it wasn't, but…"

"But?"

Lissa sighed. "She seemed to think that she could use me, if she offered the right motivation."

Lance rocked back on his heels, considering. "I don't know much about this First Lit, but personally, if I was hoping you would chase down the first lead I gave you, I would give you something that I knew you'd want to follow, whether the trap was obvious or not."

Lissa paused, remembering the encounter. "She did seem to think she could cast me as the selfish hunter who attacked without thinking."

"Because she thought she was smarter than you, or because she was afraid of you?"

"Both," Lissa said after a moment.

Lance made a pensive noise, and Lissa felt his hands settle on the back of her seat as he leaned forward. His eyes were still locked on the starmap. "So who did she give you to hunt?"

Lissa tensed, and she sensed the shift in Lance as he registered her reaction. He took his weight off her seat, and she felt his eyes on the back of her head.

I can trust him, she told herself. *I have to trust him.*

She still had to fight to get her next words out. "His name is Rosonno. He's..."

A silence played out as Lissa tried to finish the thought.

"The one who ambushed you on Yuna," Lance supplied softly.

With a start, Lissa twisted halfway out of her seat, staring hard at Lance. She had never told him that.

His voice was gentle when he spoke. "After Phan, your nightmares... Well. I didn't try to hear, if that makes it any better. I just made sure Blade was with you so you wouldn't wake up alone."

The black arkin lifted her head at her name. When she saw Lissa's distress, she half-rose from the floor, but Lissa made a calm, easy gesture with her hand and the arkin settled back down.

Lissa lowered herself back into her seat, still tense.

I have to trust him, she told herself, but she felt the resistance start to build back up.

She jumped a little when Lance placed a tentative hand on her shoulder.

"I know how hard it can be to admit to vulnerability in the past," he told her. "It's like opening the wound all over again, and it can feel like you're giving power back to that person." His hand rested more firmly on her shoulder. "As though they somehow made you who you are."

Lissa remembered the story Lance had told her about his time away from the Star Federation as a teenager. He had fallen in with a ruthless gang led by a boy who thought he could claim immortality and rule a slice of the galaxy. The kind of boy who, after a few years' time and a couple of turf wars, would have ended up on Lissa's hunting radar.

"They can scar you," Lance finished softly, "but they don't define you."

With a shuddering sigh, Lissa broke the resistance down. "It's always come back to Rosonno," she said.

Lance gave her shoulder a light squeeze, then moved his hand back to her seat. She was surprised by how quickly she missed its warmth, but she said nothing.

"Do you think the Seventh Sun would really do that?" Lance asked. "Throw out one of their own as bait for you to follow?"

"Maybe," Lissa said, a little more at ease now, "but not him. He's one of their leaders." She released a hard breath. "And he's the kind of person who would set up a trap like this."

"Okay," Lance said. "So until we know for certain what's waiting for us at the end of that ship's trail, we should focus on the one you pulled from the communication logs."

Lissa nodded, and they both stared at the starmap for a long, silent moment.

A loud groan from one of the arkins broke the mood, and both Lance and Lissa turned to look at them. The arkins glared back at them, ears flattened in irritation.

"But first," Lissa said drily, "we'd better feed the arkins before they stage a mutiny."

Lance laughed softly, obviously relieved by the break in the tension. "Your turn this time. I'll work on locking in that ship's signature and setting us on the trail."

Lissa nodded. She placed the datapad on the control panel in front of her, but her attention was locked on the device and she made no move to rise.

"If you're looking for a way to distract yourself," Lance said after a long moment, "maybe you can come up with a name for your ship."

"Our ship," she corrected him, and was rewarded with a cautious but warm smile.

Later, as she parsed out rations for the arkins down in the galley—neither of them looking particularly happy with her food choice but waiting impatiently all the same—Lissa reflected on Lance's suggestion and felt her stomach turn.

Even with the easier atmosphere between her and Lance, the prospect of naming the ship brought on a twinge of panic.

In a wash of faded memory, she remembered Aven buying their first and only starship. He'd christened it *Lightwave* before the seller had even signed off on the transaction. And *Lightwave* was a fast, beautiful ship, capable of long-distance travel and high speeds. It was very much like her and Lance's starship from the Fangs, though it had been built with more jagged lines and a bulkier hull. *Lightwave* had been hers and Aven's, completely. And *Lightwave* had brought her nothing but grief as Aven drove further and further into the hunting game, picking up far more enemies than allies. When Lissa had sold the ship, she'd felt the weight of *Lightwave's* heavily tracked signature lifted from her shoulders.

Leaving the blue-and-black patterned starship unnamed had held those memories at bay.

If the ship had a name, it had a bond, and if it had a bond, it would be almost impossible to let go.

Even *Lightwave* had put up an emotional fight. Enemies bearing down on the ship's trail or not, Lissa had felt a sharp spike of guilt and sadness as she signed away ownership of the vessel to a team of interstellar traders on Phan who'd intended to gut the ship for parts.

She did not know what the future held, and it was difficult to imagine this new ship remaining in her life for any stretch of time. She feared becoming attached to it.

There was a soft nuzzle at Lissa's hand. She looked down to find Blade nosing at her fingertips, amber eyes bright against her black fur. Lissa rested her hand on the arkin's head, remembering that there had been no hesitation when it came to naming the scruffy, little arkin kit she had adopted years ago.

Time and life had changed a lot of things, but Lissa felt the weight of the irony on her shoulders.

Blade was a living thing. Even if she and Lissa came through everything alive, she would still die one day, maybe long before Lissa did, if enemies did not catch up to her first.

The ship was different. Her ship was not a living thing. If it needed to be replaced, it could be, and named or not, a ship was just a way between worlds.

But it wasn't just *her* ship. She'd meant it when she'd told Lance that it was theirs. Together.

That was what she was afraid of locking into her life.

Returning to the task at hand, Lissa picked the food up off the galley counter and brought it into the arkins' designated dining corner. They both flanked her closely as she moved, almost bouncing as they walked with their eyes turned up to the food. They dug in hungrily before Lissa even put the trays on the floor.

Standing back, Lissa watched the arkins eat, sharp teeth gleaming dully in the light whenever they surfaced to chew a bite.

With Blade and Orion before her, Lissa thought about the other things in her life she'd tried to push away and outrun. Her eyes lingered on Blade's bad wing, and she forced herself to admit that running had never ended well.

She had told herself she would stop fleeing, but that extended beyond the hunting game.

Turning on her heel, Lissa made her way back up to the middle level of the ship, where the control room was. Lance heard her coming, and he swiveled in his seat as she stepped into the room.

"*Light Runner*," she said.

"What?"

"The ship. I want to name it *Light Runner*."

Lance blinked, then sat back and turned the name over in his mind. "I like it, but…" He studied her for a long moment. "Are you sure you want the word 'light' in the name?"

Welcome to the fight for me, Little Light.

Lissa knew that she couldn't outrun those voices any more than she could outrun her past, and her heritage as a Neo-Andromedan. It was time to accept that.

"You once told me," she said, moving to sit in her seat next to Lance's, "that shadows are faster than light." She let her gaze wander around the control room, taking in the sleek lines of the systems. Different colors lit up various parts of the controls, breaking the monotony of the soft gray interior. "I think I should remind myself of that a bit more often."

"Why not name it *Shadow Runner*?" Lance asked.

She gave him a half-smile. "It's not shadows that I need to stop being afraid of." She shifted in her seat so that she was facing him more fully. "And the Shadow is who I chose to be. When I took up the name, I thought I could shut out all the Light, and turn my back on it forever."

Lance let a small silence play out before he asked, "And now?"

"Now, I don't want to. Not all of it. Whether I want it to be or not, the Light is part of me. I was named for it. The more I try to fight it, the more it hurts me, and the ones I care about. But none of that means that I have to let it control me. And I think that, on my own terms, I could make peace with it."

Lance was quiet for a long time, but eventually, he nodded. "I think you could, too."

CHAPTER 24: INSUBORDINATION

When Jason's small fleet came down from its faster-than-light journey and began to offer images of the Daraaxi system, he initially thought that the Star Federation fleet had been met by enemy starships ahead of his arrival.

Pulse cannons blazed like newborn stars against the backdrop of small, dark Daraax Beta and massive, burning Daraax Alpha. Everything was silhouetted by the blue and red binary suns, making it impossible to pick out friends or foes from the images alone.

Remembering the ambush at Ametria, Jason ordered his ships toward the battle at a slow pace, pointedly keeping what he hoped was a safe distance away from any takeover attempts. He waited with his junior officers for the scans of the Daraaxi system to return with information on which ships were Seventh Sun vessels, and where his support was needed most. Scans of the space around the smaller Daraaxi planet returned images of starship debris, and the sickening revelation that the only ships out there were Star Federation vessels.

Not one Seventh Sun ship was present. The Star Federation fleet had turned on itself.

The Neo-Andromedans on Daraax Beta had taken control of almost every ship in the Star Federation fleet, and turned the ships' weapons on each other. Nearly every ship in the fleet had sustained damage, ranging from mild hull scorches to total destruction. Two of the three *Argonaught* dreadnoughts that had led the assault were locked in a deadly, blazing exchange of pulse cannon fire.

As for the third *Argonaught*, Jason recognized it as Keraun's flagship. Based on the images of the battle, it looked to still be under complete Star Federation control.

Jason recalled the conversation he'd had with Major Miyasato about Keraun brokering a deal with the Yukarians. Whatever the Hyrunian had done, it was working... for him alone.

The bastard hasn't shared the tech, Jason realized.

Anger burned through him, and before he had paused to consider the consequences, Jason was at the main communication terminal in the control room, driving a transmission to Keraun's ship.

A lieutenant answered him, but the soldier barely had time to accept the transmission before Jason was snarling his demand to speak to the fleet commander.

"Tell the captain," Keraun's voice clicked from somewhere beyond the capture ring of the terminal, "that I am commanding a battle and do not have time for his tantrums."

Jason felt something snap inside of him. "Tell the fleet commander," he shot back, startling the lieutenant, "that withholding critical tech from the rest of the fleet is grounds for court-martialing by the admiralty board!"

There was a heavy pause while the lieutenant looked off and waited for Keraun's response.

Finally, the Hyrunian stomped into the capture ring and flickered into the hologram. "We will discuss this—" Keraun began, voice hard with danger and denial.

"NOW," Jason cut in.

He felt every eye in the control room focus on him. The room held its breath, making Jason's rage-colored breathing loud in his own ears.

"We will speak in private, Captain," Keraun finally snarled. His putrid yellow eyes glittered even over the hologram projection. Then he stormed out of the ring and disappeared from sight.

The lieutenant gave Jason a bewildered look before the transmission ended.

Jason ordered the ships to be kept well away from the battle until he'd spoken with the fleet commander. His instruction was met with a murmured affirmative, but he still felt the room's collective gaze as he stormed out. He found a small, empty room, and waited only a few minutes for his personal communicator to intercept the incoming transmission.

Keraun's head flickered into view a moment later. The Hyrunian was already snarling before the hologram fully formed. "—middle of launching an attack on the Nandros and you dare disrespect my authority?"

"I'm sure that Yukarian tech will keep your ship safe," Jason snapped. "How dare *you* keep that from the rest of the fleet?"

"Do not question me, human," Keraun growled. He dipped his head a little, bringing his thick, curling horns to the focal point of the hologram. The *shekdan* mark burned along the back of the Hyrunian's skull edged into view, dark and twisted and horrible.

Jason stood his ground. "You jeopardized every soldier who came here today. You let them fly into battle unarmed. For WHAT?"

"More than you could ever know," Keraun said, suddenly quiet. His slitted pupils regarded Jason with clinical cruelty. "Keep your stupidity in check, *Captain*—" the Hyrunian spat Jason's rank as though it were a terrible taste on his tongue, "—and get your units ready for the raid. You're following me to the surface." He raised his head again, regarding Jason with his permanent glare. "And I will remember this."

"You'd better," Jason growled as he slammed the controls and ended the transmission. Then he checked the recording he had initiated prior to accepting.

The full conversation was there.

He almost sent it to Erica. He hesitated when he remembered the broken way they'd left things. Then he sent the recording to Miyasato instead.

If something happened, she would know what to do with it. Keraun might try to dodge the consequences, act as though he'd taken the brunt of the risk from a field test of the new tech, but anyone could worry at the holes in the story until the truth came screaming out.

Then the full impact of what he'd just done slammed into Jason, and he reeled on his feet. This was a very, very dangerous game, and he was certain that he had already doomed himself to lose.

He let himself sink down to the floor, resting his back against the wall. He pressed his hand against his forehead and took a few deep breaths, trying to steady himself. He gave himself a few minutes to recover, but he kept thinking, *Keraun is going to kill me. He is finally going to kill me.*

It was almost a relief to know that he'd finally reached the tipping point, but he strongly preferred to live.

I need to survive today first, anyway.

Jason pushed himself back to his feet, then made his way back to the control room. His voice was steady when he sent out the order for the ground strike team to suit up. He would lead them into battle on the Daraaxi surface. "Ready the dropships," he ordered the teams working in the bays. "The *Argonaught* will breach the sky, but we'll need dropships to take us the rest of the way down."

One of the team leaders gave an affirmative, then asked, "When are you expecting to breach, Captain?"

"As soon as Keraun clears a path," Jason responded grimly.

Then he went to change into battle armor.

CHAPTER 25: UNSPOKEN

A suitable replacement for Rosonno's starship was found within a few sidereal days. His new ship would be fast, reliable, untraceable, and with enough storage space to accommodate the numerous files he kept on hand.

Rosonno had a rule about his files. He never deleted any data, not even after the candidates were long dead. There was plenty to learn from a "completed" candidate's file, after all, and he had amassed an arsenal of information that reached decades into the past. Not all of the files concerned Neo-Andromedans.

Even across species, there were repetitions of certain behaviors and instincts. Rosonno had always been able to see the twists and weaves of the patterns. Sometimes, he needed to spend more time studying them in order to make correct predictions. He enjoyed the work, even when it frustrated him.

But when it came to Lissa, he could not understand her, no matter how many hours he spent pouring over her data.

Her pattern refused to come into focus. It was abnormal.

Unpredictable.

Undesirable.

Dangerous.

But soon enough, he would be safe from her. He was en route to his new ship, his new home, and with the new signature, no one—not even Lissa—would be able to track him. Maybe he would follow in Arrevessa's footsteps and disappear for a while. But unlike her, he planned to return. There was still work for him. He could leave Sekorvo and Tyrath with enough to occupy them for some time while he went dark, just long enough to throw Lissa off of his trail. Between Tyrath and Sekorvo, Rosonno was confident they could find a use for the Awakened, and figure out a new plan of attack against the Star Federation.

The isolation would give him time to try his hand at battle strategies, too.

He was taking a much-needed break from his work to daydream about what his own attack on the Star Federation would involve—they worked poorly without proper leadership, perhaps there was a way to target the officers and spark a chain of self-destruction—when a sharp knock sounded on his door.

Irritated, Rosonno rose from his desk. "You were told not to disturb me," he snapped at the agent as his door opened.

The agent looked distressed, and his words tumbled out in a rush. "Forgive me, First Lit, but it's too important to wait."

"Is anything wrong with the replacement ship?" Rosonno asked.

"No, but—"

"Then there's no reason for you to disturb me," Rosonno said, turning to hit the control that would close and lock the door.

"Daraax Beta," the agent blurted, and Rosonno's hand froze. With Rosonno's attention suddenly devoted to him, the agent hurried on. "A large Star Federation fleet is moving toward the Daraaxi system. We think they know about the base."

Numb, Rosonno found himself asking the most useless question. "How do you know this?"

"First Lit Tyrath sent us a direct message," the agent said. "She, ah… She asked that we didn't tell you until after the Star

Feds attacked, but it seemed like you should know this now."
He hesitated for a long moment before adding softly, "She told
us to tell you goodbye."

Rosonno shook his head. "No, no goodbyes. Get back to
the control room, and tell them to set us on a course for
Daraax Beta."

The agent did not try to hide his confusion. "We are not a
fighting ship. We can't help."

"We're not going to fight." Rosonno left the door open as
he rushed to his private communication terminal. The agent
took a hesitant step into the room to keep Rosonno in his line
of sight. "Tyrath lost evacuation ships when rogue agents
deserted the base."

"Rogue agents?"

Rosonno waved him off. "They're not important. What *is*
important is that *we* aren't at full carry capacity."

The agent paused before quietly pointing out that
Rosonno's ship did not have the room or the resources to take
on more than a few agents from the Daraaxi base.

"That doesn't matter if we can get to the right one in
time," Rosonno said, almost breathless. He knew Tyrath would
make the wrong choice when it came to the evacuations, and
his fingers flew as he keyed in Tyrath's private terminal code.
As he waited for her to answer, Rosonno became aware that
the agent was still in his doorway. "You heard what I said," he
snapped. "Set us on a course for Daraax Beta."

The agent squared his shoulders as though bracing himself
for Rosonno's anger. "The Daraaxi system is in the opposite
direction of the new ship."

"Is there a reason the ship can't be sent after us?"

"We haven't paid the dealer yet."

Rosonno froze.

When he'd ordered his agents to find a new ship, he had
cleared them to search all channels. That included the ones
outside of the Neo-Andromedan network. He'd forgotten that
buying a ship from an outside dealer would complicate things

and eliminate the security of an advance payment, but at the time, that had not seemed like a deal-breaking detail.

Tyrath is smart, Rosonno tried to rationalize. *She'll know to get herself off Daraax Beta.*

She was a First Lit. She knew how critical she was to the Seventh Sun's future.

And with a wave of shame, Rosonno realized that Tyrath was too important to leave to chance. She was short several evac ships, had the Awakened to account for, and would never put herself before her agents. She had also told him goodbye.

He had to go after her.

"Take us to Daraax Beta," Rosonno finally said. "We'll go back for the ship after we've secured First Lit Tyrath."

As the agent left, Rosonno hoped he was wrong, that Tyrath had made the rational choice after all and put herself on an evacuation ship. If she had, Rosonno's ship could simply turn around again and continue on to the original destination. The dealer would forgive a small delay as long as they were paid in full. The ship could wait.

The longer Rosonno's transmission went unanswered, the more hopeful he became that Tyrath really had left Daraax Beta. She could have changed her mind after leaving that message with Rosonno's crew. She must have.

Rosonno was reaching for the controls to cut the transmission when Tyrath accepted, and the hologram projectors threw her into focus before him.

She looked terrible. Exhaustion pulled at her, drooping her shoulders and turning her thin face into a gaunt caricature of its normal pristine beauty. Her hair was tied back sloppily, dark wisps hanging loose, though some were plastered to her pale, sweaty forehead. Her narrow, upturned, red-and-gold eyes were defeated, but through all of that, she smiled at him and it somehow looked genuine.

"I see they gave you my message too early," Tyrath said. "They couldn't even follow a simple instruction. Some elite crew you have there, Ros."

Rosonno's heart beat slow and heavy in his chest as he looked at her. "What are you still doing on Daraax Beta?"

She smiled again and wiped the back of her hand against her forehead, pushing some of the damp hair away. "You know that we don't have enough evac ships, and there's no one close enough to pick the rest of us up in time."

"I'm on my way now," Rosonno said. "I'm coming for you."

Tyrath shook her head, still smiling. "The Star Feds are already here. We didn't see them coming until they were on top of the system." She looked away, and Rosonno knew she was gazing out at the base.

He knew that her quarters sat above the others, and her room offered an aloof view of the entire base. He'd often wondered how she could tolerate the lack of privacy, but he also knew firsthand that she had a personal guard to keep unwelcome visitors at bay.

"We intercepted their fleet and bought enough time for the evac ships to escape. They should be able to clear the system before the Star Feds can regain control. And we gave the Star Feds enough reason to focus on the planet instead of the fleeing ships." Tyrath added softly, "They have fully charged power cells and more than enough supplies to get far, far away from here."

"Why aren't you on one of them?" Rosonno demanded, his voice almost cracking. His knees did not want to function properly and he had to grip the terminal for support.

"I had to make sure as many people as possible got out." Her chest heaved as a sudden, ragged breath wracked through her. "There are still so many here."

"Tyrath, listen to me," Rosonno said. "Listen!" When she focused back on him, he took a moment to calm himself. It was important that he keep her from panicking. "If you can't get off the planet, there has to be some way for you to get out of the base and wait for a pick up."

She frowned at him in confusion. "We don't have the resources for that. Only a small party could go. The others would have to stay."

Frustration edged Rosonno's voice when he said, "Tyrath, leave *all of them*. Get *yourself* out and find a safe location."

Tyrath drew back from her terminal, anger seeping in. "I am not going to do that."

A frustrated cry escaped Rosonno's lips. "You stupid idiot, we need you! You are a Seventh Sun leader."

"And what good is a leader if her followers are dead?" Tyrath shouted back. "The people here all volunteered to stay. That includes me. And I will not abandon them now."

Rosonno's breathing became labored. He couldn't see the way to talk her out of this. And now, he was going to lose her.

There were things people normally said when they were faced with this situation, Rosonno knew. Things that would give closure or affirm the hidden feelings that both parties were too afraid to speak of before. Rosonno did not know how to say any of those things.

Instead, he asked, "What about the Awakened?"

Tyrath frowned at him, then gave a colorless laugh and shook her head. Rosonno had the sense that he had somehow fallen below her expectations of him.

Tyrath said, "They didn't fit. I put as many people as I could on those evac ships, and there just wasn't room for the Awakened." She looked off again, out at what Rosonno knew was the drop that led down to the stasis chambers. "We assembled an amazing army, right here on Daraax Beta. And it's sitting useless in stasis. But not for long." She looked him dead in the eye, and the defeat burned away. Frenzied determination replaced it. "You know, Ros, there's some twisted, sadistic part of me that's always wanted to do this."

"Tyrath—"

"The Light awaits us all, Rosonno. I'm going to reach it a little sooner than I thought I would, but..." She drew in a deep breath. "I'm ready."

Rosonno found himself at a loss for words.

Tyrath quirked a final smile at him. "Goodbye, Ros."

Then she cut the transmission.

"NO!" Rosonno screamed. "Tyrath, no! TYRATH!" He sent another transmission to her, but this time, it went briefly unanswered before a communication block descended and threw the frequency. He tried the few codes he knew offhand for various parts of the Daraax Beta base, but they were all blocked.

It was the final procedure for a base that was about to fall. Cut and destroy all outside communications so the Star Federation would have nothing to trace.

Running as fast as he could, Rosonno fled his private quarters and charged for the control room. The agents he met in the halls jumped out of his way in shock, but they kept a respectful distance and did what they could to clear his path.

The three agents in the control room were a little less discreet. They'd all heard Tyrath's message, Rosonno realized. They had all drawn their own conclusions, but something close to pity surfaced in their gazes before they broke eye contact and focused on their tasks again.

"How long?" Rosonno panted. His attention snagged on the agent who had brought him the news of the looming attack on Daraax Beta. He edged towards the agent. "How long until we reach the Daraaxi system?"

The agent's voice was just above a whisper. "Over a day, sir."

Rosonno slumped against the wall and buried his face in his hands. He could not shake the feeling that he was somehow responsible for this.

A poison that will rot us from the inside.

That was what Arrevessa had called him. Was she right? Was this his fault?

Maybe not the attack itself—it couldn't be, could it?—but if Rosonno had resigned himself to his fate as Arrevessa had demanded instead of seeking out a new starship, he would have been within striking distance of Daraax Beta. There was a chance he could have reached Tyrath in time. Or maybe his ship could have detected the Star Federation's movements sooner. Maybe—

"Sir?"

Rosonno surfaced to find the agents in the control room all looking at him. One of them had been asking him a question.

Forcing himself to straighten, he directed his attention back to the agent he recognized. He should maybe make an effort to learn their names, he decided. "Repeat that, please," he said, his voice sounding strained and fragile even to his own ears.

"Should we continue to Daraax Beta, or return to our original course and pick up the new starship? The dealer won't hold the ship for us. We may lose it."

Rosonno looked at them blankly. His mind was starting to behave an awful lot like his knees as of late, but he forced himself to make a decision. "Keep the course to Daraax Beta. Top speed." He scrubbed a hand over his face and pushed back his hair. "We can't be too late."

And if we are, he thought as he watched the agents execute his order, *I will kill every last Star Fed with my own hands.*

CHAPTER 26: RETRIBUTION

Blocking all override attacks, Keraun's ship breached the Daraaxi sky. It didn't take long for the Hyrunian to find the transmitter on the roof of the Seventh Sun base, and once he took it out, Jason's ships were clear to follow.

Were it up to him, Jason would have sent aid to the damaged Star Federation fleet. Forced friendly fire had taken out almost a quarter of the fleet and left a third of the remaining ships in critical condition. Soldiers were already dead before they'd set foot on the planet, and the ones in the medical bays would not see the battle. Jason wanted to help where he could.

The decision was not up to him. As ordered, he followed Keraun to the Daraaxi surface.

The dropships landed Jason's units as close as possible to the Seventh Sun base. The airlocks spilled them out in clusters of gleaming, armored soldiers, with Jason spearheading the charge. The thin light of the Daraaxi suns sparked off the captain's insignia blazed across his chest, and as he led his units over the rocky plain between the dropships and the base, he scanned the soldiers that were already attacking the building. He quickly picked out the golden bars that marked the other officers directing the onslaught.

At a glance, he knew that Keraun's forces had failed to penetrate the walls. His ship may have taken out the transmitter, but if the Hyrunian wanted to take the base, he could not damage the building too much. He could not use pulse cannons to open fire without the risk of the Neo-Andromedan structure crumbling under the firepower, even if it was proving sturdier than anyone had anticipated.

A group of soldiers was trying to ram the main door down while officers took others around the perimeter, searching for an access point. Jason had some of his junior officers follow the perimeter teams, ordering them to keep an eye out for snipers and protect the others as they searched. He took the rest of his unit over to a humanoid officer standing fifty paces away from the building, watching the soldiers trying to break through the main door.

The officer's armor bore the red accents and double bars of a captain's rank. With the armor on, it was impossible to tell who the captain was.

Jason jogged to their side and asked what progress they had made.

"Not much," the captain responded, voice rough but distinctly female. "We're waiting at this point."

"For what?" Jason asked.

The captain's helmet swiveled towards him, offering him a blank, mirrored-visor stare that somehow managed to convey exasperation, resentment, and amusement all at once. "For Keraun's pet to finish." The captain nodded over her shoulder, then stalked off to the knot of soldiers at the door. "Clear the way!" she shouted at them.

Jason looked to see what the other captain had meant, but he didn't fully register what was coming towards him until it was less than ten paces away. Then he jogged out of the way and called for his soldiers to clear a path.

What roared past looked like a compact version of the armored drilling ship that had attacked the *Argonaught IV* at Ametria. It glided over the Daraaxi surface, propelled by burning engines, and Jason saw a black Star Federation insignia burned into the plating on the side of the machine.

Then he noticed the figure running next to the driller, making last-minute adjustments to a holographic display near the rear of the machine. Dressed in nothing more than an environmental suit with a special modification to allow the blue antennae to stick out of the top of the headpiece, the Yukarian form was easy to identify. In the Yukarian's wake, Keraun and a few of his non-human subordinates loped after the driller, following it to the base.

Jason realized that he shouldn't be surprised to see a Yukarian working with Keraun, given what Miyasato had told him. What did surprise him was recognizing the Yukarian once she finalized her work on the driller and spun around. She hurried past Jason, and her crystal clear visor showed the excited gleam in her eyes as she moved back towards one of Keraun's dropships.

It was Myrikanj, the Yukarian from the renegade crew that had been involved in the Ametria ambush.

What the hell is she doing here? was all Jason had time to wonder before the driller slammed into the base.

With a steady pulse, the driller bore a hole straight through the sealed doors, and when the machine backed away, a blaring alarm penetrated Jason's helmet. A forcefield shimmered over the hole in the next instant, silencing the alarm and creating a new problem for the soldiers.

From experience, Jason knew that there were two types of forcefields: the ones that were designed to let living bodies pass through, in case anyone ended up on the wrong side of the protective field; and the ones that weren't.

He could not decide which kind the Seventh Sun had utilized.

Keraun, armored from nose to tail in shining gray plate, turned and thrust the tip of his tail against the forcefield. The field sparked and darkened where it touched his armor, but it seemed to recognize organic matter beneath the plating and let him through.

With a triumphant snarl and a trail of sparks, Keraun slashed his tail across the forcefield, then dove headfirst through the shimmering divide.

Soldiers followed him, catching resistance against the field but spilling into the base when it gave way.

Jason took a deep breath, then led his units into the Seventh Sun base.

He ducked his head and pushed his way through the field, feeling the harsh resistance against his armoring. His visor darkened to preserve his vision against the cascade of sparks that fell around him. He drove his head and then his shoulders through, and his helmet flashed a warning, indicating that the push through the forcefield had stripped away the outer shielding of his armor. Then he was fully through the field. He had just enough time to take in the open layout of the base and three-story ring of balconies overlooking a central pit before enerpulse fire came from his left.

He took a shot in the shoulder, but managed to spin away from more damage. The soldiers around him were not as lucky. Even as Jason's helmet flashed another warning, indicating that his left shoulder would not fully protect him against another direct hit, he saw three soldiers fall, their damaged armor scorched and burned by enerpulse fire.

Jason brought up his rifle and returned fire with the others, taking out one of the Seventh Sun agents that had come running to meet them.

The Neo-Andromedans wore no armor, and once the Star Federation soldiers recovered from the surprise, the agents quickly began to fall. More Seventh Sun agents opened fire from the second-story balcony, offering feeble cover fire for the small wave of Neo-Andromedans that had come to meet the soldiers.

With a lusty bellow, Keraun launched himself over the fallen soldiers and bounded to meet the advancing Seventh Sun agents. He took two point-blank shots, but his armor held and allowed him within striking distance.

Unlike the other soldiers, Keraun bore no weapons. Instead, he rammed his spiraled horns into the stomach of one of the Neo-Andromedans, threw his head back and sent the Nandro flying. He braced his tail against the ground, reared back, and lashed out with his powerful legs, blasting another agent across the wide room, towards the pit in the center. The agent landed and bounced, skidding to a halt just shy of the lip of the pit. They lay still and bleeding at the edge, one arm dangling over the maw.

After that, the Seventh Sun agents who had not died in the initial skirmish tried to retreat. Keraun went after them, and a large pack of soldiers followed. There were shouts in a language that Jason could not identify and the receptors in his helmet could not translate. Then the agents at the balcony trading enerpulse fire with the soldiers on the ground floor withdrew from range.

Jason did not want to follow the slaughter. There was no question in his mind that Keraun and most of his soldiers would come out of the battle with the agents here alive, but there was something that did not sit right with him.

As the fighting migrated away from him, Jason formed up a small unit of his soldiers and moved them in the opposite direction. They needed to scout the rest of the base and flush out any hiding agents, but Jason also wanted to understand why so few Neo-Andromedans had been left to defend such an important building, let alone without proper combat training.

This was nothing like the base that had been found on Daanhymn. The reports from Erica's teams indicated that the Daanhymn base had been cannibalized from a decaying human structure, built on the foundations of what was already there. In stark contrast, the Daraaxi base was state-of-the-art and pristine, aside from the fresh scorch marks on the walls and ceiling from misaimed enerpulse shots.

Something key to the Seventh Sun's operations went on here. Jason intended to find out what, and why it had been left so unprotected.

There were hallways that branched off the open, central room. Jason sent a few groups headed by sergeants to scout the halls and any other rooms they found.

That left him with twenty soldiers. He intended to find a way to the upper levels and assign them tasks there, but the pit in the center of the room pulled at his attention until he was standing at the lip, staring down into the darkness. The soldiers followed him to the edge, fanning out around him, all transfixed by the maw. There were no railings to stop them from falling in, so they found themselves standing less than a pace away and leaning forward as they strained to see where the pit led.

"The hell is this thing?" Reed the scarred lieutenant asked. He sounded as though the mysterious awe of so much darkness was making him uncomfortable, and the discomfort was, in turn, angering him.

No one tried to answer him.

Jason studied the pit, taking note of the wide ramp that spiraled down the sides into the darkness below. The ramp began on the other side of the room, directly across from where Jason stood. A central column cut through his view. The column supported a small but sturdy lift. There was a thin walkway that led from the ground floor to the lift, the only part of the pit that sported any sort of safety railings.

Now that he looked closer, he supposed he understood the logic. To actually fall into the pit from anywhere but the thin walkway, he would have to launch himself from the edge. Otherwise, he'd land on the ramp, and there was no point around the top of the hole where the drop to the ramp was large enough to kill him. He'd twist his ankle, maybe, but he wouldn't die.

Jason was baffled by the design. He could not think of anything that would merit this kind of construction.

He was on the verge of ordering a small party down the ramp to search for answers when a flash of movement caught his eye. He snapped his head up to see a group of three Neo-Andromedans sprinting out of a hallway, shouting and brandishing enerpulse rifles. They fired off quick shots without halting to aim, hitting a couple of soldiers through the sheer force of statistics; a shot fired at a knot of people was bound to hit someone.

The armor held despite the stripping of the forcefield, and Jason's group was forming up to meet the attack before the order had fully left his lips.

Jason immediately saw that these agents were different than the ones who had initially met the Star Federation. The first agents had been clumsy with their aim, had tried to compensate for lack of skills by firing more rounds, and had stumbled backwards and run away when Keraun attacked.

These new agents knew how to dodge. They knew how to aim while running. And they knew to look for cover. They were clearly trained to fight, but with relief, Jason realized they were not Awakened. They were too calm and disciplined in their movements. Unfortunately for the three agents, they were also far outnumbered, and it did not take long for them to fall. They managed to score a few more direct hits before they went down, and one soldier was now sporting a scorched breastplate.

Jason took one look and told the soldier to leave the battle; another hit to the chest would be fatal.

The soldier shook his head, saying that he wanted to see the fight through.

Jason was halfway through ordering the soldier away when another called for his attention, raised her rifle, and began to fire.

Jason spun around, expecting to see more attacking Seventh Sun agents, but what he saw instead was a tall, lithe woman with dark hair sprinting across the narrow walkway. She moved just fast enough to throw the soldiers' aim as they opened fire, never once looking at them as she barreled toward the central lift.

In a cold snap of clarity, Jason realized that the three attacking Neo-Andromedans hadn't just been trained to fight;

they'd been trained to guard, and their final task was to draw attention away from the woman as she went for the lift.

Jason took a step closer to the edge of the pit. He raised his rifle, sighted along the barrel, shifted a little to compensate for the speed of the target, and squeezed off a single shot.

The enerpulse shot took the woman in the shoulder, drawing out a piercing cry of pain as she fell against the railing, then to her knees. There was a breath of silence as the soldiers adjusted their aim, and then, against all of Jason's expectations, the woman surged back to her feet and barreled forward. Her shoulder was black and smoking where his shot had landed, and even from so great a distance, Jason could see the agonized twist of her pale face.

The wound slowed her, but her sudden burst of movement was enough to save her from another hit, and she slammed herself against the lift. The door opened in the next instant, and then she was inside. Enerpulse shots crashed into the lift, but the door shut and the lift began to descend.

"Down the ramp!" Jason shouted.

He led the small column of soldiers around the pit, jumping over the edge to land on the ramp when he knew the drop was shallow enough not to sprain his ankle. Soldiers dropped around him, and to his frustration, Reed and a few others landed further down the ramp, risking the farther drop in order to take the lead. They stumbled, but quickly found their footing and began to run. Jason and the others went after them.

As he ran, Jason kept his head turned to the central lift, watching it slip away into darkness. The lights on the Star Federation helmets switched on, illuminating the curve of the path. Gravity sped their steps, but under the heavy battle armor, Jason could not keep pace with the lift. It was not moving fast, but it had a direct path to the bottom. For every spiraled level Jason and his soldiers took, the lift took four. He knew he could not catch it. Finally, he slowed and called his soldiers to a halt.

Reed and the others with him ignored the order, charging ahead. Disgusted, Jason saw that nearly half of his soldiers had continued the pursuit. He ordered them back again, and the response was a wild whoop from Reed followed by an audio notification that the scarred lieutenant had disconnected his communication line. The other soldiers with him followed suit a moment leader.

Fuming, Jason stood at the edge of the ramp, watching the lights of Reed's group follow the slope as it circled around the central column. The lift was still descending, throwing out its own feeble light that the darkness swallowed. It was impossible to tell how much further it had to go, but Reed and the others showed no sign of stopping.

Fine, Jason thought, *let the assholes run themselves into oblivion.*

It would have solved a number of his pettier problems, but Jason couldn't let them descend without support. He had no snipers in what was left of his group, so he would need to follow Reed into the pit. He jogged forward again, fuming at the lieutenant's insubordination.

A soldier's tense, urgent voice cut across his thoughts. "Captain?"

Jason slowed to a halt. When he turned to face the speaker, he saw that all of the remaining soldiers had remained in place, staring at the wall of the pit. He followed their gazes, and felt his heart stop.

He'd been so focused on the descending lift and Reed's group that he'd missed the sudden appearance of the uniform chambers in the walls of the pit. Jason could see a solid line of them following the ramp back up, all dark and empty. He moved closer to study the empty chamber next to him. The light from his helmet played over the back wall, revealing connecting nodes and neat arrangements of thick tubes and wires.

Jason had seen enough hibernation systems in his life to recognize what the chambers were, but the emptiness of them disturbed him.

This pit was terribly large. What use would the Seventh Sun have in building so many hibernation chambers, only to have them stand empty?

"Wait here," Jason told the soldiers. He started down the ramp again, but at a steady walk this time. The lights from his helmet flashed over one empty chamber after another, until they caught and bounced off a cloudy pearl of color ahead of him. As Jason made his way to the first occupied chamber, he saw more stretching beyond it in a broken pattern of empty and full chambers. Most were swirling gray, but he caught a glimpse of a blue one further down the line.

He stopped and glanced over the edge of the ramp. The central lift had descended far below him, and Reed's group had made it another few levels down. They had slowed to a steady jog, letting gravity dictate their pace, and Jason noticed that Reed's group was passing a long thread of occupied chambers. Their lights reflected off of the cloudy grays and blues, but none of the soldiers were paying much attention to the wall. Most of their heads were turned towards the center of the pit, watching the lift as it descended.

Is it finally slowing?

Jason could not tell. He touched the side of his helmet, trying a secondary communication line that tied him to his soldiers. "Reed?"

No answer.

He tapped again, on the tertiary final line. "Reed!"

Silence.

"Shit," Jason muttered, tapping his helmet to switch back to the primary line. He swung his attention away from the descending group to the hibernation chamber next to him.

The pod the chamber held was large enough to comfortably hold three humans, but when Jason stepped close, his helmet's scanners confirmed the presence of only one dark, humanoid figure suspended in the murky fluid. As Jason looked, the cloudy liquid shifted and cleared in uneven patches, offering him glimpses of blurry details. There was an otherworldly serenity to the body inside the pod, but that was familiar to Jason; all hibernation systems had that effect on the sleeper. It had, however, been a long time since Jason had seen suspension fluid used in a hibernation chamber. This technique had been used almost exclusively on older starships, when faster-than-light travel was still a novelty rather than the norm. To see it here, in a Seventh Sun base, robbed the hibernation chamber of all tranquility and set Jason's nerves on edge.

The figure inside shifted with the gentle ebb and flow of the swirling hibernation fluid, and for a moment, the face came close enough to the thick glass of the pod for Jason to see distinctly human features. A breathing device was secured tightly over the nose and mouth, with two long tubes extending towards the top of the pod. Long hair floated around the tubes, caressing them almost lovingly. The eyes were closed, and for a moment, Jason could almost doubt that he was looking at a Neo-Andromedan.

What the hell were they doing here?

His answer came abruptly, when a mechanical sound echoed up the pit. Jason was back at the edge of the ramp in three quick strides, and he had a clear view of the lift far below him. He could only guess how many levels there were between him and the bottom of ramp, but when the lift opened and spilled out a column of light, the lone figure that staggered out was tiny. Her shadow stretched long before her as she began a stumbling run, and the optic sensors in Jason's helmet picked up on his strain as he followed her movements. A square window popped up on the left side of his vision, offering him a magnified view of the agent, enough for him to make out the pain on her face and the heavy grip she kept on her left shoulder as she moved, but there was a singular purpose written across her posture. She was not trying to escape. She was heading for something.

Scanning along the Seventh Sun agent's path, Jason saw a small podium standing near the wall of the pit. He recognized it a moment later as a control panel, just before the agent fell across it, blocking the details. She activated the panel and began to frantically key in a complicated code. A holographic display flickered in front of her, flashing a red warning. The agent cast a deliberate look up, her face set in a snarl of pain. Then she bared her teeth in a horrible smile, slashed her hand across the warning, and slammed her fist down on a final button.

Jason tapped his helmet to clear the magnified window as a slow rumble sounded up the pit. He felt a light vibration in his boots as the sound traveled past him. Lights began to snake their way up the pit, following the curve of the ramp. The lights reached his level, brightening the hibernation chambers and revealing more pods than Jason could count, though a glance told him that there were more empty chambers than full ones. Somehow, he knew that it was a blessing that all of the chambers in the top third of the pit were all empty. That was where his remaining soldiers waited.

Jason stood at the cusp of the full chambers, blue and milky pods stretching off to his left and the wide gaps of the empty chambers to his right. With a creep of morbid fascination, Jason found himself looking down at the rows and rows of hibernation pods. And when he thought he saw movement in one of them, he almost started to look closer.

But instead, with an unnerving thought thundering in his brain, Jason spun around and stared hard at the pod behind him. He found that he was not surprised to see the fluid in the pod draining, the figure within beginning to twitch and jerk as they woke up. The breathing device disconnected, and there was a sudden hissing sound as the seal around the pod broke. The fluid drained faster, and Jason stumbled up the ramp, grip tight on his enerpulse rifle as the glass front of the pod lifted up.

The person within fell out, landing hard on the ramp. It was a woman, Jason saw, bare and vulnerable and coughing raggedly. Her light skin glistened under the thick fluid of the hibernation pod, and her hair fell in sticky ropes across her face.

"Captain!" a soldier called over the communication line.

That broke the spell, and Jason began to edge further up the ramp. He couldn't quite tear his eyes away, though, and it was through his peripheral vision that he saw that all of the hibernation pods—*All of them*—had released their occupants on to the ramp. They were in various stages of recovery, some already on their feet while others struggled to push off the floor, and while they ranged in age, gender, body types and skin tones, there was a predatory quality to all of them that sent a chill racing down Jason's spine.

He looked back at the woman to see that she was braced against the floor, legs coiled under her in a classic sprinter's launch. She had swiveled towards Jason and was watching him closely as he retreated up the ramp. Her eyes were bright, molten copper chipped with electric green. They bore into Jason with wild bloodlust.

"Awakened," Jason breathed. He began to step up the ramp faster, squeezing off a shot at the woman in front of him. To his horror, she dodged the shot and came flying at him, but his second shot was at point-blank range, and she fell and skidded up the ramp, carried forward by her own momentum. By the time she had come to a halt, more of the Awakened Neo-Andromedans had turned their attention on Jason, and were beginning to charge up the ramp. They were regaining their coordination quickly.

Jason spun around and slung his rifle over his shoulder in one clean motion. As he secured the weapon and freed his hands, he started sprinting, waving his arms wildly at the soldiers above him. "Fall back!" he shouted over the communication line, hearing the fear in his own voice. "Retreat now!"

The soldiers had seen him open fire and formed up to do the same, but at his frantic order, they broke rank and took off.

Jason brought up the rear, his muscles straining under the armor and pull of gravity as he ran back up the spiraling ramp. He dared not look back, but with the design of the pit, he always had a view of the swarm of Awakened as they chased after him. Their inhuman howls and screams filled the pit, and their footsteps thundered up the ramp as they followed his trail. Some of the Neo-Andromedans had begun fighting each other, animal-like in their ferocity, but most were fixed on other targets. And in one horrible, heart-stopping moment, the curve of the ramp brought Jason around to a view of Reed's group.

They were too far away for him to do anything for them, and though they were firing their enerpulse weapons in a storm of desperation, illuminating their lower level with white-hot flashes, they were quickly overwhelmed by the speed and numbers of the raging Nandros. Jason saw the Awakened tear the armor off of one of the soldiers before the press of bodies screened the sight, and then the curve of the ramp brought him past the view.

Reed and his group were beyond help. Despite everything, regret was bitter on Jason's tongue, but he forced the feeling away as he focused on staying alive.

"Keep going!" he shouted to the remaining soldiers, coming up to push one of the slower ones as they flagged under the weight of their armor, propelling them forward. "Do *not* stop!"

Jason's heart pounded in his ears as he urged the soldiers on, but in the end, he could not save them all. Two fell behind, overwhelmed by the unrelenting climb. Jason heard their terrified panting over the communication line as they slowed, but then one of them screamed a curse and began to open fire at the oncoming Awakened. The other started to join in, but then there were just screams of pain from one of the soldiers, and the other simply said, "I can't," and then jumped off the edge of the ramp. It was a while before Jason and the others heard the sickening crunch that signaled the end of the soldier's life. Terror drove the survivors on, and finally, they reached the top of the ramp and spilled on to the level ground.

They immediately turned to the hole Keraun's driller had made in the wall of the base, moving faster now that gravity was not quite so punishing. A second wind came to Jason's group, and he saw everything in hypernatural detail as his soldiers made a dash for the hole. Soldiers pouring into the building through fresh driller holes watched in surprise as they charged passed. Others rushed to the balcony railings, straining to see what was happening at the central pit. When the Awakened came, some recoiled, and were not fast enough to move out of the way. Others were swifter to react, and rained enerpulse fire on the Neo-Andromedans.

"Fall back!" Jason screamed, but the soldiers did not move fast enough.

He was very aware of the Awakened slamming into soldiers behind him, of enerpulse fire and pounding feet and clashing bodies and all the sounds of death. Then his armor was sparking and his helmet flashed a warning across his vision as he dragged himself through the forcefield.

He fell into the afternoon of Daraax Beta, into a world that was as dark and raw as a bleeding wound. He scrambled over the rocky ground, but he heard the whine of the forcefield behind him. He twisted around in time to see an Awakened sail through the field and land on the Daraaxi soil, but asphyxiation set in immediately, and the Awakened fell to the ground in a cloud of dust. Jason was on his feet and moving away from the building before the Awakened stopped twitching.

He frantically searched the soldiers swarming outside of the base. He barked orders for the subordinates to stay away, even as the fight raged inside. Enerpulse flashes lit the windows and the driller holes, and over his communication line, Jason heard soldiers' deaths as the Awakened reclaimed the base. He had to forcibly yank two soldiers away from the hole in the main doors as they tried to rush in and help their dying comrades.

"Retreat, damn you!" he shouted over the primary communication line, but he felt the order fall on deaf ears.

As the fight raged, Star Federation soldiers began to spill out of the Seventh Sun base. Some still wore their full armor, and some were missing pieces. Their limbs hung at awkward angles, broken and useless, but they were alive. They were helped away from the building. Before long, the base grew quiet.

A reluctant ceasefire descended on Daraax Beta as the soldiers milled around the outside of the base and the Awakened stalked the interior. Jason could see them flitting past the opening the driller had left, the forcefield distorting their shapes as they raced by.

"They're too fast," an officer breathed over the communication line. "Too many, too fast."

Damn right, Jason thought as he moved through the soldiers. They parted before him, respecting the captain's insignia blazed on his armor, but they were a confused mess as the commanding officers debated what to do.

Jason found them near a dropship. Keraun was easy to spot in his custom armor. Erica needed to be picked out by the blue-and-gold fleet commander insignia on her armor and the bars on her shoulders. She blended with the mostly human crowd otherwise.

Jason stalked up to the fleet commanders, too angry and exhausted for formalities. They were engrossed in a debate on how to best infiltrate the base now that the Awakened were a factor, but Jason spoke over their conversation, demanding to be heard. "You have to destroy that base."

They both looked at him harshly.

"I will deal with you later, Captain," Keraun clicked dismissively. "Return to your dropship and get off of this—"

Jason ignored him and addressed Erica. "You can't win against that many Awakened. You're in Neo-Andromedan territory going up against an army that's faster and stronger than all of your soldiers. You can't win."

Keraun began to snarl promises that made the Awakened seem like pacifists in comparison, but Erica looked at him steadily. She kept looking at him even after Keraun ran out of creative ways to threaten him.

"Your opinion has been noted, Captain Stone," was all she said to him.

Then she called for her units to form up, and she moved to lead a direct assault on the base.

Jason went after her. He felt Keraun's claws land on his shoulder and scrape against his armor, leaving deep scours now that the protective coatings had been stripped away, but Jason twisted out of his grasp and ran after Erica. He realized that after everything, he hated her more than a little, but she was going to get herself and all of her soldiers killed if he did not stop her.

Erica's units were rested and going in on fresh legs. Jason would learn later that they'd been delayed by the hacking attempt but had come through as the least damaged ship in the fleet, and when they'd finally been able to breach the sky, Erica had held her units back. She'd missed the critical first strike and had landed in a position to provide reinforcements, which Keraun had been in the process of assuring her were totally unnecessary when the Awakened came boiling out of the pit.

Now, she drove her soldiers into the building, determined to make up for the lost time.

Erica's armor sparked as she dove through the forcefield, and her soldiers followed her faithfully.

Jason went through a minute later, this time feeling heat as the forcefield pushed back against his stripped armor.

He was astounded by how much havoc the Awakened were able to wreak in a minute.

Slowed under their battle armor, Erica's soldiers could not hope to match the speed of the Awakened. They fired off disciplined enerpulse shots, but the erratic rhythms of the Awakened caused them to miss far more shots than they landed.

The Neo-Andromedans managed to be everywhere at once, driving at the soldiers from all sides and even swinging down from the balconies to attack from above. They dug their fingers into the seams and gaps between the plating, ripping armor from soldiers' bodies. When enough was stripped away, the Awakened went for the vitals. The thermal suits the soldiers wore beneath their armor offered a little extra protection, but the Awakened tore through them and went for bloody kills. As the fresh battle raged, the Awakened began to separate groups of soldiers and then pick those groups apart, taking down more and more with each passing heartbeat.

Through it all, Jason caught a glimpse of the dark-haired Seventh Sun agent who had unleashed this nightmare. She'd ridden the lift back up and now stood with her weight on one of the thin railings that separated her from the drop into the Awakened pit, her injured arm hanging limp at her side. She watched the Awakened tear through the Star Federation soldiers with mild interest, and Jason saw her sigh as though she regretted something. Wasted work, maybe. Then her head snapped to the side and she watched impassively as an Awakened barreled down the narrow walkway toward her. She did not flinch as the Awakened launched at her, and even turned to the berserk Nandro as though greeting an old friend. The Awakened smashed into the agent, driving them both back into the lift, and that was the last Jason saw of her.

An Awakened leapt in front of Jason, reaching for his head. Jason threw up a block, but the Awakened's hands locked on his arm. There was a burst of pain as the Nandro jumped in a new direction and began to twist his limb, but Jason forced himself to spin with the motion rather than against it. He brought his free hand around and landed a solid crack across the Awakened's jaw.

The Nandro barely flinched.

Then someone else was there, slamming the butt of a rifle into the Neo-Andromedan's head. The Awakened released Jason's arm and went after the newcomer, seizing the weapon and wrenching it out of the soldier's hands. The Nandro flipped the rifle with the grace and ease of a trained soldier, bringing the weapon up to fire off a shot at the soldier.

Jason's leg shot out and landed a solid kick to the Nandro's side, throwing off his aim. The shot missed the target, slamming into the ceiling instead.

Jason caught a glimpse of his savior's armor. His breath hitched when he registered the blue-and-gold fleet commander insignia.

Erica.

Then the Awakened Jason had kicked leapt on to his back, bringing the rifle down across Jason's throat. The Nandro pulled back, wedging the length of the weapon under his helmet.

Jason threw himself backwards, letting the Nandro's weight carry him. The Awakened was caught by surprise, and his head slammed into the ground. His grip slackened for a moment, and Jason wasted no time. He shot up, pulling the rifle away from the Nandro. He dove away, spinning his body around to line up a shot.

The Awakened was already sitting up and reorienting his legs, preparing to launch at Jason again, but the enerpulse shot took him in the face and he collapsed, finally still.

Jason looked up in time to see another Neo-Andromedan dodge a punch from Erica, lock her arm in an unnatural bend, then twist violently. Erica's hoarse cry of pain punctured the other sounds of the battle, and Jason found himself on his feet and driving punches into the Awakened faster than he knew he could move.

The Awakened moved faster. He slipped out of Jason's reach, then charged back into him, driving him off his feet and across the floor. The rifle went flying, lost somewhere in the raging battle. Then the Awakened was back on Erica, scrabbling at her armor and trying to tear pieces off. Erica went down, and the Awakened began to claw at her helmet, trying to either rip it off or break her neck. Another Awakened caught sight of Erica—pinned and losing stamina fast as she strained against the weight of the Nandro on top of her—and came loping towards the easy target.

Jason did the only thing he could think of. He grabbed Erica's legs, and dragged her and the Neo-Andromedan on top of her through the forcefield. The heat of resistance was almost unbearable this time, and Erica's armor sparked hot in Jason's hands as he pulled her through. The Awakened on top of her rode cleanly through the field. When the Nandro's head cleared the forcefield, he grew rigid. An instant later, his body jerked as he fought for air.

To Jason's surprise, the Awakened threw himself forward across the forcefield, back into the base. Through the shimmering field, Jason saw him hacking and sputtering on the ground, and the second Awakened who had targeted Erica came to an abrupt halt. She looked at the forcefield, at Jason and Erica beyond, her eyes bright with burning light. Then she turned and surged back into the battle, ignoring the Nandro that was now seizing on the floor.

Erica sat up after a moment, cradling her injured arm. "Thanks," she muttered. Then she twisted around and rose up to her knees, as though ready to dive back into the fray. She stopped when she saw what was happening on the other side of the forcefield.

"You have to call the retreat," Jason breathed.

Erica raised her uninjured arm, pressing the padded underside of her hand against her helmet. For a moment, Jason thought she would refuse. Then he heard her soft command over the main communication line. "Fall back. All of you that are still alive, fall back."

It went quickly after that. The survivors fled the battle, breathing hard and limping rather than running. They left so many fallen soldiers behind. The air was heavy as considerably less-crowded dropships began to take off from the Daraaxi surface, heading for the main ships. Keraun went with a middle group, after staring hungrily at the Seventh Sun base and fighting with Erica on another strike. She did not want anyone to go back in, and after what had happened inside the base, she had the support of nearly all of the junior officers, many of Keraun's included. Defeated, the Hyrunian stalked off and had his flagship depart before the remaining soldiers had been accounted for and removed from the Daraaxi surface.

Jason stayed back to help organize the survivors and ensure that they were not leaving anyone behind. He left on the last dropship, standing shoulder-to-shoulder with Erica as they took off. A medic had helped her out of her armor and reset her shoulder, but her arm would be in a sling until she got back to her ship and received proper medical attention.

She said nothing as their ship lifted off from the ground, only watched with Jason in silence as the dropship's scanners returned images of the base. Their ship had just cleared the atmosphere when the pulse cannons of the two remaining *Argonaughts* opened fire. The burning shots streaked down from the sky, glittering like comets, and reached out to touch the base almost tentatively. There was a flash when the shots made contact. Then, where the Neo-Andromedan base once stood, there was a massive column of smoke and rock and dust and debris, shooting high into the sky as the suns slipped towards the horizon.

There would be nothing left, Jason knew. Nothing to scan, nothing to scavenge, nothing to attack them. Just an empty world, with a fresh scar.

He wondered how many more of those he would leave behind him.

CHAPTER 27: DUSK

Even with the scans that revealed the smoking ruin of the Daraaxi base and the complete lack of life on the planet, Rosonno wanted to land. His agents stirred with suppressed agitation when he gave the order, but he let that pass. He knew that it was dangerous to go down there, even if it looked like the Star Federation ships had all left the system.

That is the worst part, Rosonno thought. The Star Feds had found the base, come for it, destroyed it, and then abandoned it. As though the base and all the lives it had held were worthless.

Which they were, he supposed he had to admit as he picked his way through the wreckage that surrounded the destroyed base's location. He was wrapped in a fully protective exploration suit, built to cycle breathable air through the helmet and keep the dangerous atmospheric pressure at bay. Walking in the suit was slow enough, but Rosonno forced himself to keep a cautious pace and pick his way carefully over the dark, dead ground. He had opted to go to the base by himself, and there was no one to help him if he sustained an injury through reckless stupidity.

The silence of total isolation pressed into Rosonno as he made his way to what was once the holding chamber for the

213

in-stasis Awakened. It was now a large crater blasted into the surface of the planet, a wound ripped open by pulse cannons. The blasts had completely destroyed the base and a large part of the surrounding land. Scorched debris rested in a massive radius around the crater, impossible to identify as rock, bits of the destroyed building, or something else.

Rosonno made his way to the lip of the crater and looked down, trying to picture where, exactly, the walls of the Daraax Beta base had stood.

Where the Awakening chambers had spiraled down into the darkness that they had promised to someday fill with light.

Where Tyrath had died.

The sting of her death had come several hours before his ship had reached the Daraaxi system. From that point on, Rosonno had spent his time in a state of numb denial, refusing to believe that the base had fallen and Tyrath was gone. He'd received messages from all of the other First Lit—except Arrevessa—but he had ignored them. Instead, he had cracked down on his agents and demanded they push the ship as hard as they could to get to the Daraaxi system.

One of the reasons he'd forced himself to disembark and walk through the wreckage was to grind the moment into his mind, and force himself to accept that Tyrath was truly gone.

His hand wandered up to his neck, but his fingers bumped against the hard shell of the exploration suit and he could not touch his collar.

There were two dark stars on it now. They were on opposite ends and added a saccharine symmetry to the row of formerly uniform white stars. The balance made Rosonno sick.

I'm sorry, he thought, hoping the feeling would suffice. He was connected to his agents via communicator in case the Star Feds returned or something happened to him and he needed their assistance, but at that moment, he did not dare speak aloud. *I should have been here for you.*

He hesitated, and then another thought thundered across his mind. *I would have been, if you hadn't banished me from the planet after you tried to oust me from the First Lit.*

Rosonno fumed at the memory, but almost immediately, he was ashamed of the anger. Even if he could pretend that Tyrath had not had a solid reason for all of that, she was still gone. If he had not gone after a new starship, he might have been able to save her.

I'm so sorry.

The maw of the crater gaped wide before him, and offered no response.

To his surprise, tears blurred Rosonno's vision. With the exploration suit, he could not wipe them away, so he blinked and forced himself to look up, into the feeble light of the setting suns.

On Daraax Beta, the binary suns set violet, small, and weak. It left the world with a cold, broken feel, and Rosonno felt his breath catch and tears dry up.

There was nothing comforting about that double sunset. Instead, it was terrifying to watch the light fail with so little flourish and power. There were no clouds to illuminate, just the clarity of a swiftly falling night and the icy stares of the emerging stars.

Rosonno watched the light die, and thought about his promise to kill every last Star Fed with his own hands. He kicked a lose rock into the crater, and watched it fall away into the dark pit. He did not hear it bounce.

He swallowed hard, and thought about how the Star Federation had done this, just as they had opened fire on the Neo-Andromedan colony Rosonno had been born into all those years ago. They'd left craters on that planet, too. And they would keep shooting holes into worlds if it meant they could exterminate Neo-Andromedans. They would do it again, and again, and again.

The Seventh Sun had tried to stop them, but they were being crushed in turn. They'd had minor victories, but where it mattered, the Star Federation was besting them.

Because Arrevessa pulled out.

Without her...

No, Rosonno decided, they could still succeed without her. She had abandoned them at a critical moment. That was the only reason why the Star Federation had gained the upper hand. They'd dealt the Seventh Sun a heavy blow, but they could still recover and set themselves back on track.

I promise you, Tyrath, I will see you avenged.

He needed to get in touch with the remaining First Lit and formulate a new plan. Together, surely they could come up with something. They were the leaders of the Seventh Sun, and together, they were strong.

A surge of confidence went through Rosonno, but he still found himself lingering to watch the horizon. By the time he returned to his ship, it was fully dark and he was stumbling through the debris, blind and alone.

CHAPTER 28: LOST

Haelin's drop ship had not moved from Crythsia. Vinterra allowed herself a moment of concern as she turned over the knowledge. She wondered if a trap was waiting for her as she drew closer and closer to the source of the signature she had tracked across a long stretch of the galaxy, but she saw no other options. She had to know what had happened to Haelin. She had to know where she was, if she was still alive, what her last actions had been if she'd died.

She had to know.

Driving the ship at top speed for the planet drained the power cells past the warning point, and as she sprinted through the last leg of the journey, Vinterra tried to tell herself to be rational. If she bled off too much of the ship's energy, she would be stuck on Crythsia until the cells recharged. That could take days if she couldn't find a supplemental power source, and she doubted one would be readily available on a planet like that.

She knew it was dangerous and foolish to rush headlong for Crythsia, but she could not bring herself to slow down. Not when she was so close.

She flew into the star system without trouble, only slowing the ship when she came dangerously close to overshooting the planet. Even then, breaching the Crythsian sky was a heart-stopping maneuver as the ship's alarms screamed at Vinterra for entering the thick atmosphere at such a high speed. Friction threatened to tear the hull apart. Frantically, Vinterra fought to bring the ship back under control as it tore through dark storm clouds. The evac ship rattled and groaned as it broke through to clearer air, and Vinterra slammed on the reverse thrusters, forcing the ship to bleed off more speed.

Finally, the alarms quieted, and Vinterra shakily steered the ship over a low mountain range, toward the flat expanse of rock where Haelin's dropship had landed. When the evac ship was safely on the ground, Vinterra shut the systems down and set the power cells to recharge, hoping the Crythsian sun would strong enough to give them a boost once the storm passed.

Then, with everything catching up to her at once, she slumped back in her seat and stared blankly at the control panel in front of her.

On Crythsia, she would either find Haelin, or learn if she could finally accept her partner's fate.

Vinterra allowed herself a moment to cry. The tears came freely, rolling in heavy streaks down her cheeks and dotting the front of her shirt. Which, she realized, was dirty and creased after days of space travel and poor sleep. Much like she was.

She almost laughed at the vanity of the thought.

After, she promised herself. *After I find out what happened to Haelin. I will deal with everything after.*

For now, Vinterra wiped the tears from her face, forced herself to rise, and found the pistol she'd set aside from the ship's meager arsenal. Her hands were shaking when she inserted the energy capsule into the pistol, the blue light wavering as her fingers slipped over the smooth, warm surface.

Blue was a lethal color for enerpulse fire, but only if it hit in the right spots. Vinterra was ready to do a lot of things to discover Haelin's fate, but she had not been able to convince herself to take a white energy capsule for the weapon.

With the pistol loaded and the barrel pointed well away from her own body, Vinterra moved to the ship's airlock, and stepped out on to the Crythsian surface.

A hot wind heralding the approach of a storm assaulted her. It pulled at her clothes and whipped her coiled hair into a frenzy, and the grit it picked up from the ground stung her skin and eyes.

Shielding her face as best she could, Vinterra squinted out at the landscape, trying to pick out the shape of the other ship. She'd landed as close as she'd dared, but there was a long stretch of open ground between her and the other vessel.

Crythsia was a minimalistic world, with an atmosphere that was breathable if a little on the thick side. Yellow grass spotted the black, rocky land, blasted flat against the ground by the bursts of wind. Blue iron clouds raced across the sky, and in the distance, three tall, dark mountains smoked and glowed fiery red at their tips and belched black smoke.

Volcanoes, Vinterra corrected herself, *not mountains.*

What concerned her more than the active volcanoes was the dark smudge of rain on the horizon, growing darker and larger with each passing moment.

Vinterra blinked against the grit in her eyes and focused on the other ship. She slumped in dismay, thinking she had managed to land even further away than she had intended. Then she realized that the ship was just much, much smaller than she had expected. But as she reevaluated the distance, she knew that the rain was likely to catch her before she completed the journey.

"Why didn't I land closer?" she moaned against the wind as she buried her face in her elbow and started forward. With her first step, Vinterra nearly slipped on the dark rock beneath her. The wind and grit had polished the surface to a glassy sheen, and Vinterra's feet nearly slid out from under her. Recovering her balance, she set out again slowly and deliberately, clenching her teeth against the frustration that boiled in her gut.

"I'm coming," she promised, but she felt a hot stab of foolishness as the wind whipped her words away.

Haelin won't be there, she told herself.

The chances were far too great, but she refused to stop. She had to know what had happened to Haelin. She had to.

Every step toward the distant ship was agonizingly eternal. It seemed that every time Vinterra peeked over her arm, the ship was no closer, but the rain was bearing down on her. The sky darkened further, and the black rock greedily drank in the remaining light of the Crythsian day. Then the rain arrived. It fell in hot, heavy sheets, drenching Vinterra immediately. It ran in black rivers through her hair and down her clothes, plastering them against her skin. The wind blew harder, as though even the weather had set out specifically to turn her back. And still Vinterra pressed on. She gripped her pistol tighter, forced herself to look up and fixate on the ship, and, with an angry cry, she ran the last hundred paces to the vessel, skidding and slipping on the rain-slicked rock.

Vinterra slammed into the side of the ship and leaned into the hull, letting the feel of metal under her arm guide her as she moved towards the airlock. She felt the seam beneath her hand as her palm slid over the edge, and she began beating her fist against the airlock.

Even to her ears, the sound was feeble and weak.

So Vinterra began to scream. She screamed and pounded on the airlock, even hitting the sealed doors with the butt of the pistol. She had no idea if anyone onboard the ship would hear her, but the thought of coming this far only to be stopped by a closed airlock made her scream harder. Her voice began to scrape through her throat, but she refused to stop. She needed someone, anyone, to hear her pain.

Then a light above the airlock flashed briefly.

Stumbling back, Vinterra stood in the downpour, wondering if she had imagined the light. Could someone have really heard her?

The airlock slipped open, and Vinterra threw her arm up in an automatic response to the sudden surge of aggressive motion, pointing the pistol at the agent who moved to block her entry.

She didn't mean to pull the trigger, but in a brilliant flash of blue, she discovered that intent did not mean much when it was at odds with action.

The shot hit the agent full in the face, and the body crumpled in a heap inside the airlock.

Vinterra was so shocked that she forgot to lower her arm. She just stood there, staring at the dead agent on the floor, with black rain pouring over her and hiding her tears. The back of her throat burned as her stomach threatened to rebel, and she finally managed to look away.

Her eyes fell on three more agents standing in the main hallway of the ship, back beyond the airlock. Their eyes were bright and shocked, flicking between Vinterra and their dead companion. Dimly, it registered that all three of them were injured in some form or other, with bandages wrapped around various parts of their bodies. The one closest to the front of the group had one of his arms in a sling.

Vinterra did not want to fight them. She just wanted to know.

"Where is Haelin?"

Vinterra almost didn't recognize her own voice. It scraped out of her throat, and the words were raw and ragged. She swallowed, feeling the tightness of the collar around her neck, and tried again, but she only managed to get one word out this time. "Where?"

The agent at the front of the trio lifted his hands in a slow, careful demonstration of non-aggression, wincing as his bad arm shifted in the sling. "We'll take you to her," he murmured, and the soothing lilt of his voice set Vinterra's teeth on edge. "Just put the pistol down, and we'll—"

Vinterra's hand was shaking again as she arced the barrel towards the speaking agent. "Where is she?" she croaked again.

The agent stood frozen, his sharp, copper eyes riveted on the pistol. "We can bring her to you," he offered. His eyes moved back to Vinterra's face, and she felt her heart wrench.

This isn't who I am, she thought desperately. *Not me.*

She wasn't a killer. Not when she'd hated the screams of Awakening candidates on Daanhymn, and snuck out to watch the sunsets and the blue pollen rise, and braided flowers into Haelin's hair when they had a moment of peace.

Haelin—

Somewhere along the fall of memories, Vinterra had lowered the pistol. She was dimly aware that the agent who had spoken to her had sent his two companions off somewhere. They could be doing anything, she realized. Signaling someone. Finding weapons. Anything.

Vinterra could not bring herself to raise the pistol again. So she and the agent stood staring at each other, saying nothing as the rain hammered down.

They took a long time to return, but when the other two agents came back, they pushed a familiar sight between them: a hovering stasis pod identical to the ones Vinterra had helped move on Daraax Beta. They pushed the pod through the airlock as quickly as they could, one of them hobbling on a bandaged leg.

Bandages, she thought. *We only use bandages when we can't get to an outpost.*

Whatever had happened to these agents, it had chased them all the way to Crythsia, and left them broken. It was too much to hope that Haelin would be with them, let alone alive, and yet…

The stasis pod bobbed up and down as it slipped over the lip of the airlock and fell the short distance to the surface. Rain drummed off the glass panel that pointed skyward, beading and running down the slick surface. Light from the airlock spilled over the pod, gleaming off the rain and the glass, distorting the figure suspended within the stasis fluid.

Clear fluid, from before Vinterra's introduction of the pollen from Daanhymn.

Moving around the pod, desperately trying to see the face through the fluid and the light, Vinterra cupped her hand over the glass. The shadow offered her an unclear glance at a round, rosy copper face and floating tendrils of brown hair. A breathing tube secured over the nose and mouth blocked most of the features, but Vinterra recognized the face immediately.

With a ragged cry, she threw her arms across the stasis pod, tears streaming freely down her cheeks again to mix with the black rain. She did not care that the agents onboard the ship could see her. She let the sobs come freely as she leaned on the stasis pod, legs shaking and chest heaving.

She'd found Haelin, and that was all that mattered.

Then she caught a flash of movement out of the corner of her eye, and she whipped the pistol around. Once again, she did not mean to pull the trigger, but the weapon was far more sensitive than she had ever expected, and the shot flew in a burst of blue.

She missed this time.

She heard one of the agents shout, "I am *not* dealing with this!" before the owner of the voice dove for the airlock controls.

The words "But Sekorvo—" managed to slip out before the airlock doors snapped shut and sealed with a hiss.

Vinterra did not spare any time thinking about that. Instead, she ran around to the head of the hovering stasis pod, angled it back towards her ship, and began to push it forward. Her feet slipped on the black rocks, but she kept her grip on the pod, refusing to fall now. She'd made it about halfway when she heard the engines of the ship behind her roar to life.

Throwing up her hand to shield her vision, Vinterra watched as the ship lifted off from the ground, angling towards the sky. She half expected it to turn towards her and Haelin and open fire, but it only sprinted up, engines disappearing into the thick clouds.

Vinterra suddenly became aware of the sound of hysterical laughter, but it took a moment for her to realize that she was the one laughing.

"I did it," she gasped, turning back to the stasis pod. "I found you."

Rain hammered on the glass panel in response.

The laughter died.

Suddenly, Vinterra could not wait another moment to bring Haelin out of stasis. Rushing around the side of the pod, she found the small control panel and began to work. At her direction, the pod lowered itself to the ground, coming to rest firmly on its back. There was nowhere for the stasis fluid to drain, so Vinterra let it spill freely over the ground as the seal around the large glass panel broke with a *hsss*, and the panel began to rise. Thick, cloudy liquid puddled out around the pod, pooling around Vinterra's knees, but she was already soaked from the rain and barely noticed. She only cared about the figure that emerged from the stasis fluid, bare and vulnerable and achingly familiar.

When the fluid had all drained from the pod, Vinterra raised the panel higher and ducked her head under the glass. She fumbled with the breathing mask over Haelin's nose and mouth, finally detaching it and revealing the rest of her partner's face.

Vinterra froze, looking down at Haelin.

Her copper-rose skin was coated in the stasis fluid, and her hair was slicked down against her skull, but she looked so peaceful. Like she was sleeping.

Smiling and crying all at once, Vinterra brushed her fingertips over Haelin's cheek, tracing the soft line of the bone and coming to rest against Haelin's red lips.

Haelin's eyes snapped open. They swiveled towards Vinterra, burning white hot with Awakened light.

With a frightened cry, Vinterra stumbled back. Haelin surged up out of the pod. Vinterra scrabbled back over the rock on her hands and feet, trying to get away, but Haelin was there in an instant, the long, bionic fingers of her hands wrapping around Vinterra's throat.

Vinterra tried to call out her name, but Haelin's fingers pressed tighter, and she could not scrape the word out. Vinterra grabbed at Haelin's wrists, belatedly realizing she had put the enerpulse pistol down somewhere out of reach. She tried to pull Haelin's hands away, but the Awakened would not break her grip.

I should have expected this, Vinterra realized with a sudden calmness that shocked her. Her vision swam and grew dark, but she saw with an odd sort of satisfaction that the rain was washing away the stasis fluid from Haelin's body. *There are clothes on the ship for you,* she thought to Haelin because she could not speak. Her grip on Haelin's wrists relaxed, and Vinterra stopped struggling. She found that she was content to just hold on to Haelin one last time, to feel her skin beneath her fingertips. It was warm with life. *I love you.*

Vinterra closed her eyes, ready to surrender, but Haelin's grip around her throat shifted. With a painful gasp, Vinterra sucked in air, her eyes flying open with shock.

She met Haelin's stare, and saw the moment the harsh light of her Awakening left her. The irises returned to their normal, beautiful white gold, and tears welled up in them.

They sat like that for a long time, rain pouring down and washing the last traces of stasis fluid from Haelin's body.

"I thought of you," Haelin breathed. "I thought of you... until... the end and then I... I almost... I almost killed—" Her voice broke on the last word.

Then they were wrapped in a fierce embrace, Haelin sobbing against Vinterra's shoulder and Vinterra pressing her cheek against Haelin's head, rocking softly. Vinterra's heart hammered in her chest, threatening to burst from the sheer force of her joy.

"I found you," she whispered into Haelin's ear. "I found you."

They stayed like that for so long that the rain thinned and finally stopped, and the storm blew past. It left an indigo sky bursting with stars in its wake, the center of the galaxy risen in a cloudy swirl of shadow and light over the horizon. Vinterra sat with Haelin—now quiet and breathing steadily—in her arms, staring up at the sky and marveling at how far she'd gone for love.

CHAPTER 29: TARGET

Lance had just finished a practice session with the arkins in *Light Runner*'s training room—he'd taken them through a series of agility and problem-solving tests made out of a combination of interactive projections and some of the various training weights—when the ship-wide intercom signaled him with a sharp, urgent tone. Lissa's voice followed immediately, asking him to return to the control room.

Lance quickly put the last of the weights away, then ushered the arkins out of the room. Blade gave him a half-irritated but affectionate headbutt to the leg before slipping into the hall with Orion. Yawning, they both sank to the floor and curled up against each other, content to let him go on without them.

He returned to the control room alone, and found Lissa pacing around the small room in agitation. "What happened?" he asked.

Lissa motioned to the starmap projected over the controls. They always kept it up now, and updated it with their target's movements. Lissa had managed to pick up the true signature and tease out the trail, and they'd been following it for days. They were gaining on the source ship, but slowly.

Or at least, it had been slowly until now.

Frowning, Lance stood before the projection with his arms crossed, staring hard at the marked trail on the map. Lissa moved into the space beside him, her fingers curled against her mouth. He had never seen her so nervous before.

"Are we sure this is right?" Lance asked after a long moment.

Lissa nodded.

The trail had shown the ship slowing to a comfortable coasting speed, which was far from uncommon for starships on long, interstellar journeys with no knowledge of a hunting ship following their trail. But abruptly, the target had reversed direction, almost completely doubling back on itself, and shot off at top speed.

Lance rubbed the back of his neck and looked to Lissa. "What do you think?"

Lissa did not say anything for a full minute, and Lance could see her silver eyes darting along the marked path, picking out every shift in speed and direction. Finally, she stepped forward and pointed at a marker on the map that signaled a planet. It sat just off the target's initial path, about halfway between the target ship and their own. "It looks like they're heading here." She glanced over her shoulder at him. "Do you know the planet?"

"Crythsia," Lance said, feeling the breathy name blur strangely through his teeth. He thought hard about the planet, then nodded, recalling the information from the Star Federation's database.

The world had fallen under his jurisdiction during his time as a fleet commander, and though he never had a reason to visit most of the worlds in his territory, he had often read through the planetary catalogue that detailed them.

"It's a young world," Lance said as he moved forward to stand next to Lissa again. "Air should be breathable, but the surface is still very active. The weather is unpredictable and often violent." His eyes narrowed as he considered the marker on the starmap. "It's on the Star Federation's radar as a protected world, although a low priority one since there's barely any life."

Lissa drew in and released a heavy breath. "What's the surface like?"

"Unlivable," Lance said, though with a small hitch in his confidence.

Lissa gave him a pointed look.

Despite his doubts, Lance shook his head.

The Crythsian surface was coated by a black, dense crust weathered slick and glassy by wind and rain. It was possible to drill into, but not easy, and building there would have been too impractical, even without the numerous active volcanoes promising to erupt. The Seventh Sun had built in unexpected and incredible places, but not on a world that was directly under Star Federation protection.

And yet...

Lance finally had to admit that there could be a Seventh Sun base on Crythsia.

He and Lissa looked at the starmap for another long, silent moment.

"They either know we're coming," Lissa finally said, "or found something to chase."

"What makes you think that?"

"First instinct," Lissa said, reaching out to trace the target's path, "is to run *away* from your hunter. Even if there's safety back the way you came, you try to avoid bringing yourself closer to your pursuer." Her finger reached the point where the target ship had abruptly turned around and put on speed. "At least at first."

Lance studied the positions of the ships and the planet. "We're closer to Crythsia," he noted. "We could probably beat them there, if we wanted to."

"*Do* we want to?" She did not drop her hand away from the map.

Lance saw her wrestling with the decision. "If you're right," he said, "we'll have total surprise on our side."

"And if I'm wrong..."

Lance spread his hands in a half-shrug. "If you're wrong, *Light Runner* still has enough power for an overdrive sprint. There's a good chance we can get away."

Lissa breathed out again and turned to him. "We try?"

"We hunt," Lance agreed.

CHAPTER 30: FRAYING

After his blatant disrespect on Daraax Beta, Jason fully expected Keraun to try to tear him apart, both figuratively and literally. Keraun had witnesses to Jason's insubordination, so if the Hyrunian wanted to rip Jason's rank away and leave him at the mercy of a military court, he had what he needed to do it. Jason suspected the Hyrunian was more likely to try to kill him before he arranged for court-martialing, and he waited for the signal that Keraun was rendezvousing with his ship for some flimsy excuse of a meeting.

Major Miyasato also thought that the Hyrunian would try something, but she agreed that Jason was safe as long as Keraun wasn't there to attempt the murder himself.

The total silence from the fleet commander was a surprise to both of them. Hours stretched to days before new orders finally came, and when Jason read them, he almost could not believe that he was being allowed to live.

Keraun's decision to send him out of the Reach was another mystery, one that Jason could not fully puzzle out, but he had an idea of why Keraun wanted him out of that sector.

His suspicions were confirmed when his ship detected a steady movement of Star Federation troops into the Andromeda Reach just as he was ordered to leave the region.

Keraun had found something, and he did not want Jason anywhere near it.

"He's sending you away, but he hasn't forgotten about you. Hyrunian grudges don't die," Miyasato warned him. "You're not in the clear."

"Neither are you," Jason told her grimly, handing her the datapad that displayed the orders from Keraun.

After a moment of tentative surprise, Miyasato scanned the message. Jason saw her eyes catch on her own name. A heavy frown cut across her brow, and she muttered a curse.

"You're one of a very small pool of medics who know enough about Hyrunians to treat them effectively in case of injury," Jason said, taking the datapad back.

"I'm aware," Miyasato said. Her tone was frosty but Jason knew it was not directed at him. She sat back in her seat and crossed her arms. "I haven't found the right moment to send out that recording yet. I haven't done anything with it."

"There will be time—" Jason began.

"Not if he kills me," she cut across him. She did not sound frightened, only irritated. "If he knows you recorded that conversation about the shielding tech, then he probably knows that you sent it to me. He's got plenty of loyal spies in your ranks."

"I know."

"So if he kills me, I'm not going to be able to get that transmission out. Or the report about the hybrid boy."

Jason shrugged. "If he kills you, I'll broadcast them myself to every corner of the galaxy." He felt oddly calm talking about this with Miyasato. "But I don't think he'll kill you."

The major studied him closely. "You think he actually found something."

Jason nodded. "Whatever it is, it's big enough to warrant organizing troops in the Andromeda Reach, and he wants me far away from it." He glanced down at the datapad.

The orders from the fleet commander stared back at him. He was to continue purge efforts by putting down a protest on a planet that hosted an open population of Neo-Andromedans that had somehow managed to remain a secret from the Star Federation. Keraun wanted them silenced. All of them.

Jason put the datapad down and scrubbed a hand over his face. "I think he wants your medical expertise in case something happens to him."

"And *then* he'll kill me."

"Probably."

They sat in silence for a time, long enough for Jason's thoughts to slip back to Firoden and the boy he had killed and the wailing cry of the father who had watched his child's body placed in a line of corpses.

Then he thought about the Neo-Andromedan Keraun had killed in the hospital on Phan.

Aven. His name was Aven.

Sick and unarmed, shielded by a doctor who had told Jason that, as a soldier, he was not doing enough.

Jason had said that he was doing his best, but what was his best?

All those risks the Star Federation had ordered him to take. Stupid risks with little payoff, from salvaging a ship on Ametria to storming a Seventh Sun base and losing hundreds of soldiers to a small army of Awakened.

Jason had killed plenty of Awakened and Seventh Sun agents that were terrorizing the galaxy, but what about all the other Neo-Andromedans? He had wanted to do some good from within the ranks of the Star Federation. What was good about barreling into a hospital and standing aside while Keraun killed a sick man? What good did the Star Federation do by ignoring Yuna until the planet was too far-gone to save? How would traveling to Saenos to silence a protest protect the rest of the galaxy?

What was he *doing*?

Hell, Jason thought, *Ashburn deserted to try to do something that he thought was right.*

If only Jason knew where that had landed the runaway officer. He did not even know if Ashburn was still alive.

"Captain?" Miyasato's voice brought him back, and he found her staring at him intently, her brow furrowed. "Are you all right?"

Jason blinked at her. "How do you do good?" he asked.

The question caught Miyasato off-guard, and she began searching his face for signs of mental fatigue. Jason did not doubt that there was more than enough evidence of strain to support any order she gave him to lie down in a dark room and stay there for three days.

Jason tried the question again.

"I don't understand," Miyasato said.

"You're a physician," Jason said. "You've learned how to treat an incredible number of species, all in the name of saving lives. How do you reconcile that with the things that the Star Federation does? All of the terrible things the Star Federation does?"

Miyasato hesitated, then nodded at the datapad in front of Jason. "I imagine it's easier when you don't have someone ordering you to do those things."

Jason thought of Erica and her signature on the purge. "From what I've seen," he murmured, "people will still do terrible things even when they're not under orders."

The major studied him for a long time. She said something, low and soft, that sounded like, "It all comes back to him," but when Jason asked her to repeat it, she shook her head. "Thinking out loud, Captain," she explained. "But I suppose, for my part, I just remember that there are soldiers who really are trying to do some good for the galaxy. And if I can keep them alive, then we all still have a fighting chance."

Jason nodded absently, then dismissed Miyasato. She had a tense journey and preparations for an upcoming battle ahead of her, which, based on the movements of Star Federation ships still coming into the area, promised to be a grisly one.

And Jason had another heartrending mission to carry out.

CHAPTER 31: DIVIDE

After the destruction of the Daraaxi base, Erica tried to find ways to distract herself, but the mission had been nothing short of a failure. They had needed the Daraaxi base to provide them with their next move, even if it was just a clue to point the Star Federation to their next target. Anything that could have helped them was now lying at the bottom of a crater, burned beyond use if not reduced completely to ash.

Erica knew that Intelligence was working on the ships she had captured from the Nandro raid on the main space station, but she had little hope for those efforts. All four of the Seventh Sun ships had come from Daraax Beta, and their communication logs had been nearly obliterated by the Nandro crews before the ships were fully captured. What little that was left pointed back to Daraax Beta.

The Star Federation was at a dead end, and they all knew it.

The other fleet commanders were organizing purge efforts, often encouraging live captures now that they were hunting for information. Thus far, all they had found were uncollared Nandros who claimed to know nothing about the Seventh Sun beyond its existence.

Harsh, probing interrogation methods that were only legal during a purge confirmed their lack of knowledge.

As the days stretched on and Erica busied herself with her duties, she often found her thoughts slipping to Jason. Specifically, how he had let that traitor Ashburn go, and the things he had left unspoken the last time they'd had a conversation off the battlefield.

That felt like a lifetime ago, those words exchanged when he had come to her before they had parted ways on Phan.

She thought about that final conversation a lot in the days that followed the Daraax Beta raid, and regretted not bringing it up with him when she'd had the chance.

After the battle, she'd ridden back to her dreadnought in the same dropship as Jason, but they had not spoken a word to each other. After docking and letting Erica and her soldiers off, the dropship had carried Jason away to his own ship. That he still had a starship, let alone his rank as captain, was a twisted sort of miracle, fueled in part by Erica's inability to speak against him.

At first, she'd kept quiet about their final conversation and her suspicions of his involvement in Ashburn's escape because she knew she did not have the evidence she needed to see him successfully court-martialed. As a new fleet commander, a display of paranoia and unsteady reasoning could have ended her career. Now, with the attacks on Sciyat and the Star Federation space station behind her, she found herself remembering the battle on Daraax Beta, and how Jason had saved her life.

She'd done the same for him, but something wasn't sitting right.

What was it he'd said to her all those months ago? Something about non-lethal Nandros?

Erica snorted at the thought. As far as she was concerned, the only Nandros that weren't dangerous were the dead ones. And even those had their secrets.

Although, in light of how he'd handled himself on Daraax Beta, Erica wondered if Jason had finally come to understand what the Star Federation was up against. What they were all fighting for.

What Jason *needed* to fight for.

She resolved to ask him, and the first chance she had to retreat to her private quarters, Erica activated the room's private communication terminal. She had Jason's personal communicator code memorized, though it took her a moment to remember the first part of the sequence. Once she sent the transmission, she only had to wait a few moments before he answered.

Jason's holographic head and shoulders flickered into focus, his dark brown skin tinged blue by the display. He blinked at Erica in clear surprise, lips slightly parted in what Erica had once thought of as excitement, but now recognized as apprehension.

"Hello, Jason," she said easily.

"Hello, Commander Anderson," he returned.

A beat passed as Erica weighed the wary tone of his greeting. She had to play this carefully. Luckily, she was ready with a plausible excuse.

"I have not been able to reach Commander Keraun for the last few days," she said, and there were no lies in the words. "I was hoping you had an idea of how to contact him."

Jason pressed his mouth into a hard line. "He's been out-of-reach since reassigning my units."

Erica did not have to feign interest when she asked, "He reassigned you?"

Jason nodded. "Continuing purge efforts." He said the words as though they burned his tongue.

"Has Keraun shifted you to live captures?"

Another long moment slipped past as Jason stared at her. "No."

That did not surprise her. Neither, she realized, did Keraun sending Jason back out into the field after the raid on Daraax Beta. The Hyrunian was the least likely to follow proper procedure when he wanted to discipline a soldier. Any other commanding officer, and Jason would have been court-martialed by now. Erica herself had considered it. But Keraun...

Keraun had other methods, and with a cold pang, Erica realized that there was a good chance that Jason would not survive the war. She sincerely doubted that a Nandro would be the one to kill him.

And Jason was not under her command. There wasn't anything she could do about it, except maybe warn him.

"Are you alone?" Erica asked.

Jason nodded. His mouth was that hard line again, and something unfathomable pulled at Jason's eyes. He was exhausted, she realized, but more emotionally than physically.

You brought this on yourself, Erica thought, more with pity than anger, but frustration blanketed the idea.

"Where are you heading?" she asked, making an effort to keep her voice low and gentle.

"Sorry, Commander," Jason said after a moment that was a little too short to be regretful. "That's classified."

Lying.

All at once, Erica was back on Mezora, blocked by a hulking Justice Keeper that tried to kill her while a couple of Terran colonists lied to her face. She was tearing through space, trying to track the shuttle Ashburn had stolen before she lost the signature and ran out of time. She was hearing about the attack on Sciyat. She was rushing to her sisters' defense. She was calling soldiers back into Star Federation territory. She was fighting a Nandro on the Star Federation space station, knowing that if she fell in that battle, she would have lost the war for the very soul of the galaxy.

Her pity evaporated.

"I'll let you get back to it, Captain Stone," she said airily. "I'm sure you have a lot of work ahead of you." She let a small pause slip into the conversation, enough to leave something forbidden unspoken. Jason was raising his hand into the formal salute when she said, "But keep in mind, Captain..."

He froze, his hand half-raised, waiting for her to finish.

"You're a Star Federation officer. You rank demands that you at least *try* to do some good for the galaxy. While you're still out there."

Jason countered with a stiff, formal goodbye, and then Erica cut the transmission.

The hologram had not fully disappeared when the terminal caught a new signal. This one was a broadcasted recording rather than a live message.

It was from Keraun.

The full Hyrunian came into focus, every scale and iron cuff rendered clearly by the projectors and the proximity of their two ships. Normally, two-way communication across lightyears' worth of space resulted in flickering holograms and distorted details, but based on the clarity of Keraun's fierce expression, his ship must have been only a few systems away from Erica's. His horns cut that permanent glare into his features, but his eyes sparked with clear triumph.

"A message for all admirals and fleet commanders," the Hyrunian said. His tail thrashed back and forth in either excitement or irritation, but Erica was willing to bet a lot of credits on excitement. "My scout ships have confirmed the location of the main Nandro base."

Erica felt her mouth drop open.

"I will send exact coordinates in a follow-up message, but all available units must mobilize in the Andromeda Reach. The Nandro base is out past the fringes." Keraun's lip curled in a deadly smile. "Where there are no stars."

The message ended there, and for a stunned moment, Erica could not move. Then her hand wandered to the ship-wide broadcast controls and she found herself ordering all active navigators and engineers to get the ship to the Andromeda Reach as quickly as possible.

She was running for the control room less than a minute later. Excitement, dread, and determination churned in her stomach. She knew this would not be an easy fight, but if Keraun had really found the main base, that battle would be the end.

CHAPTER 32: FOUND

It took far longer to recharge the depleted power cells than Vinterra had anticipated. Exhausted from the night before, she and Haelin had fallen asleep onboard the stolen evac ship, curled up against each other in one of the small bunks. They did not sleep long. Haelin was plagued by nightmares, and woke in a panic more than once. Vinterra did what she could to soothe her partner, but Haelin kept apologizing and breaking down in Vinterra's arms.

"I did this to people," she whispered after the third panic attack. "I sent them into the Light."

Vinterra said nothing and pulled Haelin in closer.

By the time the power cells had nearly charged enough for the ship to leave the planet, Haelin had recovered somewhat from her Awakening. Bathing and dressing in fresh, clean clothing helped stabilize her, although she found the most comfort in being near Vinterra and making sure she took care of herself, too. With Haelin watching over her, Vinterra began to eat regularly again, and even with Haelin's nightmares, she felt more energized after resting.

With her hope restored, Vinterra began to prepare the ship for departure, though it would still be a few hours more before they could lift off.

"Where should we go?" Haelin asked, sitting next to Vinterra in the control room, bionic fingers threaded through Vinterra's dark brown ones.

Vinterra paused. "I hadn't really thought about that," she murmured. "But there must be somewhere quiet, away from everything, where no one can find us."

In the small silence that followed, Haelin gently squeezed her fingers. "As long as there are flowers," she murmured.

Vinterra's breath hitched for a moment, but a smile spread over her lips. Before she could respond, a system near Haelin beeped out an alert.

Shifting in her seat without releasing Vinterra's hand, Haelin brought up the warning and quickly scanned the message from the system. Her brows creased in confusion. "Tracking says there's a starship on a direct trajectory for our location." She looked back at Vinterra. "Should we be worried?"

Vinterra opened her mouth to offer a logical explanation, but the words never found her voice. She found herself remembering the night the agents had given her Haelin's stasis pod, after she'd accidentally shot at them twice and killed one of them. She'd been so desperate to put that shameful mistake out of her mind. She'd wanted to talk to Haelin about the kill, but until her partner recovered more from her Awakening, Vinterra had decided to keep quiet about it. The secret of the death rubbed her raw, and even though she knew it was an accident, even though she knew there was a very good chance the agent was trying to disarm or even kill her, Vinterra could not shake the guilt.

But after she'd killed that agent, after the survivors had given Haelin back to her, one of them had mentioned First Lit Sekorvo.

All at once, the panic she should have felt at the mention of his name came flooding in.

Vinterra ripped her hand from Haelin's and dove at the controls. She tried to fully power up the engines and ready the ship for takeoff, but the systems locked her out, informing her that after the full drain, the power cells needed more time to recharge before they could sustain the ship on another interstellar journey.

They were grounded on Crythsia.

"We have to go," Vinterra said, jumping to her feet. "Right now."

Haelin did not mask her surprise, but she rose from her seat and followed Vinterra as she rushed out of the control room. "What's going on?"

Vinterra gave an abbreviated account of her escape from Daraax Beta and the events surrounding her flight, ending with the surrender of Haelin's stasis pod and the mention of Sekorvo. She ran through the ship as she talked, gathering supplies without fully understanding why she bothered. If Sekorvo was on the approaching ship, he was going to hunt them down like animals.

Haelin listened to her story in grim silence, following Vinterra as she frantically stuffed food rations, spare clothing, and anything else she could think of having any value into a pair of bags. Vinterra expected Haelin to contradict her, to tell her that it was all wild speculation, that maybe it wasn't Sekorvo coming for them.

Haelin said none of those things. Instead, she asked, "Did you say you saw other agents taking ships from Daraax Beta?"

Vinterra paused long enough to say, "I just don't understand what they were doing. And they all left together, like they had it planned, or were part of something."

"And you're sure they weren't going out on a mission?"

Vinterra shook her head. She'd seen agents who were working on long-term projects board those ships. Agents who had made plans to stay on Daraax Beta for a long, long time.

Haelin curled and uncurled her bionic fingers. "That sounds like desertion."

"But where were they *going*?"

"You and I are probably never going to know," Haelin said. She stepped to Vinterra's side and began to sift through the bags, dispersing the weight more evenly between them.

"But if that many people deserted Daraax Beta, then the First Lit must know about it, and they must have set Sekorvo on the task."

Vinterra swallowed past her collar, feeling its grip tighten around her throat.

Everyone in the Seventh Sun knew what desertion meant, and agents were encouraged to report even the smallest traces of dissent among the ranks. But for First Lit Sekorvo to personally take the task, it must have been desertion on a grand scale. Usually, Sekorvo tapped his network of spies to glean information, then organized and sent retrieval teams after the rogue agents. No one knew how far his network reached, but everyone understood that Sekorvo sat at the center, and he only moved when something terrible happened.

The last time he had headed a retrieval team, a large group of uncollared Awakening candidates had fled the main base, slipping past not only First Lit Tyrath, but First Lit Rosonno as well, back when the First Lit still lived and worked on the main base. Sekorvo had found and killed all but two of the escaped candidates; only the siblings Aven and Lissa had evaded him.

Vinterra shuddered, remembering Lissa's eyes as she'd gone into her Awakening trial on Daanhymn.

In the end, Vinterra reflected mournfully, *the First Lit find everyone. We cannot outrun the Light.*

Haelin was still packing supplies. Vinterra reached out and stilled her partner's hand, wrapping her dark brown fingers around Haelin's copper ones. Haelin blinked at her in confusion, then shook her head when she realized what Vinterra was thinking.

"We're not giving up," Haelin said, her voice firm and clear.

"We can't escape him," Vinterra murmured. "This is my fault."

"No, it's not."

"It is. I led him right to us. To you."

Haelin turned to her, one hand coming up to grasp Vinterra's shoulder. "And you came for me," Haelin said, her voice shaking a little, but there was a firmness beneath the words.

"You went into an Awakening machine for me."

"I did." She said it so frankly that Vinterra snorted with laughter. Haelin was smiling when she continued. "Now let's do this for each other. If he finds us, then…" She shook her head, and neither of them tried to finish the thought. "But we try. For each other, we try."

Vinterra squeezed Haelin's hand, then grabbed one of the supply bags and slung the straps over her shoulders. Together, they ran out of the ship, into the dark, early morning. Dawn was still a ways off from breaking, but the horizon was brightening in one corner of the sky. The stars were beginning to fade, all except one, which grew brighter and larger with each passing moment.

Sekorvo's ship was on the verge of breaching the sky.

Vinterra tore her gaze away and spun around, searching for somewhere, anywhere, she and Haelin could go. As her eyes adjusted to the predawn light, she picked out the shapes of hills behind the evac ship. Carved into the side of one of the hills, there was a darker pool of blackness that marked the entrance to a cave.

Vinterra's heart beat hard and fast at the sight, and she grabbed Haelin, pulling her over the glassy ground toward the hill and the cave. She had no idea how deep the cave was, or if it led anywhere, but the cave had to be better than running out in the open, offering prime targets for Sekorvo to shoot down from the sky.

The sky was bright enough to be devoid of stars by the time they reached the hills. They were both out of breath, but Vinterra hit the slope and began scrabbling up it without stopping, leaning forward and using her hands to gain traction as she climbed. She felt her feet slipping over the rocks, but her hands kept her steady.

There was a terrible *thud* and pained cry as Haelin went down behind her.

Vinterra reversed direction immediately, sliding more than running back down the slope.

Haelin was already climbing to her feet. "I'm fine," she gasped, but she did not protest when Vinterra took her hand again and led her up the slope.

They reached the cave as the yellow sun peeked above the horizon, and Sekorvo's ship breached the sky.

The starship came down fast, too fast for the atmosphere, and the hull screamed in protest, an awful sound that made Vinterra and Haelin clap their hands over their ears. The shriek quieted as the ship bled off speed, and it shot toward the plain where Vinterra had landed the stolen evac ship.

Vinterra got her first good look at Sekorvo's starship as it circled over the evac ship, clearly scanning for signs of anyone onboard. It was smaller than she had expected, probably housing a crew of five at most, but everything about it screamed *hunter*.

The ship boasted three pulse cannons, two on the sharply angled wings and one centered on the bow. The hull was narrow and pointed, all the better to cut through atmospheres at top speed and dodge around enemy fire. The engines looked huge compared to the rest of the ship, and Vinterra could not understand how something so small could handle that much power.

"The extra rations were a mistake," Haelin whispered suddenly.

Vinterra looked at her in confusion, then followed Haelin's gaze down the slope. Her heart stopped as she saw the bright spot of white at the bottom of the hill. One of the packaged rations had fallen out of Haelin's bag when she slipped.

Cursing softly, Vinterra looked back at the hunting ship. There wasn't enough time to go down the hill and try to get it without being seen. They had to leave it.

As the ship banked around, Vinterra turned to move deeper into the cave, expecting to see darkness reaching towards a back wall too far away to see, or maybe even an opening to a network they could hide in, but she came up short.

From a distance, and without the rising sun hitting the rock at the right angle, the cave had looked deep and safe. Now, Vinterra could see her shadow hitting the solid back wall, just a few steps away from the entrance.

They were trapped.

And Vinterra had led them there.

Tears stung her eyes and rolled down her cheeks as she looked at Haelin. Her partner gazed back at her levelly, and Vinterra saw the gentle light from the dawn shining in Haelin's white gold eyes and soft brown hair. Desperately, she drank in the details of that moment, right down to the tiny glint of sunlight on Haelin's eyelashes, holding on to something beautiful before her life ended.

Wordlessly, Haelin took Vinterra's hand and led her the few steps to the back of the cave. They sank down with their backs to the wall, looking out at Crythsia.

From that position, they still had a view of the ships, even as the small but deadly hunter ship landed. The hulls of the ships stood out against the black rock of the plain, their metal turned almost white by the contrast. The sky brightened to a pale gray-blue as the airlock of the hunter ship opened, and five figures emerged.

They were all dressed in dark clothing, and Vinterra had to pick them out by the small patches of exposed skin that stood out against the rock. She followed their movements as three of them moved towards her stolen ship. The other two hung back at the hunter ship.

Time slipped by, marked by the swift climb of the sun. Vinterra had to shield her eyes against the light as it fully cleared the horizon. Haelin did the same, but their free hands rested on the cave floor, their fingers intertwined.

As they watched, the figures emerged from the stolen ship. Two of them walked decidedly toward the hunter vessel, throwing their arms up to signal a dead ship.

The final figure hesitated well away from the group, turning slowly and assessing the landscape. Vinterra registered the exact moment when the final figure's gaze alighted on the cave, and it began moving toward them. Someone from the group called out, but the lone agent advanced towards the cave and waved them off. The others settled in to watch and wait.

As the figure drew closer, Vinterra began to pick out small details.

It was a man, she saw first. A large, physically imposing man, heavy with muscle. His skin was a deep bronze color. His dark hair was cropped close to his skull, appearing as nothing more than a shadow on his skin. He drew closer, and Vinterra saw the hard line of his nose, a heavy brow over his eyes, and the square set of his jaw. He moved with definitive purpose, arms swinging menacingly in time with his step, and the black collar around his throat looked thin and feeble compared to the rest of him.

Beyond all doubt, Vinterra knew that he was First Lit Sekorvo.

The First Lit disappeared from sight as he approached, slipping below the bottom lip of the cave entrance. Vinterra thought she heard his footsteps as he neared the beginning of the slope, but then there was a pause. Vinterra strained to hear, trying to imagine what the First Lit was doing.

Something came flying into the cave, landing hard on the ground and skittering toward Vinterra and Haelin. They both jumped, and a startled cry escaped Vinterra's lips before she could stop herself. She registered the food ration Haelin had dropped, and realized the First Lit had thrown it up the slope to startle them into revealing themselves.

Vinterra closed her eyes tight, wishing she had not made a sound.

Haelin's hand shifted up to Vinterra's shoulder and pulled her in. The sunlight against Vinterra's eyelids disappeared as her head came to rest against Haelin, and she felt her partner wrap her arms around her. Haelin's lips pressed against her forehead. "I love you," Haelin whispered.

Vinterra returned the hug fiercely, feeling Haelin shaking against her. Or maybe Vinterra was the one shaking. She did not know.

She sat with Haelin, breathing hard and listening for the First Lit's approach.

She imagined him moving slowly now, smiling hungrily as he climbed the slope, certain that he had found his prey cornered and helpless. Vinterra felt sick with anticipation, waiting for the moment he appeared in the entrance to the cave. She thought it might have come when Haelin's grip tightened even more, breath almost whistling in her throat, but then Vinterra heard something unexpected.

A low, piercing whine split the silence, and Vinterra looked up in time to see another small starship come roaring out of the sky, diving toward the two grounded starships in a graceful streak of silver and blue. A pulse cannon opened fire, and Vinterra saw the first strike hit Sekorvo's hunting ship, throwing up sparks and smoke.

Even she could see that it was a precision strike, intended to cripple but not destroy.

The next few strikes were more liberal, hitting the four agents that tried to retaliate with enerpulse fire. The white-hot shots looked pathetic next to the larger attacks from the ship's pulse cannon. The agents all went down under the superior firepower.

Exchanging a bewildered glance, Vinterra and Haelin untangled their arms and quickly crawled to the lip of the cave.

Below them, Sekorvo was flying back down the slope, arms pumping as he ran hard towards his hunting ship. Vinterra did not know what he expected to do, but she did notice that he had timed his sprint to coincide with the silver-blue starship coming out of its dive and bleeding off speed in preparation for landing.

"He's going for his ship," Haelin breathed. "He wants to try to shoot them down."

Vinterra looked at the three cannons on Sekorvo's ship. The top one was damaged beyond use, but the two on the wings looked functional. They looked like they could overpower the new ship without much trouble.

"He might actually make it," Vinterra muttered, watching the First Lit's long, powerful legs carry him over the distance.

Fall, she pleaded with fate. *By all the light in the galaxy, make him fall.*

The First Lit's steps were quick and certain, even over Crythsia's glossy surface. He would not fall. He would make it to his ship, blast the attacking starship out of existence, then come back for them.

Vinterra felt paralyzed as she watched the silver-blue ship turn, angling towards the stolen evac ship. It seemed oblivious to Sekorvo's wild run. But then Vinterra saw the airlock open and something jump out. It fell for a heart-stopping moment, then large wings unfurled and it began to glide easily through the air. From the cave, Vinterra could not tell what it was, but she could follow its movement as it swept across the sky, arcing towards Sekorvo. It aligned itself with the First Lit, then dropped into a steep dive, crossing the line of the horizon in a matter of moments.

Sekorvo saw it coming. He skidded to a halt, fighting for balance but keeping his feet. Vinterra thought she saw him raise a weapon.

An enerpulse shot blasted out from the flying figure, and slammed into Sekorvo just as he fired his own weapon. His shot went wild, disappearing into the sky as his body was thrown to the ground.

Silence reigned as the flying figure climbed back up into the sky, circling the hunter ship and looking for further threats. The silver-blue ship landed, powering down, and Vinterra dully registered that it had not fired at the stolen evac ship. After a few minutes, a second figure emerged from the airlock, quickly followed by a dark shape that Vinterra had just enough time to register as some sort of animal before she lost sight of it against the black ground. She focused on the figure she could see, and saw it raise its arms and signal to the flying one. The airborne thing turned on a slow glide and descended on a gentle angle toward the ground, alighting near the silver-blue starship. There was a moment of confused movement before the flying figure divided into two, one an animal, and the other—

"Are they Neo-Andromedan?" Haelin asked, her voice barely above a whisper.

"I don't know," Vinterra whispered back. She stared hard at the silver-blue ship, but while it was too far away to pick out any markings, she could see that the starship was not of Neo-Andromedan design. "But I don't think they're Seventh Sun."

The figures stood together in a tight group, the two upright ones gesturing towards the evac ship and the hunting ship. The one dressed in darker clothing took a few steps away, then paused, considering. It turned back to the other and pointed towards Sekorvo's body. They both moved toward the corpse, and Vinterra saw one gray animal and the near-invisible movements of a black animal following close behind. The group reached Sekorvo's body and stood looking down at it for a long time. Then the dark-clothed figure turned to the other and gestured to the smoking hunting ship. The other pointed back at the evac ship. The dark-clothed figure looked down at Sekorvo again, then turned in the direction he had been running from. Toward the hill and the cave.

"They know he was hunting something," Haelin said as the group began to move towards them. Her bionic fingers flexed as she watched the four figures approach. Then she abruptly stood up, offering her hand to Vinterra. "It would be better if we went to meet them, instead of letting them find us."

Vinterra looked back at the advancing group, still too distant to make out any definite details, but they had paused, evidently catching Haelin's movement. With a sigh, Vinterra took Haelin's hand and let her partner pull her to her feet. Together, they eased their way down the slope, slipping and sliding all the way.

Staying upright demanded all of their attention, and they were both watching their feet as they descended. They did their best to keep their hands visible, showing that they were unarmed—*Another stupid mistake,* Vinterra realized belatedly—as they neared the bottom. She could only hope their deadly saviors would show mercy.

After what felt like an eternity, the ground finally leveled off under their feet. Vinterra and Haelin took a moment to find their traction on the surface, then raised their heads and started forward.

They were close enough to see the approaching group clearly now. The two animals were arkins, Vinterra could see, one as black as shadows with deep, amber eyes, the other rich gray with yellow eyes that seemed to glow against the slash of black fur across its face.

As for the other two, one was a man, moderately tall with a lean but muscular build. He carried himself with the straight, alert posture of someone who held a position of authority, though he was dressed in undecorated traveler's clothes. His skin was pale olive, his hair dark blond, and his eyes were a deep, human green.

Human. Not good.

The final member of the group was a woman, and as Vinterra looked at her, she felt her feet slowing of their own accord. It registered that the other group had already come to a complete stop as Vinterra and Haelin approached, the man and the two arkins looking with confusion at the woman.

She stood tense, an enerpulse pistol gripped in her gloved hand dangling forgotten for the moment next to her hip. Her black hair matched the darker shades of her clothing, and was drawn back into a tight knot, showcasing the hard, angular planes of her face, which was sparking a dawning horror in Vinterra. The woman's skin was taught over her bones, a sign of a hard life and harder travel, but the golden brown color looked healthier than the last time Vinterra had seen it. Her blazing silver eyes darted back and forth between Vinterra and Haelin, shifting from horror to anger as she looked at them.

"Oh," Haelin breathed, coming to a complete halt next to Vinterra, who took another two steps forward and put herself between Haelin and the group without even thinking about it.

There was a brief, tense silence.

Then Lissa snarled, *"YOU!"* and stepped forward, enerpulse pistol sweeping up to focus on Vinterra's heart.

CHAPTER 33: UNFORGIVEN

Fight for me, Little Light.

"*YOU!*" Lissa snarled, snapping her enerpulse pistol up. She started forward without even realizing she was moving, anger burning in her gut. The sunlight strengthened rapidly, growing brighter and brighter as Lissa focused on the agents' heartbeats.

Lance was there immediately, one hand coming up to block Lissa across her shoulders, the other closing on the top of the enerpulse pistol and forcing the barrel down and away from the two Seventh Sun agents.

"Lissa, *stop!*" he shouted, voice edged with desperation. "Keep control!"

Lissa forced herself to a total halt, tense under Lance's touch, but she took a long, slow breath, allowing the world around her to cool. She knew that he was right; she had almost let herself slip over the edge, and she had to keep herself under control.

But she still wanted to kill the agents.

"Let go," she said, her voice muted in her own ears.

"They're unarmed," Lance said, his voice sharp but also low.

Lissa did not look away from the two women.

They stared back at her, hands raised, eyes wide, breathing quick and shallow. They were afraid.

Good.

To her right, Blade gave a low growl before stepping closer and brushing her wing lightly against Lissa's leg. A possessive, protective gesture. The arkin's back was arched, the hair along her spine standing rigid as she bared her teeth at the Seventh Sun agents.

Out of the corner of her eye, she saw Lance look between her, the black arkin, and the two agents. His expression changed as he took in the black collars studded with white stars around their necks, and his arm across Lissa's shoulders slackened a little. His voice was much quieter when he asked, "Do you know them?"

"They Awakened me," Lissa breathed.

The woman with the too-long fingers flinched.

Lance looked at Lissa in silence. Then he lifted his hand from the enerpulse pistol, dropped his restraining arm, and took a full step away from her. He landed out of sight, somewhere behind her, leaving a clear path to the two women.

Lissa brought the pistol up again, but the full weight of what Lance had just done sank in. She broke her focus on the two women and glanced over her shoulder at him.

He stared at the two Seventh Sun agents, his eyes hard. His breathing was a little too rapid, and there was a hard set to his jaw that Lissa had only ever seen twice before, both times after he had failed to save the lives of the Star Federation soldiers under his command as a fleet commander. It was the look of someone who had failed to protect.

Sensing her gaze, Lance's eyes slid to hers for a moment, but there was no judgment there. Only a flash of understanding.

Lissa turned back to the agents.

They had not moved beyond the shaking of their hands and the uneven rise and fall of their chests. The agent with the tight, black coils of hair and deep brown skin was standing in front of the other one. Her bottom lip trembled and there were tears in her eyes, but she held her head high, silver-and-purple eyes locked with Lissa's.

She was not going to move.

They were both there, Lissa remembered. *Both on the balcony, even if only one of them is one of the voices in my ears.*

An enerpulse shot to the heart was a cleaner death than either of them deserved, but Lissa had never been one to draw out a kill. She refocused her pistol on the agent in front, lining up the shot.

"I'm sorry!" the agent with the too-long fingers suddenly blurted.

Lissa froze, her finger resting lightly on the trigger. She shifted her gaze from the onyx-skinned woman as the agent behind her stepped forward. Her too-long fingers curled as she came to the front, placing herself directly in the line of fire.

"Haelin," the other agent whimpered, her voice cracking on the name.

The agent named Haelin was crying freely, Lissa saw, and shaking badly, but she spread her arms out like a shield, trying to block the other agent from Lissa completely. "I'm sorry," she repeated, staring down the barrel of Lissa's pistol. She said it in the Galactic Unified Voice, the words thickened by her accent.

Lissa's jaw clenched as she remembered what had happened the last time a Seventh Sun agent had said those words to her.

Haelin seemed to read Lissa's agitation. She pressed her thin lips together and nodded, tears falling from her chin to stain her shirt. "Kill me," she said, her voice surprisingly steady, "but let Vinterra go."

The other agent let out an anguished sound and began to shake her head.

"Vinterra didn't do anything," Haelin continued, still crying. "She always hated the Awakenings. I didn't. I was the one who put you through it. It was me." She drew in a rattling breath, and the tears stopped falling. "You know it was me."

Lissa did not move for a long time. She just stood with her body angled along her sight line, pistol trained on Haelin's heart, finger light on the trigger.

One small move was all she needed.

One quick shot.

But Lissa couldn't do it. Not yet.

"I still hear your voice," she said, shaping each word carefully. "You wanted me to fight for you."

Haelin's eyes squeezed shut for a moment, and she nodded. "And you did. You did fight." She opened her eyes again and they focused on Lissa with muted awe. "And you were incredible."

A surge of white-hot anger drove Lissa across the remaining distance between her and the Seventh Sun agents. The two agents cried out and stumbled back, but Lissa stepped faster and closed the gap. The barrel of her enerpulse pistol flew up to Haelin's skull, pressing into the flesh between her white gold eyes.

"I *fought*," Lissa screamed at the agent, "for the chance to *kill you!*" Her voice split the Crythsian air, and the faint echoes resounded her anger and pain.

Haelin froze, shaking, hands spread wide.

The edges of Lissa's vision began to burn, bleaching the world with brightness. The whispers swarmed into her ears again, but this time, Lance's earlier words cut through them.

Keep control.

Lissa took a long, deep breath, holding it in as the brightness receded. She did not drop her pistol from Haelin's head.

In the silence that spread as Lissa waited for the world to cool again, Vinterra moaned softly. She inched closer to Haelin, closing her fingers around Haelin's upper arm. There was nothing threatening about the gesture, but Lissa found herself focusing on the motion. There was an intimacy to the grip that she could not ignore. It brought on a sharp twist of envy.

These agents loved each other. After everything, they still had each other. And together, they had helped rip Lissa's life apart.

"Killing me would have been kinder than what you did," she growled at the agents.

Haelin licked her thin lips and slowly uncurled her too-long fingers, but she did not try to pull away from the pistol. Her voice was a dry whisper when she said, "If I'd known then what it was like, what it was really like, I would have given every candidate that mercy."

Lissa pushed the weapon harder against Haelin's skull, drawing a satisfying wince from the agent. "But you would not have stopped the Awakenings."

"I didn't want to." Haelin's voice hitched, but she kept going. "My life belonged to the Seventh Sun. I gave it to them willingly because I thought I could do great things. I thought—" she swallowed past a lump of fear in her throat, "—I thought your Awakening would be my chance for that. So I took it, and after you broke free, they offered me a choice: step into an Awakening machine, or send Vinterra to the Light in my place."

"So you ran," Lissa said. She'd realized that the man she had shot down from Orion's back was hunting someone, though she had not expected these two. The design of his ship alone had announced his intentions, and she knew from experience what the Seventh Sun promised to do to deserters. These two must have decided that deserting the Seventh Sun was worth the risk if the alternative was an Awakening.

Champions of pain were rarely willing to endure it themselves.

But, to Lissa's surprise, Haelin shook her head and whispered, "I went into the machine."

Lissa found herself staring hard into Haelin's eyes, searching for the ghosted remains of Awakening light. They were the same harsh, white gold color that she remembered from her nightmares, but they were ringed with dark exhaustion, and there was no power there. Just fear, regret, and acceptance.

She couldn't help but wonder if her own eyes had looked that way on Daanhymn, after Lance found her. After she'd almost killed him.

She remembered the complete loss of control over herself, the burning, aching need to kill before the hunger tore her apart. An Awakening was something she would never wish on anyone.

Not even Haelin, she realized with a jolt.

This agent had already gone through far worse than Lissa's vengeance. And killing her would not silence the teasing voices in her ear that tormented her and begged her to fight. The very sight of Haelin had stoked a raging fire in Lissa's heart, but she knew enough about her own anger to know that, this time, there was nothing beyond it. Once it died, it would leave her scorched and cold and empty.

With a loud breath, Lissa pushed away from Haelin. She turned on her heel and stalked a few paces away, trying to think, to convince herself to just take the shot, but she knew that, no matter what she did, this moment was going to haunt her.

She caught sight of Lance and the arkins, standing where she'd left them. Blade and Orion both watched her for some sign of how they should act, though Blade was crouched low and ready to attack while Orion cocked his head quizzically.

Lance stood with his body half-turned away from the two agents, keeping his enerpulse pistol out of their line of sight. His hand was closed around the weapon, and he had lifted it almost completely out of its holster. He was watching the agents carefully now that Lissa's back was turned to them, but he spared a glance at her to ask a silent question.

He offered to do what she could not.

Would not.

Her decision made, Lissa shook her head at Lance.

He silently slid the weapon back into the holster, though he kept his hand on the butt of the pistol, ready to draw at the first sign of trouble.

Lissa took a moment and a few shaking breaths to steady herself, but she knew that stalling for more time would not make what she was about to do any easier. Steeling herself, she turned back to the two Seventh Sun agents. "Go," she told them, low and quiet. "I don't care where, and I don't care what happens to you. But if you ever work with the Seventh Sun again, or Awaken another Neo-Andromedan, I will come for you. And I will kill you."

They stared at her in bewilderment.

"Get off this planet," Lissa snarled, each word growing louder until she was shouting at them again, "and get out of my life!"

The agents flinched, but hope sparked in Vinterra's eyes. She edged around Haelin, still gripping her partner's arm, and began to gently pull her in the direction of the ships. It took several tugs before Haelin moved, but even then, her expression was blank. Her mouth hung partly open, and she would not stop staring at Lissa.

Lissa had to turn away for fear that the staring would change her mind.

Evidently, Haelin did not fully understand how precarious her footing was between life and death. She stepped closer to Lissa and, with an awe-filled, shaking voice, said, "Thank you."

With a grimace, Lissa turned back to the agent.

Fresh tears had streaked down her round, fleshy face, leaving shining tracks against her copper skin. The black collar with the seven white stars glared out at Lissa from the shadow of Haelin's chin, tight around her throat.

Lissa's fingers found the pouch on her belt that held her own broken Seventh Sun collar. She traced the outline of the piece through the fabric, feeling the ridges of the stars on the surface. She slid her gaze from the collar around Haelin's neck back to her white gold eyes and said, "You are not forgiven."

The agent's eyes widened a little, but she pressed her lips together and nodded. Then she turned and walked away as quickly as she could over the glossy Crythsian surface, clinging to her partner's hand like a lifeline.

Neither of them looked back.

But Lance did. He pitched his voice low so that it wouldn't carry to the two agents when he asked, "You okay?"

Lissa nodded, not trusting herself to speak.

Lance lingered a moment longer before making a quick gesture to Orion, who turned and followed the departing agents. Lance went with the arkin, one hand still on his enerpulse pistol, just in case.

And Lissa had let them go.

Her knees suddenly felt weak, and she allowed herself to sink to the hard ground. Blade moved to Lissa's shoulder and gently pressed her head against Lissa's, the arkin's breath warm against her cheek. Lissa looped her arm around Blade's neck, and they watched Lance and Orion recede into the distance.

They chased the agents back to the ships, but there was a moment of confused movement as the group of four drew near *Light Runner* and the hunting ship. They broke apart, and Lissa surged to her feet when she realized that Orion was staying with one of the agents. Lance went with the other one, into the hunting ship.

Lissa slipped and stumbled on the glossy rock as she ran to the ships, Blade close behind her. As she drew near, she saw that the one named Vinterra was standing with Orion, her gaze locked on the arkin and her hands raised in a fearful, placating gesture. When Lissa yelled at her, her attention snapped away from Orion.

"What are they doing?" Lissa shouted at Vinterra. She was already rushing past the agent, toward the hunting ship, but she slowed enough to point her pistol at Vinterra's heart.

"Haelin wants to give you something," the agent said, shrinking away from the weapon. "Nothing dangerous!" she continued quickly, but Lissa was already beyond her, almost into the airlock of the predatory starship.

I'll tear them apart if she hurts him, Lissa promised herself, then skidded to a halt when Lance and Haelin emerged from the airlock of the hunting ship.

Lissa's eyes ran wildly over Lance, searching for signs of an injury. He looked back at her with mild surprise, but spread his arms to show her that he was unharmed. He had his enerpulse pistol drawn, and he turned the barrel back on Haelin, but his finger was off the trigger.

It took a moment for Lissa to accept that Lance was not hurt, and had Haelin under control. She knew from experience that he could handle himself in dangerous situations, but when the Seventh Sun was involved, she trusted nothing to go as it should.

Finally turning to Haelin, she was surprised to find the agent holding out a datapad to her. Haelin's eyes were downcast, afraid to meet Lissa's, and she held the thin machine in two hands, as though offering something fragile and sacred.

At a loss for anything else to do, Lissa took the datapad.

Haelin seemed as though she wanted to say something. She thought better of it. The agent dropped her eyes again, hurried past Lissa, and ran to embrace her waiting partner. They turned together and headed for their starship, stiff with tension. But their arms were locked around each other, and they did not look back.

Lissa felt Lance's hand close gently on her elbow, reassuring her that he was all right. He stepped past her and boarded *Light Runner* just as the two agents reached their small, clunky ship. Lance had identified the craft as an evacuation ship, and said that, from what he could tell, it was an unarmed vessel. That did not stop him from quickly powering up *Light Runner*'s pulse cannons, ready to attack or defend as necessary. The evac ship made no aggressive moves when it took off, simply angling into the sky.

Lissa lost sight of it as it shot toward the risen sun. She blinked and it was gone.

CHAPTER 34: SUNDOWN

Sekorvo's death was a hot sting against Rosonno's neck. He was in his private washroom when it came, splashing cold water on his face and trying not to imagine what Tyrath had been doing when she'd died. Then the prick came, the star filled with blood, and after a stunned moment, Rosonno looked up, hoping to see the center star in his collar turn the color of death. When he saw which star had darkened, he forgot how to think.

For that moment, his mind was blissfully calm.

Then Arrevessa's words came screaming back to him.

Selfish. Poison. Rot us from the inside.

"No," he whispered. The new red star was garish in color next to its darker companions.

Ereko. Tyrath. Sekorvo. All gone.

Rosonno, Niradessa, and Zeran. Still living, still breathing, still shining out in the galaxy.

Arrevessa. Central and bright and haunting and missing.

Poison.

Rosonno shook his head and stumbled out of the washroom. He could not bear to look at Sekorvo's dead star, but the memory of his passing lingered hot on Rosonno's skin, itching beneath the collar. The hard edges dug into his neck as

261

he scratched. He quickly pulled the collar back into its proper place, taking as deep a breath as he could against its restrictive grip. He made himself think.

"Tyrath was killed in the Star Federation raid," he said, pushing himself to accept the fact. He crossed the room and stood over his desk, frowning down at the neat lines of datapads. The symmetry was soothing, and his frown eased. "The Star Feds found her location when the raid on their space station failed, and they were able to capture ships. There is a high probability that most of those ships, if not all of them, had come from Daraax Beta. That was their lead."

Terrible luck, but not his fault.

But he still hesitated for a moment. He was reluctant to plunge down the next path, though he knew that he had to. He needed to be able to tell Niradessa and Zeran *some*thing when they inevitably contacted him. With so few of the First Lit left, it wouldn't be long.

He pushed himself on.

"Sekorvo had no communications with those ships. None of them. The Star Federation would not have been able to pull his signature from any data." He took another deep breath, and the collar tightened its grip. "So who killed Sekorvo?"

The last Rosonno had heard from him, Sekorvo was pursuing deserters from the Daraaxi base. He had locked on to one ship in particular, whose pilot had not managed to scramble its signal. Sekorvo had suspected that Vinterra, the terraform-leader-turned-botanist, was on that ship. He had based his theory on the fact that Vinterra's stolen ship was following the trail of her Awakened partner's dropship.

Rosonno knew it had been a mistake to let those traitors live.

And now, another First Lit was dead.

But Rosonno could not see Vinterra killing anyone. He'd studied her psychological profile after what had happened on Daanhymn, and nothing about her suggested a capacity for killing. She hated Awakenings, devoted herself to the study of flowers, and had been the happiest resident on Daanhymn by far. She was easily contented with menial work far beneath what her brilliant mind was capable of.

Of course, her happy life had been ripped out from under her, her relationship with her partner severed, and she had been drawn into working with the Awakened again, even if they were in stasis.

Rosonno had to wonder if there had been enough of a shift in her psyche to create a capacity for aggression.

But killing Sekorvo?

Sekorvo was too cunning and too ruthless to ever die by Vinterra's hand. He was a hunter. He would never allow himself to be destroyed by his own prey.

A hunter...

Rosonno shivered as his thoughts turned to Lissa. He immediately felt foolish for it. "That's not—" he began to tell himself, but he found the word *possible* bucking at the tip of his tongue. He knew the truth. Denying it would not undo the past or derail the present. It would only seal the future.

"Probable," he finished.

But the thought of Lissa finding and killing Sekorvo had taken root in his mind, and he found himself chewing on his bottom lip in an effort to distract himself from the idea of a bounty hunter closing in on his own trail.

Then another thought occurred to him.

If Sekorvo had died on a planet, then there was at least one ship blazing a trail back out into space. It would be so easy to track.

Quickly, he moved to his communication terminal and sent a message to Syreth's handling team, instructing them on their next move. He was glad that they were near the system in question, so picking up the trail and following it would be a swift process.

He just hoped that he'd finally set them on the right path.

CHAPTER 35: RECON

Erica stared hard at the holographic model Keraun had sent to her and the three other senior officers leading the mission beyond the Andromeda Reach, not quite believing what she was seeing. The hologram was compiled from images Keraun's scout ships had taken. It was not complete and only offered a partial view of the Nandro base rather than a full turnaround, but that was more than enough to stun her and the others into silence.

For nearly five minutes, no one on the conference transmission said a word. Erica was vaguely aware that the two admirals and the other fleet commander were openly gaping at the image. She could see their mouths working as their eyes darted left and right in the hologram projections of their faces.

Keraun was the exception. The Hyrunian's permanent glare was undercut with impatience.

"Are you certain this is the proper scale?" Admiral Araxorra finally asked. There was no fear in her sibilant voice, only clinical calculation. Since the attack on Araxii, the admiral had been obsessed with keeping her home planet secure. Now that she had the chance to avenge her people, everything about her radiated cold determination. Her pinched, beaked face darted left and right, swaying on her pink-skinned, serpentine neck. Her eyes were bright with anticipation, and the large crests of skin that edged her face and directed sound into her small ears were curved intently toward the communication terminal.

"Yes, Admiral," Keraun responded. "My scouts checked and confirmed the accuracy of their data six times over."

Erica did not know when she had begun holding her breath, but she let it out in a soft rush when she heard that. Based on the information from Keraun's scouts, the Nandro base was the size of a small planet.

It was nothing like Erica had ever seen anywhere in the galaxy. Built as a series of uneven, crystalline spikes jutting out from what she had to assume was a central core, this space station was dark and terrifying. She could not believe that anyone had actually built it, that something that massive and uneven had been manufactured rather than twisted into existence by the crueler side of nature.

A sudden curse from Admiral Lukati snapped everyone's attention to him. "Do you know what that is?" he demanded. He raised one brown hand and pointed at the Nandro base. "That's an Andromedan stronghold."

There was a heavy pause, and even Keraun looked thoughtful at the proclamation. Araxorra nearly turned her head upside down as she studied the image.

"It can't be," Ranisheden growled after thorough scrutiny. The Vareesi fleet commander tossed her head, blurring the white markings on her violet skin. "The Star Federation destroyed them all during the war."

"We must have missed one," Lukati said darkly.

"That's not possible," Ranisheden insisted.

"Then what is that?" Lukati said. He sounded more tired than impatient, but there was a harsh edge to his voice.

While Ranisheden hesitated, Erica called up the Star Federation's database and began to skim through the entries on the Andromeda War. She stopped when she found one about the end of the war, detailing the Star Federation's triumph over the Andromedans. The military had killed most of the invaders and driven the rest of them out of the galaxy, then found and destroyed every last structure the Andromedans had built. That included the four strongholds the Andromedans had built within prominent solar systems. There had never been any evidence to suggest a fifth.

Erica pulled up images of the four known strongholds. At a glance, she knew that Lukati was right. There were differences in the shapes and orientations of the structures, but they all had the distinct, crystalline spikes jutting out from a core.

If Keraun had not found a fifth stronghold, then he'd found a damned good imitation of one.

Ranisheden still looked doubtful, but she had to either accept the facts, or submit to the authority of her superiors. Either way, the Vareesi gave up the fight. "How are we going to destroy it?" she asked.

"I don't think we can," Lukati said.

The admirals frowned, and Erica felt a muted sense of dread wash through her.

The other strongholds had proven impossible to breach digitally. They'd withstood pulse cannon fire and all other forms of weaponry. Desperate to destroy them, the Star Federation had finally turned every ship in the military on the strongholds. They used a combination of tractor beams and pulse cannon fire boosted to dangerous levels to push the strongholds off orbit, and crash them into stars. They finally succeeded, but more than a third of the starships were destroyed in the attempts, ripped apart by overexertion of their power cells. The Star Federation spent years rebuilding the fleets.

Looking at the images of the final stronghold Keraun had provided, Erica knew that the same tactics would not work, no matter how far their technology had advanced since the end of the war; there was nothing near the stronghold. Out beyond the edge of the galaxy, the Andromedan structure was surrounded by empty space for lightyears.

And if Keraun's coordinates were correct, there was only a small percentage of starships that could safely make the journey to the stronghold.

They needed another way to destroy the base, but Erica's mind came up blank.

She watched Lukati work through an idea. Based on his dark expression, she had the sense that his solution was a bleak one.

But before he could speak, Araxorra murmured, "We could take the deal."

Keraun and Lukati both snapped their attention to the Araxii, but while the Hyrunian had an intense and hungry gleam in his eye, the human admiral was livid.

"We agreed that was too high a price," he spat.

"That was before Commander Keraun found a fifth stronghold," Araxorra returned coldly. "As things stand, I'm sure the other admirals will agree that the reward outweighs the risk."

Lukati shook his head, and Erica was shocked to see a shadow of defeat cross his expression. "I am against this," he said.

Araxorra dipped her head in acknowledgement. "We will discuss with the other admirals before proceeding, but I grant Commander Keraun permission to open the lines of communication again."

Erica noticed that the Hyrunian now had an amused curve to his signature snarl. She had the feeling that Araxorra's promise to bring the other admirals in was more of a formality than a chance for Lukati to sway the leaders of the Star Federation against the mysterious bargain, and Keraun knew it.

Ranisheden the Vareesi officer, on the other hand, looked as confused as Erica felt.

"For now," Araxorra continued, "we need a strategy to get into that base. The deal is worth nothing if we cannot penetrate the stronghold."

Lukati grimaced, but agreed.

As the admirals began to discuss the base and what little success the Star Federation had previously found against the Andromedan structures, Erica focused on the image of the crystalline stronghold again. There was nothing close enough to throw light on the station, and the only illumination came from the base itself. That was feeble in comparison to the sheer size of the structure; lights dotted three of the massive spikes, and the dozens of others were dark. Keraun's scouts had only found the stronghold because they had noticed a large, black mass where the faint light of other galaxies should have been, made distinct from the rest of the dark matter out in space by the concentrated glow of power on those three spikes.

How he had known where to look was beyond her.

When Erica tuned back into the conversation, she found that the admirals were focusing on the illuminated areas of the base.

"It's likely the Nandros were holing up there after the first purge, and now are abandoning the station," Lukati said. "At this point, we know they've spread throughout the galaxy in large enough numbers to sustain their population. What we're looking at is probably the highest concentration of Nandros we'll ever find, but it's far from the core of their numbers."

"How many do you think are living there?" Araxorra asked.

"Impossible to say without knowing how much of the station is automated," Lukati said without missing a beat. "But at that size? Maybe a little more than two million."

Erica frowned. With numbers that high, it was unlikely that every single Nandro on that base would be trained in combat, certainly not at the same level as the ones she'd come across in the field, but all Nandros were dangerous for one particular reason that sat nestled against their hearts. Erica was not one to charge in and forget that.

"We need a way in that will give us some protection against any berserk Nandros," she said.

Lukati nodded in agreement. "Thoughts on that, Commander Ranisheden?"

"From what we know of Nandros," Ranisheden growled, "they'll see us coming when we move within a certain range. What we need are ships with heavy firepower to decimate the populated areas before they can react. We strike hard and destroy the base, crippling the heart of the Nandros."

Araxorra tipped her head to the side, narrowing her electric blue eyes. "If that base really is Andromedan build, we're not going to be able to destroy it with our ships, even if we brought every *Argonaught* to the location." Her head tilted even further off kilter. "With this stronghold situated beyond the Reach, most of our ships won't even be able to make the journey."

"What do you propose, then?" Lukati asked her.

The Araxii admiral thought for a long moment, then snapped her serpentine neck straight. "Three waves," she declared. "We need enough ships for three waves of an attack. The first will engage the Nandros, draw their focus, and do as much damage to the base as possible. Striking the populated areas may be a good preliminary tactic for us, but we'll use it as a distraction.

"The second wave will bring in the armored driller Commander Keraun captured from Ametria. That thing's been able to cut through everything we've put in front of it. We don't know everything about it yet, but I bet it'll get through the stronghold. We can use the driller to penetrate the base here." She reached out and touched the projection on her own terminal, and Erica's responded by highlighting a spot on the Nandro fortress. The base of one of the dark spikes glowed where the admiral had indicated. "We'll move troops into the populated area from the access point. From there, they'll look for a main power core. A structure that size must have multiple cores, though I suspect only one is active. Once our troops find it, they'll need to seize control and prepare for a payload delivery. They'll activate the payload, retreat, and at least the populated side of the base should be destroyed."

"What happens if the driller can't cut into the stronghold?" Erica asked.

A shiver rippled down Araxorra's neck. "Then we use the old fashioned way and ram it with an *Argonaught*."

Lukati nodded, but he was frowning. "We don't know what the interior of that base is like. We may not be able to even get in to the populated areas."

Araxorra inclined her head. "That's why we'll need a third wave, larger than the others, to provide support and continue blasting the base. If the driller gets us in, I suspect the bulk of our progress will be made with laser cutters and foot soldiers. We'll need to give them all the support and protection we can."

Lukati hesitated before agreeing. "Commander Ranisheden," he said, and the Vareesi snapped to attention. "You will oversee the first wave and draw the Nandros' attention away from Commander Keraun, who will lead the second wave and drill into the base." Lukati focused on Erica then, and she felt a twist in her gut at being given the last wave, but she held her tongue. "I will lead the final wave with the assistance of Commander Anderson."

"And I will join Commander Ranisheden in the first wave," Araxorra finished. "Everyone, take some time to prep your units and ensure your ships are stocked for the voyage. We're going to be spacebound for a long time. Ranisheden, you and I will discuss the details of the first strike on another transmission before coordinating with Keraun." Admiral Araxorra disconnected after that, and the two other fleet commanders followed suit.

Before Erica could move, Lukati asked her to remain connected. "We need to talk about how to handle the third wave in a number of situations," the admiral said. "We're taking the most crucial role, Anderson. It's very important that we are prepared for anything when we join the battle."

Erica nodded, relief and pride swelling in her chest. She'd thought that Lukati was keeping her out of the battle for all the reasons she did not like to think about. It seemed he had more faith in her than that.

"Where would you like to start, Admiral?" Erica asked.

Lukati grinned wryly. "With a break. Take a few hours, clear your head, and come back refreshed. We have some time before the rest of the fleet arrives in the Reach, and we'll need to make sure that they're ready for the journey."

"Yes, sir," Erica said, but she had the feeling there was more on the admiral's mind. "Was there something else, Admiral?"

Lukati narrowed his eyes and pressed his lips into a thin line. For a moment, Erica thought she had somehow offended him, but then he nodded and said, "Keep your eye on the Hyrunian. I don't trust him."

"Sir?"

Lukati sighed and held Erica's gaze, as though measuring how much he wanted to tell her. "There have been some... *developments* with the Hyrunians that I'm not particularly excited about."

"Hostile developments?"

"No," Lukati said, wincing, "not on the surface, at least. There have been some exchanges between them and the Star Federation that I did not approve of, but the other admirals decided to proceed with."

Erica frowned. The alliance with the Hyrunians had moved much faster than she had thought it would. "What are they giving us?" she asked before she could worry if she was overstepping her rank.

Lukati offered no reprimand if she was. "They've offered to provide more open trade and technology exchanges. Some of it should arrive in time for the battle outside the Reach." The corners of the admiral's mouth turned down. "Anderson, that deal that Araxorra mentioned? That's for a Hyrunian bomb that just might annihilate that entire stronghold for us, if we can get it inside."

Erica felt her mouth fall open. The idea of a weapon doing that much damage to something out in the total void of space numbed her, and she struggled to close her mouth again.

The admiral caught the gesture and smiled sympathetically, but there was no levity in his voice when he said, "I think it's too good to be true, too."

"What are we going to give *them* for something like that?"

Lukati's face creased with anger, but he kept his tone level and controlled. "The Hyrunians want access to all human-developed tech from recent years. They said it's unlike anything they currently have, and they felt that it would go a long way towards strengthening relations between Hyrunians and the Star Federation."

Erica frowned. "I'm surprised the Yukarians haven't been leaking those things to them already."

"Oh, they have," Lukati growled, "far more than they've leaked Hyrunian tech to us, but that's not what worries me. What keeps me up at night," he said, dropping his voice low and leaning in, even though the communication terminal destroyed that kind of conspiratorial gesture, "is that the Hyrunians want all of our captured Nandro tech and data, too."

This time, Erica did not bother to close her mouth. "We can't give them that when we don't completely understand it ourselves! What if they figure out a way to turn it against us?"

"I know," Lukati said, cutting her off before she got any further. "Believe me, any reason you come up with now about why that's a terrible idea, I've had two extra months to be sick over." He sighed, deep and heavy. "The other admirals were torn on the idea, but we finally agreed to only hand over what we've already thoroughly examined and determined to be—" he grimaced again "—*safe*."

Erica held his gaze steadily. "But we don't know that for sure."

"No. We don't." Lukati straightened up. "But the bigger problem is that the Hyrunians already have a potential source within our leadership for that kind of classified tech, even if we manage to keep the Yukarians away from it."

It took Erica a moment to realize that he was talking about Keraun. She saw a lot of cracks in the theory. "But Keraun is a *shekdan,*" she said. "He's banished from their society, and a champion grudge carrier. Why would he even *want* to help them?"

"I've always thought there was more to the *shekdan* than they let on," Lukati said darkly. "Mark my words, Anderson, the Hyrunians are up to something, and we need to watch them."

Erica nodded, but she felt a twinge of doubt. This sounded more like a conspiracy theory than anything else. She had nothing but respect for the admiral, but he was quite a bit older than her, his mind more seasoned than hers, certainly, but also more susceptible to paranoia. She agreed that the exchange with the Hyrunians was a bad idea, and handing over Nandro tech was out of the question. But the thought of Keraun betraying the Star Federation to the species that had branded him as nothing and cast him out had a bitter taste to it that Erica could not swallow. She did not tell Lukati that. When she signed off, she promised the admiral that she would watch Keraun to the best of her ability.

"Human and Nandro tech in exchange for whatever the Hyrunians deign to give us," she grumbled as she stepped away from her private communication terminal. "They'd better hand over some fucking *amazing* schematics."

Taking a deep breath, Erica ran through the tasks she still had to accomplish before she met with Lukati again to plan the assault on the Nandro base. Hyrunian demands aside, they had a galaxy to protect and war to win, and Erica was determined to see them victorious.

CHAPTER 36: PREDATORS

Sweat beaded on Lance's forehead. He was breathing hard, but he knew he could keep going. It was Lissa that he watched for signs of exhaustion. She was sweating too, dark patches showing on the gray, sleeveless shirt she wore, and her breaths were faster than his. She wasn't conditioned to this level of physical training yet, but her eyes were alert and she stepped lightly over the sparring mat.

Once more, Lance thought. Then he launched himself across the short distance between them.

Lissa danced sideways, turning into the defensive stance he'd shown her. She ducked past his first punch, threw her arm up to block the second, and landed a jab to his stomach. He pushed his breath out and stiffened his core muscles to absorb the blow, but the hit still drew a grunt from him.

Lissa jumped back, putting herself out of his reach again.

She was getting better.

Lance told her as much when he called an end to the sparring session.

She nodded in agreement, but looked like she was already thinking about water, fresh clothes, and some rest before they put into port.

Lance led the way off the mat, nearly losing his feet to Orion and Blade as they darted into the center of the room, eagerly taking over the cushioned training mat to jump and swipe at each other. Once they were safely away from the arkins, he took Lissa through a cool down and their stretching routine.

He was pleased with the progress she had made since the beginning of their training sessions a few months earlier. He could feel the strength building behind her attacks, but it was her defensive moves that showed the most progress. Lissa was eager to learn and had picked up the basics quickly, and now was honing them to perfection. Lance could still break her guard with combination attacks, but she was holding her own against him now.

With his breath and heartrate leveled out, Lance took a swig of water before passing the container to Lissa. She was frowning at the floor and did not notice the gesture. He had to say her name twice before she jerked back to awareness, and Lance realized that the distracted look in her eye ran deeper than physical exertion.

"You all right?" he asked.

Lissa took the water and swallowed a long draught. "I keep thinking about those agents," she murmured. "I don't know if I should have let them go."

Lance leaned back against the wall, studying her.

They had left Crythsia five days ago, and *Light Runner* had taken them far, far away from the planet. Lissa had been reserved throughout the journey, but it wasn't the dangerous quiet she had slipped into before plunging them into the uncharted system. When they weren't sleeping, Lissa had spent most of her time either keeping Blade and Orion entertained, or sitting with Lance. She spent a lot of her time lost in thoughtful silences. When they spoke, she'd kept the conversations centered on the arkins, their training sessions, where to put in to port, and which supplies they were running low on.

She had not told him what was on the datapad Haelin had given her.

He sensed that this was not the time to push.

"From personal experience," he finally said, "I can tell you that even if you'd taken the shot instead of sparing their lives, the moment would still be haunting you."

"I know," she said, "but I'm not sure which is worse."

Lance considered that for a long while before answering. "In time, you'll decide what the answer is." He took the water ration back from Lissa and swallowed another sip as he let his gaze slip to the arkins.

They swatted playfully at each other and ran in tight circles around the sparring mat. Lance noticed that, even when he managed to flank Blade, Orion avoided striking at her injured wing.

"For whatever it's worth," Lance said, focusing back on Lissa again, "I think you made the right choice."

Lissa frowned at the floor. "How do you know?"

"Because it was *your* choice."

She looked at him then, her golden brown skin shining under the harsh light of the training room. Her breathing had leveled out, and though she held herself straight and tense, there was total control in her silver eyes.

Lance quirked a bitter half-smile. "Remember, I made a similar choice years ago." His gaze flickered to Orion again, and he caught a glimpse of the rough patch of dark gray fur on the arkin's flank. "I chose differently."

"Do you regret it?"

He held her frank, open stare for a moment. "The moment will never leave me, but no. I don't regret it. And I think," he said, pushing off from the wall, "you won't, either."

Lissa nodded, but he could tell from the way she watched Blade and Orion spar that there was something else on her mind. "Come with me," she said, and led Lance out of the training room.

There was a lull in the arkins' movements, and then Lance heard them bounding after him and Lissa.

Lissa took them to her personal quarters. As the door slipped open and they stepped over the threshold, Lance couldn't help but notice the total austerity of Lissa's room.

Everything was packed neatly, ready to go at a moment's notice, including a few food and water rations she had taken at some unknown point and laid out in careful arrangements next to a decent-sized traveler's bag. The food was the plastic-tasting, long-term travel provisions Lance had always hated, but Lissa had set it aside, just in case. There wasn't a sense of abandonment to the supplies; it seemed to be done out of sheer habit of preparing for the worst to happen. In sharp contrast, her bunk was messy and unmade, though Lance supposed that bounty hunting and a life in constant motion rarely demanded military-grade bedmaking.

Lissa shifted the blanket on her bunk aside, pulling out a datapad. She activated it, swiped through a few commands, and handed Lance the machine.

"This is what the agent gave me," she murmured.

Lance found himself looking at a database of names and locations, some of which were paired with pictures of people. All were Neo-Andromedan, and some wore black collars around their throats. Most did not. Lance scrolled through the database, and bright, metallic eyes stared back at him.

With a start, Lance remembered the ship they had chased to Crythsia. It was a hunting ship, outfitted for fast travel, stealth, and proficiency in dogfights. Now he knew what—and who—that ship had been hunting.

"I think we killed Sekorvo," Lissa said.

Lance brought his gaze up and saw that she had started pacing in front of her bunk, taking slow, measured steps from one side to the other.

"You knew him?" he asked.

"I knew *of* him," Lissa said. "He was the one every uncollared Neo-Andromedan was taught to fear. The one that I thought was going to come after Aven and me." She paused and raised a hand to her neck, but stopped herself before she started scratching. "But he wasn't the one we were really afraid of."

"Rosonno," Lance said after a small pause.

She nodded and turned to face him. "Sekorvo hunted people for the Seventh Sun. For Rosonno." She pointed at the datapad in Lance's hand. "And those are the people he was going after next." Her breath caught in her throat, and Lance took a step towards her, but she waved him off. There was anger in her voice when she spoke again, but it was cold and controlled. "He was going to hunt them down, and give them to Rosonno so he could put them in Awakening machines."

Lance felt a shiver of disgust at the thought. He frowned down at the datapad. *So many people,* he thought. He scrolled a little further into the database, and came up short when he found a familiar face with copper-rose skin, brown hair, and white gold eyes. Next to Haelin was a picture of Vinterra.

He showed the images to Lissa, halting her mid-stride. She stared at the database for a long time.

"You're right," she said suddenly. "I don't regret letting them go."

Lance touched Haelin's picture, bringing up her full database entry. A large block of text appeared next to her image. It was written in a language that Lance had no hope of reading, but he had seen wanted lists before. "Do you think Haelin was trying to redeem herself in your eyes?" he asked as Lissa paced in front of him.

Lissa shook her head, but then she hesitated. "Maybe," she finally admitted, "but why the rest of it? Why not just part of the database, or a smaller part if this isn't the whole thing?" Her hand wandered up to her neck again, but she clenched her fingers into a fist before she could start tearing at her skin. "I don't know what to do with it."

Lance considered the database again, all the names and locations and lives it held within its entries. As he looked, a wild, dangerous, fiery idea came to him. He watched Lissa pace, and wondered if she would accept it. "If you could keep any of these people from an Awakening," he said, each word slow and careful, "would you?"

"Yes," she said immediately. Then she looked at him sharply. "Why?"

He put the datapad down before answering. "You're good at finding people," he said, holding her gaze. "I'm good at organizing them. Together, maybe—"

But Lissa had turned away.

Lance caught her arm. "Listen to me," he said, and waited for her to look at him again. He was surprised to see that there was more fear than anger in her eyes this time. "We could help these people. We could stop them from going anywhere near an Awakening machine, and maybe even keep them safe from the Star Federation." He loosened his grip on her arm, but she did not pull away. "We could give them a future."

With a hard sigh, Lissa looked away. "How, Lance?" She shook her head. "The time, the resources... How would you ever...?"

"We could figure it out," he said, and there was no doubt in his voice or in his mind. He shifted his hand down to hers, holding it gently. "It would take time, and a lot of work, but we could do it."

She met his gaze again, and there was nothing but fear in her eyes.

"I know you don't like to think about after," he said, closing his other hand over hers, "but give this a chance. Just think about it, and what you could do for them."

"And if I say no?" Lissa asked quietly.

"Then that's your choice," Lance said. "But give yourself the chance to *make* the choice before you say no."

Lissa wanted to be alone after that, but there was no hostility in the request. She simply wanted time and space to think, and Lance gave it to her.

When the time came to put into port, Lance knocked softly on Lissa's door. She emerged a moment later, but said nothing about the database. Lance did not ask.

They took *Light Runner* into port at a trading outpost on Zuftal, a popular but relaxed world with a wide range of biomes covering its surface. They chose a forest-based trading post, and Lissa joined Lance when he set out to restock their supplies. When they disembarked, Lance saw that *Light Runner* was one of the larger ships at the ground port, taking up almost a tenth of the landing pad, but they had managed to find a port with few visitors that day.

Lofty buzzes of conversations mingled on the breeze with the earthy smell of the nearby forest. White trees with fiery leaves scratched against a pale, bright sky. It was a beautiful day, and they lingered at the ground port, basking in the clean sunlight and fresh air.

When they were ready to head to the market, Lissa suggested letting the arkins out to stretch their legs and hunt the forest, but Lance wasn't completely at ease with sending Orion out on his own. He ultimately agreed when the gray arkin planted himself in the airlock and refused to let Lance close up the ship.

When he and Blade were let loose, Orion turned his face to the sun and spread his wings in the breeze. Then he sprinted after Blade and chased her off the landing pad.

Lance watched them go, an unsettled feeling snaking through his gut.

Lissa elbowed him in the side. "Orion's an apex predator, and he has Blade with him," she told him teasingly. "He'll be fine."

Lance allowed himself a smile, but stole one final look after the arkins before heading into the market with Lissa. He was glad to see her at ease, almost free of stress, but he knew that she had not made a decision about the database. Whenever they bartered for supplies, she kept her focus and helped Lance ensure a good deal, but more than once, he caught her staring absently beyond the various offerings of the market. Sudden sounds would catch her attention, but she was more relaxed than Lance had ever seen her in a crowd, and she allowed herself to be distracted.

It was mid-afternoon by the time they had finished their trades and purchases, and both the market and the ground port had grown busier. Lance and Lissa threaded their way through the crowds back to the port, *Light Runner*'s blue, black, and silver hull standing proudly above the dull grays of the other ships and the gaudy colors of the sky cruisers. As they closed the distance to their starship, Lance saw two men standing at *Light Runner*'s bow, looking up at the ship with interest.

He almost called out to them, but his steps dragged to a halt. He stared hard at the strangers. Lissa froze beside him, looking between him and the two men.

"What is it?" she asked, fully focused and wary again. In his peripherals, he registered her lifting her pistol half out of its holster.

Lance shook his head, frowning at the men.

There was something familiar about them. The way they both seemed to carve through space rather than occupy it, but Lance could not place it.

One was sandy-haired and narrow in frame, very sharp in his limbs. His pale hand gestured at *Light Runner* with quick, cutting motions, and even his fingers were locked into hard angles.

The other man had deep bronze skin, and his hair was shaved to reveal the full sweep of his skull. He was squarer in build than his companion, but the sharp, knife-like quality was in him, too. He looked as though he was built more for cleaving than slicing.

"Why do I know them?" Lance murmured.

Somewhere behind him, the airlock of a nearby starship hissed open, cutting through the quiet drone of the market. In that moment, realization slammed into Lance.

They were at Ametria.

Lance dropped his pack. He was reaching for his enerpulse pistol when the two men abruptly turned and waved to him and Lissa, their metallic eyes sparking in the sunlight.

Black collars glinted around their throats.

Before Lance could fire, Lissa cried out and pushed Lance off balance. He stumbled but kept his footing, turning just in time to see a very tall, dark-haired man slam into Lissa and drive her off her feet. She landed hard on her shoulder. Her pistol went flying out of her hand, but she managed to roll to her feet and take off at a desperate sprint. The tall man followed her.

Without pausing to think, Lance fired after them, and managed to clip the shoulder of the man, but after a stumble that should have been a collapse into howling pain, he kept going. Then enerpulse fire from the Seventh Sun agents in front of *Light Runner* drove Lance into cover behind a low shuttle. He heard civilians screaming and scrambling away from the ground port, and chaos broke out at the market beyond. Lance ignored the turmoil and peeked over the shuttle just in time to see that Lissa had led her pursuer off the landing pad. They disappeared into the tree line. Enerpulse shots slammed into the shuttle Lance hid behind, and he ducked down again.

One of the men called out in an unfamiliar language, and there was a lilting response from a female voice somewhere else on the ground port. They both laughed.

"Come out, little Star Fed," one of the men shouted in the Galactic Unified Voice.

Lance listened hard, trying to gauge his distance and position.

"Play with us!" the other man called, throwing off Lance's tracking of the first agent. "We'll make it faster than our friend will."

The female voice did not return.

"He's been waiting to see Arrilissa again," the first agent said, and Lance was startled to hear how close he'd come. "He's been waiting a long, long time."

"The waiting almost killed him," the other agent called, already in a new position.

"It almost killed *us*," the first agent returned. He sounded like he was just on the other side of the shuttle now. "Repeatedly."

Lance shuffled along the shuttle, towards the stern of the vessel. His pulse roared in his ears when he jumped up and fired, but the agent closest to him had moved away again, ducking behind a sky cruiser. Lance barely had time to register the agent as the one with bronze skin before he dove down again, narrowly avoiding the white-hot enerpulse shot from the pale-skinned agent who had moved back to *Light Runner*.

Between the two of them, they could keep Lance pinned for a long time.

Where's the third? Lance wondered, before more shouts and soft footsteps drew his attention again. The agents sounded like they were moving to flank him, and Lance crept back along the shuttle, moving towards the nose of the squat vessel.

Then Lance saw movement out of the corner of his eye. He snapped his head around, and found himself staring down the barrel of a pistol held by the female Seventh Sun agent. He had not heard her sneak around.

There was a rolling, quicksilver quality to her movements as the agent tilted her head and smirked at him. "Caught you," she purred. Her blue-flecked silver eyes laughed at him, and she rolled her finger onto the trigger of her pistol.

Lance braced himself, but before the shot came, there was a deep roar and a loud *whoosh* as Orion dropped out of the sky, knocking into the agent and sending her flying. She came down hard in the middle of the central aisle of the ground port. Orion quickly landed behind a ship on the other side of the port, keeping the vessel between himself and the two male agents.

Lance took his shot the moment the female agent pushed herself up, offering a clean target with minimal risk of hitting Orion. The enerpulse shot took her fully in the side of the head, and she fell still, lifeless.

There was a moment of silence before the other two agents screamed in outrage.

Lance dared not expose himself by trying to look around the shuttle again. Instead, he signaled to Orion, and set the arkin up to wait for the right moment to take flight again. Orion unfurled his wings and crouched, waiting.

A low sound near Lance caught his attention, and he looked around to see Blade huddled at the edge of the ground port, almost flat in the grass. Her ears were pressed down against her skull, and her pupils were dilated as her gaze darted from Lance to Orion, to the ships around the ground port, to the howling Seventh Sun agents, and back to Lance. Her claws sank deep into the dirt as she crept even closer to him, whining softly.

"Here, Blade," Lance whispered, waving the arkin to his side. "Come on."

Blade shivered, staring hard at him.

No, not at him. At the empty space next to him.

Lance reached toward the black arkin, but before he could blink, she shot to her feet. "Blade, no!" Lance shouted, lunging for the arkin, but she took off running.

Without pausing to think, Lance jumped up and fired at the Seventh Sun agents, missing them completely. He shot wildly, making it impossible for him to fully lock on to a target, but all that mattered was that he threw them off balance and kept their focus off of the black arkin. He couldn't let them shoot Blade down.

Blade ran for the tree line, unfolding her wings. She beat them hard and leapt into the air. She fell, leapt again, staggered, strained to keep the rhythm, and then, against all of Lance's expectations, managed to settle into an unstable flight that took her over the tops of the trees.

Orion bellowed after her. Lance dropped behind the shuttle again looked across the way at Orion. He thought he saw a triumphant gleam in the arkin's yellow eyes.

Lance began to hope against reason that Lissa would be the one to return from the forest.

"Come back to us," he whispered.

Then he jumped up and fired another shot.

CHAPTER 37: OMEGA

Undergrowth tore at Lissa's boots as she sprinted through the forest. Light filtered in through the thin canopy overhead. Fueled by pure terror, Lissa leaped over fallen trunks and low bushes, never once daring to look back.

She didn't need to. She could hear the Phantom following her, tracing her path even as the enerpulse wound from Lance finally took its toll.

But even through her fear and the pounding of her own heart—loud, too loud—she heard the erratic, lumbering quality to the Phantom's movements. He crashed through obstacles more than he jumped or dodged them, and the sounds he made...

Like an animal.

An exhausted, half-starved animal.

Lissa heard the low growls and grunts from the Phantom, and she suddenly wasn't certain if it was just him on her trail, or if his arkin Jet was there, too. The Phantom was always silent, completely submerged in the Light. Jet was massive and loud and impossible to lose.

But the one pursuing her was too agile to be that arkin. She did not know where Jet was, but if the Phantom had fallen as far into the Light as she suspected he had, he may have killed the arkin to stave off some of his bloodlust.

The thought pushed her to run faster.

Lissa's breath raged in her own ears, washing out the sounds of the chase and forcing her to focus on the path ahead of her. She wove through trees and bushes, diving for small openings that she knew the Phantom would have trouble with, but he always stayed close.

Until, suddenly, he was gone.

Lissa did not know when he vanished, but she felt herself slowing down, unable to keep up the breakneck pace any longer. Her heart hammered in her chest and she gasped for breath, but even through that, she heard the silence behind her.

She came up short, panting hard, and looked around frantically.

Forest stretched all around her, pale light slanting through the white trees. Everything was silent. Nothing moved.

Another spike of fear hit her, threatening to pierce her heart, but Lissa forced it down.

This was what a hunter relishing the chase did. They pulled back, and fed on the challenge, or they ran ahead, and set a trap, and waited. Anything to let them feed on their prey's fear.

Lissa whipped her head around, searching everywhere, even the thin branches overhead, but she saw no one. Leaves crunched under her feet as she moved, and she forced herself to be still, afraid she would give away her position.

If she had shaken the pursuit at all.

Desperate for some cover behind her, Lissa stepped to a tree, wincing at every crackle of the fallen leaves beneath her boots. She pressed up against the trunk, feeling the roughness of the bark bite through her clothes.

Listen, she told herself. *Wait and listen.*

She pushed back the panic and closed her eyes, though try as she might, she could not slow her shallow breathing. She settled for filling her lungs as quietly as she could, and tried to let the sounds of the forest wash over her.

There was nothing. No creatures scurrying or wings flapping, not even a breeze playing through the leaves. The world held its breath, the way animals did when predators drew close.

Too close.

Lissa's pulse roared in her ears. When she cracked open her eyes, the world had grown brighter, the shadows harsher. Light burned her sight and her heart, and the voices crept back in.

Welcome to the—

"No," Lissa whispered. She shut her eyes again, blocking out the light. Scared as she was, she would not go back into an Awakening.

Keep control.

Lissa focused on the rough resistance of the white tree bark against her back and the solid feel of the ground beneath her feet, broken by the twisting network of tree roots. She held her breath and listened.

Finally, there was a low keening sound, and unsteady wingbeats.

Lissa opened her eyes to a cool, normal world, and looked up.

Some distance to her left, an arkin was circling over the treetops, its wings beating erratically. It looked totally unstable, as though it had not flown in a long time. It circled close, dark against the bright sky, and loosed another low keen as it wobbled along its path. It was almost overhead now. With a quick jerk of its body, the arkin evened out into a steadier glide, then beat its wings again as it tried to gain height, losing the smoother flight pattern almost immediately, but that moment was all Lissa needed to recognize the arkin.

"Blade?" she whispered, not quite trusting her own eyes.

The arkin keened again and began to move away.

"BLADE!" Lissa screamed.

She saw the arkin jolt again.

Then movement flashed in the corner of her eye and Lissa dove for the ground. Light gleamed off of a long knife blade as the Phantom's arm plunged into the space where Lissa's throat had been a moment earlier.

She landed and rolled but misjudged her own momentum, and ended up scrabbling backwards on her hands and feet as the Phantom came at her again. His golden eyes burned hungrily into hers, standing out so severely against the dark circles around them that Lissa almost overlooked the scar she'd given him years ago. It ran long, thin, and white down the side of his face, from the corner of his eye to his chin. Dark hair hung greasy and unwashed around his face, exacerbating the hollowness of his cheeks and the sharp angles of his bones.

She did not remember him being this thin, but she felt her heart squeeze tight as she took in his haunted stare.

He shifted his grip on the knife, and lunged for her.

Lissa rolled and shot to her feet, sliding into the stance Lance had taught her. The first blow almost sank the knife into her gut, but she managed to twist away and the blade only skimmed her shirt. The flick and pull of the knife she was able to block, but the Phantom's other arm came around to strike the side of her head, and then the knife sliced across the top of her arm.

With a gasp of pain, Lissa leapt away, trying to ignore the warm, red trickle that now moved down her arm. She had no time to see if it was a deep wound or not, but it stung enough to bring tears to her eyes. She blinked them away, shifting back into the defensive stance.

The Phantom circled her, bent spine curving him into a beastly shape. He kept his eyes on her as he brought the red edge of the knife up close to his nose, and inhaled deeply.

As he smelled Lissa's blood, something shifted behind his eyes. It solidified, became more controlled.

That terrified Lissa more than his closeness to starvation. Her feet moved of their own accord, bringing her a few steps further away from the Phantom, and she felt herself beginning to turn as she made to run again. She stumbled on a protruding root, and fell back against another tree.

The Phantom jumped after her, and it was all she could do to block the next knife swing. It came faster this time, and though Lissa drove her hand down and to the side, as Lance had taught her, she did not move her leg out of the way fast enough. The knife bit through her leg, slicing deep across her thigh before embedding itself in the trunk of the tree.

Screaming with pain, Lissa forced her hand to close around the Phantom's wrist. She tried to twist his arm off the knife hilt, but he let go willingly. Both hands came up to wrap around her throat, and Lissa felt her feet leave the ground. She kicked at the Phantom with her uninjured leg, but he pressed her against the tree and drove his knee into the deep cut on her thigh.

Lissa screamed again, or tried to. The Phantom's fingers were tight around her throat, and she could not find the air as the world darkened around her, so unlike an Awakening, and the pain, so much pain…

She scratched weakly at the Phantom's arms, gasping for air. His eyes burned into hers even as her vision faded, and she felt a muted sense of rage that his hungry smile was the last thing she would see. She couldn't turn her head, but she slipped her eyes up and away, which seemed to anger him and make him squeeze her throat harder.

But it was enough for her to see the black arkin tuck her wings and drop into a familiar dive.

With a roar, a crash, and a shower of branches, Blade ripped through the canopy and slammed into the Phantom.

The momentum knocked him off his feet and sent Lissa sprawling. She landed on the forest floor, knobby tree roots bruising her ribs and shoulder, but she only felt relief as she sucked in a huge gulp of air. Coughing as tears streamed down her face, Lissa rolled gingerly on to her stomach, lifting her head as she watched Blade struggle with the Phantom.

The hunter was on his back, Blade on top of him. The arkin had her claws hooked into his chest and had managed to sink her teeth into his arm, but even in his half-starved state, the Phantom was stronger than her. He got his feet under her, and kicked Blade off of him. She yipped as she was thrown back, but she bounced off the forest floor and kicked up a spray of dirt and dead leaves as she lunged at the Phantom again. He lashed out at her with his fist this time, hitting her beneath the jaw and stunning her. Then he twisted and brought his foot around in a kick that sent Blade sprawling.

Lissa felt the spark of anger again, and pushed herself to her hands and knees. The cuts on her arm and leg screamed in protest, but she grit her teeth against the pain and crawled back to the tree. Back to the knife that was embedded in the trunk. She closed her hand around the hilt and tugged, but it did not move.

There was a howl behind her, and Lissa looked over her shoulder to see the Phantom kick Blade again. He aimed for her wing. The one that had been broken.

With a snarl, Lissa gripped the knife harder, shifted her position, and shouted at the Phantom. He whipped around to stare at her, Blade forgotten as he zeroed in on Lissa's heartbeat again. He gave a low growl, then ran at Lissa. He launched at her when he was still a few paces away, flying through the air and reaching for her throat.

Lissa clenched her fist, twisted as hard as she could, and ripped the knife free.

The Phantom hit her hard, and then the tree trunk scraped Lissa's back as his momentum drove her off the ground again. The bark snagged the fabric of her shirt and the skin beneath, slowing her down and drawing an agonized gasp from her. They landed, and the knife wrenched out of Lissa's hand as the Phantom overshot her.

For a stunned moment, they both lay still. Then the Phantom shifted, pushed himself up, and dropped again.

Lissa shakily rose into a sitting position, wincing at every new scrape along her back. The deep cut on her leg openly wept blood, but at a glance, she knew that the knife had missed her femoral artery.

Lucky, she thought numbly. *So lucky.*

She looked at the Phantom, and saw that he was still trying to push himself up. His eyes, hungry as they always were, held a note of bewilderment now. A dark pool of red was steadily growing under his chest, seeping into the dirt and staining the dead, fallen leaves.

Lissa made to crawl away, but froze when she saw the knife on the ground near the Phantom's knees, the long blade wet with shining red. She reached over and grabbed it.

The Phantom caught her movement, and he twisted around, trying to catch her.

Lissa pulled away. She shuffled back as fast as her injuries would allow, sliding over roots as she went.

The Phantom tried to follow her. As he twisted toward her, she finally saw the large gash in his chest, ripping across his breast where the knife had gone in. Blood pumped steadily out of the wound, soaking his clothes and the dirt beneath him. But it was his eyes that Lissa watched.

As the life drained out of the Phantom, the Awakening light began to fade from his eyes. They darkened to a deep, burnished gold. The hunger died, replaced by confusion, fear, and, shockingly, relief. His mouth moved, the animalistic grunts slowly giving way to half-formed words.

"I—i—it—"

His hand crept forward, reaching for Lissa's ankle, but she drew away again and his fingers closed around air.

"It's dark," he finally breathed.

The last traces of the Awakening light drained from him. And for a moment, his eyes went wide, clear and gold and peaceful. Then he collapsed in the dirt, and his life fled.

Lissa stared at the body for a long time. Then everything caught up to her at once, and she was suddenly scrambling away from him, the knife abandoned on the ground between his motionless form and her frantic retreat. Lissa's whole body screamed in pain and tears fell freely down her face as bile rose in her throat. Coughing and gasping, she bent over and waited for the nausea to pass, but panic soaked the places it left behind.

A low keen sounded behind Lissa, and she jerked her head up to find Blade creeping towards her.

With a cry, Lissa lunged for the arkin, and Blade shot forward to meet her. Lissa sat with her arms wrapped around the arkin's neck, shaking and sobbing as the arkin whined softly in her ear and gently rubbed her cheek against Lissa's head. The arkin's fur was soft and familiar, her breath warm against Lissa's skin, and Lissa found herself slowly regaining control as she focused on Blade's smooth breathing.

When Lissa managed to take a few deep, steady breaths, Blade lightly disentangled herself. She dropped her head to sniff at the cut on Lissa's thigh, ears pressed back against her skull. With another whine, Blade licked at the blood, trying to clean the cut.

Lissa stilled the arkin with a hand against her muzzle. She gently stroked Blade's head, taking note of the small swelling that was already forming over one of her amber eyes. Lissa felt another surge of anger when she saw that, but she forced herself to stay calm.

She felt along her belt, and found the large pocket with the medicinal supplies.

There wasn't enough to treat all of their injuries, but Lissa was able to clean the worst of her leg wound and apply a thick bandage to each of her cuts. For Blade, she had a stimulant shot to help keep the swelling down until they could get back to *Light Runner* and properly treat her wounds.

Light Runner.

And Lance...

With a deep breath to brace herself, Lissa pushed to her feet. A wave of dizziness washed over her, but Blade pressed against her hip to steady her and Lissa's head cleared soon enough. Lissa limped back towards the Phantom's body, stopping when she reached the knife. She scooped it up and stood looking down at the face that had lived in her nightmares for so long.

One of the faces, she corrected, now locked out of the Light forever, but not before it had destroyed him.

And it angered her all over again.

Lissa forced herself to look at the Phantom's face, to sear into her mind that he was really gone. That he could not hunt her anymore.

She found herself focusing on his blank, staring eyes.

It seemed unfair that someone who had haunted her for so long, who had fed on her fear and her pain, should find peace at the end.

Lissa clenched the knife in her hand, bringing her arm up and aiming the blade at the Phantom. Her arm shook as she prepared to plunge the knife into him, somewhere, anywhere that would ruin his unearned tranquility.

She held the knife over him for a long time before slowly lowering her arm to her side.

There had been no peace in the Phantom's life, she knew. He had been a Seventh Sun hunter, set upon irredeemable targets to feed his bloodlust before the Light destroyed him completely. He had a handling team and a leader who had seen him as an asset, but nothing more. Even his arkin had been an angry, broken-willed beast. Lissa had seen that the very first time she had met them. There had been no companionship. And with the way the Awakening had starved the Phantom by the end of his life, she knew beyond doubt that Jet was no longer alive. That arkin had probably lost his life in a desperate, wild fight as the Phantom attempted to satiate the hunger, but Awakenings like that could not be satisfied. They claimed everything, including the Neo-Andromedans who burned in them.

Reflecting, Lissa realized that she had never even known the Phantom's name. His Awakening had robbed him even of that.

That could have been her, if things had gone differently.

Lissa shifted her grip on the knife, and turned away from the Phantom for the last time. She limped back to Blade, and let her free hand rest against the back of the arkin's neck. Blade moved slowly as she traced a path through the trees, letting Lissa keep pace.

Dully, Lissa became aware of the sounds of the forest, picking up where they always should have been: small, skittering creatures; tiny wingbeats; distant cries and chirps. The forest was heavy with life, and Lissa and Blade moved through it all.

Lissa turned her face up to the sky, and breathed in the fresh, clean air. She suddenly remembered Blade's dark silhouette against the bright sky, wobbling and unstable, but airborne. "You flew," Lissa murmured.

Blade made a soft, low noise in response, tossing her head back to look at Lissa with her bright, amber eyes.

As they continued on, a spark inside of Lissa flared up, something she had not felt in a long time. But she couldn't fully embrace it.

Not yet.

Staying close to Blade, the two of them picked their way through the trees, both injured and a little broken, but whole.

CHAPTER 38: MESSAGE

Lance was locked in a stalemate with the two male Seventh Sun agents. He had managed to clip one of them, get Orion back up in the sky, and move himself to a new position, but no one had been able to gain the upper hand since then. Lance faced a storm of enerpulse fire every time he moved anywhere near the edge of the small starship he now sheltered behind, but with Orion circling overhead, ready to dive at a moment's notice, the two agents were forced to stay close to each other and watch their partner. As long as they stayed together, Orion could not dive without one of them firing at him. The other kept a close watch over Lance.

Leaning back against the ship, Lance cast a hard look back at the market. Based on how fast the stalls had emptied and how long it had been without any sign of local Zuftali law enforcement, Lance suspected that he and Lissa had managed to choose a not completely legal market for their patronage. It was a mixed blessing. On one hand, there was no risk of arrest if he scraped through his battle with the Seventh Sun agents. On the other, he and Orion were on their own.

Lance looked at the forest again, straining to see any sign of movement through the white trees. He thought he saw the flicker of a shadow, but couldn't be certain that his mind wasn't playing tricks on him.

Squinting up at the bright sky, Lance picked out Orion's circling form. The arkin was just high enough to be out of range of most enerpulse shots, but low enough to catch a signal from Lance, as long as it involved a lot of frantic arm waving.

Lance looked back at the forest again, back to where he'd seen the flicker in the light, and he jumped when he saw the faces staring back at him from the very edge of the tree line. A dizzying wave of relief came when he recognized Lissa and Blade, but it was short-lived. Blade had a nasty swelling over one of her eyes, and Lissa's golden brown skin was blanched with pain. Lance looked harder, and saw dark stains on Lissa's clothing.

Blood, he realized. *A lot of it.*

Even with the distance between them, Lance could see that Lissa was breathing hard, and leaning against a tree for support. But there was a hard set to her jaw as she glared at the two Seventh Sun agents who had him and Orion pinned. She turned back to Lance and gestured to him.

He nodded his understanding.

Lance shifted toward her, careful to keep his head ducked below the tiny starship. He locked the safety on his pistol and shifted his grip on the weapon. He brought his arm back, braced himself, then shot to his feet and hurled the pistol towards the tree line. He used the momentum to dive to the ground, just managing to dodge the searing heat of an enerpulse shot. He landed beyond the nose of the starship, exposed, but he heard one of the Seventh Sun agents shout in confusion. As Lance scrambled back behind cover, he saw enerpulse shots streaking after his spinning pistol, trying and failing to hit the weapon as it arced toward the trees.

Blade did not hesitate. She jumped out of the forest, closed her jaws around the pistol, twisted even before she hit the ground, and sprang back to safety. Every enerpulse shot missed her comfortably.

There were more confused, angry shouts from the agents, but Lance kept his attention on Lissa as she took the pistol from the arkin's jaws and quickly set off through the trees. She was limping badly, but she moved fast and Lance soon lost track of her and Blade as they crouched low and flickered through the undergrowth.

One, Lance thought, just before the shot cracked out and one of the agents gave a strangled scream of pain.

Two.

The second agent did not scream, but Lance heard him fall.

Peering over the edge of the starship, Lance saw that the bronze-skinned agent was still standing, but he clutched at his arm and moaned in pain. The agent's hand had been blackened by Lissa's enerpulse shot, the fingers locked in a disfigured claw. He had dropped his enerpulse pistol, but even as he sank to his knees, he clenched his teeth against the pain of his wound and made no move to touch the weapon. He sank forward until his forehead was pressed against the landing pad, howling in agony.

Lance moved out from behind the tiny starship. He ran to where Lissa's pistol had fallen when the Phantom tackled her. He snatched it up before jogging toward the remaining Seventh Sun agent. He took note of the pale-skinned one on the ground, of the preciseness of the shot that had taken him fully in the throat and left him staring up at the sky, his red-splashed gunmetal eyes still and lifeless. Lance knew that Lissa had purposefully aimed to keep the last agent alive.

He could not fathom why.

He looked around for her, and slowed to a halt when he saw her crossing the small stretch of yellow grass that separated the ground port from the tree line.

She moved slowly, taking her time, though even with the bad wound on her leg, Lance doubted that it was from pain. She kept her eyes fixed on the Seventh Sun agent as she advanced, her jaw set and nothing but anger in her eyes.

The agent rocked back, raising his head and catching sight of Lissa. He whimpered with discomfort, but he registered the danger and twisted around, reaching for his enerpulse pistol.

"Leave it!" Lance snapped, focusing the pistol in his own hands on the agent.

The agent froze, staring at him through streaming copper eyes. Lance stepped forward and kicked the fallen pistol away before moving back out of reach.

Orion swooped down out of the sky and landed a few paces away, lips curled into a snarl as he crept forward.

The Seventh Sun agent rose to his feet when he saw the gray arkin. Gasping with pain, he stumbled away from Orion. He spun around to find himself face-to-face with Lissa.

They stared at each other for a long, silent moment before Lissa raised her hand. Lance shifted uneasily when he saw that she held a knife. He knew she had not been carrying one when she'd gone into the forest, at least not one that size. The knife was long and dark with drying blood, and for a moment, Lance worried she would use it against the agent.

That was not like her.

Lance's eyes flickered to the agent's blackened arm and he tightened his grip on his enerpulse pistol.

But Lissa only held the knife up in front of the agent with the tip of the blade pointing to the ground, giving the agent a few moments to absorb the details before she dropped it. The knife struck the surface of the landing pad with a metallic clatter, and the agent stared at it hard. His breathing quickened, as though he recognized the knife.

"Tell Rosonno," Lissa said, and the agent's eyes snapped back to her face, "that I am coming for him."

The agent swallowed hard, then edged away from her. Blade snarled at him from Lissa's side, and he stepped more quickly. He barely looked at Lance as he rushed past.

Lance stepped to Lissa's side, and she surprised him when she reached for his arm and leaned heavily against him. She hissed with pain as she shifted her weight off of her injured leg.

They needed to clean and rebandage that wound quickly, but Lance couldn't help glancing at the retreating Seventh Sun agent.

The agent stumbled past the vessels of the ground port, never once looking back. He made his way to a white-and-gray starship that had the off-balance elements Lance recognized in a Neo-Andromedan ship trying to camouflage: an airlock that was off-center; proportions tipping toward asymmetry; and a flatter, stockier hull than the sleek models humans had designed within that starship class. It was all obvious, once Lance actually looked at the ship.

He should have paid closer attention to the ships at the port, he reflected.

"You're really letting him go?" Lance asked, watching the Seventh Sun agent flee.

Lissa hesitated long enough to look at the dead, pale-skinned agent a few paces away. "We didn't come here to hunt, and I've taken enough lives today."

Lance frowned as he entered the security codes to open *Light Runner*'s airlock. The seal broke and the airlock hissed open, but he hung back.

"And what about that warning to Rosonno?" he murmured.

Lissa limped inside ahead of him, Blade at her side. "I'll explain," she promised. "But for now, we need to leave."

CHAPTER 39: REMEDY

Lissa found herself grateful to Lance for running back for the packs of supplies they had dropped when they had been ambushed by the Phantom and his handling team. *Light Runner* had accumulated a decent store of medical supplies over the course of their journeys, but in the market on Zuftal, Lance had found a gel that soothed pain from burns and cuts alike, along with a range of immunity boosters. Down in the storage hold, resting on the floor with medical supplies spread around her, Lissa cleaned the swelling over Blade's eye and gently smeared some of the gel on the wound before selecting one of the milder immunity boosters and giving Blade the shot.

The arkin hissed and nipped lightly at Lissa's fingers, then whined softly when she smelled the dried blood on Lissa's arm.

Blade had faired far better than Lissa in the fight against the Phantom. Her bad wing was tender after the uneven flight, and she had a few tender spots on her side and under her jaw, but the swelling over her eye was the worst of it. Now that Lissa had taken care of that, she turned to her own injuries with a grimace.

The bandaging around her thigh was soaked with red, and her leg throbbed agonizingly as she peeled the sticky gauze away. Fresh blood welled up along the ragged line of the wound, and Blade whined again when she caught the scent.

Lissa grabbed a small pair of scissors and cut away her bloodstained pantleg. She began to clean the wound more thoroughly, gasping at the sting of the antiseptic. When she'd cleared most of the dried blood and sterilized as much of the cut as she could stand, she looked around for the tool that would knit the torn flesh back together. She groaned when she realized she had forgotten to take it off the shelf.

Bracing herself, Lissa began to push to her feet, but her leg was stiff and threw her off balance. Her vision swam as the dizziness from blood loss caught up with her. Panting, she sank back to the floor.

Lance's voice came from the entrance of the storeroom. "Want some help?"

Lissa closed her eyes, taking refuge in the dimness behind her eyelids, and nodded.

She listened to his footsteps as he crossed the narrow interior of the storeroom, halting in front of the shelf that held the protective cases of the medical tools. There was a soft *clnk* as he opened the mending tool's case, then a shuffle and low murmuring as Lance displaced Blade. Lissa felt the air stir as the arkin jumped over her outstretched legs, and then a warm muzzle nudged its way under Lissa's hand. Lissa rubbed Blade behind one of her long ears, feeling herself relax as Lance knelt next to her.

She heard him move some of the supplies around, but then, instead of the intense but bearable burn of the mending tool that she was expecting, Lissa felt another sharp, hot sting in her leg.

Her eyes flew open and she gasped at the fresh pain, her spine rigid. "I already cleaned it!" she snapped at Lance.

"Not well enough," he returned calmly, liberally applying antiseptic to the wound.

Lissa groaned again, but she balled her hands into fists, bit back her complaints, and let Lance work. A light sweat had broken out on her forehead by the time he finished, and she felt lightheaded all over again, but now that it was clean, the wound looked better than Lissa had initially thought. It would heal, and her leg would return to full strength, but the burn of the mending tool was almost a relief after Lance's heavy-handed nursing.

Lance slowly ran the machine over her leg, watching the readout closely as the thin, white device hummed along. Lissa's skin felt taught and hot under the mending tool. She pressed her head against the wall and took several deep breaths as the machine slid down her leg, leaving a cold, itching sensation in its wake. She fought back the urge to scratch. When Lance finished, Lissa inspected the jagged line of pale, new flesh across the top of her thigh. It stood out against her golden brown skin, but the pain had already lessened. With a sigh of relief, Lissa settled back against the wall again.

Lance took her arm and gently unwrapped the bandage from the second cut. He inspected the wound briefly before checking the supply levels left in the mending tool. "This will heal well enough on its own," he said. "You okay if we let it?" When she nodded, he rose to his feet and replaced the mending tool in its case.

"How long until we come out of the overdrive sprint?" Lissa asked, reaching for the antiseptic before Lance could drench her arm with the terrible stuff.

They had agreed to use *Light Runner*'s overdrive feature to erase their energy signature from the trackable spectrum, but it burned through the ship's power cells at a dangerous rate. With their signature already tracked once, they had not felt as though they'd had another choice.

"We're already out," Lance said, sinking down beside her again. "I brought the speed back down after we cleared the system."

"Is that far enough?"

"For now," he said, helping her clean the cut on her arm. "It's enough to throw the signature without burning too much power." At her skeptical look, he said, "We can run another sprint later if we need to." After a mild struggle over the antiseptic, he dabbed at the wound in silence for a while before asking, "Why did you tell that agent to warn Rosonno?"

Lissa had been expecting the question, but she let a few beats slip by before answering. "I want him to feel what it's like. How it feels to be hunted."

Lance's hand tightened on her arm, but not enough to be painful. "That's a dangerous path, Lissa." Her name was soft in his voice, but she heard the catch of wariness. "And I've already seen what a revenge hunt does to you."

Lissa watched him closely as he wrapped a clean bandage around her arm, the tips of his fingers grazing lightly against her skin.

"I need him to understand," she murmured, focusing on Lance's touch rather than the pain of the cut.

Lance secured the end of the bandage with a small clip before meeting her eye. His gaze was intense, almost challenging. "Why?"

Lissa looked back at him calmly. "If I find him, it will be because he wasn't afraid to be found. But if I can't find him, or he gets away, I need him to understand what it's like to always be afraid. I need him to know what that does to people." She shifted, drawing herself up a little straighter. "I need him to not want to come back."

Lance's eyes were dark under the stark light of the supply room. "What will this do for you?"

She shook her head. "It's not just for me. Not anymore."

Lance frowned but waited for her to continue.

"The Seventh Sun has done terrible things," Lissa said, "but the worst has always been the forced Awakenings." She hesitated, holding Lance's gaze. "You might not agree."

His lips pressed into a hard line, but something behind his eyes softened. She saw the memory of the Ametria ambush pass through his mind, all those soldiers dead at the hands of the Seventh Sun. But then that memory was eclipsed with something else, and his green eyes burned into hers. "Actually," he said, his voice low, "I do."

After a moment, Lissa shifted her arm, bringing her hand around to rest on top of his. "I killed the Phantom in the white forest," she said. "I watched the light drain from his eyes."

Lance turned his hand, lightly threading his fingers through hers. "I know you did," he said, his gaze flickering over the enhanced scar tissue on her thigh.

She shook her head before he could continue. "No, I saw the *Light* drain from him. He came out of his Awakening. He was at peace when he died." Her throat suddenly felt tight, but she pressed on. "I kept thinking that it wasn't fair that he died at peace, not after all the fear and wild killing he fed on, but I know what he felt. I know the hunger that drove him to that." She swallowed past the hard lump in her throat. "And I know that, in the end, it doesn't come back to him. It all comes back to Rosonno."

She paused, waiting for Lance to disagree, but he only waited for her to speak again.

"That database full of people," Lissa continued. "They're all in there because Rosonno marked them fit for Awakenings. He wanted to drown them in the Light, and kill them if they couldn't fit his purpose. I can't let him do that. Not to me or anyone else. Never again.

"But if he gets away, there needs to be a chance that he'll finally understand what he's done to people. I don't know how many others he's fed to the Awakening machines, but I know it wasn't just me. I need him to understand what it's like to fear something more than death. If he escapes, I need him to be too afraid to ever come back."

Lance considered this for a long time. But he slowly nodded in agreement before asking, "And what if you find him, and he doesn't get away?"

Lissa tightened her grip on Lance's fingers, but he did not flinch or pull away. "Then I do what I need to, to give those people in the database a future."

Lance searched her face, looking for any cracks in her resolve. There were none to find. "Just don't lose yourself in this, Lissa," he finally whispered.

"I won't," she promised. She held his gaze steadily. "It's my future on the line, too. And I'm finally thinking about what will happen after."

Lance leaned forward until his forehead gently pressed against Lissa's. "I'm glad."

She gave a small nod of agreement, leaning in to strengthen the point of contact between them.

CHAPTER 40: RIFT

Rosonno was left to boil in his own fear and paranoia for days before Niradessa and Zeran finally contacted him. By that point, he was seething with anger over the loss of both Sekorvo and the Awakened Syreth, and he was at his breaking point.

He never considered contacting the other two First Lit. If he wanted to step into a leadership position, he needed them to come to him. It infuriated him that they took so long. By the time they did reach out, any hope of support he had from Niradessa and Zeran evaporated the moment he accepted their transmission. Neither of them even attempted to initiate the proper greeting.

"Why is Sekorvo dead?" Niradessa demanded before Rosonno had fully registered that she and Zeran were standing together at the same communication terminal.

That was unusual for them. They both resided permanently on the main base, evenly dividing up the massive amount of work that went into overseeing resource allocation to the rest of the Seventh Sun's population. They handled it well, and Niradessa even took on morale boosting and information control while Zeran headed the population regulation and genetic sequencing departments. They often interacted with each other, but they kept their distance and, as far as Rosonno knew, rarely met face-to-face.

That they were together now set him even further on edge. He knew they'd been talking about him.

"Why did it take you so long to ask this question?" Rosonno shot back at Niradessa.

Her silver-flecked eyes glared poison at him, but it was Zeran who offered a counter. "You did not reach out. We waited. You were silent."

Rosonno opened his mouth to respond, but the words died under the echo of Arrevessa's parting words in his skull. He clenched his jaw and said nothing.

"And still he is silent," Zeran snarled, turning away. Their shared communication terminal was cramped with the two of them in there, and Zeran had to contort his way past Niradessa. She did not move as his limbs brushed against her hip and shoulder. "He clearly has nothing to say that I want to hear," Zeran quipped as he went. "I am done."

"I'm not," Niradessa said. Her voice was low, and even with the distortion of a long-distance transmission, Rosonno could hear the menace in her tone.

Zeran grunted and flickered out of sight as he stepped out of the capture zone of the terminal.

May your death be dark and cold, Zeran, Rosonno thought. He focused back on Niradessa while he waited for her to speak again. For as long as he'd known her, she itched to fill long silences, and he would not have to wait much at all for her to get to the point of their conversation. Her anger burned brighter than the violent death of a star.

Moments after Zeran was gone, Niradessa tried to rip into Rosonno again. This time, she succeeded, and Rosonno went cold at her words.

"We know what Vessa said to you before she disappeared," she said.

"She was wrong and abandoned us to—" he clamped his mouth shut when he saw the flash of triumph in Niradessa's eyes.

The cold under Rosonno's skin changed to a burning flush.

He'd forgotten that Niradessa played with minds when she wasn't distributing resources. She'd made a lucky guess, but he had confirmed it for her without even pausing to think.

Niradessa straightened and laced her fingers together as she regarded Rosonno. "So you do know why she left. You know and you haven't said a word to us." Her speckled eyes hardened. "Did you know before Tyrath died? Did you let her—"

"Tyrath made her own choice!" Rosonno snapped. "She stayed on that planet when she knew the Star Feds were bearing down on her."

"She stayed because she could not evacuate everyone," Niradessa replied calmly. "The deserters took too many ships, but she stayed to give others a chance."

"How do you know that?" he demanded.

Niradessa frowned and cocked her head, as though faced with a puzzle so simple she did not want to deign to solve it. "She told us, as soon as she realized the Star Federation was approaching the system. She wanted to know if we could provide support for the base, or more evac ships from our network. We sent what we could, but they were too far from the Daraaxi system to be of any help." There was no trace of sadness in her voice. In her eyes, Niradessa had done all that she could to help her fellow First Lit, and she had nothing to be ashamed of.

Rosonno felt sick.

Tyrath had asked for help. She had asked, and the Seventh Sun had failed her. But after everything, she had not asked for *him*.

Niradessa's eyes lit up as she reached the same conclusion. "Tyrath knew better than to look to you," she said. Now her voice was slow and deliberate, cutting him deeper with each word. "She knew you'd never give her the help she needed. She knew—"

"Enough!" Rosonno shouted.

Niradessa flinched in surprise, but her lips curved into a wicked smile. "You never could read her as well as you pretended to."

"Darkness take you," Rosonno muttered.

He cut the transmission before Niradessa could reply.

Rosonno's hands shook with rage as he stepped away from the communication terminal. He half-expected the incoming transmission alert to flare up again, signaling that Niradessa wasn't willing to cut him out of the First Lit just yet, but the terminal remained dark.

He sank down on the edge of his cot, taking deep breaths as he tried to calm himself. He told himself that he'd had every intention of telling Niradessa and Zeran about losing Syreth and the message Lissa had left with the sole surviving member of his handling team. He'd meant to advise them to fortify the main base, possibly even evacuate it.

She'd told Syreth's surviving handler that she was coming for them.

He leveled out his breathing, and with a spike of clarity, he knew that Niradessa and Zeran would have laughed at him.

The main base was impossible to find. Lissa may have been born there under Zeran's population directions, and spent her early life wandering the stronghold's halls, but that was a long time ago, and she had no hope of finding her way back.

Niradessa and Zeran were safe.

It was Rosonno who was in trouble.

But first Lissa had to find him.

Well, then, Rosonno thought, standing up and brushing his clothing smooth, *let her come.*

He stepped to his desk and lifted the datapad that now occupied a permanent place in an upper corner. This was the one that held information on a number of threats to the Seventh Sun, including Lissa. He brought up her information and sat down to study it with fresh eyes. It had been awhile, and Rosonno made himself take it piece by piece, editing his own notes until he had erased the frenzied paranoia that had seeped into the data, until he was left with simple, rational paragraphs.

He had to remember that Lissa was acting out of fear. They'd backed her into a corner, and now she was trying to fight her way out. But more than anything, more than any*one*, she was afraid of Rosonno.

He had seen the way she'd looked at him on Yuna. He had a power over her, one that he'd almost surrendered when he allowed *her* to strike fear into *him*. He would reclaim it. He knew he could still wield that advantage if he played their next meeting carefully.

He could still forge her into what he wanted. This time, he would do it by himself, for himself.

And after that, he would do whatever it took to see the Star Federation fall. Niradessa and Zeran would return to him eventually. The three of them were all that was left of the Seventh Sun's leadership. Whether they wanted to admit it or not, they needed him.

He smiled at the thought of them begging for his help.

Then he returned to his work.

CHAPTER 41: OBLIVION

Lance stood over Lissa's shoulder as she opened the storage locker near the control room. The datapad from the uncharted sector rested within, untouched since the day she'd left it there. For a moment, she was still, staring down at the machine as though reluctant to touch it. But only a moment. She pulled out the datapad and gripped it firmly as she limped into the control room.

"Are you sure you're ready for this?" Lance asked as she activated the machine, bringing up the starship signature and last known locations that made up the entire cache of information on the datapad.

Lissa nodded and brought up a starmap. As she plotted the locations of the ship, she said, "It's long overdue. Not just for the others, but for me, too."

Lance searched her for signs of distress or uncertainty, but Lissa was calm and steady as she began the hunt.

It took hard travel and intense searching, but Lissa honed in on the target's signature, matching up the faint traces in space with the sample from the datapad. As the days bled into the trail of the target ship, they discussed what they would do if they encountered a trap. There was a chance that *Light Runner* could withstand a hacking attempt, given that the ship was of a unique design and benefited from Mezoran technology hybridized with human-designed systems. But neither of them were willing to risk the ship or their lives on that kind of gamble, and they searched for ways to maintain control if the Seventh Sun managed to take the ship.

They came up short, but somehow, that did not crack Lissa's tranquility.

He watched her closely as they bore down on Rosonno's starship.

They chased its trail to Daraax Beta, and from there, picked up a stronger trace of its signature leading back out into space. *Light Runner*'s tracking system projected a couple weeks' worth of travel before they caught up.

Lissa took everything calmly. She handled the controls expertly whenever they needed to adjust the navigation system and take manual control of the ship for a while, and never made a move to push *Light Runner* to a breakneck pace. Even when they needed to slow the ship to allow the power cells to recharge, she was unrattled.

It seemed that nothing could shake her after Zuftal, not even her nightmares. Lance had expected her run-in with the Phantom to terrorize her sleep, but she was more at ease than ever. She woke rested each day and filled most of her time by rehabilitating the medi-stitched muscles in her leg until she no longer moved with a limp. Then she picked up sparring lessons with Lance again, focusing on her defensive stances and moving around and away from strikes.

When she found a rhythm that worked for her, and was able to dodge most of Lance's attacks and successfully block the rest, she began to take up target practice. She built a simulation in the training room that tracked the barrel of her unloaded enerpulse pistol, indicating when she was successfully targeting a moving object. She practiced on marks of varying size and speed, and while she started out stronger than most of the soldiers Lance had served with, he noticed that she was only getting better, until she was honing in on the smallest targets in less than two seconds.

Target practice was the one time she wanted to be alone, and even Blade kept her distance. Lance often found the arkin outside of the training room, dozing and waiting for Lissa to finish.

On the day they planned to put into port for the final time before catching Rosonno's ship, Lance joined Blade outside of the practice room, watching Lissa through the open door.

He had seen Lissa shoot before, and he would never forget the shot she had made that night on Mezora when she traded a bounty contract for *Light Runner*. He wondered what she could possibly get out of a simulation that she could not already do.

The answer came as he watched her run through the exercise, and he realized that Lissa's calmness did not extend beneath her surface.

She had combined Lance's sparring lessons with the target simulation, and was now having the simulator shoot beams of light at her as she tracked moving objects. Her skin gleamed with sweat as she pushed herself to dodge and take cover where she found it, but the simulator kept her moving, always flushing her out of hiding. She responded by taking out target after target, and the simulator steadily dropped the intensity of its onslaught as she picked off the virtual enemies.

Lance knew what this was. She was doing incredibly well, but he knew that even she could not keep it up. Sure enough, the moment came when she did not move fast enough, and a shot from the simulator hit her in the gut.

"Critical strike," came the smooth announcement. "Simulation terminated."

Lissa gave a frustrated growl. She straightened up and wiped the sweat from her forehead, stretched her arms, and prepared to go again.

"You can't train for this," Lance called as he stepped into the room.

Lissa turned to face him. She was breathing hard, and her eyes had some of that unnerving brightness in them, but he was relieved to see that she had control over herself.

She'd lose it if she kept trying to push herself to do the impossible.

"You can't train yourself for an ambush," Lance said, coming to a halt several paces away. "Not like this. You know how to recognize traps and I've seen you fight your way out of them, but you're never going to be able to prepare for a full-scale assault coming out of nowhere." He glanced around the room. "Especially not here. You know too much about the room, you know the situation is controlled, and even if you managed to program a basic simulator like this to randomize attacks, you're still going to be able to feel the rhythm of the automation." He focused on Lissa again, and saw that she was listening intently. "You know that ambushes are meant to take you by surprise. No matter what you do, there's always going to be something that's unpredictable."

Lissa sighed and nodded. "I can still expect it, and try to prepare for it."

"Not with this you can't." Lance gestured to the simulator. It was a good model, all things considered, but it paled in comparison to the military-grade machines Lance had trained on. "You'd need something more advanced, something you could program to act like real people. People make mistakes. They shoot too soon or misjudge their aim, they panic, they break, they lose themselves in battle and rush in. They sometimes keep going after you've shot them in the gut, or they drop everything and run after you've barely clipped their arm."

"I get it," Lissa murmured, turning away. She walked to a bench along the wall where she'd left a small towel and a container of water.

Lance followed her. "You're trying to train yourself for a battle, but there are a lot of factors you're not thinking about there, too."

She took a deep swallow of water and scrubbed her face with the rough towel before turning back to him. Her gaze was hard and unforgiving but he pressed on.

"For one thing," Lance continued, "you're not alone anymore." He looked at her pointedly.

She dropped her gaze and turned away. "I'm not going to ask you to put your life on the line to take down Rosonno."

"You don't have to," Lance said, stepping closer. "I'm here for you, no matter what. I promise."

Lissa did not seem to know how to respond to that.

"And in the future," Lance continued, "there are going to be other people fighting with you. You have a database full of Neo-Andromedans who did not want to join the Seventh Sun. At least some of them are going to want to fight."

Lissa shook her head. "That's not something I can ask them, either."

"I'd be surprised if you had to."

Lissa frowned and half-turned away again. "You don't know anything about them. What makes you so certain?"

"It's a database full of people who are not part of the Seventh Sun but were marked for Awakenings. People who would rather die before they let the Seventh Sun bring them anywhere near one of those machines." Lance shifted so that he was back in her full line of sight. "People like you."

Lissa did not look convinced.

"I promise you, you're going to be surprised by the number of people in there who will get behind you to fight for a life free from the Sun."

"And what if none of them want to fight?"

Lance shrugged. "Then you'll still have me."

Lissa held his gaze for a long moment. Then she burst out laughing. "You and me against a galaxy that wants Neo-Andromedans dead, and two militaries that are hunting for them."

"Sounds about right."

"We're going to die."

Lance shrugged. "Eventually, but not until we say so."

"Is this how you talked to your soldiers before you went into battle?"

"This is actually a very effective way of speaking to soldiers."

"But not bounty hunters." Smiling, Lissa stepped away. She hesitated in the middle of the room, looking at the battle simulator. Her smile faded. She took a deep breath before she gave the verbal command to shut down the simulation for the day.

The machine obliged, and Lance followed Lissa out of the exercise room.

While Lissa went to bathe and change into nondescript traveler's clothes, Lance brought the ship in to port on a planet with a healthy and stable economy and population. They were cleared for entry into the atmosphere, and touched down at the ground port without trouble. A flash of uneasiness rippled across Lance's mind as he remembered the ambush of the Seventh Sun agents back on Zuftal, but they were running low on food. He and Lissa had both agreed to keep a more careful watch, but even with the prickle of anxiety, Lance was not certain that it would be needed. Three of the four people that had attacked them were now dead, and with *Light Runner*'s overdrive capabilities, there was no trail for the Seventh Sun to follow.

The arkins stayed behind to guard the ship while Lance and Lissa set off to replenish their supplies. They found what they were looking for and paid without incident, though Lance noticed that Lissa was more on edge this time. He mirrored her alertness, and almost simultaneously, they both noticed the nearly silent crowd around an open-air street bar.

With a small, curious glance at each other, Lance and Lissa made their way to the edge of the crowd, peering over heads and through antennae to see what was going on. Lance saw a large projection of one of the main galactic news sources, but from the back of the crowd, he could not hear what the story was about.

But the Star Federation insignia shown next to the anchor's head was enough to keep his attention.

Someone called for a higher volume, and there was a soft chorus of agreement. One of the bartenders adjusted the controls, and the news story flooded out into the street.

"—too far away for us to track the story as it unfolds," the anchor said in the Galactic Unified Voice, staring solemnly ahead, "but we have confirmed that the Star Federation is launching an attack on what is believed to be a previously undiscovered Andromedan stronghold, which the Neo-Andromedans have taken over. Star Federation units mobilized in the Andromeda Reach before moving en masse beyond the outskirts of the sector, past the edge of the galaxy."

Lissa went rigid next to Lance.

"The strike is already under way," the anchor continued, "and the Star Federation has confirmed that there is no need for secrecy at this time. Admiral Darattadan, one of the three admirals *not* leading the attack, had this to say."

The image cut to the Vareesi admiral, all blunt, broad edges and skeletal markings over his deep purple skin. "As I speak," Darattadan began, "Admirals Araxorra and Lukati, with the assistance of Fleet Commanders Keraun, Ranisheden, and Anderson, are leading the attack against the core of the Nandro threat. We will win this battle, and the war in turn, and we will complete the purge of the Nandro population. They are too dangerous to be allowed to remain in this galaxy."

Murmurs of assent rippled through the crowd, but Lance heard someone say, "That's a load of arkin shit," off to his left. To his surprise, he saw two humans and one Rhyutan watching the broadcast with dark expressions. Someone hissed at them to be quiet, but one of the humans shot back a venomous reply that drew ugly looks from other parts of the crowd.

Lance took that as the cue to leave before the tension broke and a fight began. He turned to suggest as much to Lissa, only to find that she was already gone.

He found her on the other side of the street, half a block down and away from the crowd. She was breathing hard again, bouncing from one foot to the other with her hands balled into fists. She looked ready to fight someone, but as Lance approached, he realized that the look in her eyes was not anger, but despair. Her breath caught and became shallow, and she shook her hands loose before rubbing her left shoulder.

"They found the main base," she whispered as Lance drew close.

He put a gentle hand on her shoulder, and she gripped his wrist hard, keeping his hand in place. He could feel her fingers shaking.

"There are people on that base who are not part of the Seventh Sun," she said. She breathed in sharply, let it out in a ragged rush. "People who had nowhere else to go, or couldn't get away." She squeezed her eyes shut. Then she took a step forward, pressing her forehead against Lance's chest.

He circled his arms around her and held her tight.

She did not pull away. "I didn't think they would find it. I really didn't."

Lance did not know what to say, other than a whispered, "I'm sorry."

She looked up at him, her gaze fierce. "Promise me we're going to give those people in the database a future. Promise me we'll find them, and we'll fight for them, and we'll keep them safe from the Seventh Sun and the Star Federation and everyone in the universe if that's what it takes."

Lance looked her in the eye, and nodded. "I promise." He squeezed her shoulders, and she pressed her face against his chest again. He rested his cheek against the top of her head as she wrapped her arms around his waist. He felt her shudder against him, and he held her tighter. "I promise."

CHAPTER 42: STRONGHOLD

After all their coordination with Admiral Araxorra and the hurried integration of the Hyrunian tech that arrived just before the battle, Erica thought that she and Admiral Lukati were prepared for anything.

She was wrong.

When the fleet under her command arrived at the battle site, she expected a raging dogfight between the Star Federation and an equally massive force of Nandro fighters and starships, with Keraun's units struggling to get the driller into position despite the edge the new Hyrunian weapons and defense systems gave them.

By the time she arrived, the small defenses the Nandros had put up were already decimated, the new system shields from the Hyrunians were holding strong against any override attacks, the driller was through both the outer shell of the base and the inner walls, and Keraun was well on his way to the populated arms of the base. His units were reporting continuous need for their laser cutters as they encountered sealed doors dividing each closed sector, but they were boring through without trouble and making steady progress.

Erica did not believe that it could be this easy. Lukati agreed and sent her to provide backup for Keraun's units.

Shuttles brought Erica's soldiers to the rear airlock of the driller, and from there, they followed Keraun's trail through the stronghold.

With the power off in this part of the station, Erica and her soldiers relied on illumination from their helmets to help them avoid obstacles, along with alerts from infrared scans for any lurking surprises. Erica would have preferred to find debris and hidden enemies rather than the clean, silent, sweeping hallways that brought them closer and closer to the core of the base.

The main hall was massive, easily five times Erica's height with a floor that was borderline spongey but easy to run on. The elegantly curving walls had massive symbols etched into them, and large, semi-transparent seals that divided off what Erica assumed were once living quarters. Huge numbers of living quarters. She wracked her brain as she ran, trying to imagine the Andromedans who had originally lived here, but without any firsthand experiences with those extragalactic beings, the image she called to mind was flat and sterile. They were very tall, she knew, spiny and angular and completely unlike anything she had seen anywhere else in the galaxy. Try as she might, she could not picture them drifting up and down this hall, could not imagine what this station had looked like when it was fully operational. It was dark and mostly dead now, and the sheer unfamiliarity of it sent shivers up her spine.

We don't belong here, Erica found herself thinking. It was an odd thought, but it kept reverberating in her skull as she led her soldiers down the path Keraun had carved through the sealed, massive sheets of alien metal that divided off each sector of the stronghold. She tried to ignore the sense of being completely out of place, but it gnawed on her mind and was impossible to fully drown out in the crushing silence of the Andromedan fortress. She actually welcomed the sound of her own breathing as she ran on; it helped keep that invasive thought in the background.

Gradually, Erica caught up to Keraun. The edges of the cuts in the sector dividers shimmered with residual heat as she drew nearer, and she felt a small surge of anger that he had not waited for her before proceeding. He knew that she was following him, and that the admirals wanted him to have extra support. But the Hyrunian had pressed on, and with a startling abruptness, Erica found the sharp corner that connected the dead space station spike with the one that held the Nandros. Light spilled from the final hole Keraun had cut, harsh and white after the darkness of the dead sectors. Her helmet adjusted the tint of her visor to preserve her vision, but it still took a moment for her to pick out the bright flashes of enerpulse fire from the rest of the light.

"Keraun's units have engaged the Nandros," Erica barked over her communication line, relaying the message back to the admirals as well as her soldiers. "Moving to join the battle."

With a surge of adrenaline, Erica charged through the hole. She found herself in another massive hallway, lit by glowing panels in the ceiling and the curving walls. Some of them flashed a violent color, throwing spots into Erica's vision despite her helmet's best efforts. She turned her head away from those panels and took in the battle before her.

Keraun's units were clearly holding their own, and Erica saw the Hyrunian charging through the clusters of enemy Nandros, enerpulse fire glancing off his custom armor. There were a few bodies on the floor, but none of them wore the Star Federation gray.

Erica looked closer, and realized that Keraun's units outnumbered the Nandros four to one, and that number was quickly skewing even more in the Star Federation's favor. The Nandros were ragtag and desperate. Some of them had armor on, Erica realized, but the majority of them wore light clothing and were firing at the advancing soldiers with little thought to their targets. Almost as if they were an army of volunteers with little to no combat training.

Not one of those Nandros was one of the berserk ones. There was desperation and fear in their metallic eyes, but none of the savage light Erica had seen on Daraax Beta.

This was not what she had expected.

Keraun's units made swift work of the Nandros. Erica's soldiers provided a little assistance, but it wasn't long before the Hyrunian bellowed a war cry and pushed forward again. Soldiers from both commands followed him, and Erica ran after them, feeling a sense of wrongness resonate through her.

It's this damned station, she told herself. The otherness of the structure was overwhelming and confusing her. She made herself concentrate on getting to the head of the advancing group, trying to filter out the flashing light panels and the size and emptiness of the space around her.

Nandros kept meeting them at each sector, and Erica kept registering their desperate terror as they tried to fight back. There were always too few Nandros to stand any chance against the Star Federation. That sharpened the sense of wrongness in her, but she was more bewildered by the lack of berserk Nandros than anything else.

"They must be keeping them in reserve," she told the admirals over her communicator. Keraun had not sent them any information after breaching the active area, so the responsibility fell to her. "I'm worried they're luring us in with these small skirmishes and planning to set the really dangerous ones on us once we're farther in."

There was a brief silence from the admirals before Araxorra said, "You're aware that we're not expecting you to take this base, Commander?"

"Yes," Erica said.

They'd all known that. It was too big, too far out from the galaxy, too dangerous. Their mission wasn't to capture it; they needed to destroy it. The Hyrunians had provided them with a way to do that. A way that, if Erica stopped and thought about it for too long, made her equally as paranoid about the Hyrunian's intentions as Admiral Lukati was.

"Based on what we know of the internal structure," Lukati said, his voice rough in Erica's ear, "we may be able to send a couple of fighters to fly the payload to you. Find where it will do the most damage and prepare to receive."

Erica acknowledged the order and rejoined the battle.

As the fighting dragged on for the better part of a day, stretched by the sheer size of the space station, Erica found that they were steadily making progress across the populated spike. She needed to divide the soldiers and send some to hold the main hallway as the rest fought their way into the next one, cutting off any chance of a rear ambush. The Nandros were growing increasingly frantic as the Star Federation drove on, but they still were not sending out the berserk ones.

What are they waiting for? Erica wondered.

She did not allow herself to dwell too long on the question. Instead, she pressed on and listened to the updates from the promised fighters as they followed her into the base. They arrived before she and Keraun had found a good location to set the bomb.

With the roars of their engines echoing down the hallways, the fighters came gliding to meet the field soldiers, carrying the bomb between them in a flexible net hastily attached to the noses of the vessels. Erica's stomach tightened at the sight, and she had four soldiers move in to assist with the delivery of the payload. When it was safely removed and lowered to the floor, the fighter pilots offered to stay and help with additional battles, but even with the size of the Andromedan space station, Erica knew they would have trouble maneuvering. How they had managed to deliver the bomb safely was beyond her, but Erica had seen how slowly the fighters had moved. They were made for faster travel, and bringing the bomb in would have put a lot of strain on their power reserves. She doubted there was enough left for more than one or two shots, which the pilots confirmed for her.

She sent them back out of the stronghold, then turned her attention to the bomb.

The bomb was surprisingly compact, but came with the promise of wiping out the fortress. From the little she understood about the Hyrunian weapon, Erica knew that it required a manual code input before it could detonate, but she still had to resist the urge to step away from the bomb. The weapon came in an armored casing for protection, a dark, squat cylinder of armor that shimmered with cold colors in the light and was icy to the touch. Hyrunian symbols wound around the casing, glowing against the dark shell.

The weapon was oddly pretty, for something so deadly.

She wanted nothing more than to leave it and run.

With a shudder, Erica turned away. She assigned five soldiers to oversee the transport of the bomb, ordering them to hang back until she and Keraun had confirmed that any Nandros up ahead had been cleared out. Then she followed Keraun. Once again, he had not waited, but Erica caught up quickly enough.

Keraun found what promised to be a central power core, and guarding the location was the largest group of Nandros Erica had seen since setting foot in the stronghold.

The Nandros put up their hardest fight at the entrance to the power core. As they engaged the Star Federation, Erica noticed that these Nandros seemed like they'd actually picked up a weapon a couple of times in their lives. A lot of them knew where to aim, and more than a few Star Federation soldiers went down, but as with the other skirmishes, there were no signs of the berserk Nandros, and the sheer press of Star Federation numbers smothered the resistance.

When the last Nandro fighter had fallen, Erica and Keraun focused on the large plate that sealed off the room beyond. The solid covering in place of the semi-transparent seals of the other areas betrayed the room's significance. It had to be what they were looking for.

They were stopped by a set of controls demanding an unlocking sequence they had no hopes of knowing, let alone being able to read.

Keraun snarled a curse and kicked at the plate, rearing back on his tail to deliver a crushing blow. He did not leave so much as a scratch on the surface. He cursed again and began stalking back and forth in front of the plate, muttering to himself as he moved.

With a tired ache spreading through her muscles, Erica stepped away to relay the situation to the admirals. "We may have hit a dead end," she told them. "We don't have a way to—"

The sound of a laser cutter activating and sheering away at the metal plate cut her off.

Erica whipped around and charged up to Keraun. "Are you crazy?" she shouted at the Hyrunian. "You don't know what's on the other side of that! If you damage a power core, you could kill us all!"

"I will not be stopped by some lesser species," Keraun growled.

He stomped past her, knocking hard into her shoulder as he went, and as Erica recovered her balance, she had the feeling he was talking about her as much as he was the Nandros. Maybe even more so.

"Get back!" Erica shouted at the soldiers around her. She pointed at the group coming up with the bomb. "You especially."

It was an empty gesture, she knew, but it made her feel better as she stood by and watched Keraun risk all of their lives.

Heedless of the danger, Keraun ordered the laser cutter pushed to a higher speed.

The cutter whined as the rhythm of its motion increased. Heat rose off the plate as the cutter carved through the metal. Erica realized that she was holding her breath, but she dare not let it out as the seconds dragged on.

Any moment now—

With a loud rush, the lasers cut through the metal, penetrating the room beyond. Keraun ordered the machine switched off, and Erica waited to hear the sound of a ruptured power core thrumming erratically as it spilled plasma or some other deadly substance, ready to explode.

What she heard instead were wails and screams.

As the laser cutter was lifted away, pulling a thick section of the plate with it, Erica ran to the opening and peered inside, almost shoving Keraun away to do it. The Hyrunian growled next to her, but she barely heard him as she registered what she was seeing.

People. Thousands of people, all inside a room so large, Erica could not see the far side. It stretched away into hazy distance, and a sea of faces stared at her, metallic eyes bright against every human skin tone Erica had ever seen. Men and women, old and young, all stared at her in open horror. They pushed away from the opening, trying to get as far away from her as they could. They wrapped their arms around themselves, around their neighbors, around—

Children.

There were children in the room, too. A huge range of children, from teenagers to toddlers. No infants, but that didn't mean they weren't somewhere else, hidden from her sight.

We aren't supposed to be here.

Slowly, Keraun pushed past her and stepped into the room. Erica tried to speak, but she found her mouth dry. She tried to move, but her feet felt rooted to the ground. So she watched as the Hyrunian stood in the shallow clearing formed by the crowd pressing as far away from him as possible. He surveyed the Nandros, almost disinterested in what he saw. He tipped his head towards the ceiling, and Erica followed the motion to see a power core suspended high above the crowd, pulsing blue from a central sphere out along a spiderweb of feed lines. In the distance, she saw more power cores, but they were darker than dead stars.

It was dangerous for these people to be in here. Prolonged exposure to a core was a risk even if regular maintenance was performed on the casing, but they must have felt that they had nowhere else to hide. They had all come here, and now that they were found, they were prime targets.

Children, Erica thought. And then a modifier forced itself through her mind. *Nandro children.*

They would all grow up deadly.

Erica's gaze slipped to one of the younger ones, wide-eyed and tearful as he clung to a man's leg and stared open-mouthed at her. She quickly glanced away.

Her attention snagged on Keraun, who had turned to look at her again. No, not at her. Beyond her.

His voice scraped in her ear over the communication line as he ordered, "Bring the bomb."

There was a shuffle behind Erica as the soldiers moved to carry the Hyrunian weapon through the opening. Erica moved in front of them, blocking the way.

Keraun stepped to her immediately, pulling himself up to his full height tower over her. "Move," he growled. His helmet blocked his eyes, but Erica was very aware of the wicked curve of his horns and the muscles flexing in his legs.

"Admirals," she said, not daring to turn her head away from Keraun, "there are children here."

There was a brief silence before Admiral Lukati said, "Unfortunate, but we knew that was a possibility."

Erica felt her mouth go dry all over again. "Sir?" she managed to croak out.

"Complete the mission," Araxorra said. "That's an order, Commander Anderson."

Time seemed to slow for Erica after that. She felt detached from herself as she stepped out of the way, and watched the bomb slide into the room. "I will have no part in this," she muttered as she walked away, listening to the sounds of enerpulse fire as the soldiers drove back the Nandros. She assumed at least some of them had tried to stop Keraun as he moved to activate the bomb. Screams undercut her voice as she ordered the remaining soldiers to begin the retreat back to the driller. A captain from her fleet confirmed that they would have shuttles ready and waiting to receive the soldiers at the entry point.

The journey back to the driller took some time, but it was much faster now that there were no dividers to cut through or Nandros to slow them down. There were only the bodies where they had fallen, and the remaining soldiers who had branched off to block any potential ambushes from the rear. Erica saw how unnecessary that was now, and she called them back and sent them to the waiting Star Federation fleet.

Other than the first wave of Nandro ships that the Star Federation had easily destroyed, no additional starships had left the base. Erica could not help but wonder if that small Nandro fleet had been a counterattack as everyone had thought, or an evacuation attempt.

As Erica had saw her last soldiers on to a shuttle, Keraun and his units arrived at the entry point. They were panting as though they had run hard to catch up, but they filtered through the driller with quiet efficiency. As they boarded the next shuttle, Erica noticed that Keraun was moving with a heavy limp. She hung back as he stalked into the airlock, then pulled a soldier aside and asked him what had happened.

"This one Nandro came to the front of the crowd," the soldier told her. "Blonde, pale skin. Called herself Neera-something. Spoke Galunvo, and said she wanted to make a deal with us. Keraun did not want to hear it. We tried to push her back but she managed to get around us, and she pulled some sort of blade on the commander. She got it into a gap in his armor before he fought her off."

"She got past how many of you?" Erica asked.

The soldier shuffled sheepishly. "Three of us, ma'am. We were watching the crowd and didn't expect her to move so fast, so she caught all of us by surprise before the commander landed a kick. We think she was leadership, since her collar was different from the others."

"Her collar?"

The soldier nodded. "Hers had some dark stars on it. The commander took it if you want to get a look at it."

"He... *took* it?"

The soldier nodded again. "Used the same blade on her that she stabbed him with. Wasn't pretty to watch, ma'am."

Erica tried not to picture that. "What did you do with the bomb?"

"It's active and counting down. We used the laser cutter to seal it back in the room."

Erica wasn't able to keep the horror out of her voice. "With all of the Nandros inside?"

The soldier nodded.

The shuttle ride back to the fleet passed in a blur of nausea and guilt. Erica spoke to no one, but she kept replaying the conversation she'd had with Jason what felt like an eternity ago, back on Phan after she'd just received her promotion to fleet commander. Her memory was fuzzy, but she remembered that he had tried to warn her about this.

Innocent people, he had said.

Nandros, had been her response.

When Erica stepped onboard the *Argonaught IX*, she still wore her armor, which was pristine and looked like she had not seen a battle at all that day. She supposed she hadn't. What she had seen was a slaughter.

And it wasn't over yet.

The moment she was in the control room, Erica ordered a visual display of the base brought up, along with a scan for signs of life. As she expected, the scan showed that all of the living beings on the base were concentrated in the massive power room. The rest was devoid of life, even though the two main spikes still glowed with light.

The sudden explosion flared with a terrible silence, engulfing the core of the base in white fire that died immediately in the vacuum of space. Secondary explosions came from the ruptured power core, but the life scan had gone dark with the first blast. The space station splintered and burst, breaking apart into massive chunks of frozen metal and billions of debris shards.

Erica made herself watch.

There was a mild cheer from the soldiers in the room, and the soldier at the communications station patched through a broadcast from the admirals that congratulated them on a successful mission.

"We did today what we all swore to do," Lukati said via a hologram projection, holding himself tall. "We stood, and we protected. Now let's go home."

Another cheer went up from the soldiers, and the navigators plotted a course back to the Andromeda Reach.

Erica stood in the middle of it all, numb.
Stand and Protect, the Star Federation always said.
She couldn't help but ask, *From what?*

CHAPTER 43: RESOLUTION

With the Star Federation attacking the main base, Lissa found herself faced with the same choice she'd always had: run and try to hide from who and what she was, or embrace herself—all of herself—and make a stand.

This time, it was easy to decide.

She still felt a tiny bubble of fear lodge itself in her throat when Rosonno's ship finally came up on *Light Runner*'s scanners, but she took a deep, unrestricted breath, ran her thumb over the broken collar in the pouch on her belt, and reminded herself that this time, she would be the one with control over the situation.

Welcome to the fight for me, Little Light, voices whispered in her ears, but this time, there was a softer, more encouraging note to the female voice that undercut the others and asked her to fight. It still made her skin crawl, but it helped drown out the rest, and solid hatred for one voice made the others seem flimsy and faint.

Lissa changed into her hunting clothes, the smooth black fabric stretching over her frame. She had put on some weight thanks to Lance's cooking, and the days spent training with him had thickened her muscles. She felt stronger, more whole. Lissa slicked and coiled her hair into a tight bun at the base of

331

her skull, fastened her boots, pulled on her gloves, and snapped her belt and enerpulse holster into place.

Blade was waiting for Lissa in the hall. Her injured wing still rested awkwardly at her side, but they had worked to stretch and strengthen it since Zuftal. She wasn't ready to fly again just yet, and Lissa was not certain that the arkin would return to her full grace and agility in the air, but she would be able to take to the skies again someday.

Blade rose to her feet and nosed Lissa's hand when she extended it to the arkin's head. Lissa rubbed the arkin's face and ear, feeling the gentle push of Blade's head against her fingers. Fondly, Lissa remembered a time when a scruffy black arkin kit had snapped and hissed and refused to let anyone near, including her.

How things had changed.

"Time to go," Lissa said.

The arkin's amber eyes flashed as she gave a soft grunt. Then she turned and padded down the hall, leading the way to the control room.

Orion met them at the doorway, butting heads playfully with Blade before nuzzling her neck affectionately. Blade responded by putting her mouth over Orion's muzzle and refusing to let go until the gray arkin had pushed her off with his paws.

Lissa stepped around them into the control room, smiling a little as their mock fight took them further down the hallway. "We're going to end up overrun with arkin kits," she murmured.

Lance groaned from the ship's controls. "We'll cross that chasm of bad sleep and hairballs when we come to it." He had a starmap up and was checking their path against the trail of Rosonno's ship. Based on the distance left, there was only a sidereal hour or two at most before they caught up. "It looks like our cloak is holding. We're coming up behind them in the dark." He glanced over his shoulder at her. "Are you ready?"

Lissa nodded and stepped closer to the controls. Her hand came to rest on Lance's shoulder as she checked the ship's speed and power reserves.

Lance followed her gaze. "Everything looks good for *Light Runner*," he told her, "but you and I have a problem. This far out in space, I'm not seeing us taking more than five shots with the pulse cannon and having enough left in the power cells to make it to another planet."

Lissa nodded. She knew that *Light Runner*'s weapons were powerful, but they had their limits. All the ships they had destroyed in the past had been grounded on planets and powered down with their shields off. *Light Runner* had never gone against a spacebound ship before, and Lissa did not know how the starship would fair in a dogfight, but she trusted Lance.

"If I can't destroy that ship," he continued, "we're going to have to find another way to take out Rosonno." He hesitated, looking Lissa up and down. A faint line appeared between his brows, and his eyes darkened with worry. "Without a nearby planet to ground them on, I can only think of one way to get you on that ship, and it means that we're going to do something that's a little crazy, and very, very dangerous."

Lissa shrugged. "That sounds right for us."

Lance's mouth twitched into a half smile, but it faded quickly. "You ever jump airlocks before?"

"No."

"Then you are in for the worst experience of your life." Lance outlined what the maneuver entailed, and Lissa felt her calmness cracking.

According to Lance, he needed to remotely override the target ship's outer and inner airlocks, leaving them open long enough for a good part of the interior air to vent. Ideally, hostiles would be blown out of the ship, making the situation onboard the target ship easier to handle. Then the attacking ship would swing in dangerously close, until the hulls were almost touching, and open its own outer airlock without draining the air inside. The result would shoot anyone in the airlock into the target ship, ideally with enough force to overcome the rush of wind from the interior of the target ship. Then the remote override would reverse and allow the target ship's airlock to close again.

The Star Federation adopted the maneuver after studying the tactics of the more successful pirate crews. The soldiers trained for airlock jumps in case they needed to board a hostile ship and did not have the ability to incapacitate the target with a tractor beam. It tended to take the enemy by surprise and leave the survivors stunned for a critical moment, regardless of whether or not the maneuver was successful.

But it was dangerous enough that Lance had never seen it performed. Usually, the Star Federation opted to destroy the hostile ship if they could not incapacitate the target and board it safely. There were very few shields that could stand up to pulse cannon fire from a Star Federation starship.

"There's an infinite number of ways it can go wrong, and only one way it can go right," Lance finished. "And of course, someone has to pilot the attacking ship." He held Lissa's gaze for a long moment. "If we do this, you have to go alone."

Lissa hesitated.

"If you're not sure about this, even a little bit, I can turn us around and—"

"Actually," Lissa interrupted, "I was trying to figure out how much time I have to practice getting out of a spacewalker suit without help."

Lance blinked.

"They restrict motion and the visor may throw off my aim. I'll need to make the jump, be able to take out anyone in the immediate area, then rip the suit off and keep moving before reinforcements arrive."

"Lissa—"

She shook her head. She took a deep breath, held it for a moment, then released it slowly. She was very aware of her own heartbeat, fast and hard with anxiety. She refused to let Lance see that. He would not let her go if he did. She admitted to herself that she was scared, but her life had proven to be stronger than Rosonno's desire to snuff it out, time and time again, and she held on to that knowledge. She might not even need to face him, but if Lance could not destroy his ship with the pulse cannons, she would not let her fear control her.

Not anymore.

Fight for me, Little Light.

Lissa took another deep breath. "I need to do this," she said. "For me, this time." She fixed her gaze on the starmap, on the yellow triangle that marked Rosonno's starship. "I'm ready."

CHAPTER 44: DEFIANCE

After watching recordings of the marches and demonstrations on Saenos, Jason knew that any other protest like this would only warrant the attention of the Star Federation if the leaders suddenly took over governmental buildings in major cities, revealed themselves to be cultists of the blood sacrificing nature, and somehow managed to gain control of every complex machine on the surface of the planet in order to make good on their gory promises to whatever higher being they worshipped.

The Saenese protests had none of those characteristics. They were peaceful except where onlookers tried to disrupt them, but those skirmishes were easily handled by the local police forces. They were small, cropping up in thirteen cities around the planet out of hundreds. And they barely disrupted anything, given that most of the population traveled via sky cruisers and the protests were staged on the ground. Even with the gatherings in key locations and the advertisements they took out on the cloud boards, these were some of the mildest protests Jason had seen in his life.

The only problem was that Neo-Andromedans were leading them.

Saenos was an unusual planet. Tiny and remote at the edge of Star Federation territory, almost across the border into Yukarian-controlled space, Saenos was a mild world that the Star Federation paid little attention to. It was well-developed, but it had no notable resources and was too far removed from the next closest systems to serve as a waypoint between destinations. It was in Star Federation-controlled space, but the Star Federation simply did not care enough about the planet to monitor it.

All things considered, it shouldn't have surprised Jason that a Neo-Andromedan population had managed to take root there. Hybrid children were almost common, now that the Star Federation knew to look for them. And while they clearly weren't living free of prejudice and harassment, the Neo-Andromedans and their children were openly *living* on Saenos.

That was the most incredible thing Jason had seen in a long time.

When his dropship touched down in Raethon, one of Saenos's main cities, the protest there had been going on for three sidereal days, which translated to five Saenese days. Protests in the other cities had broken up, but they were still holding on in Raethon. From the data sent by local police, there were less than one hundred people still camping out in front of the capital building. Most of them were Neo-Andromedan.

Jason wore the armor that the Star Federation now labeled as "standard outfitting" when facing Neo-Andromedans. His soldiers wore the same. They looked like they were heading into another battle on Daraax Beta. Aside from slightly slimmer shielding and more flexible plates, there were no differences between the armor they had worn to storm a base full of Awakened and what they were dressed in to quell a peaceful protest.

It was odd to think that out of all the soldiers who had set foot on Daraax Beta, Jason's ranks held the majority of the survivors.

And now they were going to fight unarmed protestors.

No, Jason corrected himself, *we're going to* kill *unarmed protestors.*

His stomach was in knots as he led his soldiers off the dropship. They formed up behind him in a formidable column, stepping in unison so that the strength of their numbers echoed off the glassy skyscrapers bordering the pedway. The sky was very blue overhead, cruisers cutting oblivious crisscrosses against the color. The capital building was another tall, glass-covered building with two vertical, golden stripes running its length. It was set back from the street with a white stone plaza in front of it. There was a holographic projection of the seal of Saenos over the plaza, hovering directly over the crowd that sat shoulder-to-shoulder on the white stones. Onlookers at the very edges of the plaza watched the protest, remnants of midday meals clutched in their hands as they stretched their lunchbreaks a few minutes longer. Three people stood in the plaza, facing the crowd. Their voices were amplified by the small disk microphones stuck to their jaws. They were chanting something in the Saenese dialect with muted enthusiasm, and the crowd was responding with equal force, but the voices died away as Jason and his soldiers drew close. A sea of faces rippled toward him, and Jason saw metallic eyes of every color staring at him.

Jason came to a halt at the edge of the plaza, where the white stones met the black surface of the pedway. He held up his hand, and his soldiers fell still behind him. Total silence descended, and even the onlookers seemed to be holding their breath. Neo-Andromedan gazes locked on him with open defiance, waiting for him to give the order.

He couldn't do it.

He wouldn't.

Not this time.

Jason turned to his soldiers, looking up and down the line. They all wore helmets, and the mirrored visors made it impossible for him to see any of their expressions. "Step back," he ordered.

There was only the briefest of hesitations before the soldiers obeyed, but now, Jason thought he could sense the confusion radiating off of them. White sunlight glinted off of their gray armor as they moved, gleaming and perfect and so devoid of humanity.

Jason reached up to remove his helmet as he turned back to the protestors. As he tugged it off and stood blinking in the bright daylight, he saw that several of the protestors had risen to their feet, but only one of them was moving toward him.

She was one of the three people who had been chanting to the crowd, and she approached him with slow, cautious steps. Her hands were raised to show that she carried no weapons. Behind her, the other two leaders were watching her anxiously, hands pressed to their mouths.

Jason placed his helmet on the ground, followed by his enerpulse rifle. He took a step forward.

As they drew close, Jason studied her details. She was of a medium build with dark olive skin and curling brown hair. Her face was round with a pert nose and a smooth forehead. There were no lines on her face, suggesting that she was in her early to mid-twenties, but her eyes, bronze flecked with brown, had the stubborn tenacity of someone weathered by years of aggression and no more tolerance for it. She wore a loose, flowy dress patterned in blue and white with a crisp, short, black jacket slashed with white over her shoulders. There was no collar around her throat.

She took Jason in at a glance, her eyes lingering for a moment on the red-and-gold captain's insignia on his chest before she looked him in the eye. "Is there—"

She and Jason both winced as the mic disk at her jaw whined and amplified her voice again. Her cheeks reddened as she reached up and gently pulled the disk off of her skin. She tried again.

"Is there something we can help you with, Captain?" she said in smooth, unbroken Galunvo. There was a lilt of fear in her voice, but she held herself steady.

Jason tried to keep his gaze soft as he said, "You all need to leave."

"We have a right to be here," the woman said. The lilt became a light tremor, but she still held herself firm. "We are not breaking any laws, and we are all Saenese citizens. We have every right to—"

"I know," Jason told her. "But I don't just mean that you need to disperse from the premises." His attention slipped over her shoulder, to the crowd of Neo-Andromedans that were now all on their feet and watching him. "You need to put your heads down, and keep yourselves safe."

The woman gaped at him.

Jason reached for the mic disk she held. "May I?"

Numbly, she extended the disk to him, and when he took it, she looked down at her empty hand with open confusion.

Jason stepped past her, placing the mic disk against his own jaw. He felt a light tickle as it secured itself to his skin. "I need you all to listen to me," he said, his voice carrying over the crowd. As he drew closer, he began to pick out solid-colored human eyes, along with the split gazes of adult, human-Neo-Andromedan hybrids. "Anyone with Neo-Andromedan genes needs to leave. The safest thing for you would be to go into hiding. Keep your heads down, and keep yourselves safe."

The crowd stared back at him without comprehension, but he doubted a language barrier was the issue.

"I know this isn't what you want to hear," Jason told them, "but there's a purge on, and it's not safe for any of you. It won't be for a long time. This is not the time for you to put your lives on the line in the name of a revolution. You will lose them." His gaze fell on a teenaged boy with one brown eye and one silver eye. "All of them."

The boy swallowed and ducked his head.

"You need to survive this. Put your heads down, and survive." He picked the humans out from the crowd again, making sure to lock gazes with each of them. "There are others who can stand up for you, and do it without dying in the process." He focused on the Neo-Andromedans again. "This does not need to be your fight."

"No."

The voice came from behind him, clear and steady. He turned to see the Neo-Andromedan woman in the dress staring at him.

"This *is* our fight." Her feet were planted firmly on the white stones, and there was a fiery undercurrent to her voice now. No trace of fear. "It's our fight, and our lives, and our futures, and we will not let them go."

There was a murmur of agreement from the protestors.

Jason shook his head. "I admire your courage, but you need to be smart about this. It's a very dangerous time for you, and it's certainly not the right time."

"We're tired of waiting for permission to live!" someone shouted from the crowd.

"I understand," Jason said as he turned back to the others. "But you also need to watch out for the *wrong* time, and now is definitely the wrong time."

"It's always the wrong time," another voice said, and Jason found himself looking at the teenaged boy again. The boy swiped at his brown and silver eyes, hiding angry tears, but he did not look away this time.

"The galaxy doesn't see us as people," the woman in the dress said as she came around to stand in front of Jason again, between him and the crowd. "Here on Saenos, we're more accepted, and it's because of that we can actually make them see us. Here, we can speak, and people just might listen." She pushed her hair behind her ears as a light breeze washed across the plaza. "And if enough people here listen and see us as we really are, as *people*, the rest of the galaxy will, too."

But you shouldn't have to forfeit your lives to put an end to that, Jason thought. He did not think the protestors would respond well to that. Instead, he asked, "How do you know they will listen?"

The woman's lips twitched into a small smile. "You did."

Jason held her frank, open gaze for a long moment before he took in the crowd behind her again. People stared back at him. Scared and determined and exhausted and hopeful people.

Jason reached up and tugged the mic disk from his jaw. He handed it back to the young woman, and she accepted it with a brighter smile.

"Thank you, Captain," she said.

"My name is Jason."

"My name is Calyra."

He nodded and looked past Calyra at the protestors one last time. "Please try to keep them safe. Good leaders do that for their people." He focused on her again. "The Star Federation will return here, I can promise you that. I don't know how long it will take them, and I won't be able to stop them. With the purge on, you will absolutely be a target."

"I understand," Calyra said.

There was no trace of fear left in her voice, and Jason had to wonder if she or any of the others truly understood what could happen to them. But he could not force them to make a choice they had already rejected. He could only leave them with their lives today, and hope for them in the future.

"Good luck, Calyra," he said.

"You too, Jason."

When he turned back to his soldiers, he saw that they were as rigid and unmoving as he had left them. "Fall back," he called out, emphasizing the order with the corresponding hand gesture.

This time, there was a longer hesitation, and Jason saw three soldiers tighten their grips on their rifles. Jason stood at his full height and stared down the line, daring any of them to disobey him.

He was relieved when the soldiers turned and began marching away, but he did not let it show. He picked up his helmet and his rifle, pausing long enough to ensure that no rogue soldier would turn and fire back at the crowd. He had just gone against purge protocol. It would not be entirely unexpected, and the Star Federation would not consider that kind of insubordination completely unforgivable.

But it did not happen.

As he walked away, Jason heard cheering from the plaza, carried to his ears by the breeze.

When he boarded the dropship again, most of the soldiers had already slipped into their seats and pulled their helmets off. A good number of them sat with tight jaws and stared straight ahead, refusing to meet Jason's eye. But what held his attention were the soldiers who looked relieved when they put their rifles away. There were quite a lot of them, almost as many as the angry ones.

That was a start.

CHAPTER 45: STRIKE

The pulse cannon was fully charged, the target ship was only a few minutes away, and *Light Runner*'s cloak was holding beautifully. Lance needed to return to the control room soon to take over the strike, but he lingered at the airlock with Lissa and the arkins.

They both knew that there was a good chance she would not need to jump airlocks, but if *Light Runner*'s pulse cannons were not enough to destroy the target ship, she needed to be ready. Lance would have a very small window between the initial attack and Rosonno's agents regaining control. In that time, he needed to override the enemy airlock, and send Lissa into Rosonno's ship.

Then he needed to retreat to a far enough distance to keep *Light Runner*'s systems safe from a Seventh Sun attack, leaving Lissa stranded on the target ship with nothing but a spacewalker suit and an enerpulse pistol to protect her.

His heart thundered in his chest as he watched Lissa check the light spacesuit she wore over her black outfit. She was decked out in full hunter's garb minus the mask, which betrayed her clenched jaw. She was avoiding Lance's eye, trying not to speak, and Lance did not push her.

She was not as good at hiding her emotions as she thought she was, but Lance knew that he could not change her mind on this. All he could do was try not to let his concern for her distract him from what he needed to do.

Lance knew that she could get in and out of the spacesuit on her own. She'd been practicing in the time leading up to the strike, and he was confident that she had broken a galactic record for getting out of a spacesuit. She'd tried teaching herself to shoot with the suit on, opting for the more efficient and less dangerous solution first, but as flexible as the lighter spacewalker suit was, it still slowed her down and disrupted her aim without offering any protection from enerpulse fire to compensate. She had quickly given that up and focused on the riskier option, training herself until she could remove the suit with her eyes closed.

Of course, she had not been able to practice removing the spacesuit while disoriented, which was what worried Lance. Standing in the training room was one thing. Jumping airlocks and racing out of a suit while enemy agents closed in was another.

Lance did not voice the concern. Lissa already knew.

But if anyone could pull off this kind of stunt, it was her.

She finished checking the suit, which was designed for sleekness and mobility but looked bulky compared to what she usually wore. She lightly tapped the respirator pack on her chest, and it lit up at her touch, signaling a full cycle of breathable air.

She was ready.

Blade whined and bumped against Lissa's hip, who dropped her hand to rub the arkin's neck. Orion stepped forward to sniff inquisitively at the boots of Lissa's spacesuit, but he backed up and fixed his attention on Blade when she cried again. Lissa rubbed her other hand under the black arkin's chin, looking down into Blade's amber eyes and hushing the arkin with soothing whispers.

Lance gave them a moment before he stepped forward and handed Lissa the spacewalker helmet. She accepted it, but did not put in on. She drew in a deep breath, held it for a moment, then let it out in a quiet rush as she met Lance's gaze. She looked like she wanted to say something, but kept biting down on the words.

She surprised him by stepping closer, cupping her hand around the back of his neck, and pressing her forehead against his.

It was awkward and a little painful with the thick, rough gauntlet on her hand and the hard bulk of the space suit pressing against his chest, but Lance slipped his hand behind her head and leaned in to the gesture.

"We'll be here when it's done," he murmured.

Lissa shut her eyes and nodded against him.

They stayed like that for another breath, and then pulled away. Lissa hit the airlock controls, opening the inner door. Blade tried to follow her inside, but Lance grabbed the arkin and gently pulled her back. Blade whined and resisted, but Lance did not release her until Lissa had closed the airlock.

Through the thick, transparent pane that made up half of the inner airlock door, Lance watched as Lissa pulled on the helmet and locked it in place with a gentle twist. She hit her respirator pack again, then gave Lance a thumbs up. The mirrored visor obscured her face, offering only a distorted, blue reflection of Lance's return signal. Before she could turn away, Blade scratched at the barrier between her and Lissa, whimpering.

Lissa paused when she saw the arkin. She sank down to one knee in front of the transparent panel, pressing her hand against the glass. Blade sniffed at the glove and cried again, scratching harder at the airlock doors.

Lance gently touched the arkin between the shoulders. Her muscles twitched under his fingers, but she calmed enough to stop scratching.

Lissa lingered for a moment, helmet turned to the arkin. Then she stood, and even through the mirrored visor, Lance could feel her silver stare on him. He nodded once at her, and she dipped her helmet in return before turning her back on them firmly.

Lance left Blade and Orion behind as he made his way back to the control room. Blade's whimpers faded as he rounded the corners, and it was silent when he slipped into his seat.

Before seeing Lissa off at the airlock, he'd left the navigation system and visual displays from the ship's scanners open and ready for his return. Now, he took manual control of the ship, watching the target starship swell as *Light Runner* stalked closer and closer.

Rosonno's ship was set at a light cruising speed, the pace a starship often took when the navigators were waiting on the energy cells to recharge before they could bring the ship back up to faster-than-light travel for the next leg of their journey. Lance had settled on an approach from below, giving him a wide target and a good chance to cripple the engines if he lined up his shots correctly.

But there was no if.

He had to get the initial strike right or Lissa would not have a window at all.

Lance adjusted *Light Runner*'s speed and course, bringing the pulse cannon's aim around and settling it at the back of the target ship, at a crucial juncture where the engines met the hull of the ship. He was banking on the shields to be weaker in that area, with most of their power directed to the bow in order to deflect debris as the ship coasted through space. If he had guessed right, he would not need to send Lissa to face Rosonno.

Light Runner would give him five rapid-fire shots. That was all a non-combat starship of this size would allow before drawing on the main power cells, and he could not risk stranding them in space. *Light Runner* had been designed to evade and escape, but its pulse cannons could wound if not outright cripple a pursuer. Lance hoped the ship could hunt, too.

When the ship was as close as he dared bring it to the target, he hit the firing sequence. *Light Runner*'s visual displays showed five white-hot shots streaking toward the enemy ship. Four were absorbed by the ship's shields, throwing ripples and distortions around their strike areas, and Lance saw that he had guessed wrong; the enemy's shields were spread evenly over the starship.

He went cold as he watched the final shot approach the ship. He almost did not believe it when the shot slammed through the weakened, distorted shields, and burned into the engine joint with a fiery pulse that died immediately in the vacuum of space. That gave Lance a clear view of the damage he had wrought, and even as the target ship quickly powered up its engines, Lance knew it was not going anywhere.

He felt no relief. He had aimed to destroy that ship, and now he needed to get Lissa inside it.

Light Runner rolled and arced around the target ship as the engines flared, but a blue pulse surged out of the hole Lance's shot had left, triggering another small explosion that snuffed out in the vacuum. The engines sputtered and the ship began to spin uncoordinatedly.

Lance kept *Light Runner* a safe distance away as the target ship struggled to right itself. A thorough scan revealed that Rosonno's ship had no pulse cannons of its own, so Lance only had to wait patiently until it was safe to move in close. He dreaded that moment; as long as the Seventh Sun agents were fighting to keep their own ship under control, *Light Runner*'s systems were safe.

But safe wasn't enough, and Lance knew that this was his chance to overtake the enemy airlock. He did not hesitate, and was glad for the chaos that helped mask his less elegant attempt. He broke into the system, and waited for his opening.

The moment Rosonno's ship steadied, Lance pushed *Light Runner* closer and angled the starship to pass so close to the target's hull that the two crafts would almost touch. Alarms screamed warnings as Lance began the maneuver, but he ignored them in favor of triggering the airlock override.

For a moment, he wasn't sure it had worked. Then a new warning sprang up, informing him to exercise caution around fresh debris from the interior of the target ship.

Lance gripped the controls, hoping he had made things a little easier for Lissa, then pushed *Light Runner* right up next to the enemy airlock. He kept the ship as close as he could as he sent the signal to Lissa. Barely an instant later, a final alert from the ship told him that *Light Runner*'s exterior airlock had been opened.

Lance released control over the enemy's airlock, letting it shut. He piloted *Light Runner* away, taking the ship back out into space. He settled the ship at what he hoped was a safe distance from the target, and tried not to think of all the ways Lissa could die from that moment on. He tried, but the sound of Blade's anguished howls reaching even the control room turned his mind to dark places.

I don't even know if she made it into the airlock.

Lance pressed his face into his hands, not daring to allow himself to hope. "Come back to us," he whispered.

Blade's cries answered him.

CHAPTER 46: JUMP

When the signal came, Lissa slammed the release on the outer airlock and dove forward. Her breathing was the only sound as the doors opened and the air rushed out, shooting her into space. She had to trust that Lance had lined the ships up perfectly, compensating for both ships' momentums. But the moment she launched out of the airlock and found herself facing the blank hull of Rosonno's ship, her mind filled with pure terror. With her movements beyond her control, her body flipped and offered her a view of *Light Runner*'s flaring engines as the ship sailed past, leaving nothing but distant, icy stars in its wake.

There was nothing that could help her if her jump was off. She'd be left a broken smear against Rosonno's hull, and a rupture in the space suit would be a blessing at that point.

She forced her eyes to stay open as she somersaulted through the void between the ships, but she couldn't help flinching at the thought of smashing against the body of Rosonno's starship. She fought the urge to fling her arms out to try to steady herself. It would do nothing for her in space, except increase her risk of breaking a limb against the ship.

Her breath was loud and shallow in her ears, and she swore her heart was on the verge of bursting out of her chest, but then she shot past the outer hull, sailing neatly through the open airlock into the interior of Rosonno's ship.

The rush of air from inside the ship was powerful enough to drag Lissa's speed to a halt much sooner than she had anticipated. She should have made it further into the ship. She twisted again, searching for the airlock controls, and her heart stopped when she saw that they were out of her reach.

The escaping air began to push her back out into space.

No!

Lissa switched on the travel jets of her spacesuit, trying to force her way to the control panel, but the rush of the wind was too strong, and all the jets did was slow her a little. She lashed out, landing her feet against the closer wall. She pushed off as hard as she could, but the escaping air carried her back into the airlock.

"No, no, NO!"

She turned again, trying to find any sort of handhold, but even through her panic, she knew her grip would fail against the vacuum of space.

Then the outer airlock snapped shut.

Lissa fell to the ground as the ship's artificial gravity reclaimed her, her momentum bringing her to a crashing halt against the outer airlock. The impact jarred the suit's jets off, saving her from further damage. She lay there for a moment, stunned. She was breathing hard, and her stomach felt painfully tight, but she forced herself to her feet and staggered out of the airlock.

She allowed herself another moment of hazy relief at not being blown back out into space, then took a deep breath to steady herself. Readouts from her suit informed her that the air on the ship was too thin to breathe, but that would not last long. The ship only needed a chance to stabilize the atmosphere again. Then the trouble would come. Lissa reached for the secure holster Lance had attached to the back of the spacesuit. She felt another wash of relief when her hand closed on the pistol, and she unlocked the weapon. Wielding it was awkward with the extra bulk of the space suit, but until the air approached normal levels again, she would have the advantage of full lungs and a steady pulse.

She looked up and down the narrow hallway of the ship. There were no rooms off this hall other than the airlock, which she knew was close to the stern of the ship. She turned right, toward the middle of the ship. The seal of her suit blocked all sound, which set her nerves on edge, but they had caught Rosonno and his agents by surprise, Lance had gotten her on the ship, and she was protected from the depleted atmosphere.

It was time to hunt.

CHAPTER 47: CORNERED

Rosonno was out in the hallway when the airlock opened. The attack on his ship had drawn him out of his private quarters, angry and shouting for someone to send the ship into a faster-than-light jump. A few agents scrambled down the halls, calling to one another as they raced to assess the damage. They dodged around Rosonno with barely a glance and disappeared around a bend in the hallway. Even through his outrage, a slow ripple of dread washed over Rosonno. If his agents were ignoring him, there was a chance that the damage to the ship was greater than he realized.

He was running for the control room when a rush of air yanked him off of his feet and pulled him down the hall, slamming him into the floor and walls. He came to a momentary halt at the corner as wind raged around him, and his leg made a sickening crunch before the wind dragged him against the wall. Pain raced up his leg and he opened his mouth to scream, but the air was thin as he tried to pull it into his lungs. His chest spasmed as he gulped for air.

The wind stopped as abruptly as it started, leaving Rosonno in a heap on the floor with black stars in his vision.

His gasps became easier as the seconds slipped by, but the dark spots took a long time to clear. His leg throbbed and burned, but he gradually became aware of a chill in the air, as well as an announcement blaring over the ship's communication systems. His head refused to clear enough to let him register the words. All he could focus on was how thin the air was, how each breath felt too shallow.

What are they saying?

Rosonno drew in ragged gulps of air, trying to fill his lungs. Pain formed a lattice up and down his leg. Everything was cold.

I can't hear...

Rosonno's sight faded completely.

Then there was a gentle wash of warm air, and Rosonno pulled in a deep breath. He coughed and drew in another, then another. The air was still thin, but it could sustain him. His vision cleared. He rolled on to his back, groaning.

"—at critical levels. Protect airlock at all costs."

Airlock? Rosonno wondered. *What is wrong with the airlock?*

"Repeat. Intruder detected on main level. Airlock breached, leaving air reserve at critical levels. Protect—"

Rosonno sat up with a jolt. It left his head swimming and his injured leg flaring in protest, but his mind raced.

Intruder through the airlock, all the way out here.

They were at least a sidereal week away from the nearest star systems. Their ship was small and so easy to overlook against the background noise of space. They should have been safe.

Rosonno swallowed as his head cleared. He felt cold all over again, despite the warmth the ventilation system had flooded back into the ship.

It can't be...

The first enerpulse shot snapped his head around. The second brought him staggering to his feet. The third sent him limping through the halls, desperately trying to remember where he could find a weapon on the ship.

CHAPTER 48: SHADOW

Lissa pulled off the spacesuit with one hand while she swept her enerpulse pistol up and down the hall. The first three agents she'd found lay crumpled at her feet, lifeless. They had not fully recovered from near asphyxiation when they came, their movements had been erratic, and they had gone down easily. Lissa had made sure they were clean deaths.

It was quiet now. Lissa doubted that Rosonno only had three agents protecting him, but there was a chance the open airlock had claimed more.

Free of the suit, she stalked through the halls. The emptiness began to fray at her nerves. She kept expecting someone, anyone, to be waiting for her around each corner. She was hunting a Seventh Sun leader, the one who had sent her into an Awakening machine and done the same to countless others, the same man who had haunted her nightmares for most of her life. She could not believe that this hunt would be so easy.

Fear kept trying to worm its way into her movements. She managed to keep it out, but it sat coiled in her gut, ready to paralyze her the moment she heard Rosonno's voice or caught a fleeting glimpse of him.

I am alive, she told herself. *I am alive, and I am stronger than him.*

Rosonno had tried to drown her in the Light, had tried to kill her in an Awakening machine, and sent a gold-eyed hunter to chase her down and feed on her life.

But she had resisted, she had survived, and she had overcome.

I am alive, she repeated like a mantra, until she had drowned out the voices that whispered in her ears, begging her to come to the Light. Then, suddenly, her thoughts turned to the database with all the Awakening candidates. Once, she had been a name in a list like that. She had broken free, and now she would give all of the rest of them a future.

She would fight for it long past the end of this hunt.

I am alive, and I have so much to do.

The fear began to fade. When she heard the first echo of Rosonno's shouts, she hesitated only a moment before pressing on.

Rosonno had tried to define her life, and when that had failed, he had tried to shape her death. She would not let him touch either of those things. Not now, and not ever again.

They were hers, and hers alone.

The fear hissed in her stomach, but she drowned it in a wave of serene determination.

She followed Rosonno's shouts to the control room, which turned out to be a small cluster of systems and seats in an alcove near the center of the ship. As she stalked along the wall toward the area, she made out other voices responding to Rosonno's anger with urging, pleading tones, but it sounded as though there were only two agents with him. When she peered around the final corner, Lissa saw that her estimation was correct; Rosonno stood off to one side of the control room, and there were only two agents with him.

Lissa saw the way Rosonno hobbled and winced as he moved, favoring a recent leg injury. A bad one, from the strain on his face. She did not think she would ever see Rosonno vulnerable; he worked hard to hide his own mortality.

"She is one person!" Rosonno shouted as Lissa looked on. "There must be someone on this ship who can deal with her!"

One of the agents shook her head and said something too low for Lissa to catch.

"Of course there's someone left," Rosonno snarled. "I'm looking at two people right now."

The agents balked. "We're maintenance engineers!" the male agent protested. "Everyone who had combat training is already dead!" There was a tense pause, and then he said something softly.

Rosonno's face reddened. "I will NOT abandon this ship! *No one* will. My work is too important, especially now. I am the one who will save the Seventh Sun, and I will not have that taken away from me by someone who was never anything more than a shadow of her brother!"

It took Lissa a moment to realize that Rosonno's words had failed to impact her in any way.

She was, finally, no longer afraid of him.

But before Lissa could step around the corner, the two agents turned away from Rosonno, postures tight with anger and defiance. "We're not dying for your delusions," the female agent said as they stalked away.

Lissa raised her pistol, but the agents were angling away from her, toward the other side of the hall. She pulled back from the corner, taking aim just in case, but as the agents came into view again, she knew they were not a problem. They weren't even looking in her direction. She let them go.

Rosonno did not.

The agents were about to round the corner when the first enerpulse shot took the woman in the back of the head. She died immediately. The man cried out, stumbling away from her and throwing his hands up to shield himself. Rosonno's next shots took him in the shoulder and in the leg. Then in the hip. Then two more enerpulse shots slammed into the wall as the man crumpled, moaning with pain.

Lissa's teeth clenched as she watched the man on the floor writhe. The smell of burnt flesh and clothing hit her nose, bringing on a small wave of nausea, but what sickened her most was that another enerpulse shot did not come. She heard Rosonno talking to himself between the agonized moans, and the sound of him moving around the control room, but he left the agent on the floor to die, slowly. Painfully. Inconsequentially.

Lissa stepped away from the wall. She didn't look at Rosonno as she walked silently up to the man on the floor. She stopped next to him, and aimed her pistol at his head.

His eyes—silver flecked with blue and brown—were very wide as he stared up at Lissa, at the weapon in her hand. He did not look afraid.

The mercy shot drew Rosonno's attention. When Lissa turned to face him, he was staring at her, his mouth hanging open as though he did not quite believe she was there. His hands were frozen above the control panel, some sequence half-entered into a command field. The enerpulse pistol was sitting on the panel in front of him.

Rosonno realized that an instant too late. He grabbed for the weapon as Lissa fired.

Her shot hit the control panel, exploding on contact and leaving a scorched mess where the pistol had been.

Rosonno jumped away from the control panel with a pained cry, clutching his hand to his chest and turning his face away from the sparking systems. He nearly fell as he stumbled back, but he managed to keep his feet. He was breathing hard when he faced Lissa again, a mixture of anger and fear swelling behind his eyes.

Lissa looked back at him impassively.

"You won't survive this," Rosonno told her, but she heard him struggling to keep his voice level.

"I already have," she told him.

He shook his head. "My agents will—"

"You have no agents," Lissa said.

Rosonno fell silent. She could still see his fear, but his dark, gold-flecked eyes shifted. He began calculating. "Why haven't you shot me yet?"

Lissa shifted her grip on her pistol, but did not bring the barrel up to aim at Rosonno. She found herself considering the question seriously, even though she recognized what Rosonno was doing. It was a much clumsier attempt than the one she had encountered in the uncharted sector.

Lissa knew that she could make him suffer. Shot by shot, each one placed carefully, she could leech the life out of him. She could make him scream.

But she was so tired of pain. She didn't want his, too.

"I want to know if you understand why I'm here."

Rosonno made a jagged motion with his uninjured hand. "Because you belong to me," he said. "That's why you haven't killed me yet."

Lissa felt a flare of disgust, but she forced herself to keep calm.

Give him nothing. Nothing at all.

"If I belonged to you," Lissa said, "I would have died a long time ago. You know that."

Rosonno swallowed hard, the collar around his throat bobbing with the motion, the seven white—

No, she saw, *two white stars. The rest are dark.*

Seven stars.

Seven leaders.

All but two dead.

Rosonno was saying something about Awakenings, but Lissa was not listening.

"Who is she?" Lissa interrupted. "The First Lit from the uncharted sector. What does she do?"

To her surprise, Rosonno's face went red, and saliva sprayed from his mouth when he screamed, "DO NOT SPEAK OF HER!"

Lissa did not flinch.

"She is nothing!" Rosonno rambled on. "*I* am the one who gave the Seventh Sun the Awakened. *I* am the one who built the strength of our light." He took a step forward, nearly falling on his injured leg. "*I* am the one who made *you*!"

Lissa laughed softly. "You really don't understand," she muttered.

"You're a killer," Rosonno said. "An assassin. Dangerous. Deadly. *I* made you that way." He nodded at her, almost manic, and Lissa saw that he had actually convinced himself. "You're exactly what I wanted you to be."

This time, Lissa flinched. "I was never who you wanted me to be."

Rosonno's eyes lit up, sensing weakness. He moved to press his advantage. "I *made* you who you are."

He went too far.

"No," Lissa said, anger creeping in, but it was cold anger, controlled. "That was my brother, who was broken but protected me. And a family, who took us in when everyone else chased us out." She took a step forward, and Rosonno recoiled. "And an arkin who defied death to stay with me." Another step, and Rosonno was stumbling back. "And a Star Fed who threw everything away to join the hunting game with me." Rosonno fell, and she stopped. "But more than anyone else, it was *me*." Lissa reached into the pouch on her belt that held the broken collar. She ran her thumb over the seven little stars one last time. "*You*," she said, withdrawing the hard piece from the pouch, "were always nothing."

Lissa tossed the broken collar to him. His eyes snagged on the piece as it arced through the air, and he reached for it mechanically, even as fear blossomed across his face and he flinched away from something so harmless.

Lissa raised her enerpulse pistol as he caught the broken collar. He looked at it, then at her, and she saw that he finally understood.

One quick shot.

CHAPTER 49: RETURN

When the signal came from the enemy starship, Lance almost thought that he was imagining it. But he was on his feet before he realized that he had moved. He threw away caution and accepted the transmission, not caring what would happen if Lissa was no longer alive. If she was gone, the Seventh Sun could take the ship for all he cared. He would gladly give it to them, preferably down their throats at faster-than-light speeds. But no matter what, he would give them hell before he died.

Lissa's voice came over the connection.

His knees buckled in dizzying relief. She was alive, and they had so much to do together.

Lance told her to wait for *Light Runner* to come in closer. They kept the transmission open as Lance approached the Seventh Sun ship again. Blade and Orion came running when they caught the sound of Lissa's voice, and the black arkin stood with her gaze riveted on the communications system.

When the two ships were close enough again and Lance was holding *Light Runner* steady, Lissa exited the other ship and used the jets on her spacesuit to make her way back to *Light Runner*'s airlock. Lance picked up on her progress on *Light Runner*'s scanners, and tracked her as she went. It was a slow journey for her, and Lance kept waiting for something to go wrong, for the small, Seventh Sun starship to spring back to life and chase after Lissa. But the enemy ship remained still and silent, and finally, an alert from *Light Runner* informed Lance that the outer airlock had opened.

Lance ran with the arkins to meet Lissa, arriving just in time to see her step into the ship and brace herself. Blade reared to wrap her front legs around Lissa's shoulders and rub her head against Lissa's jaw. Lissa dropped the helmet of her suit to catch the arkin, burying her face against the arkin's dark fur.

Warmth swirled through Lance's chest as he approached. He slowed enough to give Blade time to drop back to the floor, then he was face-to-face with Lissa. She did not smile, but she nodded in answer to his unvoiced question, and then they were embracing. The respirator pack dug into Lance's chest, but he pressed his cheek against Lissa's hair, too relieved to care.

Until that moment, none of it had seemed real.

But she was solid and alive in his arms, and there was so much they had to do.

They needed to destroy the Seventh Sun ship to keep anyone from stumbling upon it. They needed to find and protect the people in the database. They needed to figure out their next moves, where they would go, what they would need, how they would succeed. It was a wide, uncertain future before them, but it was finally an open one that invited their action instead of demanding their sacrifice.

But it all could wait. Lance stood with Lissa, and let everything outside of that moment fall away.

CHAPTER 50: STARBORN

Erica did not sleep well in the days that followed the destruction of the main Nandro base. She kept seeing a sea of faces in front of her, all metallic-eyed and harshly alien, but soaked with fear and looking too human for it. The adults called out to her, begging for mercy, and the high, piercing cries of children undercut the pleas. Erica tried to reach out to them in her dreams, but her limbs felt like lead and it took every fragment of her strength to move a finger. When the explosion came, as it did every time she dreamed, she had no strength left to turn away. She had to watch the bodies rip apart in front of her. Then the fire engulfed her, too.

She always woke up sweating and breathing hard.

After a particularly vivid nightmare, one where she felt hot, red blood spray across her face, Erica sat on the edge of her bed with her head bent over her knees. She tangled her fingers through her hair and tried to quiet the pounding thud in her head.

The dreams will pass, she told herself. *This can't haunt me forever.*

The pounding would not stop.

It was frustratingly irregular, and only seemed to be increasing the longer she was awake.

Then a muffled shout came from the other side of the door to her private quarters, and she realized with a guilty jolt that the pounding wasn't in her head. Someone was knocking.

When Erica opened the door, the human soldier that met her had the decency to look momentarily horrified at catching her in an undignified state. Then the soldier drew herself up and offered Erica a sharp salute.

"I'm sorry for disturbing you, ma'am, but we could not reach you on your comm."

Erica ran her knuckles across her forehead, too tired to be self-conscious of the rumpled undershirt she had greeted this soldier in. "I set it to silent," Erica mumbled, offering the explanation as much to herself as the soldier. She pushed her hair out of her eyes and forced herself to stand up straighter. "What's happening?"

"It's Commander Keraun, ma'am."

Erica groaned. "He can wait." Nightmares or not, she would not sacrifice any more sleep for the Hyrunian.

"No, ma'am," the soldier said, an urgency undercutting her apologetic tone. "He's dead."

Erica forgot her exhaustion.

The soldier informed her that the admirals and other fleet commanders were waiting for her on a private transmission as Erica hastily rinsed her mouth in her washroom, splashed cold water on her face, and scrambled into a clean uniform. Erica smoothed her hair down as she dismissed the soldier and bolted to her private communication terminal. The door to her quarters shut as Erica called up the waiting transmission. She was panting lightly when the other officers came into view.

"Good of you to join us, Commander Anderson," Admiral Lukati said with a hard edge to his voice.

"My apologies," Erica began, but the admiral waved a dismissive hand.

"As you all know by now," Lukati said, addressing the group, "Fleet Commander Keraun is dead. It seems the wound he sustained in the Seventh Sun stronghold suffered an infection, and he died a few hours ago. The physician who treated him reported that it was some sort of microbe that's common enough throughout the galaxy, but deadly to Hyrunians if it enters their bloodstream. Her report speculates that it may have been on the blade the Nandro used to cut him, and it was already deep inside the wound when they bandaged him up."

Erica's mind prickled at that. "Who treated him?"

Lukati's attention flickered to a datapad he held. "Major Malia Miyasato," he read off. "She's one of very few medics who can treat Hyrunians, but we're having others confirm her report." The admiral addressed the group again, but Erica sensed that he was speaking to her in particular when he said, "We have no reason to suspect foul play among our own ranks. Keraun was killed by a Nandro, and bad luck."

There was a pause as that sank in, and Erica noticed more than one other fleet commander shifting uneasily. They all knew there was more to this abrupt call for a conference transmission than just the fleet commander's death; there were other, more efficient ways of announcing something like that.

"The reason we called this meeting," Admiral Araxorra said, picking up the expectant thread, "is because of this."

The communication display changed, shrinking the officer's faces into a single row across the bottom as a rotating view of a collar filled the main projection. A black collar, studded with seven stars.

"Keraun took it from the Nandro base and was studying it before he died," Lukati said.

Erica stared hard at the hologram as it rotated before her, noting the ragged edges where a serrated blade had sawed through the hard material. She thought she saw dried blood there, but the dark color of the collar made her think that she was just imagining it.

The stars, though…

Only one of the seven stars was white. The rest were varying shades of deep red, with the exception of one blue star.

"Five of the stars are filled with Nandro blood," Araxorra went on, rattling off the facts from the analysis report with clinical detachment. "It's all from the same Nandro, the one who was wearing the collar, but tests confirm that the blood was not all drawn at the same time. The most recent sample corresponds with the Nandro's exact time of death, Keraun noted that this star—" the hologram projection highlighted the star on the far left, "—turned red as he was, ah, removing the collar." There was a delicate silence before another star was called to their attention. "The oldest blood dates as far back as nearly seven months ago."

Erica wracked her brain, trying to match that up to the events she remembered. Seven months ago was the attack on Sciyat, when this all began, but she did not remember anyone reporting a Nandro with a special collar.

"What about the blue star?" another fleet commander asked.

Erica looked at the star in question: second from the right, cobalt blue in color.

"One of Keraun's physicians was examining the collar when it pricked him," Araxorra said. "He feared that it had injected him with poison, but as of now, he is stable, and all tests have come back negative."

"So that's his blood?"

Araxorra nodded. "We don't know if he triggered the collar by accident, or if it pricked him in response to a remote signal."

"When did this happen?" Erica asked.

"Right about when Keraun died," Lukati answered. "The physician was going to report the finding to Keraun, but he found the commander unresponsive and Major Miyasato trying to revive him. Keraun was pronounced dead not long after."

Erica studied the collar again, turning her attention on the remaining white star. "What about the central star?" she asked.

Araxorra toggled her controls so that she and the other admirals dominated the center of the display again. "That brings us to the single most important discovery this collar has given us." All five admirals looked grim as Araxorra delivered the news. "There is still at least one Seventh Sun leader alive somewhere in the galaxy, and as of now, we have no idea how to find them."

Erica drew in a sharp breath. "How does this collar tell us that?"

"We think the collar draws blood from the leaders whenever a Seventh Sun head dies," Lukati answered. "The timeline of the blood samples corresponds to major battles we've had with the Nandros, all the way back to Sciyat, with the exception of these two." The blue star and a dark red star on the other side of the collar glowed on the hologram. "We don't know what happened to these two," the admiral murmured darkly, "but the others likely died during those battles."

"So, the middle star...?"

"Represents the last surviving Seventh Sun leader," Lukati finished. "We're sending ships back to the destroyed stronghold to scavenge for any data we can find that might point us to their whereabouts, but we don't have much hope for that."

"We have other sources we can tap," one of the fleet commanders said. "We'll find them."

Erica and the others nodded in determined agreement.

"I would expect nothing less," Lukati said with a note of pride in his voice.

Erica almost reached for the controls to cut the transmission, ready to begin the search for the surviving leader, but the other admirals traded uneasy glances, and Araxorra's head tilted sideways.

"There is one more thing," the Araxii admiral said. "Someone has leaked a... certain report." Araxorra paused delicately. "It seems that it contained information on human-Neo-Andromedan hybrids, and the confirmed viability of their offspring."

There was a murmur of confusion among the other officers, but Erica felt herself go cold as the admiral's words sunk in.

Nandros and humans.

That couldn't be. It was impossible.

Nandros weren't human. They masqueraded as humans, imitated them almost perfectly except for their horrible, metallic eyes, and were nothing but a twisted experiment from another galaxy.

That had been ripped from human genetics...

Erica suddenly remembered her nightmares.

Children.

The murmur of conversation turned into a buzz, and Erica felt the universe closing in on her as she stared at Admiral Lukati. He alone was silent.

Did he know?

As she studied the human admiral, she was aware of the other fleet commanders demanding to know whose report had been leaked, what evidence supported the claim, and how they would keep the information out of the hands of the galactic media.

"We can't," Araxorra said in response to the final question. "It's only a matter of time." She ignored the other inquiries.

Erica tore her eyes away from Lukati and studied the other admirals. There was something about the way they were holding themselves. They seemed... unsurprised. Oddly resigned, almost accepting.

As though this were an unpleasant but unavoidable development instead of a star-shattering—and dangerous—discovery.

"You knew," Erica whispered. No one acknowledged her. Her tongue felt thick and fuzzy in her mouth, but she made herself speak louder. "You all knew, and you did not tell us."

The other fleet commanders fell silent, and Erica felt their attention rivet on her.

Four of the admirals regarded her grimly, and Araxorra tipped her head sideways. "Admiral Lukati?" she said, sliding the responsibility into his lap.

The human admiral was quiet for a long time. When he finally spoke, his voice was low and gravelly. "It makes no difference. Nandros are dangerous, and they need to be destroyed." His eyes were dark and fierce when he looked up. "All of them."

Children.

Erica broke in before anyone else could, and her voice was hot with anger. "You kept that from us, and you let us initiate a purge. You let us define them as monsters, and now people are going to start asking how we can keep them separate from humans."

Lukati shook his head. "We are entirely different species. You know that, Anderson."

"Different species can't produce fertile offspring, and yet, there they are!" Erica shot back. Her mind raced, and a horrible thought spun into focus. "How long before the galaxy starts seeing humans and Nandros as the same thing?"

Lukati started violently. "That's a far leap in stupidity, Anderson," he snarled at her.

But Erica saw the exchanged glances between the other officers, and knew that the prediction wasn't as far-fetched as Lukati wanted to pretend. Humans had been the blueprints for Neo-Andromedans, after all. It had been easy to imagine that they weren't same species, but the evidence could not be ignored now.

Once the report on hybrids hit the general population, it would cause a rift, even among humans. Erica did not know if it would be enough to spark a civil war, but it could put pressure on the Star Federation to remove those responsible for the genocide. And purge or no purge, what would stop leadership from ousting human officers from the higher ranks altogether? Human may have made up a majority of the military, but here in the higher ranks, Erica and Lukati were severely outnumbered. The others could claim that humans were not far enough removed to look at the situation from an impartial distance. It would be so simple for humans to lose control of the Star Federation.

The military had been built in response to the birth of an alien species derived from human genetics. Turning the perception of the galaxy and making the other species believe that humans had initiated two wars and destroyed countless lives for the sake of infighting was only a breath away.

The fate of the Star Federation was on unstable ground, and Erica knew she had to tip it further off balance.

"We have to stop the purge," she said.

There was a stunned silence, then arguments erupted on all sides.

"They're too dangerous," Lukati spat, and three fleet commanders voiced their agreement.

Darattadan the Vareesi admiral made a case for the Star Federation being too far in to the purge to pull out now.

Two other fleet commanders argued that the purge had been a mistake to begin with. With a twinge of irony, Erica recalled that both of those officers had signed off on the initiation of the genocide without hesitation.

"This is not what Keraun died for!" a fleet commander snarled.

"Well he certainly didn't die for the Star Federation!" another shot back.

"Enough!" Araxorra cut in, her voice cracking like a whip. She glared at each officer in turn until the bickering had died. "Regardless of how we proceed, we need to be very careful." Her gaze lingered on Erica. "Our human representatives are clearly divided on the matter, which should give you all a clear indication of things to come. The hybrid report will create chaos, and the Star Federation may lose control of key territories if we do not handle things properly."

Erica's eyes narrowed. Araxorra had twisted her concerns beyond recognition, but she had to admit that this information did not cut the other officers as deeply. She gazed at their projected images, all so different from her and Admiral Lukati. If she wanted the others to side with her, she knew she should let the Araxii speak.

Her tongue burned with unspoken words.

"We are running out of time," Araxorra continued. "Whatever we decide, it has to be now."

Lukati opened his mouth.

"For my part," Araxorra hurried on, "I happen to agree with Anderson."

Lukati tripped over his surprise, but his eyes smoldered under a deep frown.

"Stop the purge, and we jeopardize our alliance with the Hyrunians," Darattadan warned.

"The Hyrunians are war-hungry, unstable *ishthath*," another admiral fired back, not bothering to find the right word in Galunvo for his curse. "Ally with them, and we'll find their claws in our backs the moment we look away."

The crests around Araxorra's head flattened for a moment. "That is a risk we would face if we discontinue the purge."

Erica swallowed past the lump in her throat and looked to Lukati again. The admiral was suddenly torn between his choices: annihilate the Neo-Andromedans, or destroy an alliance with the Hyrunians?

Araxorra seemed to be waiting for him to reach a decision as well. She held the discussion until the human admiral finally gave a defeated sigh, and threw his favor into allying with the Hyrunians in order to continue the purge.

Erica shook her head. "We may not even lose the Hyrunians if we stop the purge," she pointed out. "Keraun opened the channels for communication. We can continue without him. The risk is worth it."

Araxorra tipped her head thoughtfully, then turned to the next admiral. One by one, they cast their votes, deciding the future of the Star Federation.

In the end, Lukati and Darattadan wanted to continue the purge.

Araxorra and the other two admirals did not.

The orders to end the purge were sent out immediately, and Lukati gave Erica a scathing look before he and Darattadan disconnected. Erica knew she had lost an ally, and Lukati would likely make her life painful for the foreseeable future, but he would not be an admiral forever.

Someday, Erica told him silently, *I will take your place, and never make the mistakes you have.*

If only she could say that aloud without losing her command.

Someday, she promised herself.

"The purge may be over," Araxorra informed the fleet commanders, choosing to ignore the two admirals' disrespectful departures and jarring Erica back to the present, "but you all have a lot of work to do." Her head swung toward Erica again. "Especially you, Commander Anderson."

Erica nodded. "I understand, Admiral."

"Negotiations with the Hyrunians will be difficult without Keraun," Araxorra concluded, "but I am confident that we will see a new era of peace in the galaxy. Make it so, commanders."

When Erica broke her end of the transmission, she felt a wave of exhaustion hit her. She sank back down on her bed, but did not let herself lie down. The admiral was right; there was a lot of work ahead of her.

As she gathered herself to address her soldiers and give them new orders, her thoughts turned back to the collar Keraun had taken from the Nandro in the stronghold, and the single white star. She hesitated, tracing a circle on her kneecap.

She may have disagreed with Lukati on the purge, but he was right, too; Nandros were dangerous, and there was a Seventh Sun leader roaming the galaxy unchecked. A sour taste came to the back of Erica's mouth when she thought about letting the final Nandro leader go.

Continuing the purge was out of the question, but destroying the last traces of the Seventh Sun might be enough to quell the Neo-Andromedan population, and minimize future bloodshed.

It needed to be enough.

I will find you, she promised her final, faceless enemy. *Wherever you are, I will find you.*

Then she stood up, and went to meet with her captains.

CHAPTER 51: AFTER

It took months for the chaos around the destruction of the main Seventh Sun base and Keraun's death to calm enough for the Star Federation to finally turn its focus on Jason. He was ordered back to the main space station, removed from command of his ship, and kept under close surveillance while he waited for his fate. He knew what was coming, but all things considered, the general discharge he was finally given was the best outcome he could have hoped for.

Especially since the only real issue that formed the crux of his misconduct seemed to be that he did not murder every Neo-Andromedan he saw on Saenos.

The officer who was sent to finish what Jason had refused to start reported that he was only able to find a small fraction of the Neo-Andromedans that were supposedly living there. The rest had somehow vanished. Jason smiled when the news reached him.

Once he was stripped of his rank and privileges, the Star Federation arranged to put him on a ship and send him to Earth. Before they had smoothed out all the details, Major Miyasato managed to make her way to his quarters and pay him one final visit. Their conversation was supervised, but Miyasato said more than enough to confirm the suspicions he'd been fostering ever since he had learned about the Hyrunian's death.

"Some are speculating that I failed to save the fleet commander," Miyasato told him, solemn and stoic. "But I can say, truthfully, that I did my best."

Jason held himself very still at her words. "Unfortunately, I don't think I'll be able to speak to your credibility any more, Major."

"I know." She smiled at him then, sadly, but her dark eyes were intense. "But I wanted you to know the truth, Captain."

They said brief, formal goodbyes, knowing that they would not see each other again. As the soldier who had stood guard in the room escorted the major out, Jason studied the straight line of her back and the iron gray streaks in her hair, and remembered what she had once told him.

I try very hard not to be the best.

She did not look back.

Days later, Jason sat at an outdoor bar near a ground port on Earth, dressed in civilian clothes and waiting for the ship that would take him to Sciyat. He'd spent less than a day outside the Star Federation before he knew where he wanted to go. Ranae and Tomás were both eager to see him and willing to host him for as long as he needed, although if the rumor Ranae had heard about an opening at the Sciyati piloting academy was true, they would not have to support him for long. Jason's experience as a Star Federation captain was more than enough to qualify him for a position as an instructor, discharged or not. The academy was a prime recruitment center for the Star Federation, but Jason was starting to see that less as a disadvantage and more as an opportunity. It seemed like a good place to impress on a younger generation what really made an enemy.

The communicator Jason had purchased to replace the one the Star Federation had confiscated beeped to alert him to an incoming message. He lifted the cheap device, the bulkiness of it an unpleasant but not quite resented sensation, and saw that his ship was ready to board. He'd booked cheap passage on one of the large transporters. He would spend the journey sharing meals and quarters with three bunkmates, but it would be worth it.

He stood up and reached for the bracelet on his wrist. A holographic display rose around his arm, and Jason swiped until he found the credit transfer. As he paid for his drink, his eye caught on a news broadcast projected on the back wall of the shallow street bar. Bottles obscured the banner that displayed the headline, but next to the Araxii news anchor's pink head was an image of a group of Neo-Andromedans with their arms linked and determined glints in their eyes. With a jolt of surprise, Jason picked out Calyra, frozen in mid-shout. One of her eyes was blackened, but she was holding herself tall.

"Could you turn that up?" Jason asked the bartender.

"—rising number of protests against the Star Federation in the wake of the report released on Neo-Andromedans and the viability of their offspring with humans."

The bartender made a startled noise, then crossed his arms as he turned his full attention to the broadcast.

The Araxii anchor continued, "Protestors are demanding that the Star Federation pull back from all Neo-Andromedan areas, saying that they just want to be able to live without fear."

The broadcast cut to an interview with Calyra, recorded sometime before she'd received the black eye. "There's this idea that we're somehow not people," Calyra said, "that it's okay to slaughter us. We're here to show the galaxy that we're not nothing. We live peacefully, we care about our neighbors, and we never wanted a war. In response, the Star Federation committed genocide against us. *Again.* We just want to be able to take a breath without someone trying to kill us. I really don't think that's too much to ask."

The report cut to a young man Jason had not met, but his mismatched copper and blue eyes revealed his heritage. "My mother is human," the man said, "and my father is Neo-Andromedan. They loved each other, more than anything, and they were never ashamed of it or thought that they were doing anything wrong. But I grew up wearing colored contacts and watching them try to hide what my dad is from everyone. They never knew who they could trust. And all throughout my life, the galaxy tried to make me think that their love was somehow wrong, that *I* wasn't supposed to exist." He looked straight into the camera. "But I'm here, and I'm proud of my heritage. No one will ever take that away from me."

The story wrapped after that, and the bartender pulled the volume back down with a low whistle. "Humans and Nandros," he said.

Jason stiffened, waiting.

"I can't believe no one ever..." the man trailed off, shaking his head. "*Somebody* had to know, right? And we just let the Star Federation hunt them down?"

Jason relaxed. "We do terrible things when we're scared," he said.

The bartender grunted, then eyed Jason. Even out of his uniform, he cut an impressive figure. "Bet you've never been scared a day in your life," the man said.

"You'd lose that bet," Jason told him, raising his glass in a mock salute before downing the last sip of his drink.

The bartender gave a light laugh, but he sobered as he watched Jason. "You're military, aren't you?"

Jason carefully placed the empty glass on the counter. "Former," he said, and was surprised by the bitter taste the word left on his tongue, fleeting as it was. He supposed that it would take some time before the sting truly faded.

The bartender nodded thoughtfully. Jason watched a thousand questions rise to the man's face, but all he said was, "Good luck out there."

Jason thanked him.

On his way to the ship, Jason thought about Calyra and the black eye she had. His mind twinged as he wondered if she was still alive after the broadcast of her protest, but he felt a small swell of pride in her for throwing her voice as far as Earth. He was glad she had stood up to him on Saenos. He resolved to find out more about the Saenese protests the next chance he had. The Star Federation could not control everything, and that information was bound to surface if he dug far enough.

He knew that Calyra and her followers had a long fight ahead of them, if they were still alive.

Abruptly, his mind flicked back to Aven, the sick Neo-Andromedan in a hospital on Phan. And from him, to the Shadow.

Lissa, Ashburn had called her.

Jason remembered the name with a pang of clarity.

It was strange, but out of all the Neo-Andromedans he had come in contact with over the past year alone, he'd only learned the names of three. One was dead. The other two, he might never know.

Calyra.

Lissa.

He hoped that, wherever they were, they were alive, and safe.

EPILOGUE: BREATH

When *Light Runner* touched down on the planet, dawn was mere minutes away, the sky already brightening on the horizon. The dark shapes of distant mountains rose black against the spreading glow, and the stars slowly faded into silence.

Lissa and Lance needed to restock and let Blade and Orion out to stretch and hunt before heading to their next destination: a remote world where one of the Neo-Andromedans from the database was hiding.

They had already found three others from the database, all safe and happy but terrified to learn that the Seventh Sun had known where to find them. But with the destruction of the Seventh Sun and the end of the purge, they had chosen to stay where they were. One of them had asked to be left alone from then on, no matter what, but the other two pledged to help Lissa and Lance in any way they could. Things had started to grow from there, with the people they spoke to giving them information about other Neo-Andromedans that might be in trouble. There was a strange, new feeling that came with these connections, but Lissa did not try to pin it down. Instead, she put the information into the database, and began to sort through those who were in more dire situations.

There was a heavy cloud of danger over their next target's head. The Neo-Andromedan was deep within Anti territory, and had decided that trying to blend in with hostile humans was better than facing an Awakening. He would need protection, maybe an extraction if he was still alive. Lance was already strategizing for every situation he could imagine, and beginning to tap their steadily growing network for help. They were in the process of setting up a safe location for the Neo-Andromedans who needed new homes, and there would be someone to receive this man.

If they could get to him in time.

"We'll get him out," Lance said, and Lissa agreed.

She trusted his promises.

After *Light Runner* was fully powered down, Lissa helped Lance gather their supplies and money before ushering the arkins out of the airlock. They could not spend long on the planet, but Lissa found herself drawn to the edge of the ground port. There was a drop-off some three hundred paces away, across a sea of short, soft grass. Beyond that, the air was clear, offering a view all the way to the horizon as the dawn came on.

"You go ahead," Lissa said to Lance. "I'll join you in a few minutes."

He followed her gaze to the strengthening light. A flash of concern crossed his face for a moment, but it faded when he saw her expression. With a nod, he motioned the arkins off, releasing them to hunt. They took off with eager yips, chasing each other off the ground port.

"I'll wait for you," Lance said, giving her hand a gentle squeeze.

Moments later, Lissa stood near the edge of the cliff, facing the anticipation of the rising sun. She felt Lance's gaze on her back, always watchful and protective but never invasive.

As the light strengthened, turning the sky from deep blue to pink, a strong wind rushed across the land, sweeping up the side of the cliff to whistle over the dark rocks and ruffle the dewy grass and tug and tangle Lissa's hair. It was a cool night wind that chilled her a little and put tears in her eyes, but it carried the promise of early summer warmth and the smell of a world heavy with life.

The dawn came with a startling swiftness, cracking open the sky and spilling molten gold over the land. In that moment, Lissa felt lighter, freer than she had in a long, long time. The sunrise touched her skin, gentle and warm and seeming to promise that it would be better from now on. There was a future ahead, and it would not drown that out.

Lissa closed her eyes for a moment, feeling the whisper of dark wind through her hair and the warmth of the sun against her skin, and breathed in the light.

ABOUT THE AUTHOR

K.N. Salustro is a writer from New Jersey
who loves outer space, dragons, and good stories.
When not at her day job, she runs an Etsy shop as a
plush artist, and makes art for her Society6
and Redbubble shops.

For updates, new content, and other news,
you can follow K.N. Salustro on:

Wordpress: https://knsalustro.wordpress.com/

Facebook: https://www.facebook.com/knsalustro/

Twitter: https://twitter.com/knsalustro

Made in the USA
Columbia, SC
24 June 2018